Coming Together

"Y'all, these characters. They are so messy and complicated and REAL. Watching Ava develop over the course of the previous two books, and now this one, made my character-driven-novel-loving heart explode." – Eva Seyler, author of *This Great Wilderness*

"My only complaint is that the story has come to an end." – Deborah Klée, author of *The Last Act*

"[M]asterfully intertwines the looming international crises of the late 30s and the personal lives of the two protagonists. With an eye to the details that matter, Heenan recreates the streets and cafes of Paris, a littered dressmaker's workroom, or the streets of working class Philadelphia all with the same skill and attention." – Marian L Thorpe, author of *Empire's Legacy*

"A resounding and poignant finish to the story of two sisters coming to terms with one another, the choices they've made, and the choices that have been forced upon them, all set against the backdrop of the Great Depression and the looming threat of war." – Laury Silvers, author of *The Sufi Mysteries Quartet*

Coming Together

KAREN HEENAN

~CONTENT WARNING~

This story is intended for mature audiences. This story contains situations and/or references that some readers may find objectionable, including rape, unplanned pregnancy, miscarriage, abortion, and mention of sexual assault (implied/off-page).

E-book ISBN: 978-1-957081-20-5
Paperback ISBN: 978-1-957081-21-2
Hardcover ISBN: 978-1-957081-22-9
Audiobook ISBN:

Typeset in Garamond and Lemon Tuesday

Coming Together

KAREN HEENAN

Also by Karen Heenan

The Tudor Court Series

Songbird – Book I
A Wider World – Book II
Lady, in Waiting – Book III

Ava and Claire

From This Day Forward (newsletter exclusive novella)
Coming Apart – Book I
Coming Closer – Book II
Coming Together – Book III

For the women in my family.
You told stories without realizing.
I heard them without understanding.
Now I'm here. Thank you.

1

Ava

Pale afternoon sun leaks through the curtain, casting a strip of light across the freckled shoulder next to my cheek. The shoulder, and the chest attached to it, rises and falls in contented slumber. I lie still for a moment longer, trying to guess the time by the light, but it is February and the day was not bright to begin with.

I stretch, nudging him, and he snorts to abrupt wakefulness. "What?"

"Can you see the clock?"

"No." Max rolls to one side, taking most of the covers with him. "Yes. It's just after two. Time for the kids to get in?"

"Almost." I sit up, gathering the sheet to cover my nakedness. If I live to be a hundred, I will never be comfortable without clothes during the day. "It's also time for something else."

"What's that?" Awake now, he springs from the bed, scooping his discarded underwear from the floor with one hand.

"It's time you made an honest woman of me." I push the hair back from my face. It will require a good brushing to undo the damage he has done. "We can't keep doing this."

He stops in the midst of putting on his socks. "Are you sure?"

It's a reasonable question. The last time I agreed to marry him I was in such a state that he called off the wedding to give me more time. But I've had eight months to work through my hesitation, to mourn my darling Daniel, dead two years this past November, and to sneak the occasional afternoon in Max's bed.

The saving grace is that my sister is away. Otherwise I'd have to deal with her knowing about these illicit meetings. Not to mention that she'd be at me about dresses and rings and receptions again—all the frills I'd fought so hard last time. Had I really not wanted it, I wonder, or was I making excuses because I wasn't ready?

Max has caught me in his arms and borne me back onto the bed, kissing me with an enthusiasm that doesn't bode well for my plan to get home in time for the kids. I return his kisses, then shove at his chest.

"Put your clothes on." I struggle into my girdle. "Or don't, if you want to lay here and make plans. But I've got to get home."

Always amenable, he dresses quickly and produces a brush from his drawer. "You might want to see to—" He gestures at my head. "That."

I catch a glimpse of myself in the mirror. "Lord, I look like a haystack." I button my dress, then drag the brush through my curls. They droop limply at my jawline. Maybe I should get another permanent wave—I certainly don't want to sleep in pins every night once we're married.

Heat rises to my face at the thought. Marriage, again. Spending every night in bed with this man. Not having to fit love into snatched moments between my dressmaking and his patients at the clinic.

"Where will we live?" he asks, reading my mind.

"My house was good enough before." Claire offered us the use of her home when she and Harry went abroad last June, but I wasn't comfortable living with Max, not if we weren't married.

"I thought so." He knots his tie, raising a quizzical eyebrow. "Will we all fit?"

"We'll manage," I say, though I'm not sure how well. Dan, Toby, and George have the top floor, and I share the second floor with my daughters. Last year my eldest son started to divide the space but the project hadn't advanced beyond the framing stage when the wedding fell through. Dan works for our landlord—a builder, not a coal miner like his father. When I signed the lease on the house, my son put in the wall on the ground floor, giving me a workroom where, over the last two years, I've built my business. "I'll talk to Dan."

Max waits by the front door while I retrieve baby Grace. She has been in the kitchen with my friend Esther, who also happens to be my sister's housekeeper. There is no reason to flaunt my afternoon activities by letting him follow me downstairs, even though Esther knows we were together.

When I return, my cheeks hot with embarrassment at her knowing smile, I hand over my squirming child. Nearly two, she is a handful, willing to go into her coach for anyone but me.

"Who's a darling?" Max coos, swinging her up and around, narrowly missing a shelf of the fragile ornaments Claire acquires as easy as breathing. As Grace giggles joyfully, he swoops her into the coach, then bumps it down the single step to the sidewalk.

"Shall I escort you home, my lady?" He settles his hat and reaches for his bicycle, which leans against a stone planter containing a winter-saddened shrub.

I shake my head. "You've got a long ride back to the clinic. The sooner you're there, the sooner you'll be done. It's not going to get any nicer today."

Max tilts his head back, looking at the gray sky. "It's a beautiful day," he declares. "The most beautiful day ever—my girl has decided to marry me." He bends me back over the coach and kisses me until I'm breathless and Grace is goggle-eyed.

"Enough of that," I say finally, pulling on my gloves. "You've given the neighbors plenty to gossip about for one day."

His laughter lingers in my ears long after his bicycle has disappeared, turning off Delancey onto Eighteenth and heading south to the clinic he runs for my sister.

"Mama!" Grace's imperious voice returns my attention to the present. I wrap my fingers around the handle and set off for home.

The house is quiet when I get in. The kids will trickle in soon: Toby first, for a quick snack before he vanishes to the garage; Thelma, on his heels, to walk the dog and do her homework until she sets the table; Pearl next, her school further away, to sew silently with me. Dan and George won't return until suppertime, Dan from his job and my youngest boy from the firehouse where he is both help and hindrance to the men of Ladder Five.

Moving through the living room, I pick up a book, two abandoned socks, and a spool of thread. I smooth the cushions on the blue davenport, which I must remember to call a sofa. It was a gift from Max, delivered the day after our canceled wedding, along with a matching armchair. The pieces have been in the house now for months, but they still feel new; I've never lived with furniture not owned by someone else first, and it takes some getting used to.

As does everything, these days.

Claire

Ava's letters are terse but regular, giving me news of the children and occasional society gossip gleaned in her fitting room. They also contain an infuriating lack of detail about her relationship with Max Byrne. "I don't know if she'll be any more ready to marry him by the time we get home than she was when we left!"

Harry smiles and pushes up his glasses, which have slid down his nose as he scanned the European edition of the *New York Times*. The availability of his precious American newspapers, in addition to the *Manchester Guardian*, *London Times,* and *Le Monde*, is the reason we have ventured as far as Les Deux Magots, rather than a café closer to our apartment. "Your sister will do things in her own time, and we both know it." He shifts in the rattan chair, placed in a lucky spot of February sunshine, and tips his head to the waiter. "What do you say to a perusal of the bookstalls? Maybe you can find something to sweeten Pearl's mood."

"What a good idea." My book-loving niece was disappointed that she couldn't come with us; I had thought her the perfect traveling companion, as she would enjoy Paris as much as I would, and would be available to watch Teddy when we wanted to go out at night. But Ava wouldn't allow Pearl to miss months of school because we had—in her words—decided to flit halfway around the world on a whim.

Her reaction was understandable. Pearl is the brightest of all her children, and she loves school. Under normal circumstances, she wouldn't consider missing all that time, but when her mother vetoed my proposal without discussion, Pearl threw what could only be termed a tantrum. She and Ava are still snappish with each other, according to her letters, and my own notes to Pearl—including a postcard of Shakespeare & Co., the bookstore she'd longed to visit—have gone largely unanswered. The few times she has written, her words are stiff and unforgiving, as if I could have changed her mother's mind about anything.

Their relationship will mend, but I hate that there is enmity between them, and that I caused it, however inadvertently. It's shocking to see Pearl behave like a normal, moody adolescent; she's always been a level-headed, helpful girl. I'm sure she won't hold her mother's good intentions against her forever.

Harry scatters coins on the table and I take his arm. We cross the cobbles in front of the café, and I cast a look up at the bell tower of St. Germain des Prés. We turn onto the crowded Rue Bonaparte and walk until we reach the Seine, where the bouquinistes have set up their wares in painted stalls along the quays.

I adore the booksellers; browsing the stalls on either side of the river is one of my favorite activities in Paris, after the museums. And on an unseasonably warm day in the middle of winter, even I cannot be lured inside to contemplate art, not when the air is balmy on my cheeks and the scents of strong coffee and baking bread waft toward me on a breeze laden with the promise of springtime.

Pearl

February 16, 1935

Being mad all the time is exhausting. I don't know how Mama did it all those years. I don't want to be like this but I can't help it. It's like every bit of good, well-behaved Pearl went up in flames the instant Aunt and Uncle left for Paris without me. Grace and Thelma are the only family I can stand to be around. That's because Grace is too little to understand and Thelma doesn't care if it's not about dancing.

Dandy keeps telling me I need to get over it, that there's no point in being upset about something I can't change. That's rich, coming from someone who still feels guilty about his own survival. Not that I'm comparing Daddy's death to being excluded from a trip to Paris. That hurt all of us. Paris only hurts me.

But don't I matter sometimes?

Mama said it was because of school that she said no. But it was only for a year! I would have learned as much in France as I am at Girls High. She rolled her eyes when I signed up for French in September and said if I wanted to rub salt into my wounds, I could do it just as easily at home.

And that's it, really. Why she said no. She wants me at home, to be a second mother and backup seamstress so she doesn't have to do everything herself. I missed out on the most amazing opportunity of my life because of that.

Not only did I lose out on the trip, which I will never forgive, but I lost my job caring for Teddy and I was supposed to work in Uncle's office last summer. So I have no income at all now, just the allowance Mama gives to all of us, except Dan, who makes enough money to pay her.

It's not fair.

Ava

My sister may be thousands of miles away, doing who-knows-what, but we still have Friday supper at her house. It's my one concession to her ongoing interference in our lives—that and her dog, Pixie, who stayed behind with us when she went away. It means that our tiny kitchen, and my workroom, will not stink of fish for two days. Once Dan comes in from work, I round up the rest of the kids, check that they're reasonably clean, and we head over to the Warriner house, where Max will be waiting.

The kids treat it like a family dinner, even though we will go home at the end and leave Max in that huge empty house. I'm pretty sure the older ones understand, but Thelma, who lived with Claire for months while undergoing treatment with Max, mutters about all those bedrooms sitting empty.

I think about them, too, especially after Max asked where we would live. I can't imagine being anywhere but the house on Ringgold Place. It's only the second house I've ever known, having married and stayed in my childhood home until my husband's death. This house, although Harry helped me to find it, is paid for by my labor and has become a symbol to me of everything my family has achieved since we moved to Philadelphia in November, 1932.

Max knows all this, which is why he's willing to move himself into a house that is too small for so many people. He knows my past, my fears, and the occasional stumbling blocks that turn me stubborn as a mule. The house is one of those blocks, and I'm not willing—yet—to talk about it.

We haven't seen each other since our intimacy the other afternoon. I don't regret saying that I would marry him, exactly, but I wonder again if it's not too soon.

He opens the door and welcomes us into the hall like the master of the house, taking Grace from me and swatting the little boys with his free hand. "Go check on Mrs. Hedges," he tells them. "I need to talk to your mama." He kisses Grace on her nose. "Hello, dumpling."

Dan and Pearl exchange glances. "Come on, Thelma. Let's set the table and let them be."

I follow Max into the living room and settle into the deep cushions of the sofa before the cold fireplace. On his own, Max makes do with the central heating; I prefer a fire, but the clanking metal radiators are more practical.

He drops down beside me, tucking Grace in between, tickling her and sending her into floods of giggles. "You've been avoiding me," he says over her head.

"I've been busy." It's not a lie, but I could have found time if I'd wanted to.

"Hmm." He stretches his arm across the back of the sofa, brushing my neck with his fingertips. "Are we still engaged?"

"Of course!" I look up, shocked he would even ask. Any second thoughts will not be shared this time; he's suffered enough over my delaying.

"Good." He visibly relaxes. "I had to be sure."

I feel bad that he's worried for no reason. "But I'm not ready to tell the kids," I warn. "And you're not to go writing to Claire, either."

He smiles impishly. "Are you sure *I'm* allowed to know?"

"Just you, for now." I kiss him quickly, pulling away before the door is thrown open.

"Mrs. Hedges is coming!" Toby shouts, whirling back toward the dining room, as excited as always at the thought of food. "Suppertime!"

The meal—a platter of grilled trout with vegetables and extra mashed potatoes for my bottomless boys—is delicious, as always. Esther is a fine cook. She and her husband, Mason, will be in the basement kitchen eating a duplicate meal. I have asked them to eat with us, but Esther refuses. "Mrs. Claire wouldn't like it," she says.

"Mrs. Claire isn't here," I counter.

She shakes her head. "That's not how it works."

Even in France, Claire complicates things.

After we have finished, Pearl and Dan stack the dishes and carry them downstairs. We may eat in the dining room, but the kids aren't allowed to treat this house like a hotel, and despite Esther's objections, they clean the table and do the dishes each week, under her watchful eye.

We return to the sofa. Thelma and Grace are in the corner with some blocks brought from Teddy's upstairs nursery, their soft murmurs a backdrop to our conversation.

"They're going to figure it out," Max says quietly. "They're your children. They're not stupid."

"I know that." I persuade him to wait a few more days. "A secret," I say. "Between us."

He raises an eyebrow. "You'll have to tell them eventually."

"I will," I assure him. "I just want to get things straight in my head before I let everyone else in on it."

"What about Claire?" The second eyebrow joins the first. "If we do this before she gets back, she'll take the clinic away from me."

Last year, Claire organized and opened a free clinic for the city's poor, and hired Max as the chief physician. It makes me uncomfortable that my soon-to-be husband is my sister's employee, but as her trip was extended once, and then again, I have become used to it. Max is an excellent doctor and Claire, at this point, is no more than an absentee landlord.

I lean against his chest, inhale his familiar scent of soap and disinfectant. "You're too good at what you do. She'd be a fool to let you go."

2

Claire

After almost eight months, Paris feels like home. When we first arrived, we stayed at the Hotel George V, and it was everything I could have hoped for—the second honeymoon of my dreams. Still, opulence can be wearing over time and so Harry found a large apartment for us on the rue Balzac. Across from the walled garden of a private mansion and close to a park for Teddy, it has three bedrooms, airy living spaces, and a full staff, and suits us far better than the hotel.

Occasionally, after a day of wandering the markets, I upset the cook by making dinner myself, but most of the time I allow her to work her magic unassisted; even Esther Hedges cannot top Madame LeClerc where food is concerned.

The last time we were in France, the country appeared untouched by the economic turmoil that had struck the United States and then Britain. Due to their disastrous losses in the war, France didn't have the same unemployment problems faced by other countries. It is different now; everywhere I look, shadows encroach on the glamorous world I had so missed. Refugees from Spain and Germany have added their language to the babel of tourists on the sidewalks and in the cafés.

In our luxurious apartment, our lives are much the same as they were at home, yet there is a difference in the air around us, a brittle gaiety infecting those who are not yet destitute. It saddens me to know what will come of it, before too long.

The city of light has cast its healing properties over us all. Harry and I are closer than ever before, the rifts brought about by my overenthusiastic creation of the clinic smoothed over. Indeed, he has almost completely relaxed the iron control he exercises over his emotions, laughing and joking and even occasionally kissing me in public—which, of course, makes me tease him that he's becoming very French.

Teddy is thriving. Just past three, he is sturdy and energetic and talks non-stop, in French and English, until he is overtaken by exhaustion and falls asleep mid-sentence. I am proud of how quickly he has acquired a second language.

Katie, too, has found her place in this strange city. When I first invited her, after Ava refused to let Pearl accompany us, she was hesitant. But she is one of Teddy's favorite people, and while I would never threaten her employment, I made it plain that if we were to be away for a significant period, we would not need to pay all the members of the Hedges family to live in our empty house. She changed her mind quickly after that, but I think she does not regret it.

The French are more accepting of colored people than we are at home, and Katie is a pretty, personable girl. She does not have Teddy's facility with language, but she has learned enough French to get around and, as she says, to either be polite or rude enough to drive away unwanted admirers.

We have spent this chilly afternoon at the park, reading on a bench while Teddy sails his model boat in the pond and throws baguette crumbs to the ducks that populate its islands.

"Would you like to eat in or out this evening?" Harry puts his newspaper aside, surfeited with dire news. Mr. Hitler's antics do not seem so far away in Paris, and he has become more and more concerned as our visit has worn on.

"Out, I think." Katie has spent the day at her own devices and so will have no problem staying in with Teddy. Madame can also, for a small fee, be induced to watch our son.

"Allard?"

"Oh, yes." The small bistro in the sixth has become a favorite destination. Despite its relative newness, it looks like any other established place in the neighborhood—mustard gold walls, lace curtains at the windows, a long zinc bar, abundant flowers. Tall, thin, serious waiters with long aprons. "Maybe we could try the duck this time."

We arrive ahead of our eight-thirty reservation and hand our coats to a cadaverous young man. He spirits them out of sight. Waiting at the bar with a glass of wine until we are called to our table, I let the long day slip away and become present in the dining room with its low murmur of dinner conversation, the clink of silver on china, the soft-footed waiters.

France is a civilized country. Even more so than England, which we have visited several times during our stay. America is brash and raw in comparison, our oldest habits and traditions mere knockoffs of the best of these ancient cultures.

"Madame, monsieur." The headwaiter stands before us. "Votre table est prête."

"Merci." Harry falls in behind me as we weave between tables in the intimate space. Candles cast shadows on snowy linen and heads bent over plates of beautifully-arranged food. The waiter tucks my chair beneath me, surrenders two large menu cards, and vanishes. He will reappear when we are ready for him; French waiters have a kind of sixth sense.

"The duck, you said?" Harry's voice rises above the menu.

"You don't have to." Duck isn't his favorite.

"It's meant to be shared." The menu lowers. Light glints off his lenses. "And it's fine. I've seen it and it looks quite appetizing."

I've seen it and it made my mouth water; I would have regretted my meal except that it was a chicken so perfectly roasted the juices ran from it as it rested on the plate, waiting to be carved.

"Escargot to start, for me," he says. "For you, darling?"

I scan the menu quickly, lost in a daydream of duck with olives. "The foie gras, I think."

Our waiter appears, bang on time. Harry hands back the menus and places our order, then asks for a bottle of burgundy to go with the duck. "The same for the starters?"

"That's fine with me." I don't know a lot about wine, only that I like it more in France than in Philadelphia.

When the food arrives, all conversation stops. We have learned that much from the French: to address our meal when it is at its best. The duck is everything I had hoped for—savory, swimming in a sauce made tangy with olives. I eat an embarrassing amount, topped only by Harry, who uses the last of his bread to clean the sauce from his plate.

"That," he says, "was far better than I expected."

A waiter steps in to clear our table, and we are left with the remainder of our wine and the question of whether or not we want dessert. The waiter returns to seat someone at the next table, and turns to us, murmuring the selections. When he says *île flottante*, I immediately find a small corner of my stomach to accommodate it.

"Where do you put it?" Harry asks, reaching across the table to take my hand. "Slender as a reed, and the appetite of a stevedore."

"It's all the walking." I never ate like this at home; I was always afraid of putting on weight and not looking my best for him. But here, I eat and eat and walk and walk, and nothing seems to stick to me. And I would sacrifice an inch here or there for the Allard pastry chef's meringue.

The man at the next table lowers his menu at the waiter's approach. "The rest of my party will arrive shortly," he says in accented French. "I will have a sazerac while I wait."

"Very good, monsieur."

While they are speaking, Harry has turned to the man, peering at him with a directness most unusual; I am the one who eavesdrops in restaurants, gleefully regaling him with overheard conversations on the way home. And this man hasn't even said anything interesting.

"Leo?"

The man looks up, recognition on his face. "My God! Harry!" He stands, reaching between the tables to grasp my husband's hand. "How good to see you."

"And you. It's been years." Harry shakes his hand, then turns to me. "This is my wife, Claire Warriner. Claire, this is my friend, Leopold Vollmer."

"How delightful to meet you." He raises my hand to his lips. "Please, you must call me Leo."

His accent and the precise arrangement of his words gives away his nationality, but I have never met a German so casual with his name upon first meeting. He must be a very good friend, although I cannot recall Harry ever mentioning him before.

They dive into conversation and I occupy myself with watching the other diners, none of whom are as animated as my husband and his friend. I am content to not listen too closely, as there are all-too-frequent mentions of Hitler in their flood of words. Of course, Harry will want to hear the news from a German perspective.

When we finally leave, Harry turns back to speak to Mr. Vollmer one last time, joining me at the door where our coats have been whisked out of hiding. "Would you like to walk back, or take a taxi?"

I am foggy with food and wine, and tired from our excursion earlier, yet a walk sounds like a good idea. I tell him so. "You're lucky I'm in comfortable shoes."

He looks down at my suede t-strap heels. "If those are comfortable, I'll sit down and eat another duck."

The night air is chilly, but there is no breeze and it is almost pleasant as we set out. Crossing the Pont des Arts, we follow the Quai des Tuileries along the deserted gardens. My feet object, somewhat, to the cobbled streets and uneven curbs, but this night—walking through a darkened city on Harry's arm—is what I dreamed of when I proposed the trip. Sore feet are nothing; I have my husband back.

The streets grow busier as we turn onto the Champs-Élysées, the city's beating heart during the daylight hours. Even now, nearing eleven, the sidewalks are dotted with people: couples going home after a late dinner or a show, artists wandering the streets for inspiration, tourists needing one last glimpse of Paris before putting their head on a pillow.

Katie has left a lamp burning in the hall, but the rest of the apartment is dark. I visit the bathroom, then change into a blue satin negligee. When I emerge, Harry is nowhere to be found. I throw on a matching peignoir and go in search of my errant husband, knowing where I will find him.

The living room is an elegant space with high ceilings and tall windows overlooking the garden of the Hôtel Salomon de Rothschild. Dark mahogany furniture glows against the cream damask walls, setting off two paintings of Degas ballerinas and a large, vivid Renoir—our purchases, to replace the staid French country scenes which now reside in Katie's room; she likes art that looks like real places.

In the center of the room is a massive fireplace with a carved mantle. The fire is banked, glowing red in front of two velvet armchairs and a matching Louis XV sofa, perfect for lounging away the afternoon—or brooding, which is what I find him doing.

I settle in beside him, hoping that my warm presence will induce him to come to bed. "Tired?"

"Mmm." He stares, unseeing, in the direction of the heavily curtained windows. One hand rests lightly on his stomach. "I'm sorry, darling. What did you say?"

"I asked if you were tired."

"Exhausted," he says, without a sign of moving. "Did you listen to any of our conversation?"

"Not really." When it becomes obvious he is not ready to sleep or make love, I rise and pour a whiskey for him, adding a touch of water. "Tell me about your friend."

Harry takes the glass with a look of gratitude and drinks deep. "I've known Leo since my days at Princeton. He was in his last year, but our rooms in the fraternity house were close together, and we kept similar hours. Neither of us liked the party atmosphere at college, though we were always willing to celebrate a victory over Penn, especially on the river."

I had forgotten that Harry rowed; when we first married, he was part of a group that got together on Saturday mornings to go out on the Schuylkill, but that pastime faded as he and his friends got older and busier.

"He was taking a degree in economics and then returning to Germany. Further study at Gottingen, I believe, before joining *his* father's company." He drains the glass and sets it aside. "I've run into him over the years, once in London, once in New York, before the war, and we've exchanged occasional letters ever since."

It must have been difficult to have a friend on the other side of the war, with no way to contact him or know if he'd survived.

"Did he fight for Germany?"

I switch off the light and stand for a moment at the full-length window, looking through the cold glass. A couple crosses the street, walking very close together, their hands joined. I turn away.

"Not directly." He shifts, puts a cushion behind his head. "He's a few years older than me. But his company supplied war materiel to the army, as did mine."

Not so different, after all. Just on different sides.

"And what about this friend he was waiting for tonight?" I rest my head on his shoulder. "He seemed upset."

"He was." Harry shifts so his arm comes around me, his fingers playing absently with my hair. "He asked me to meet him for lunch tomorrow."

"Do you want me to come along?" Even though Mr. Vollmer was pleasant enough, I dread the thought of sitting through a dull business conversation. It's one of the things about home that I've missed the least. "I'm sure that Katie could take Teddy to the park again."

"I think he'd rather it be the two of us." He stands, stretching. "If it's anything interesting, I'll be sure to fill you in."

As if two men talking about manufacturing could be interesting. I stifle a yawn. "Shall we go to bed? That duck was delicious, but it's not doing anything to keep me awake."

Pearl

February 25, 1935

I signed up for the Peace Club today. It will keep me after school until 4:30 every other Tuesday, and I won't be able to do any sewing at all because I'll have homework after supper. And if I don't have homework, I'll make some up.

Mama didn't want me to miss school, so she can't complain if I'm busy. If I could find another after school club, I would, but this will be enough, I think, because it has speakers and debating and I'll have to read the newspapers to keep up, the way I'm still in Latin Reading Club with the 9As because I started late. I wish Uncle was back home. He could talk to me about what's going on in the world. Peace Club is supposed to be "an exchange of ideas." Whatever that means.

I wish there was another play. I'm not much of an actress, as I found out in January when I tried out for *A Midsummer's Night Dream*, but I can make costumes. That would keep me out of the house.

Ava

Missing Daniel Kimber has been a privilege. My pain honored him until, one day, it began to feel as though I clung to it from selfishness, from habit; that Daniel, what remains of him, will not achieve his place in heaven with me clinging to his heels in a way that I never did when he was alive.

It is time to let my man go. He will be with me, always, but not in such a way that he stops me from living my life or from moving forward and making my family—his family—happy. My mother remarried less than a month after learning of her husband's death, but she had just arrived in America and had a baby at the breast besides. And Mama was always more pragmatic than I am, though both my sister and my daughter use "practical" as a term of abuse where I am concerned. For the bulk of my life, I have carried others, been responsible for mother, husband, children; I have been practical out of necessity.

But our lives are different now. Since Daniel's death in the collapse of that bootleg mine, I have tried my best to plan our futures, but life moves quickly in the city, and Claire and others will not let me sit silently and gather my resources; by the time I am ready, they have moved on, dragging me with them.

Max is the exception. He is *of* this place—I can't imagine him elsewhere—but he gives me what I need most: time. Last June, when we stood before a judge, watched by almost everyone I knew in Philadelphia, he was the one to step back and tell them I wasn't ready, when I couldn't bring myself to say it.

In the late morning, after I have finished what work I can on my current commission, I tidy myself up, settle Grace with Mrs. Malloy, our neighbor, and take the streetcar down to the clinic before I lose my nerve.

It's crowded as always, at least a dozen men in the waiting area, a communal cloud above their heads, their smokers' coughs a chorus reminiscent of my old life in Scovill Run, where the men also coughed like that, and smoked, when they could afford it.

"Mrs. Kimber!" Lucille Gordon, the clinic's nurse, looks up from her desk with a smile. "Do you have an appointment?"

Casting a glance over the room, I say, "I didn't think I'd need one."

"Don't worry," she says, standing. "Come with me."

I am shunted into a small examining room to wait. Max's voice comes, muffled, from the other side of the wall. It rises and falls, then there is the sound of laughter. He has a way of getting the most obdurate of men to loosen up. I hitch myself up on the table to wait; even if Lucille has told him I'm here, he won't duck out on a patient.

Finally, he appears, drying his hands on a towel. At the sight of me, he shuts the door, comes over to the exam table, and kisses me soundly. "This is a surprise," he says, when he stops for breath. He rubs his fingers through his hair. "What did I do to deserve this?"

"I wanted to tell you," I say, and stop.

"What?" He sits beside me on the edge of the table, his hip warm against mine.

I take a deep breath, let it out in a rush. "I don't have a problem anymore with the ring."

"What?" He looks at me, clearly not anticipating my words. "What ring?"

I remember how hard it was to say no to him last year, how worried I'd been that he would take it the wrong way, and he's...forgotten all about it? "The engagement ring," I tell him. "The one I didn't want."

"And now you do?" He is with me now, a smile splitting his face.

"I won't say no." I glance down at my hand, at the cheap metal band Daniel gave me when we wed. "But I don't want a diamond, if that's all right."

Max raises my hand to his lips. "The lady will have whatever she wants," he declares. "Diamonds, rubies, sapphires, you name it."

Now he's complicating things again. I don't want to think about all these jewels, what they cost, how careful I'll have to be. "Does it have to be like that?"

"Like what?"

I look at my hands again. Even taking better care of them, it's obvious that I've spent my life working. My hands are tools, not something easily ornamented with jewelry.

"I don't know." I sigh. "I can't think beyond the kind of jewelry Claire would wear. I don't want something that would look ridiculous." Or make *me* look ridiculous, I add silently.

He nods. "There are semi-precious stones," he says. "Not as expensive but just as pretty. Probably more likely to stand up to wear and tear, too, if that's what you're afraid of."

It's close enough. "That sounds perfect."

"Come with me to pick it out?" he coaxes. "There's this little place near Jewelers' Row where we could have lunch."

"No." I shake my head. "I have a lot to get done between now and the wedding. You pick out something that you think will suit me."

Max bursts into laughter. "I don't think they sell anything with spines on it like a porcupine. I'll have to come up with something else."

"You do that."

The ring, presented a few days later, comes in a dark blue leather box. I hesitate to open it—what if it's awful?—and slowly lift the lid.

Three dark red stones glint in the low light, set in a line on a slim gold band. "It's beautiful."

"Garnets," he says. "My birthstone, but I thought they suited you."

"Why?" What is my birthstone? I didn't know such things existed.

"It's a tribute to all the times you've drawn my blood." His grin tells me he's joking, but barely; in the beginning I was often unkind and even now I am pricklier than I need to be. He is a forgiving man, one of many qualities I love about him.

"Are you gonna go through with it this time?"

Since the ring would give it away, Max and I had decided to tell the kids at supper. I expected excitement, not disbelief, and stare at Toby until he reddens with embarrassment.

"It's a question worth asking," Max says, breaking the tension. "But it's okay, this time she proposed to me. She can't change her mind."

That starts them off. The tiny kitchen rings with laughter and questions as the kids take their places at the table. George shifts Grace's high chair to one side to get to his seat and immediately starts poking Toby with a fork.

"Knock it off, you two," I say automatically, though the occasional poke with a dull fork could do Toby no harm. "Sit still, so Pearl can dish up."

Pearl turns from the stove, holding the pot of stew in mitted hands. She moves to the left, where a folded dish towel awaits, then strikes the table with her hip and lurches. The pot flies from her grasp, hits the edge of the table, and spatters across the floor, the wall, and the bottom of the cupboard.

For a moment, there is silence.

"Damn it!" she cries, then claps her hand over her mouth. "Who moved Grace's chair? I caught my foot." She looks at the floor. Pixie has bounded from his bed to enthusiastically lick at the mess that had been our supper. "Pixie—"

Max pushes away from the table, his back coming up against the window sill so that he has to edge sideways. "It's all right, Pearl," he says. "Let's take it as a sign that we should go out to celebrate." He glances at me for confirmation. "Who wants to go to the automat?"

A chorus as the kids trip over each other in their eagerness.

"I'm sorry, Mama." Pearl leans against my shoulder, tears glistening on her lashes. "I'll clean it up. You all go without me."

"We'll do it when we get home," I say, squeezing her to me. "If the dog doesn't do it for us."

Pearl

March 9, 1935

One good and two bad things happened today. First, the bad things: I swore in front of Mama and the littles. Toby moved Grace's chair and I didn't see it and tripped and our entire supper went all over the floor. The second bad thing: I was so upset about it that I was accidentally nice to Mama. But she didn't rub it in, although Dan hasn't let me go about that "damn" yet.

The good thing is that Mama and Dr. Max have decided to get married. For real this time. She's got a ring and everything, although it's not a diamond like Aunt's. It's little red stones, but it's pretty. They haven't set a date yet. They're probably waiting for Aunt and Uncle to come home, but who even knows when that will happen?

I want them to get married, I just look at what happened tonight and wonder where we'll put another full-sized person in this house. It wasn't his fault what happened, but it keeps getting more and more crowded, and it's not like any of us are done growing, either.

3

Claire

Teddy and I went to a museum after lunch, but he is too young and his legs are too short to properly appreciate the experience. I bribed him with a carousel ride, but he grew cranky once the sun went in and I brought him back to the apartment before he had a tantrum. His mood cleared immediately upon seeing Katie and I gratefully left him in her charge.

A low fire burns in the living room, and I curl up on the velvet sofa with a book—I'm trying my best to read Colette in the original French—and am not quite dozing when Harry finally returns.

"You look chilled through." I take his overcoat and press a kiss onto his cheek. "Let me call for coffee."

"I wouldn't mind," he admits, rubbing his hands together. "We had lunch and then walked for what must have been hours. I'm frozen."

Madame LeClerc has coffee ready in minutes, and it arrives on a tray with a carefully-chosen assortment of pastries. I choose a buttery croissant and push the rest of them toward Harry; I'm beginning to worry about my waistline in this country that refuses to let me go hungry.

"Did you have a nice time," I ask, "other than the frostbite?"

"Nice enough." He sips his coffee and sighs with satisfaction. "At least until we got to talking about last night. He was supposed to meet some people at Allard. They were already late when he sat down, and they never appeared."

"How rude," I say, remembering a time when I had been stood up by dinner guests; it didn't bear thinking about. "He appeared more worried than angry."

Harry nods. "The man he was supposed to meet is an old friend. And a Jew. Josef Adler and his wife have been out of the country since he lost his university position in the 1933 purge. They recently returned to find their apartment ransacked. Adler asked Leo to help them."

I swallow my thoughts about rudeness and try to imagine what it must have been like for this couple. It is so uncivilized, and Europe has always meant civilization to me. "And they were to meet at the restaurant last night?"

"Yes. The Adlers were coming from Heidelberg. They had agreed it was best not to meet in Berlin. Apparently the Chancellor's men are everywhere."

"Goodness." I shrink into my sweater, chilled by what feels too much like a film about spies in wartime. "Is Leo in any danger?"

"He's been careful," Harry says. "But his history with Adler is known. If pressed, he would have to denounce him, or risk losing everything his family has built over the last century." He squeezes my arm. "And he wants his friend to be safe."

"Goodness," I say again. "What a mess."

Harry finishes his coffee, then lights a cigarette. I can tell that he hasn't finished thinking about Leo or the Adlers, and eventually he says, "He's making some calls today, trying to locate them. I hope you don't mind that I asked him to dinner tomorrow—I'd like to do what I can to help him."

"Of course," I say. "Is he comfortable at his hotel? Would you rather he stayed here?"

"I'll ask him." His gaze is tender. "I didn't want to impose on you. This is supposed to be our time alone."

I reach over and help myself to his cigarette, taking a quick puff and then handing it back. "We're all right now, aren't we? And why shouldn't we help this friend of yours, if he's in need? It's not often one gets a chance to be of use."

Leo Vollmer decides to remain in his hotel. "I appreciate your kindness, Mrs. Warriner," he says, "but my friends, they know I will be at the Meurice. I do not wish them to be unable to find me."

It makes perfect sense, but I'm disappointed; Harry's friend, with his worried brown eyes and precise mustache so unlike Mr. Hitler's, has rapidly grown on me. "But you must dine with us any night you're free."

"That I will do. Thank you." He wraps his fingers around his after-dinner brandy and gives me a tired smile. "But I do not know how long I will be able to remain in Paris. My business cannot run itself."

My husband's business apparently *can* run itself, or very near to it, but he always had an army of vice presidents and assistants and lawyers, so I am not surprised. He spends several hours a week on very expensive, complicated-to-schedule long distance calls, and I believe we could wallpaper our bedroom with the amount of cables he receives.

Leo is a widower, I learn over the next several days, which he spends with us while waiting for the Adlers. He has two daughters and one son; the girls are married, with children of their own. Thinking of him as a grandfather is surprising, as he is Harry's contemporary.

"Is your son married?" He has mostly talked about his daughters, Magda and Amalia, named for his wife, who died ten years ago.

"My son is in the army," Leo says. "Manfred's devotion is to his country."

I take that to mean he is a follower of Hitler's policies, and am sorry. Leo is a good man and his concern for his friends puts him in direct conflict with his son's beliefs.

"He takes no interest in the family business?" Harry has explained in more detail the nature of the Vollmer works—mining and steel production, like Thyssen and Krupps—which could be easily turned to weapons manufacturing.

"None at all." Leo rubs his temples distractedly. "Perhaps it is for the best, considering what is likely to come."

Leaning forward, Harry asks, "What will happen if the Adlers arrive after you leave?"

Leo shakes his head and a lock of hair flops over his brow. "That is my fear. I have made what arrangements I can, but certain of the papers—visas and permits, you understand—are dated, and could expire if they do not come soon." He sighs heavily. "And then the whole process must begin again."

Harry tops off his glass. "Do tell me if there's anything I can do to help, Leo. One reads such terrible things in the papers, it is difficult to know what's true and what has been exaggerated."

I go to the windows and tug the heavy velvet curtains closed. Immediately, the room is more snug, a safe place for this haggard man to tell us his story.

"It is all true," he tells us, "and there is more that is not known outside Germany or you would think that, too, is an exaggeration. Hitler wants all of Europe under his thumb, not just Germany and his own Austria. Poland is at risk, as is France, eventually."

They lose me again as they discuss the previous war, the Maginot line, and French and English defenses, but there is an undercurrent of worry in their conversation that does not let me drift completely away. When Harry speaks again, I return my attention to them, afraid to miss something crucial.

"There's been talk of rearmament," he says. "Not in the papers, but from other sources. It would never be permitted."

Leo smiles thinly and finishes his brandy. "You'll find that the Chancellor doesn't take kindly to being told he cannot do something he's set his mind to." He unfolds himself from the sofa. "And now I have encroached upon your hospitality long enough."

Three days later, Harry wordlessly proffers the morning paper for my perusal. The front page of the *Times* reads, *"Germany To Rearm: Hitler Defies Treaty of Versailles."* My breakfast turns over in my stomach. "Does that mean war?"

"Not yet," he says. "But eventually, yes, I think it does."

Ava

I rub my tired eyes and consider the fabric spread out on the table. No matter how I arrange the pattern pieces, there's not enough left to complete Prue Foster's evening jacket. I'll have to buy more. Should I wait for Pearl to get in or take Grace with me to Fourth Street? Her hours lately are inconsistent; often she and Dan get in at the same time, when before she would have been back early enough to start supper.

I don't call her on it, though. She was disappointed—angry—when I refused to let her go to Paris with Claire, and she's not over it, all these months later. It's understandable, but I miss the girl who always had time to help, who could take the burden, however briefly, from my shoulders, who had been growing into a friend as much as a daughter. I try not to think about whether her busyness after school is simply a way to avoid coming home.

This morning, as she was dealing out breakfast plates, she asked me, "How are we going to manage?"

Since the night of the spilled stew, she has been more like herself—I don't flatter myself that I have been forgiven, only that she is pleased about Max and probably also tired of the effort that anger takes, a feeling I understand too well. My daughter had less practice at maintaining anger; I could have held on for years.

"What do you mean?" I poured tea in some cups, milk in others. It was good to be able to afford milk for the youngest.

Her light brown eyebrows raised. "How are we all going to fit? Dr. Max can't take us out for dinner every time it's too crowded or something happens."

"We managed before." I thought of the tiny kitchen in Scovill Run, where the iron stove took up most of the room and Dan had eaten his meals standing. There was far more space now, and we still used every inch of it.

"We were smaller," she pointed out. "And Daddy and Dan were hardly ever home at the same time. We're going to need to eat in shifts."

I'd considered that option, but what did that say about family, if we couldn't even eat together? "We'll manage," I said again, and turned toward the stairs. "Breakfast!"

The weather is pleasant for this time of year; a walk will do us good. I button myself into my coat, add gloves and a hat. Thelma comes in as we're leaving. "The boys said they'll be home for supper." She leans over the coach, tickling her baby sister. "Where are you going?"

"Mendel's," I tell her. "Do you want to come?"

She shakes her head, blonde curls tumbling. "Can I go back to Aunt Claire's? Mrs. Hedges asked me to help her bake cookies."

I send her on her way, pleased she has acquired a domestic interest in addition to her consuming love of dance. Thelma will never be a seamstress, even grudgingly, but I don't want my daughters to work at my business if it can be helped. Thelma learning to bake and keep house is to be expected of any girl her age, and will help me out in a different way.

By the time I reach Fourth Street, I have begun to regret my decision to walk. While it isn't cold, the air is damp this close to the river, and when I park the coach outside Mendel's door and enter, Grace in my arms, I'm chilled through.

The bell jangles, but Mr. Mendel's customary greeting is absent. The tall stool behind the cash register is unoccupied for the first time that I can remember.

"Mrs. Kimber!" His assistant bustles out from the shelves, straightening his vest self-importantly; he is rarely permitted to welcome customers. "I'm so sorry. How can I help you today?"

I smile and set Grace down. She clings to my leg for a moment, then staggers toward the long cutting table, crawling underneath to content herself with the scraps of cloth that have fallen to the floor.

"I need another half yard of that black silk velvet," I say. "Please tell me there's some left."

It was my own carelessness that caused me to not have enough. Carelessness and distraction. I'd cut the jacket's collar incorrectly, thinking about Pearl, and there was no way to salvage it.

"There is plenty," he assures me. "Five yards at least."

I confess my mistake, though not the reason, and follow him to the rear of the shop, pausing to confirm that Grace is occupied. "Where is Mr. Mendel?"

The assistant, Mr. Friedmann, whose name I have recently learned after more than two years of patronizing the business, stops with his hand on the bolt of velvet. "He is...occupied." His brown eyes slide away from mine. "Family business."

"Mrs. Mendel is well, I hope." We have only met once, at City Hall last year. It had touched me that Mr. Mendel brought his wife to the wedding, and I had briefly worried what they must have thought.

Mr. Friedmann tugs the velvet free and carries it to the table, where he drops it with a soft thump. "My aunt is very well," he says. "It is my uncle's family, in Königsberg, that concerns him."

"I thought his family was here." I had asked, once, how long Mr. Mendel had been in the United States, and was surprised to learn, because of his archaic clothing and heavy accent, that he had been born in Philadelphia. His father had come from Germany around the same time my mother journeyed from Ireland, and set himself up as a cloth peddler. In time, success brought a cart, then a small shop, and now this prosperous business which has come down to Aaron Mendel, his son, and Levi Friedmann, his wife's nephew.

"His brother went back to Germany when he was a young man," Mr. Friedmann says. "To study. He is a doctor now, with several children." A wheezing sigh escapes his lips. "Is not good where he is."

Max speaks often of what is going on in Europe, but Claire's letters, posted from Europe, have no mention of unrest. My sister is unlikely to notice these things, unless they touch her directly; Mr. Mendel's family, on the other hand, are bearing witness first hand to the evils of Mr. Hitler.

"I hope that things go well for them." My words are inadequate in the face of their probable reality. "Please tell him that I will pray for your family."

"Thank you." Mr. Friedmann, like his uncle and employer, seems to have no problem with my Catholic prayers. "I will do that."

Claire

Back home, parties were a necessary social evil, but here, they are thrown—and attended—for the sheer pleasure of it. I ready myself for each one knowing that at any time, I could meet an actor or a famous musician or one of the impressionists whose work hangs on our walls both here and in Philadelphia. When I was introduced to Picasso I nearly choked on my drink. His work does not touch me in the same way as Renoir or Degas, but Harry teased that I was no more immune to his unnervingly masculine presence than any other woman in the room, and he was right.

Seven o'clock. I turn this way and that before the mirror, admiring my new gown, a Norman Hartnell purchased during a recent weekend in London and delivered yesterday. Made of the palest oyster gray satin, it flows like water over my body and pools around my feet.

"You look pretty, Mama." Teddy careens into the room, Katie on his heels. She catches him before he wraps himself around my legs, picks him up and inspects his hands.

"You know better than to grab at your mama when she's fancied up," she scolds gently. "Fais un bécot à maman."

Her French is clumsy, but Teddy leaps to obey, stretching from her arms to kiss me on both cheeks.

"A proper Frenchman!" I exclaim as she puts him down. "Un bon français!"

"Oui!" He charges away. Moments later there are shouts of, "Papa!" and I smile; back home Harry had been "Daddy."

Katie looks at me appraisingly. "I'll have to get higher shoes," I say to her. "Ava's hems never droop like this."

"You might have to get different underwears, too."

I peer more closely and see what she means. Everything is visible; if I had a mole on my backside, it would stand out like a pebble. "Goodness."

"Mr. Warriner, I'm sure he'll like it." Her smile is just this side of cheeky, and I love her for it. There has been a distance between us since we came to Paris; I'm not sure if it came from her discomfort at first or if she felt bad, knowing Pearl had wanted to come with us.

"I'm sure he will. It's everyone else I'm worried about." I hear Ava's voice, telling me I should wear it and not care what people think, that they're probably not even looking.

By the time Harry reaches me, I've finished my hair and retrieved the black velvet box containing my diamond parure.

"Let me," he says, reaching past to retrieve the necklace and kissing my neck as he does up the clasp.

I add earrings and a bracelet of baguette diamonds, and Ava questions whether I need all that glitter. Lifting my chin, I decide that I do. This is Paris, after all.

"I didn't get a chance to ask," I say, as we stand to one side of the grand drawing room, the party going full tilt around us. "Did Leo's train get off all right? There were no…complications?"

Leo had been called back to Berlin—a tersely worded cable which gave no reason for his summons—and Harry had gone with him to the Gare de l'Est after a farewell luncheon from which I had begged off, knowing my presence was unnecessary.

"None at all." Harry takes a swallow of his drink. "I asked him to call when he got in, no matter how late. I should have warned Katie."

He should have; she hates to answer the telephone, and a late night call always strikes fear.

"I hope it goes well for him." I lean against him for a moment, offering what comfort I can in a room filled with wealthy people carrying on conversations in multiple languages. "And that his friends make contact soon. What will happen if they come to Paris now?"

Harry shrugs, his shoulders moving easily in his fitted tuxedo jacket. "He left a message for them at the Meurice. If he is not there, they should come to me." He meets my eyes. "It's the least I can do, Claire."

"Absolutely!" We have both become invested in Leo Vollmer's missing friends. If they turn up, we will do what we can to carry out his plan for them. "Now"—I remove the half-empty glass from his hand—"I think it's time to put all that out of your mind and dance with your wife."

Parisian society parties attracted the best musicians, either those on tour and willing to sing for their suppers, or hired jazz bands of a quality never heard back home.

After several dances, a stir at the door catches our attention and we retreat to one side to observe. A young woman has entered, flanked on both sides by men in evening attire. Our host greets her effusively and she passes through the room, exchanging kisses and conversation with nearly everyone.

I recognize her face from the society pages, but she's neither a Philadelphian nor a New Yorker. "Harry, do you recognize her?"

He peers at her through his glasses. "Mary Jayne Gold. Chicago."

Miss Gold wears a column of unadorned blood red velvet—1933 Molyneux, at my best guess—with long, trailing sleeves. Her dark blonde hair is coiled in a chignon both precise and careless, and her lipstick matches her gown.

"Is she rich?" Her tan is surprising. At this time of year, that means either skiing or an early trip to the south to catch the sun.

"Richer than we are, certainly," Harry says softly. "Her family is in radiators and heating. You have her father to thank for your warm winters."

We are rich, I have learned on this trip. I always knew we had money, but until my sister re-entered my life, I had never questioned how much, or how it was spent. Now I know that our apartment on rue Balzac costs more per month than Ava makes in a year, and that our passage on the *Île de France* cost more than Max is paid for the same period.

No wonder Harry wants to help Leo's friends; we have not done all that we could.

"With what little you have, be a blessing to others," I murmur, and feel his eyes on me. "It's something Mama used to say."

"She was a wise woman, your mother. I wish I'd known her better."

"I wish you had, too." It is a lingering regret, that I kept my husband and my family apart for so long, afraid of what each would think of the other.

4

Ava

Another night, another crowded supper. Pearl is careful now when she serves, and checks the location of every leg—furniture or human—before turning from the stove to dish up the food. It makes her already erratic temper even worse, and by the time we are done eating, the boys volunteer to do the dishes so she can go upstairs to hide in a book.

Max and I take our coffee out to the front steps so he can smoke. We sit shoulder-to-shoulder on the cool white marble, talking little. The snow of less than a week ago has melted like a magician's trick. Today it was in the low seventies.

"Claire's most recent letter asked when we were getting married," he says. "I feel bad that we're leaving her in the dark."

"I don't." I need to know that I'm doing this without my sister's good intentions to prop me up. "She's too involved in our lives."

He sighs, patient with me. "And she suggested that you all move in with me after the wedding."

I snort. "And how would that be less crowded than living here? Moving six kids into her house?"

"She wants to help." He puts his hand over mine. "Be patient with her."

Unspoken is the statement that Claire—and no doubt everyone else—is endlessly patient with me.

"Daniel and I wouldn't come to the city because he didn't want to be obligated to them," I explain. "We never wanted that. And now I'm marrying a man who works for my sister."

"Would you rather I didn't?" He stares at me, considering, and I wonder if being compared to Daniel has hurt him.

Would he leave the clinic, abandon Claire after all the work they've done? "No. That's not what I mean."

"Good." He exhales. "Because I would do it for you, but I wouldn't like it."

"I would be disappointed if you left because of me." The clinic means as much to him, or more, than it does to Claire. For her, it's a project, an achievement. For Max, it's his chosen work.

Healing.

As he has healed me.

After he goes back to Claire's and the kids are in bed, I sit at the kitchen table with a cup of tea and write a hard letter. I've made my choice, but the people I need to hear from cannot tell me it's the right choice.

Dear Father Dennis,

I should apologize for not writing before now but you saw Dandy and Jake at the memorial. You know we've made our way and are doing well.

I am going to be married soon. You may remember the doctor who came with Claire after the collapse. Max Byrne isn't Catholic but he's a good man. He loves me. He's willing to raise kids he didn't father. More than that. He loves them. And they love him.

So I am writing to share my news, but also to ask - is it right, what I'm doing? Would God approve? Would my mother? Would Daniel? We almost married last June but it felt too soon. It still does, but I can't spend my life living for a dead man. He wouldn't want that. Would he?

Tell me what to do. I might not listen, but I value your opinion.

Ava Kimber

Four days later, there is a knock at the door. A boy in a drab green Western Union uniform stands on the top step, an envelope in his hand. I turn cold. What if something is wrong with Teddy? Why couldn't Claire have stayed home to mend her marriage instead of dragging my child halfway across the world?

Getting a grip on myself, I give him a nickel—all I have on hand—and watch as he bounds down the steps to the bicycle leaning against the house. Once he is weaving his way down the street, I tear it open with numb fingers.

It's not from Claire. I exhale, seeing the priest's name on the bottom of the folded buff sheet.

"I can't perform the ceremony this time but allow me to give you away."

When the kids come home, I gather them together and ask, "How would you like to see Father Dennis?"

There is more shouting and excitement than when Max told them we were getting married. I forgot how the kids loved him.

"Are we going home?" George asks.

"This is home," Pearl tells him. She glances up. "Right? We're not going back?"

"We're not," I confirm, happy that for all her resentment, she thinks of Philadelphia as home. "He's coming for the wedding."

Dan leans forward to pour more coffee, topping up my mug and Pearl's. "It'll be good to see him."

My son is like his father, a believer who rarely attends church, but even Daniel had been fond of the priest.

"He's offered to give me away," I tell them. "But I was going to ask you, Dan."

"Let him do it," he says easily. "He was Granny's friend, too, so it's like he's family."

Pearl

March 19, 1935

We got another letter from Aunt Claire today, along with a small parcel. She sent something for everyone, including an old copy of *Great Expectations* for me which she said she bought from a secondhand bookseller. It has that wonderful old book smell, and something else, which I like to think might be Paris.

I didn't smell it until I brought it upstairs. The boys would laugh, and even Thelma would think I was strange. Mama would just believe I'm trying to make her feel bad about keeping me home. And not that I don't want her to feel bad, but–

I put the pencil down and shake out my fingers. My hand is cramped from writing. I've kept a diary since I was ten, when I first started feeling like I had words I didn't want to share, and in this last year it's been a life saver because I wouldn't have a family if I'd unleashed all my poison anywhere but in these pages.

But lately it feels like I'm hiding here. Not going out and experiencing whatever life I can in Philadelphia. So what if it's not

Paris. It's what I've got. And I don't want to look up one day and realize I missed my high school years going to classes and hiding my head in a book.

I have friends, better friends than I ever expected, even without Katie. Hazel wants to meet on Saturday and go to the movies, and I'm going to say yes. I didn't want to, at first, because she only invited us so she can spend time with that Charlie without it looking like a date, but why can't I enjoy myself too? Maybe I'll meet a boy and stop moping over dumb Tommy Marinelli, who wouldn't notice me if I walked naked down Broad Street.

I think I'll write to Katie tonight. I'm not ready to forgive Mama or Aunt Claire, but Katie works for Aunt. It's not her fault. She'd have rather I'd gone so she could stay home with her parents. Who even knows what Paris is like for colored people, it might be worse than here.

Claire

A cable comes from Berlin. Leo had assured us of his wellbeing upon his return, but this transparent slip of blue paper, carefully worded, relates that the expected package has gone astray. *Parcel may be picked up at Brussels Midi on 20 March at 12:30.*

"I suppose that means we're going to Brussels," I say, looking at the cryptic words. "Tomorrow. He didn't give us much time to prepare."

"There's not anything to do but get on the train." Harry looks at his watch, already plotting how to rearrange the next few days to serve these two strangers. "And you don't need to come with me, Claire."

"Why not?" I ask, stung. "Don't you want company?"

"I always want you around." His smile is uneven. "But I'm a bit nervous about this, truth be told, and I think I would feel worse with you there."

He leaves before dawn the next morning.

Spring has come to Paris. The trees are covered in new green leaves; the air of the Parc Monceau is heavy with the sweet, nutty aroma of chestnut blossoms. Teddy and I spend an intoxicating hour with the ducks, and when we return to the apartment, he is wet and muddy and thoroughly happy. Before Katie bustles him away to change his clothes, she asks, "Are you lunching in, ma'am? I didn't know what to tell Madame."

Madame is as far as she has gotten with the pronunciation of *LeClerc*, but the cook likes her enough to not fuss too often.

"I'm going for a walk," I say. "I'll eat at a café."

"Will Mr. Warriner be back in time for dinner?"

Her guess is as good as mine. "I hope so," I tell her. "Tell Madame to make something that will keep. They might get in very late." I look at my reflection—I have somehow escaped my son's spatters, and I will go out as I am, rather than waste time in changing. "Is everything ready for our guests?"

"Yes, ma'am," Katie says. "The guest bedroom is all made up. I'll go out for fresh flowers before the stalls close, so they're nice and fresh."

And half price. The cost of everything appalls her, even though I've told her over and over that fifteen francs is around the same as one U.S. dollar. I suppose I should be pleased that she is so thrifty with our money.

I shut the door behind me, glad to be out in the fresh air and away from my thoughts. If I stayed inside, they would circle like Pixie, wondering what Harry had found in Brussels. Had the parcel—Josef and Renate Adler—arrived on the 12:25 train? Has my husband been on time to meet them? What had caused their delay?

My heels clack on the pavement as I walk—where? I turn onto the Avenue de Friedland, thinking to look in shop windows until hunger sends me to a café. Before long, an arrangement of paintings in a window lures me inside.

The Galerie Georges Petit is a small space, but the white walls, cleverly lit by high windows and artfully hung lights, make it feel larger. The paintings pulse with color, drawing me along as surely as a magnet. A large Chagall hangs alone on one wall. I position myself in front of it, trying to make sense of the fantastical figures, rendered in colors unknown to nature, or at least to the forms and people being portrayed.

Like Picasso, Chagall's work both intrigues me and leaves me cold. I know with certainty that someday it will be on the walls of every museum, but unlike my beloved Renoir and Degas, it would not be comfortable art to live with.

"Mrs. Warriner, isn't it?" The voice is American, slightly rough. "We met at Mireille Vachon's party."

"Yes, of course." Recognition dawns as I take in a blonde in a beautifully tailored suit ornamented with beaded insects—Schiaparelli, surely. "Miss Gold."

"Call me Mary Jayne," she says with a smile. "Everyone does."

I smile in return. "Then I am Claire."

"Are you thinking about the Chagall?" she asks. "I adore his work."

"I'm having thoughts about it, but I'm not looking to buy anything today—at least not for me." Over Mary Jayne Gold's shoulder is a series of smaller paintings. "Excuse me, I want to look at those."

She follows, still talking about the Chagall, as I survey the half dozen Parisian street scenes on the adjacent wall. They are similar in style and subject to the paintings seen on every easel around the city, but the skill level is markedly better. Something about them plants me in the scene to the point where the café chatter and the bells of Notre Dame are audible.

The paintings are drenched in the colors of Paris, golden lamplight spilling across wet pavements, evening skies of perfect blue spread like silk behind buildings as familiar to me as those of my home city. It is the work of a man who loves Paris and is blessed with the talent to render that love on canvas.

"My sister is getting married," I explain. "We've been in Paris since last June and I want to buy her a wedding present before we have to go back." In truth, it is more a gift for Pearl than for Ava. I don't even know if my sister appreciates art, but my niece will worship in front of this painting until the day she leaves home.

"Edouard Cortes," Mary Jayne says. "Another Spaniard who made good in France, like Pablo." She tilts her head, looking at what must, to her, seem like perfectly average paintings if her tastes run to Picasso and Chagall. "Day or evening?"

There are three of each. Ava would kill me if I bought two paintings. "Evening," I think, my gaze drawn to a particular scene of the Pont Neuf. "And rain, for the reflections."

"Yes. Paris is at its most beautiful in the rain."

"I think so, too."

The gallery's clerk, alert to any chance of a sale, drifts gently toward us.

When the transaction is complete and arrangements have been made for the painting to be delivered to rue Balzac, I turn to Mary Jayne. "My intention when I came out was to treat myself to a café lunch. Would you care to join me?"

Paris proves its beauty by pouring rain on us almost immediately after we leave the gallery. There is no careful choosing of a café; sprinting in heels, we dive into the nearest one to get out of the downpour, happy to admire the glistening sidewalks with a sheet of glass in between.

"A glass of wine?" I ask Mary Jayne, after the attentive waiter has delivered menus and extra napkins with which to blot our faces and hair.

"At least one." She looks in dismay at her napkin, which bears a scarlet smear of lipstick. "Oops."

Over croque monsieur and wine—Mary Jayne's crisp "une autre" ruffling not a single waiterly feather—we discuss Paris and Philadelphia and Chicago and why we are both so far from home. I tell her a little of my last year, though not the silliness that had damaged my relationship with Harry, while she relates an escape from stifling family expectations and a single life that strikes me as something out of a novel.

"You really fly your own plane?" I ask admiringly.

She shrugs. "How else would I be able to ski as often as I like? Trains are a bore. Flying is spontaneous. I can go anywhere at a moment's notice."

"What about hotels?" I push my plate away, replete with cheese and ham. "Isn't that a problem?"

Her merry eyes meet mine over the rim of her glass. "Hotels always have room for their best customers."

She is far richer than I'd imagined, even after Harry's whispered explanation. "I suppose I don't travel often enough."

We'd gone down to the Cote d'Azur last August, when the summer heat drove Parisians from their city, but other than the beach, I hadn't truly enjoyed it. The Fitzgeralds, whom we'd met years ago, had spent summers there; perhaps I didn't like it because it reminded me of the forced gaiety of the rich people in his books.

"Paris is enough for me." I tell her that we will have to return to Philadelphia before too long, certainly by the autumn. "I don't want to waste a moment."

"I haven't gone home in years." She looks up, her tricorne hat tilting wildly. "Une autre verre, s'il vous plaît."

"I shouldn't." But the rosé has just come in, and I can't resist; it's a seasonal wine rarely available in Philadelphia. I accept a third glass. "I can always take a taxi."

"Is your husband expecting you?" Mary Jayne leans back in her chair, the very picture of a woman at home no matter where she goes.

"He's away today." I bite my lip. Is it safe to tell this shining creature of Harry's activities? "In Brussels."

"Oof!" She rolls her eyes. "I loathe that city. It's everything bad they lead you to believe about Paris."

The waiter hovers by our table, waiting to see if another bottle should be opened. I shake my head slightly and he vanishes.

"I've never been," I say. "What's wrong with Brussels?"

She straightens, placing her palms on the table, serious. "Have you ever been told—by multiple people—that you'll absolutely adore so-and-so, you have so much in common, and when you finally meet them, they're...terrible?" Her expression is intent, with the singular focus of the slightly intoxicated. "It makes you question yourself, and the taste of all those people, for thinking you're like that." She smiles again, shaking it off. "That's Brussels."

I know exactly what she means. "I'll pass, then." I make a decision, confide. "My husband has gone to meet a couple, friends of a friend, who need to leave Europe."

She blinks, suddenly alert. "Jews?"

"Yes." I sketch the barest outline of their story, giving no names. "If all has gone according to plan, they'll be here sometime this evening."

"Well, then," Mary Jayne says, pushing her chair back abruptly and scattering coins on the table. "You should get back, in case they're early. They'll need some coddling. Your husband, too."

I reach for my purse but she holds up her hand. "Next time's on you," she says firmly. "I want to hear all about your guests."

5

Ava

The wedding date is set: April 27. A Saturday, this time, to make it easier for everyone to attend. I had thought about Easter Monday, as school would be closed and Max could miss a day from the clinic, but Father Dennis couldn't be away from his congregation on the holiday, and after discussion, we agree that his attendance is absolutely necessary.

"Don't you want to wait for Claire to get back?"

"I thought you wanted to marry me?" I return, bristling. "How long are you willing to wait? She's said nothing about coming home."

Max stretches, sliding his arm around my shoulder. "She'd be on the next boat if she knew."

I resist the temptation to snuggle against him. "Well, I'm not telling her—and neither are you. Let her come home in her own time and find out that we can run our lives perfectly well without her interference."

"If we're doing things differently this time," he says, "let's not have a big luncheon after the wedding."

"All right." I look at him from under my eyebrows. "Why not?"

"Because *when* Claire and Harry do come home, they'll want to throw us a party." He squeezes me close. "This way I can take my new wife out to a restaurant of my choosing, just the two of us."

"Nothing fancy," I warn.

Max bursts into laughter. "The first rule of Ava," he says. "Nothing fancy. I promise."

Even more important than Father Dennis, though I have neglected to mention it to anyone, is the Fashion Congress being held at the Bellevue Stratford, for which I have a commission from a new customer. The last day of the Congress will be on Friday, so there will be no distraught young matron trailing me to City Hall to have her hem adjusted. Mrs. Walter Fishwick (Celia to her friends) came to me after having seen several of my dresses at a charity ball; she wanted something for the Congress that could also be worn in regular society. "My husband wants me to look good, but also to be practical with his money," she confided, embarrassed. "He's a junior partner."

We have gone shopping together, something I don't often do with clients, but this young woman needed special handling. Also, she has the potential to bring a whole new clientele to my doors: Claire's friends, for the most part, are the over-thirty crowd; if I can get the just-married set, I will have enough customers to keep me until I am too old to sew.

Her dress will be simple, but elegant. Lilac satin—this year's fashionable color, and a perfect choice for her peach-blossom skin—with almost-invisible straps and a caped jacket on top with insets of lace. Mendel's did not have the lace we needed, but Mr. Friedmann pointed me to a shop further down the street which offered a wider selection and would dye it to match the satin.

"What are you going to wear?" Thelma asks, stacking dishes on the table. "Please, not the green dress."

I laugh in spite of myself. "No, not the green dress," I agree. I am fond of it—it was the first new dress I'd had since Claire's wedding when I was twenty—but it is showing its age, and also, I had insisted on wearing it the first time. I don't want to repeat any of my mistakes. "I suppose I'll have to get something new."

"Yay!" My daughter dances joyfully around the room, a plate in one hand. Thelma has my sister's passion for shopping.

"We'll see." I take in the fact that I *will* have to have a new dress for the wedding, and that I actually don't mind. "Maybe there's something I can—"

"If you're going to make something over," Pearl interrupts, "why not go to Aunt's and look through the attic again? That's where your black dress came from, isn't it? And she said we could go up there and take what we wanted."

I don't like that Claire has given us permission to root through her possessions. The girls have been barred from going into the attic without me, for fear that they will come home draped in beaded 1920s dresses or bustle skirts or something even more impractical and bizarre.

"We can't run barefoot through her things," I warn, but I am warming to the idea. There are plenty of garments up there that predate my sister's residence in the house, and their fabrics are more to my taste than Claire's pastels anyway. "I'll meet you at the house after school tomorrow—unless you have a club, Pearl?"

Her face falls. "I do," she says, but hastily adds, "The world won't end if I miss one meeting—I'm ahead in French anyway."

Thelma arrives on time and waits in the kitchen with me. Esther Hedges cuts fat slices of chocolate cake and sits down with us. "I hope Mrs. Claire comes home soon," she says. "I'm gettin' tired of cooking for the doctor and you all, no matter how much those boys eat." Her eyes crinkle. "I'd even welcome one of those jellied salads of hers. It's gotten that bad."

"Not one of those," Thelma says, her fork upraised. Crumbs dot her upper lip. "They're *awful*."

She's not wrong. I understand, too, Esther's feeling—missing something that she would normally grumble about, because overambitious, often unsuccessful dishes are part and parcel of my sister's domestic style. It's been ten months since Esther has cooked for anyone other than us; fortunately, Claire has made their situation so good that they aren't tempted to leave. Boredom would have done me in by now.

The slam of the front door echoes through the empty house and Pearl thumps down the steps, shedding the veneer of a young lady she dons most days. "The bus was late!" She snags the last bit of cake from Thelma's plate, dodging her defensive fork, and drops her books on the table. "You haven't been up there yet, have you?"

"We were waiting for you." Pearl hasn't been this eager to spend time in my company in months. I'm not likely to ruin the day by going exploring without her.

We leave Grace downstairs and make our way up the narrow stairs to the attic. Two doors present themselves at the landing. To the left, the door to Esther and Mason's rooms, overlooking the back alley. To the right, a second door leads to the open area running the length of the rest of the house. I push it open, still uncomfortable with rooting through the Warriner family's possessions when there is no one here to supervise.

The attic smells of trapped air and aging fabric, of old wood and mildew and a faint hint of perfume. It is, as I remembered, chock full of trunks and cast-off furniture. "Careful," I warn. "Don't go pulling things out of boxes."

"What are you looking for?" Pearl asks, keeping a hand on Thelma's arm. "Dressy or not?"

I close my eyes. "Not *too* dressy," I say. "I'd like to be able to wear it more than once." The gown I made for the clinic benefit last year nags at me; I will likely never put it on again, no matter how different my life as a doctor's wife may look. "Nothing too bright."

Pearl meets my eyes across the room. "Right. Drab, sad, practical. Maybe this?" She holds up an old sheet that had been draped over a mirror.

"Don't be rude."

I try to visualize where I'd found the black dress and head toward the small front window overlooking the street. There are several trunks there of earlier vintage, possibly belonging to Irene Warriner or Harry's aunts on his father's side. Lifting the lid of the first one, I am met with the smell of old wool. A drift of moths flutters upward, and I slam it shut. Not that one. The next trunk is no better, being full of linens kept so long in folds that they have shattered at the creases.

"Mama, look over here." Thelma is half inside a wardrobe, holding something out to Pearl. "What about this?"

I make my way over to them, ready to object to whatever they've found. My girls would prefer if I dressed like Claire, but the ruffles and candy colors she loves are suited to her coloring and personality, not mine. I would feel old and tired and *hefty* in such things. I don't know how to explain that without sounding negative; I don't want them to acquire the same voice I have in my head, which always has something critical to say about my appearance.

They have spread several garments over the nearest trunks. While not completely to the girls' taste, they obviously find these pieces acceptable enough to show me, and I draw in an excited breath.

Sadly, I have to eliminate the first dress, which I love; the fabric is too fragile. But their second choice is a nubby gray walking suit from the early part of the century—definitely before the war. Two rows of black velvet ribbon circle the hem of the flaring skirt, which, when held up against me, nearly reaches the floor. I drop it and reach for the short, double-breasted jacket, hoping against hope that it will fit and I won't have to take everything apart and remake it from scratch. It pulls against my shoulders and doesn't close in front. For a moment, I want to cry.

"You've got a sweater on, Mama," Pearl points out.

I pull it off and try the jacket again over my slip. The black velvet frog closures reach, and I exhale in relief. The length isn't fashionable, but I can use the extra fabric from the skirt to add a peplum, and I'll take some fullness from the sleeves or it will look like I'm wearing something from a dressing-up box. That is easily done, even while working on Mrs. Fishwick's dress. "This is...workable."

"Let's look at it in better light," my daughter says. "It could be all over moth and we wouldn't see it up here."

Thelma is back inside the wardrobe again, handing one hatbox after the other out the door. "Look at these," she calls, muffled. "You need a hat, Mama."

"I don't need a *Victorian* hat," I say, lifting the lid on the first box. A mass of broken feathers meets my eyes; another piece which has failed to survive decades of neglect. The next two are no better: a squashed felt with moth holes and a dyed straw whose brim has unraveled. "I think we should give up on the hats."

"No!" Thelma staggers out with one last box held before her like an offering. "This one. This is the one, Mama."

Pearl takes the box and opens it the rest of the way. Her expression tells me nothing. "Yes," she says finally. "It's perfect!"

I'm not sure it's perfect, but the black straw hat is undamaged, its wide brim as crisp as the day it was made. Hats are getting bigger—there was an article in a recent fashion magazine about cartwheel hats—and this could be re-trimmed to more resemble my taste. "The roses would have to go."

"I'll sew them to my dancing dress," Thelma says and sneezes explosively. "Can we go downstairs now? My nose itches."

Claire

Madame LeClerc held dinner until eight, by which time my head had cleared from the unaccustomed assault of the rosé. I ate alone, the empty chairs a silent reproach. Where were they? If they had met as planned, their train should have arrived in Paris by seven.

What if something had gone wrong? If so, it would be with the Adlers and not Harry, but my husband is my chief concern. He's been a bit off lately—tired and complaining occasionally of stomach pains. What if he became ill on the train? Would anyone think to contact me?

By the time the door opens, just past ten, I have worked myself into a state. He enters slowly, speaking over his shoulder as I launch myself from the sofa and into his arms.

"Darling." He kisses me, then holds me at arms' length. "I missed you, too. These are the Adlers, Josef and Renate."

My face heats at the judgment on Mrs. Adler's face; I have behaved like a silly, giddy woman before people who have been fleeing for their literal lives. "I'm very glad to meet you," I say, offering my hand. "And even happier that you are here. Leo will be so pleased."

"I sent a cable from the train station," Harry says. "He'll know soon enough."

Josef Adler is a thin man of middling height. His cheeks are stubbled and his eyes ringed with tiredness. His wife is a slim, olive-skinned woman who barely reaches his shoulder. Despite her travel-stained dress, she is neatly made up and her black hair has been wound into a fresh chignon.

Katie appears from behind me, and looks around the entry. She meets Mr. Adler's eye and he hands her a small suitcase.

"Is the rest of your luggage being sent on from the station?"

"There is nothing else," Mr. Adler says. "It's gone. It's all gone."

Renate Adler speaks up. "It is only clothing, Josef." Her dark eyes scan the room—not nervous, perhaps, but thorough, looking in corners. The mannerisms of someone who is hunted, or has been.

"Let me show you to your room," I say. "You can freshen up, and if you're hungry, I can have something ready in a few minutes."

Mrs. Adler's eyes flutter closed. "I would like to sleep," she murmurs. "If, perhaps, I could borrow a nightdress?"

Ava

I deliver the wedding invitation to Mendel's in person. "My children say to tell you I'm going through with it this time."

He takes the card and tucks it into his pocket. "My congratulations, Mrs. Kimber. I will do my best to be there, but my niece is expected very soon and I may have to travel to meet her."

I look up from the selection of trims by the counter. Resistance is difficult, but I have little use for ornament myself and can't afford it without a commissioned garment. "I hadn't heard that she was coming," I say. "Mr. Friedman told me she was having difficulty getting here."

"Papers." He throws his hands in the air. "On her end, she needs visa, passport, permission to leave Germany. On my end, she needs financial guarantee, residence, and a job." He smiles then, his face lighting. "You work so hard, Mrs. Kimber. Your new husband, wouldn't he like you to have an assistant? Sonia, she is a good girl."

I didn't realize how much was involved in emigrating from a country like Germany during these unsettled times. Although I try to avoid the news, it is impossible not to know at least some of what is going on there—for Jews and for the Germans who work and live with them without prejudice. I try to imagine that happening here, kind people like Mr. Mendel and his nephew, who want nothing more than to live and worship and run their business, being stripped of not only that business, but of their citizenship. The hair prickles on my arms.

"I have daughters," I say. "I don't need an assistant." His face pinches, and I hurry to assure him. "I'm sure I can give her at least some work. She's a seamstress?"

"Yes, yes," Mr. Mendel says. "And a very good one. My brother's children are good children."

"I'm sure they are." I want to put a comforting hand on his arm, but I have learned that his religion makes him uncomfortable with such things coming from a woman and a non-Jew. Instead, I give him what he wants. "Of course I'll give her work," I say. "And if she is not happy with it, she can tell me what she would like to do, and Dr. Byrne and I will help her find a different job."

Max will be useful in all this. He loves a project, and never seems to run out of goodwill toward his fellow man. It might as well benefit my relationship with my fabric seller, and his unfortunate niece.

Pearl

March 26, 1935

School was awful today. I can't get algebra to make sense in my brain. It's even worse than Latin. But I have to pass it if I want to graduate well. And I do.

I also need good grades if I want to join the Service Club. It's the best club in the school, the one that ranks over all the others, and only the most important juniors and seniors get in. I'm a sophomore, so they wouldn't let me in anyway, but also I'm not important and my grades aren't good enough. I'm not even as smart as I thought I was, or as my teachers said I was.

Latin kicks me in the teeth, no matter how much time Hazel spends tutoring me at lunch and after school. She likes Latin, because of her father being a lawyer, but I'm going to be a writer and probably a teacher and I don't know where conjugating Latin verbs will get me. *Amo amas amat.* What does that have to do with anything?

Claire

For the first few days, the Adlers are more ghosts than guests, encountered in the hall near the bathroom, clutching our spare robes, barely awake. Katie delivers food and manages to extricate their clothing from the room while they are asleep so she can wash them and, having checked their sizes, I can do some shopping.

On the third day, Mrs. Adler pauses in the doorway as we are sitting down to breakfast. "May I join you?"

Harry stands, pulls out a chair. "Please. I hope you're feeling well?"

"Better, thank you." She is wearing the dark blue dress I purchased for her at the Galeries Lafayette. Catching my eye, she smiles faintly. "And I assume it is you I must thank, Mrs. Warriner, for the clothing?"

"We can get other things once you've rested," I tell her, pouring coffee all round. "But I wanted you to have something other than your traveling clothes."

"Thank you." Mrs. Adler adds cream and stirs her coffee. "I do not know if your husband has told you everything that happened—"

"I did not," Harry interrupts, and it's mostly true. "It is your story to tell, when you're ready."

After our guests had gone to bed that first night, Harry himself was so done in that he wanted nothing more than a drink and to go to bed. The next morning, he told me that the Adlers had been arrested at some point in their original journey toward Paris, and after their release, another friend had assisted them as far as Brussels.

Katie brings in a tray with two plates of bacon and eggs and a rack of toast. Her eyebrows raise at the sight of Mrs. Adler. "I'm glad you're better, ma'am." Realizing she might have spoken out of turn, she looks from me to Harry. "What can I get you for breakfast?"

Mrs. Adler's eyes are on our plates. "The same for me. Thank you."

"But Mrs. Adler," Harry says, "the bacon—"

She looks at him, her expression serene. "My husband and I do not keep kosher," she says. "It is too difficult, with all the traveling. And my family were secular Jews. We went to synagogue on the high holidays, no more." Her shoulders raise in a tiny shrug. "That somehow makes our situation even more insulting."

It had never occurred to me that they might have dietary restrictions. I push my plate toward her while Katie sprints back to the kitchen for another serving.

Harry polishes off his breakfast quickly. "I have some calls to make," he says, excusing himself. "Could I speak to you for a moment, Claire?"

I follow him out of the dining room, understanding that I'm going to be responsible for the Adlers while he takes care of whatever has come up. "What is it?"

"Over the last two days, I've been searching for a ship to get them to New York," he says. "Because of the delay, their visas expire in three days."

"Have you found anything?" It had taken Leo months to acquire those visas. I'm more than happy that we can help them, but I don't want them with us long term any more than I'm sure they want to be there. "That's not much time."

"Nothing this close to departure." He looks grim, with that pinched look around his mouth that is becoming more frequent. "Even third class is fully booked. The man I spoke to says a lot of Americans are going home, and the number of refugees is also high."

I want to cover my face with my hands and sink into a soft chair, but that will help no one, including me. "Who are you going to call?"

"Leo, first," he says. "Very carefully. But I've got an acquaintance at the consulate. I'm going to attempt everything short of outright bribery to get those visas."

"And if you can't?"

His shoulders raise. "Then I'll try outright bribery."

Josef Adler joins us in the dining room while his wife and I are finishing our coffee. Katie brings another plate of eggs and refreshes the toast without being asked, and I pour him a cup of coffee. He looks exhausted, but he has shaved and Harry's suit fits him reasonably well. The sun streaming through the window makes his hair gleam like polished wood.

"You've been very kind." His accent is similar to Leo's; perhaps his wife is from a different part of Germany. "Both of you."

"Nonsense." His stiffness, I think, may be fear; whatever happened to them haunts them both, but particularly him. "Leo Vollmer is a friend. We are happy to help."

He nods, accepting my words. "It is imperative that Renate reaches America."

"You both will." I hope I sound more reassuring than I feel, and that Harry's phone calls bear fruit. "It is simply a matter of time and paperwork, that's all."

"I thought our papers were in order?" she asks, and I want to shake myself for my stupidity.

"The tickets Leo purchased were for a ship that has sailed, that's all," I say. "Harry will have to find passage on another."

We lapse into silence. Josef Adler eats like a man who has not had adequate food in some time; if they don't share their story soon, I will have to shake it from Harry. Not only am I curious, but knowing what topics to avoid will make it easier to speak with our guests.

Harry reappears. I catch his eye and he gives a tiny shake of his head. "I've been looking into a new passage for you," he says, as if he hasn't already told me of the difficulty. "It may be some time before it can be arranged."

"I have said to your wife, it is imperative that Renate reaches America."

Harry repeats my earlier assurance. "It's a clear day, Adler. Why don't we get out of the apartment for a while, leave the women to do some shopping if they like."

"Renate is a treasure," Josef Adler says, ignoring the invitation. "She is my wife, and I love her, but more important than our marriage is her talent. It must not be snuffed out"—he looks around wildly—"in this hell that was once a civilized world."

"You're Renate *Steiner*," I say, realizing why her face is familiar. "We have several of your recordings. Your Mimi makes me weep every time. And *Lohengrin* is—"

"I no longer perform Wagner," she says, her accent sharpening. "He was an anti-Semite and is beloved by the Nazis."

"I will see you both onto a ship," Harry says calmly, but his heart is breaking for them, the same as mine. "Your passports are valid, as well as all necessary paperwork to get you into the United States. Leo has left funds to purchase passage, and Claire and I will provide housing in Philadelphia until other arrangements can be made."

"What arrangements?" Josef Adler asks bitterly. "There will be safety in the United States, but little else. "

The room darkens, as if his mood has blacked out the sun. Then, a sound. Renate Adler uncoils from her chair, her sleek, silk-clad legs shining in the dim light. "Don't be negative, Jojo." She slides a hand through his arm. "It's very unattractive."

"You said it yourself, Mr. Adler," I say. "Your wife is a treasure. She is well known in the United States. Philadelphia, where we live, is a center of culture." They exchange a glance. "Not like Europe, perhaps, but we have an orchestra and an opera company, and we are a short train ride from New York, where a red carpet would undoubtedly be rolled out in her honor."

"Not only that," Harry says, "there are universities in Philadelphia who would be very interested in hiring an economics lecturer from Heidelberg."

Mr. Adler purses his lips. "It will not be what we had."

"Of course it won't," Renate says sharply, with no hint of the honeyed sweetness of her singing voice. "But we will not return home to a ransacked apartment, with the threat of arrest or worse hanging over our heads." She looks at me, arched black eyebrows raised. "And if Mrs. Warriner is correct, I will be able to work."

Unspoken are the words, "*And that is what matters.*"

6

Ava

I fold Claire's latest letter and put it on the mantel to be read aloud after supper. It's her usual rush of words, telling of people she's met—an artist named Picasso who I'm sure Pearl will have heard of—and informing me that a couple will be coming to visit, possibly even before they get home.

"They are friends of a dear friend of Harry's," she writes. "If they reach Philadelphia before us, as I hope they will, please make them welcome. They will be staying in the house with Max, but darling that he is, a woman's presence is what they will need."

A woman's presence: something that is sorely missing in my life. Though I am surrounded by women, they are clients, not friends. I can't speak honestly to them about my life any more than I can Esther; the differences in our situations—race, but more importantly, her employment—are often insurmountable.

I miss my sister far more than I expected. In the beginning, it wasn't as noticeable. Pearl's unexpected anger at being left behind kept me distracted, along with the addition of Claire's dog to our household. Pixie moved in with a cushioned bed, a bag of toys, three collars, and an assortment of leashes apparently chosen to coordinate with Claire's dresses. Every other week, a regular, prepaid delivery of Ken-L-Ration arrives from the grocer; Claire was taking no chances that her precious dog would go hungry.

The dog had been a nuisance at Claire's, yapping and getting underfoot and needing to be walked, but Thelma loved it, and when Claire suggested it stay with us while she was away, the kids loudly outvoted me.

Truthfully it isn't so bad having her in the house. Pixie eats in the kitchen before we have our meals, and sleeps on the floor beside Thelma's bed. Judging by the amount of silky black and white hair I find on the spread, he sometimes sleeps on the bed, but I haven't caught him in the act. He is less whiny and demanding, probably because there is always someone available to play or take walks.

Then there is Max. The thought of him makes me smile. But even so, a daughter and a dog and a man are not the same as a sister.

It's been ten months now. Will she ever come home? It appears that Harry can run his businesses perfectly well from anywhere in the world, but what about Claire? Does she miss her life? Her house? Does she miss me?

And what about Teddy? He will have forgotten us all by now. My darling boy, my sister's child. It hurts deep in my bones to be without him for this long. The photos Claire has sent of the three of them, feeding ducks in a park, standing in front of the Eiffel Tower, show how he's grown, but they make him feel further away.

I should write and tell her to come home. I won't. It's not in me to beg, no matter how much I feel her lack. And I've told Max that he's not to ask her, either, in those monthly reports he sends. He listens, smiling, and obeys, because he knows how I would react if he went behind my back.

It will be better once we are married. He will be in the house with me. I'll have someone to talk to, and to lean on. I'll have a lover again—properly, not in moments stolen from our busy lives. My kids will have a father.

A sharp pain in my shin snaps me out of my thoughts. Grace is leaning over the side of the playpen Dan has constructed, an alphabet block in her hand. Another one lies at my feet.

"Oh no, you don't," I say, as she hurls the next block. It bounces off the chair leg. I scoop her up and hug her to me until she starts to squirm, then shift her to my hip and carry her downstairs. "Mama has to get to work, and you get to keep me company."

She likes that, likes the bits of fabric and ribbon I give her to play with. Grace is a precocious child, her bright eyes constantly on our faces, trying to understand her world. Max adores her, and the feeling is mutual.

I put her down on the rag rug I've added to the workroom, to cushion her falls, and reach into the scrap basket. "Here you are," I say absently, thinking now of Max and the way he lights up when he sees Grace, when it comes to me: the perfect wedding present for him.

Pearl

"I was thinking," Mama says when we are all seated around the table, "I was thinking that maybe after we get married, Max could adopt Grace."

So that's why this family meeting was called.

"Why?" Thelma asks. "She's not his."

It would sound rude if I didn't know she absolutely adored him. "Let Mama explain."

She looks around the table, at each of us, and I think how relaxed she looks lately. There's still a wire that runs up her spine, quick to anger, but she's softened in the last year.

Daddy would scarcely recognize her.

"Grace never knew her father," she says. I know now how much effort it takes to keep that smooth expression. "You all had him for years, you're Kimbers, but Max will be the only father she'll remember."

Dan nods; he almost always agrees with Mama.

"Will you tell her about Daddy?" George wants to know.

"Of course," she says. "Her name will be Byrne, same as mine will be, but that doesn't make either of us any less a Kimber." She lowers her eyes for a second, then gives us the whole truth. "Max can't have kids, and even if he could, I think there are enough of us."

"He can't?

"Why don't you—"

"Did you want—"

It is shocking how much noise they make. I glance at Dan and he drops one palm heavily on the table. "Quiet," he says. "Let Mama finish."

She smiles gratefully at him. "There's not a lot more to say. I think it's a good idea—it will tell Max he's truly a part of the family, and Grace will grow up with a father of her own. Are we agreed?"

"Yes," says Dan. "Pearl?"

I lower my chin, my eyes burning. "Yes."

"S'okay by me," Toby says.

"Me too." George peers over my shoulder. "Can we eat now?"

"No." I glare at him. "Thelma?"

She slides off her chair and goes to Mama, leaning her head on her shoulder. "Yes," she says. "We had a daddy. She needs one, too."

Mama exhales, and her cheeks shine suddenly with tears. I hadn't realized how much it meant that we accepted her marriage; we accepted Dr. Max long before she did. But this is different.

"One thing." I am careful to speak in such a way that she understands I don't mean to be hurtful. Even though I'm mad at her, this is family business and I need to make myself clear. "I don't know if I can call Dr. Max Daddy."

She blinks. It hasn't occurred to her that we would. "What would you call him, Pearl?"

I consider it, put on the spot without having had a chance to confer with Dan. "I'd like to stick with Dr. Max, if that's all right."

"Me, too." At seventeen, Dan is a grown man. It would be hard for him to call someone else Dad after our father.

"I'll call him Papa," Thelma says, her eyes dreamy. "There was a girl in a movie I saw that—"

Toby interrupts. "Papa is too fancy pants for Dr. Max. I'm gonna call him Pop."

And there it is, out of my little brother's thick skull, the name Grace will grow up using for the only father she will know. Dr. Max will make his own place in our hearts and our family.

Daddy is safe.

Claire

"Do you mean to tell me"—Mary Jayne pushes away her bowl of moules mariniere, my news so shocking that she cannot eat—"that you have *Renate Steiner* staying in your guest room?"

We have met, at my instigation, for the first time since our soaking café luncheon. Harry is working himself to the point of exhaustion trying to get new visas for the Adlers and gave me permission to speak about our guests to anyone who might be able to help.

"I do," I confirm, "though you wouldn't know it. She speaks, but since we don't have a piano, or anyone to accompany her, she doesn't sing."

Even without accompaniment, I had expected to hear her—didn't a singer need to sing?—but other than polite conversation at meals, the Adlers keep to themselves.

Mary Jayne stretches inelegantly. "I'm sure I could rustle up someone with a piano," she says. "Amongst our crowd, that wouldn't be hard to come by."

"What about an accompanist?" I take a sip of my wine—white this time, as I am avoiding any further overindulgence in rosé. "Do you know anyone?"

Her brow wrinkles. "Not offhand, but I've got an acquaintance at the Conservatoire. I'm sure he could find someone, especially when I tell him who needs it."

When I return home and share the news, I receive my first genuine smile from Renate.

"That would be wonderful." She clasps graceful, red-tipped hands. "You have no idea, Mrs. Warriner, what you have given me."

"Have you missed it?" I ask, unable to resist. "Singing?"

"Like I would miss breathing." Her expression tightens for a moment. "I was afraid the Nazis had stolen that joy from me, but it is coming back, the desire. I need it."

She crosses to the living room window and looks out. Although we have been to the stores and purchased several new dresses, she wears her black traveling suit, which has been cleaned and mended. The seams of the jacket show wear, but the fit is flattering in the extreme, the only reason she doesn't look as shabby as the other refugees arriving in Paris. The mustard silk blouse beneath it—which should have washed out someone with her complexion—glows like a forgotten sun.

"What happened?" Harry still hasn't given me all the details. "I'm sorry if that's intrusive—"

"It is all right." She lets the curtain drop back against the glass. "I thought your husband would have told you."

I shake my head. "He is very respectful of your privacy."

Renate sinks down on the velvet sofa, tucking her legs to one side and crossing her ankles. Every movement is calculated; she is a performer to her bones.

"Leo told you that our flat was vandalized?" She continues without waiting for my response. "Jojo came to my concerts when his schedule permitted, but once he was dismissed by the university, I insisted that he come on tour with me." She gives a small shrug. "Otherwise he would have stayed in our flat, brooding.

"So we spent a year going from place to place—Vienna, Prague, Budapest to start. Even though we knew what was happening at home, it was a respite. Leo kept us abreast of the news from Berlin, and I spoke frequently with my manager." Her lipsticked mouth pinches. "We knew it was bad, but it has been bad for Jews before. We thought it would fade by the time we returned, but instead it was worse."

I remember Leo's growing worry when they didn't appear in Paris. "Why were you not able to meet Leo?"

"We were arrested," she says shortly. "After we returned from Geneva and found our flat destroyed, that was when Jojo approached Leo. He did not want to meet us in Berlin—too dangerous for him, because of his business and the Nazis being headquartered there—and so we left ahead of him." She takes a deep breath, holds it for a long moment. "It happened in Munich. We were separated, questioned. Kept locked up. Finally, one day I was brought into a room. Dieter, my manager was there. I hadn't eaten or slept—hadn't seen Jojo in days—and I begged him to get us out." Her mouth pinches again. "He did, for a price."

I am cold, listening to her. She speaks calmly, the way Ava used to talk about the harsh realities of her life, and because of my sister I understand this is the only way Renate can bear to speak of it at all.

"They forced me to perform for them. If I did not, Jojo would be sent to a work camp and I would die forgotten in a cell." She shakes her head. "If I had been alone, I would have refused. But it was not just me." She launches off the sofa, pacing to the window and back again. Her breath is quick but her words are slow and deliberate. "They filmed me, laughing as I took requests like a cheap cabaret singer. I gave them Wagner and the *Das Deutschlandlied* until I wanted to spit in their faces. I sang the *Horst-Wessel-lied*."

Her face is pale, ghastly. I want to embrace her, but although she has warmed to me, a show of emotion would not be welcome, particularly now.

"They released you, after that?"

"They did." She swallows. "And Dieter, he handed us two tickets to Brussels and said to forget we are German." Her eyes flutter closed. "I have known him since I was sixteen, longer than I have known my husband. I entrusted my career to him, and when he put us on the train, he called me a filthy Jew, and told me he had confiscated my earnings as repayment for getting us out."

They had arrived with one small suitcase and the clothes on their backs. I understand now that is literally all they have left. "So you were—"

"Robbed by a man I thought of as a father." Her voice is harsh, the Germanic edge more pronounced. "May God erase his name from The Book of Life for such a betrayal."

Renate will not accept my embrace, but I know what she will accept. I pour some of the schnapps Harry has acquired for them and hand it to her. She knocks it back in one swallow.

"Thank you." She looks exhausted, but somehow more at peace. "I appreciate everything you and your husband are doing for us. I will repay you, when I am able to work again."

7

Ava

Considering that I have come to make my living from dresses, it shouldn't be the case, time and again, that I have nothing decent to wear. It's the training of decades though, that keeps me from making myself a couple of inexpensive, presentable day dresses. Motherhood says money should be spent on the kids first; they're growing, they need clothing more than I do. When I gaze at the shelves of bright spring cottons and rayons at Mendel's, I hear my mother's voice: *you just want, you don't need*, and I turn away and buy what the business requires.

But I am my business, and Prue Foster has reminded me of that fact. Prue is a good friend of Claire's and my first paying customer in Philadelphia. She sent over an invitation for tea on Thursday. On the back of the card, she scrawled, "The usual crowd, plus a few new ones you should meet. Come prepared."

Does prepared mean I should bring a tape measure and a notepad in case I have the opportunity to take down their measurements? More likely, as she knows both me and Claire, her intention is to warn me that I will be on uncomfortable display, judged by strangers whose potential work could keep my family fed.

I sigh, cataloging the meager contents of my wardrobe. My two best dresses—the black taffeta and the blue satin gown I wore to the clinic gala last year—are inappropriate for a daytime event. Most of my time is spent in skirts and blouses, with a pale gray smock over top so my customers don't notice what I'm wearing. That also won't work. And because I have been busy sewing for others, my suit is far from finished—and I refuse to wear it before the wedding.

"What are you looking at, Mama?" Thelma peers in, Grace attached to one leg. By the amount of toddler visible beneath her skirt, I realize her hems need to be let down again.

"You remember Mrs. Foster?" I ask. "She's invited me to tea and I have to figure out what to wear."

She detaches Grace carefully, hikes her up onto one hip and comes into the room. "You're going to wear the green, aren't you?"

That had been my intention, but if a nine-year-old can criticize it, perhaps I should rethink.

"Life was easier, sometimes, when we didn't have so much," I tell her. "Back in Scovill Run, I had two dresses and I never had to think about what to wear."

"Back in Scovill Run," she says, placing her sister carefully on the quilt, "you were usually going to have a baby."

Thelma was my youngest for a long time, before Teddy, and then Grace. But even so, she can look at her older siblings and understand how little time I hadn't spent in stretched out maternity dresses.

"It's a different world here." I sit on the edge of the bed, one hand on Grace to keep her from squirming. "Do you ever miss it?"

Seated, I am almost eye to eye with my tall, slender daughter. Her blue eyes, so like Claire's, open wide. "Only Daddy," she says, causing my heart to clench in my chest. "And Granny. But I don't remember her real clear anymore."

"It's been almost half your life." So much has happened in a few short years—Mama, Daniel. The move to Philadelphia. Max. The kids have adjusted better than I have. "I lost my father when I was fourteen, which is way older than when you lost Granny, but I don't remember him clearly anymore." In some respects, that may be a blessing. Tata was an angry man who, when he'd had enough to drink, had no trouble showing his anger to his wife and children. I can't tell her that. "I remember the love," I say. "That's what's important."

She gazes at me thoughtfully, then, with a lightning fast change of mood, asks, "Are we poor?"

"Poor?" Thelma is too young to be worrying about money. "No, baby. We have to be careful, but I'll make sure there will always be money for your dance lessons."

"I'm not worried about that," she says, gracefully lifting her shoulders. "Aunt would pay for them if you couldn't. I was wondering, can't you buy a dress, just this once?"

I could. And I wouldn't have to overpay, because I know fabric and fit, and because I can improve on anything that I bought in a store. "Do you think I should?"

Thelma's broad smile gives me her answer. It's not often I have time alone with my younger girl. I should snatch this advantage when it presents itself.

"Then let's go shopping."

"What about her?" She tilts her head toward Grace, who is wetly gnawing on the bed's metal footboard. "You can't have her chewing on things in the stores."

"She's teething. You did it." Perhaps not with the same enthusiasm—between her physical limitations and a simple difference in personality, Thelma was an easier baby.

"Eww." Her nose wrinkles. "Can't we leave her with Mrs. Malloy?"

I consider a moment, then nod. "We did watch her baby for a whole day last week, when she visited her sister in the hospital. She won't mind."

Grace crankily disposed of in Betty Malloy's kitchen, rubbing her sore gums on a crust of stale bread, Thelma and I set off toward Market Street.

"Are we going to Wanamakers?" she asks, practically dancing along. "Or Lit Brothers? Gimbels?"

Because of the months she spent with Claire, undergoing treatment with Max, my daughter is better acquainted with the department stores of Philadelphia than I am. I wonder if she has been to the Bonwit Teller store, where my sister once strong-armed me into the very green print dress everyone now thinks is so tired.

"We're going to Snellenburg's." Of all the department stores, it is the least intimidating to me. Their slogan, *The Thrifty Store for Thrifty People*, appeals to me, even as I am being induced to go there and spend money. We are not, as I told Thelma, poor any longer.

That hard times are not universally over is obvious by the unemployed men lingering on the corner by the Reading Terminal. Next door, the store is bustling, even on a weekday afternoon. Thelma is immediately drawn to a display of ladies hats, and I have to catch her by the sleeve to drag her to the dress department.

"But your hat is awful," she protests. "It's the same sad one you've had since I was little."

It's the same hat I've worn since Claire left it behind after Mama's funeral. I've re-trimmed it several times and it's perfectly good, but I understand what my daughter means. Between her addiction to Hollywood movies and the time she spends with Claire, Thelma thinks everything should be pale and covered in flowers, and my dark felt is sad by comparison.

"We can look on the way out. Let's see what this dress is going to cost first."

The saleswomen in the dress department are charmed by my beautiful girl, and I stay well back as she explains to them that I need a day dress for an important tea party.

"My mama is a dressmaker," she proclaims, "but she never makes things for herself."

One of the clerks smiles in sympathy. "Like the shoemaker with the barefoot children."

"Exactly," I tell her, "except my children aren't naked." I color, thinking how that must sound. "And neither am I, but I've got nothing suitable for this party, and there will be women there whose custom I would like."

"You will, by the time you pass through these doors again," she assures me. "Now, what colors do you like?"

"She likes green." Thelma's eyes crinkle. "She's got a green dress she loves, but it's old as the hills."

"No it's not," I correct automatically. "But I do like green. I like other colors—just nothing too showy and nothing so light it will be difficult to keep clean."

"Understood." She gestures for us to follow. "We have some lovely spring florals that might do the trick."

Was this Claire's life, I wonder, before the clinic? I stand in the dressing room in my slip, Thelma perched on a stool at my feet, surrounded by riotous color. "It's like a candy store," I whisper to her, and she grins back at me. "But I can only buy one. Help me choose."

She bounces up, and ruthlessly subtracts three dresses from the array. "Not these."

"Why not?" I have opinions on their suitability, but I'm curious what she thinks.

"You don't look good in yellow," she says, dismissing the first one. "The blue one pulls on your bottom. And this"—she holds up a pastel floral—"is my favorite, but it looks more like Aunt Claire than you."

She is right on all counts. I select the one nearest to me, a rayon floral in shades of blue and violet, which obscurely reminds me of one of Claire's French paintings.

"What about this?" I hold it up against me. The colors are flattering, the depth of the violet brings out the blonde in my hair, and the cut is slimming, although I will never have my sister's enviable waistline.

"Either that or the stripy one." She rubs the skirts of both dresses between her fingers, a gesture I recognize as my own, and shakes her head. "The flowers. This doesn't feel as nice."

"And I'm not sure about me and stripes, anyway." I resume my clothing, and take up the hanger with the winning dress. "Can you get the rest, Thel?"

She pushes the curtain aside. "They'll put them away," she says confidently. "It's their job."

On the way out, she drags me back to the millinery department. "Just try a few on," she begs. "Please."

Another clerk swoops in, black-clad and glistening like a beetle.

"I'm not certain I'm buying," I preface, "but I purchased a new dress upstairs and might like something to go with it."

"May I look?" She looks into the bag as I part the tissue paper. "Hmm. Something you can wear through the spring and the summer."

"You can save the old felt one for winter," comes my daughter's loud whisper.

I glare at her over my shoulder, and then give in to the lure of the mannequin heads before me. They wear candy-colored felts—pinks, blues, minty greens—or pale straws with a variety of decorations. I am drawn to the straw hats, thinking of the summer humidity and the fragility of my curls.

"What are the prices?" I ask, before I fall in love with something and get my feelings hurt. To temper my words, I turn the store's slogan around. "I am a thrifty person."

"As are most of our customers." She directs me to another selection, equally attractive. "These are imported peanut straw. It wears very well, and looks as nice as some of the more expensive straws."

"What about this one?" I pick up a golden straw with a shallow brim and a scrap of veil. It has a wide ribbon band in dark blue which would suit the dress, but would also be easily replaced with other colors or flowers, as I saw fit.

"One dollar and thirty-nine cents," she says smoothly. "It's on special this week."

I swallow a lump in my throat the size of one dollar and thirty-nine cents in pennies. "I don't know…"

"Try it on!" Thelma claps her hands. On her blonde curls she wears a wide picture hat whose entire underside is ruffled lace.

"You look like a box of candy." I seat myself before the mirror, smoothing my hair and settling the hat on my head.

It looks *good.* I'm not accustomed to looking at my reflection with approval; generally, it is enough that my face is clean and my hair is combed. But this hat, tilted slightly, the veil arranged over my nose, is flattering.

"That's very nice, ma'am." The clerk fetches a hand mirror to show me the back of my head, as they do at the beauty salon. "And it will look a treat with your new dress."

It will. And that's the problem. I'm not used to spending on myself. I remember my conversation with Mr. Mendel, when I bought the blue satin for my gown. He counseled that I should think of it as an investment, that I was advertising my business. Shouldn't I then be advertising my business in a dress I have made? Or is it enough that I am appropriately dressed, which will render me invisible to these women?

"I'll take it." I sigh, and look over at Thelma grinning shamelessly at me from beneath her candy box hat. "And take that off, you little bad influence. You can carry the hatbox home."

Pearl

Dan and I strike out toward the river once supper is finished. He gives the boys a look and they meekly volunteer to do the dishes. Thelma, who had expected to be stuck with them, giggles and skips upstairs to practice her dancing in the brick backyard.

"So, are you good with this?" he asks, as we turn up Spruce Street, passing blocks of brownstone houses similar, but not as nice, as those on Aunt's block.

"With what, them getting married? Or Dr. Max adopting Grace?" It is hard to keep pace with Dan; his legs are so long.

"Both, I guess." He removes his cap, shoves his hair out of his eyes, and jams it back on.

"Why wouldn't I be? It's not that different from the last time, except I think they'll go through with it now." Grace taking Dr. Max's name hadn't been part of the agreement last year, but I'm wholly in favor of it. "Aren't you happy for them?"

"I'm thrilled." With a mischievous grin, he adds, "Father Dennis can give her away. It's a weight off my shoulders either way."

My brother has carried an adult burden in this family since he was thirteen. I shouldn't be surprised if he is a little tired of his role.

"Do you mean that?"

"Maybe." He grabs my elbow and guides me across the street. "I like knowing someone else is responsible from here on out."

"You're part of the family," I remind him. "You'll always be Mama's favorite."

It always makes him blush, to be reminded that he's her pet. "She's going to have to manage without me for a while."

"Why? You're not still thinking about going away, are you?" It's something he's threatened since we were back in Scovill Run, but I thought he was over it.

"Yes." His tone is assured. "Me and Tommy, we've been talking about it for months. We've put it off until Ma finally got hitched."

Wonderful. Not only is my brother going to leave town, but he's taking Tommy Marinelli with him! Without Dan around, I probably wouldn't see him, but a girl can dream.

"I don't think you should go." I loop my arm through his, hoping to slow him a little bit. We don't need to bolt toward the river. "Mama won't like it—and what about your job?"

He slows unwillingly. "Mr. Howe said he'd take us back on, if we weren't gone more than six months."

"Six months! Would you really leave for that long?" We move to the right as a couple approaches. They nod. We nod. When they pass, we resume our place in the center of the sidewalk.

"It's not that long." He shrugs. "I want to see someplace different, Pearl. California, or Florida. Some place that's not Pennsylvania."

"You could just go across the river to New Jersey." I sound prissy, and wrinkle my nose. "Take the train to the shore. Hop a train to the shore, if you want. But don't leave—don't leave the family."

He stops dead, and I stumble. "That's rich, coming from you," he says. "Little Miss I Want To Go To Paris."

An ice wagon rumbles by, a group of boys following close behind. From habit, I check to make sure George and Toby aren't among them.

"I didn't go, though, did I?" I've gone from prissy to sullen, not appreciating the reminder of my lost opportunity.

"Not for lack of trying," he says. "And you were miserable for a solid six months after Ma said no, so I don't think you have any room to talk about me wanting to blow this town for a while." When I don't respond, he pokes me in the ribs, hard. "Right?"

We are within half a block of the path that runs along the Schuylkill, but all the pleasure has gone out of the walk for me. "No," I say. "Go ahead and go. Have the time of your life."

Claire

Harry has been trying for weeks to obtain new visas for the Adlers. The consulate is dragging its feet; not unwilling but not rushing, either. Hoping the problem will solve itself, that they will give up and return to Germany or flee to some other part of France, petition some other government for assistance.

"They are obdurate," he complains over lunch. "Pleasant enough, but each time I appear at the office, I have to start over. They've mislaid the paperwork or the vice consul is in the country and the person available to speak with me knows nothing about the refugee visa process." He rubs his temples. "A consular official, knowing nothing about visas."

"Is there anything I can do?" I caress his shoulders through his shirt; his muscles tighten when I rub too hard.

"I can't imagine there is." He drains his wine and again he tenses under my hand.

"What is it?"

"Nothing." He shakes his head. "My stomach. I think the vice consul is in there."

Harry takes an aspirin and retires to the bedroom with a book—I have removed all the newspapers, which do nothing but upset him—while I move quietly to the living room and make a telephone call to Mary Jayne Gold.

The neckline of my new gown stretches from shoulder to shoulder, a shallow dip over my breasts giving the illusion of skin without revealing anything. The sleeves are full, girlish, banded tight above my elbows. All semblance of girlishness ends there, as the clinging lilac silk satin splinters into godets of matching chiffon, rendering the skirt simultaneously opaque and transparent. Only my purple Delman evening shoes confirm there are legs under the shifting layers of fabric.

"Where did this come from?" Harry asks, turning from the mirror, his bow tie hanging around his neck. "Is it new?"

I knot his tie for him, and brush the dull satin lapels of his tuxedo. "Recent," I say, thinking of the orgy of shopping that had taken place on the Champs-Élysées. "Do you like it?"

He kisses my cheek, then my neck. "As if you have to ask."

"You don't mind another party?" I ask anxiously. "Mary Jayne and I have arranged this one especially."

I do not tell him that she has invited every man of her acquaintance associated with the American consulate, and every other U.S. government official in or near the city. We have determined, between us, that the evening will not end until we have made someone promise to renew the Adlers' visas.

"What's one more?" He steps back from the mirror to take another look at me. "In a city full of beautiful women, how could I not want to show off the most beautiful one of all?"

"You *are* a darling." I nuzzle his neck, with its faint scent of cologne. "Let me see if the Adlers are ready. Would you call for the car?"

The party has been in full swing for over two hours. At eleven, the singer steps back to take a break, but the band continues playing. Harry and I linger near the drinks table; his stomach is bothering him again and despite his protest that he is fine, I insist on a rest from the dancing.

Renate appears at my side, splendid in the deep blue sequined gown Mary Jayne convinced Chanel's fashion house to loan her for the evening. Her hair is swept up, pinned on both sides with my diamond combs, and my favorite bracelet adorns her right wrist.

"She knows how to give a party, that one," she says, jerking her chin toward Mary Jayne. "But I think something else is needed."

I raise my eyebrows. To me, Mary Jayne has thought of everything. "What?"

We watch as she maneuvers through the crowd, slipping around so she is facing the band leader. There is a whispered conversation. His baton never stops moving and the band continues to play *Night and Day*. When the song ends, the room falls silent. The bandleader steps back, his arm outstretched, offering the stage to Renate.

She nods crisply and steps toward the microphone. A murmur ripples through the room as she is recognized.

"Good evening," she says, unsmiling. "You have all been informed, I have been assured, that this evening is a benefit to assist people like myself—Jews—who wish to leave Germany."

Another murmur, this one not so pleased. People came because Mary Jayne invited them, and because they like parties and are used to being asked for donations; most of them don't want to think about what is going on in Germany.

Renata knows this. Drawing herself up, she continues. "But this is not why you have come tonight. And it is time for me—what is your English phrase for it?—to sing for my supper."

Wild applause breaks out. Harry and I are clapping as loudly as anyone in the room. He glances at me. "Did you know—"

"That she was going to sing? No."

She steps back, gazing over the room. Her expression makes clear that she does not see the glittering crowd in a Paris apartment, but instead a concert hall in Vienna or Prague. When she speaks again, her voice carries clearly, without the microphone. "This is *O Mio Babbino Caro* from *Gianni Schicchi*. Puccini."

I draw in a breath and curl my fingers around Harry's arm. Puccini is a favorite, although I've never heard this piece performed.

She begins to sing and the hair on my arms stands at attention. When she hits the first high note, my eyes fill with reflexive tears and I forget where I am, letting myself drown in her glorious voice. I'm not musical, though I have developed a deep appreciation over the years. After our marriage, Harry took me to frequent concerts, and I was struck by the way some people could listen, unmoved, whereas I always became deeply emotional about what I heard.

Until a single violin takes up the song, I have not even noticed that she is singing alone. A young man stands among the seated musicians, his violin at his chin, eyes closed in rapture.

Renate acknowledges his accompaniment, tipping her head back and letting her voice climb until it fills the room and all of our hearts to a point where it is almost difficult to breathe.

When she finishes, there is utter silence before the room breaks into madness. I beat my gloved palms together, still crying, until Harry hands me a handkerchief from his inside pocket.

"You'll ruin your gloves," he whispers. He is not unaffected by the music; tears rim his eyes, but mine have overflowed, tracking mascara down my cheeks. I look at the black-smeared handkerchief in my hands and shake my head. I do not have enough cosmetics with me to repair the damage.

The telephone rings the next morning before breakfast. I am awake but in my nightgown, unwilling to face the day. Harry is asleep, the covers twisted around him. When we got home from the party, he complained of stomach pains again and I insisted that he sleep in. He's been wearing himself out over this visa business; I sympathize with the Adlers, but if something doesn't happen soon, I may have to put a stop to it—though how I will convince him to cease his efforts, I have no idea.

Katie knocks softly on the door. "Ma'am?"

"Coming." I grab my robe and shut the door on my sleeping husband.

"It's Miss Gold," she says. "She wants you."

It's not even seven. Mary Jayne doesn't strike me as a morning person. "Hello?"

"My head is ringing like I have the goddamned bells of Notre Dame between my ears." Her voice is hoarse from drink and the sing-along Renate led after she finished her impromptu concert. "Do you know why I'm up this early?"

"I can't imagine." Now that I'm upright, my head is pounding and I drank far less than she did. "Why?"

"Because"—her voice rises triumphantly—"I stayed on after you left, drinking with some of the consular staff. They couldn't believe they got to sing Cole Porter with Renate Steiner."

I think of the circle of joyous, drunken faces around the piano, Renate in her Chanel gown taking requests like a cabaret singer. "Neither can I."

"Get Harry over to the office with them at ten." She yawns in my ear. "Their visas will be waiting. I'm going back to bed."

My shriek wakes Harry, and soon the Adlers' door cracks open.

"What is it?" Despite our late return, Renate's face shows no trace of makeup. Her dark hair is covered with a flowered silk scarf. "We have not yet had enough sleep for you to disturb us, Mrs. Warriner."

Her ungraciousness rolls off me. "You don't need sleep," I tell the three astonished faces before grabbing Renate's chilly hands and dancing her around the hallway. "You need breakfast. You're going to America!"

8

Ava

It was difficult not to tell Prue that Max and I are getting married, but I have to assume she and Claire exchange letters as gossipy as their conversations and I'm not comfortable asking her to keep a secret. I'm also not ready for my sister to know my business. If she were here, it would be different, but as she's taken herself off to Europe with no sign of coming home, I have no need to share my life. Her life, despite frequent letters, is unimaginable.

Prue's gathering was pleasant enough, and useful in the end. No one commented on my dress, which blended in well with the absolute garden of other floral dresses in the room. Most of the women in attendance were, as Prue said, the usual crowd, but there were three new faces—a young bride and two women, already friends, whose husbands' joint business brought them north from Baltimore.

The bride was easy; Prue leaned on her gently and she is coming on Tuesday morning to discuss a dress or two for the summer season at her mother-in-law's house in Cape May. The other two were older and not as willing to be led, but I think one of them will come around. She caught me as I was leaving and asked if she could call. I gave her one of the cards Claire insisted I have printed. I'm not holding my breath, but if she comes through, her friend will follow.

Pushing my chair away from the sewing machine, I lean back and stretch, my neck and upper back crackling with strain. I need to stand up more frequently or I'll end up a hunched old woman before I'm forty.

The sound of a car draws me to the window, just in time to see Claire's roadster stop by the front step. Max must have borrowed it to go to the clinic because of the rain this morning. The car door slams, and quick feet run up the front steps and through the door over my head.

"Is it safe to come down?" Max calls.

"If it wasn't, the sign would have been on the door." I appreciate that he always checks. "Why are you here? It's the middle of the day."

He comes downstairs and through the kitchen, gathering me into his arms and backing me against the sewing table. "I'd always rather ask," he says, kissing my neck. "You're the only woman I want to catch in her underwear."

"I'm not likely to be sewing in my underwear," I tell him, though in truth I have done it when making something for myself, so I can get up and try it on without the bother of getting undressed. "And again, why are you here?"

He steps back, his expression faux-wounded. "Aren't you happy to see me, woman? Is there a man hidden in here you don't want me to find?" He stoops to peer under the table, using the opportunity to run his hand up my leg and under my skirt.

"Get up, you fool." Warmth fills my chest at the sight of him, but my gray wedding suit is in pieces on the table and I don't want him to see it. "Let's go upstairs. I spend enough time down here."

He allows me to lead him up, patting my bottom once at the turn of the stairs. "I have no real excuse to be here," he says. "I stopped back at the house to pick up my lunch. You're a bonus."

I drop onto the couch, enjoying the welcome give of the new cushions. "You'd see me tonight. You're coming for supper, aren't you?"

"I am." He sits beside me and puts an arm around my shoulders. "But I won't likely get you to myself. I love spending time with the kids, but I'm looking forward to being married so we can be alone sometimes."

"And when do you think that will happen?" I still marvel at the fact that Daniel and I managed to produce so many children with the other ones in the house.

He strokes my arm, his fingers curling possessively around it. "At night, I hope. Conversation in bed before"—he kisses my neck again—"or after. Your choice."

"The kids do have ears, you know." I'm equally looking forward to alone time, but I think of it more in terms of taking walks in the evening or going for a drive in Claire's car on a Sunday afternoon.

Marriage, for me, has never been solely about the relationship between husband and wife. When Daniel and I married, we lived with my mother until he went to war, and by the time he came home,

Dan was born. We lived in the same house for our entire marriage, and it kept getting more and more crowded. What little alone time we had was furtive, and under the covers, and most likely with the knowledge of at least half the people in the house.

Max seems to want something different. As an only child of older parents, my chaotic household is probably an interesting change of pace, but I worry that he won't be able to cope with it long term. His days are often hard—he can't always be upbeat and willing to entertain the kids; sometimes he'll want peace and quiet, and we have very little of that.

I come out of my thoughts as he undoes the first button on my blouse. "So this is what you came home for?"

A second button follows the first. He leans over to plant a kiss on my chest, above the edge of my slip. His eyes sparkle with mischief. "Not specifically, but if the lady would throw a few crumbs of time my way, I'll do my best to make it worth her while."

He has already made it worth my while. I am melting into the sofa, though I refuse to show it.

"Let's at least take it upstairs," I say. "If anyone comes home early, I don't want them to catch us up to no good."

Taking my hand, he pulls me up with him, spinning me toward the steps. "Oh, trust me, it will be good."

I follow, helpless with laughter and anticipation, but have to ask, "You wouldn't rather wait for the wedding night?"

He stops, and I collide with him. "Woman, you dragged me to the Jersey shore and relieved me of my virtue and *now* you want to wait?"

"I didn't say that." I yank down his garishly striped tie and start on his buttons. "I just thought I'd give you the option."

Pearl

April 17, 1935

I'm almost too tired to write, but everyone's in bed and I finally have some peace and quiet and I feel like I've been neglecting my diary lately. Besides, I'm too sore to do anything else. I pulled a muscle today and my leg hurts. It hurt when I left school, but then I couldn't find my carfare and had to walk home.

It was physical training, of course. My least favorite subject. Not only because of the awful bloomer suits we wear (over white blouses, no less) but because I don't want to run or play ball. I'm here to learn. And I get enough exercise going to and from school and chasing kids around the rest of the time.

If I have to do it, though, I would actually rather run than anything else. I don't have to be coordinated the same way, or know the rules to games we never played back home. I don't understand soccer. And when we play field hockey I always get hit in the shins. Good things my skirts are longer these days, to cover the bruises.

Running is okay, unless I trip over my feet like I did today. There are a couple of other girls who run at the same time. Miss Armstrong usually lets us, because most of the time we're no loss to the games being played. Two of the girls are colored and the other is Jewish. None of us fit in, but I blend in better.

We talk sometimes when we run, but not about not fitting in. Zenobia, one of the colored girls, she wants to be a singer. She's in the Bible club, because her family is very religious but also because they go to different churches and she gets to sing. She wants to join the Treble Clef Club, but her parents say no. Singing for the Lord is acceptable. Singing for an audience isn't.

Zenobia is beautiful, with the smoothest skin I've ever seen. Nellie, who's her cousin, is taller than most girls in school and barely brown at all. They snipe at each other sometimes about that, about Nellie's father, but a boy on the street called her yellow, and Zenobia lost all her Christian kindness. We had to pull her off him, and she got a discipline mark because one of the teachers saw her. Girls High girls don't do that. There are a lot of things Girls High girls don't do. Rolling their stockings and eating on the street are two of them, but making a spectacle of yourself probably tops the list.

Malka Zimmerman lives and breathes arithmetic. Not just numbers, but the kind of math I don't understand. Algebra, calculus. Geometry. She's in all the advanced math clubs. She's also tops in 10B biology and is taking chemistry classes. She says her grandfather was a scientist in Germany but when he came here, he worked in a shop. No one would hire him because his English was bad.

I'd never tell Mama, but sometimes I feel like I'm seeing all the world I need to here at school.

And now I'm going to bed because my leg is cramping. Maybe it'll be better in the morning.

Claire

Once the visas are obtained, everything moves rapidly. The same afternoon, Harry buys passage on a freighter whose eventual destination is New York. He apologizes for the accommodations, thinking speed of departure more important than luxury, and they quickly agree. The Adlers would likely climb into a rowing boat if it would get them across the Atlantic; they will reach New York, that is all that matters.

"There is no point in cabling," I remark. "I've already warned everyone you're coming, and you won't arrive before my next letter anyway."

Esther Hedges will do her utmost to make them comfortable. If my sister would get around to marrying Max, they could have his rooms instead of the smaller guest room. Perhaps he'd be willing to swap...

I shake my head. There are more important things to worry about than the sleeping arrangements at my far-off home. Turning my gaze to Renate, I say, "We'll need to do some shopping before you leave."

Harry travels with them as far as Le Havre. I stay behind with Teddy, chewing my nails until he returns, triumphant. I suggest a celebratory dinner and he agrees, not even wanting to bathe or change his clothes before heading out.

After we eat, we walk for a little while along the quay. My husband, who was animated during dinner, has grown quiet.

"Is it your stomach again?" I take his arm. Now that the Adlers are gone, he needs to take better care of himself.

"Yes," he says shortly. When a taxi swerves to the curb in response to his upraised arm, we get in and travel the short distance in silence.

Katie meets us at the door, taking our coats and asking if we'd like tea.

"No." Harry pushes past us to the bedroom. The slam of the bathroom door echoes through the apartment. Katie and I both listen for Teddy's voice, but he does not wake.

"Is Mr. Warriner sick?" she asks.

"His stomach is bothering him again. He says it's nothing."

Katie looks uncomfortable. "The other day, ma'am, I saw him over there"—she indicates the double doors which lead to the tiny iron balcony outside the living room—"holding for dear life to that railing. I asked was he all right and he snapped at me." She shakes her head. "He's the kindest man. That's not like him."

No, it is not. "Thank you, Katie. I'll try to make him listen." I put a hand on her arm. "You go off to bed now. I'll manage from here."

The bathroom door is shut, and the sound of my husband vomiting is audible. I close my eyes, consider the awful possibilities. Could he be truly ill? He'd had the first of these bouts before we left for Paris and had put it down to the stress of dealing with Irene, but it has occurred every few weeks since our arrival, and with increasing frequency since the Adlers entered our lives.

"That's it," I say, as he staggers back from the bathroom, his face gray and sweating. "You've worn yourself out. You're staying in bed for the next few days."

He gets into bed willingly enough, but immediately objects. "I'm fine, Claire. I'm just a little run down, and it was a rich meal."

It was; we'd gone to a restaurant near the Les Halles market and Harry had ordered a tower of shellfish and demolished it with a boy's gleeful enthusiasm. My Dover sole had been sufficiently light that I'd filched a few winkles from the tower.

I put my hand on his abdomen and he flinches. "Bed rest," I say. "Or I'm calling a doctor."

"I don't like doctors in English," he grumbles, removing his glasses and putting them on the bedside table. "They're even worse in French."

"You like Max." I turn off the lamp. Moonlight streams through the parted curtains, tracing a path across the carpet and over the foot of the bed. "Not all doctors are bad."

Harry rolls over and sighs. "No doctors, Claire. I'll be fine. I'll rest tomorrow and I'll be fine."

I slide down further under the light cover, too worried to sleep. My husband sounds like he is trying to convince me, and perhaps himself, that everything is all right.

9

Ava

Because everything is different this time, we get ready for the wedding at Claire's, where there is more room for the inevitable fuss and bother that a wedding entails. Father Dennis arrives at eleven. Dan has been keeping an eye from the front window, and rushes out to pay the taxi. The kids immediately mob the priest. Even Grace staggers forward, looking up at him curiously, and he bends with effort and a cracking of knees and settles her on his hip before turning to me. "There's the bride," he bellows in his rich Irish voice. "Come and give me a kiss, Ava."

It is astonishingly good to see this remnant of my old life. I obey, threading my way through the kids and planting a kiss on his red-veined cheek. "How are you, Father?" I blink back unexpected tears. "How was your journey?"

He squeezes me close, squashing Grace against me until she squeaks in protest. "I would have walked over hot coals for this day, so I consider it very civilized."

"Sit down, Father," Pearl urges. "Let me bring you some tea."

"I wouldn't say no," he agrees, following her into the living room and looking around at the elegance of Claire's home. "And I wouldn't turn down a bite to eat, if it's to be had. Mrs. Metzger packed a sandwich for me, but I gave it away on the train."

"How is Trudy?" I take Grace from him so he can sit in Harry's big chair.

"She's blooming," he tells me. "Her son came back to visit a month or two ago, did her and the kiddies a world of good."

While Pearl fetches tea, he catches me up on the doings of our old home. The mine is operating on a reduced schedule, giving the remaining men enough work that they're not tempted to leave. Prices at the store have gone up, so what little money they make doesn't go very far, and there are persistent rumors of rent increases on the tied houses.

"It's good you got out." He accepts the cup from Pearl with a smile. "It looks like you're doing well here."

"This isn't us," I say, aghast. "This is Claire's house. We live more modestly."

"Even so." He stirs sugar into his tea. "So tell me, where will I be sleeping tonight? In this fine palace, under a canopy, like the Irish kings of old?"

I explain that Max and I will spend our wedding night here, and he will stay at our house with the kids. It's as much a punishment as a blessing, but they'll behave for him and Max and I will get one night together without a dozen ears being pricked for our every move.

"I've got a special supper planned for us," Pearl says. "Mama and Dr. Max are going out to a restaurant together."

"Where is the bridegroom?" Father Dennis asks. "I'd like to meet him properly before I hand you over to him."

"Max went into work this morning," I say. "He should be here in time for lunch, and then we'll all get changed and drive to City Hall."

He's not quite that timely, arriving at a dash as we're already at the table and sliding in beside Pearl. "Sorry." He smiles at me, then focuses on the sandwich and potato salad on his plate. "My bicycle got a flat. I should start using Harry's car. He told me I could."

Father Dennis clears his throat and Max looks up. "I hope you don't treat Ava like an afterthought all the time, young man."

"Not generally, no." He gets up and shakes the priest's hand. "It's good to see you again, Father. Thank you for coming—it means a lot to Ava and the kids, and to me, that you'll do this for them."

"She's as dear to me as the daughter I never had." Father Dennis gives him an appraising look. "Now finish your lunch, man. I need to take you aside and ask you your intentions before I let this wedding go forward."

Esther leaves the dishes for later and comes up to help the girls get me ready. My suit has been laid out on Claire's bed. She puts a smoothing hand on the gray wool. "I can't believe you made that out of what you brought down from the attic," she says. "You're a miracle worker."

The jacket is unrecognizable. I removed the frog closures and used the excess fabric to extend the overlapping front, hiding the seam beneath some of the velvet trim removed from the skirt. This assures that I will be able to breathe once the jacket is buttoned. A remnant of black velvet—the mis-cut fabric from Prue's jacket—has been fashioned into a flattering portrait collar.

"It's my something old, that's what it is," I tell her, turning before the mirror to check the hang of the narrowed skirt. "My something blue is my blouse."

"And the something new is this!" Thelma shows Esther the blue silk flowers the girls bought to decorate my black straw hat. "What's your something borrowed, Mama?"

I hadn't thought of that. "The suit, I guess. The whole thing is borrowed from Claire's attic."

"That won't do," Esther says. "Let me get you my church gloves. I can wear my everyday ones."

"No." Pearl reaches into the neck of her best dress and unclasps the tiny gold cross Claire sent her for Christmas last year. "Between this and Father Dennis, it makes up for not getting married in church."

"Put it on me?" The gesture makes me want to hug her, but that would call attention to her kindness and she might withdraw again. I settle for the touch of her hands at my neck, and the warmth of her skin on the crucifix as it settles between my collarbones.

When we come down the steps, the girls flowerlike in their best dresses ahead of me, Max and Father Dennis are in the living room with their heads together. I stay in the hall, twisting my gloved hands, while Thelma goes to fetch them. Max will travel in Claire's car with the girls, and Hedges will drive the rest of us in the Packard.

"See you at the church!" Max whispers, kissing his favorite spot under my ear. "I think he likes me."

"Go on with you." I push him away. "It's bad luck to see me before the wedding."

"Superstitious nonsense." He grins at me, letting his eyes roam from the brim of my hat to my polished shoes. "You look nice."

He's wearing his best suit, the one he bought for our first wedding. The only one that doesn't belong in a vaudeville show. I nod. "So do you."

I settle onto the plush rear seat of the Packard, with Dan on one side and Father Dennis on the other. I could have no better escorts; between the two of them, any nerves I might feel this time will stay well in abeyance.

"Did he pass muster, Father?" Dan's tone lets me know he is joking. "Is Dr. Max good enough for her?"

"He is, indeed." Father Dennis looks closely at me, his eyes crinkled in a smile. "Your mother would be proud of you, lass."

Claire

"I got a telegram from Burt." Harry looks tired, the fine lines around his eyes more pronounced than usual. "We have a problem."

"What is it?" He and his lawyer are in constant communication. I think immediately of Ava, the children. Max. Even the clinic.

"It's Mother." He sighs. "Her birthday is coming up, and she's making noises about contesting the contract if I'm not home in time to celebrate her big day. At our house. With me."

Irene Warriner had been a thorn in my side since I married her son. I was never good enough for her, but for years she satisfied herself with making me feel inadequate in myriad small ways. Last year, however, she hit a new low when she tried to convince Harry that I was unfaithful. It hadn't worked, and Harry finally got her at his mercy by threatening to expose her to the newspapers. Her penance was to support the People's Clinic for the rest of her life, and beyond, with a few caveats. One of them was that Harry had to give her dinner every year on her birthday, in our house, from which she was barred for the rest of the year.

"Oh. Can she do that?"

"Possibly," he says. "She can at least make trouble, which will cost time and money, and make more talk when it's finally died down." He sighs again. "I can go home for a week, give her what she needs, check on the business, and catch the next French Line ship back to rejoin you and Teddy."

I want to agree, to extend our idyll for as long as possible, but I've known since the night we encountered Leo Vollmer at Allard that Europe would not be our home forever. As much as I want to keep my head in the sand, I cannot. War is coming. If not war, then something equally unpleasant that will displace good people and ruin lives on a massive scale.

"No," I tell him. "We'll come with you. It's time." I smile with a cheer I don't entirely feel. "After all, Ava will never marry Max if I'm not there to push her into it."

His face clears. "Will you, darling? I'd stay here forever if you wanted, Mother notwithstanding."

"We're going home?" There is a hesitation in Katie's voice; despite her reluctance to come with us, I believe she has grown to love her time in Paris.

"Yes." I drop down on the bed, wishing I could pat the place beside me, but Katie has a better sense of propriety than I do. She stands, her hands clasped in front of her. "It's almost a year. We'd never intended to stay this long."

"No, ma'am." Her bottom lip rolls in. "When are we going?"

Is there a reason she doesn't wish to leave? "Mr. Warriner is looking into tickets today."

She nods, accepting the unknown. "I should take Mr. Teddy to the park. He's going to miss the ducks."

"No ducks in Rittenhouse Square." Will he even remember our local park? "He'll miss a lot of things."

"We all will." Katie moves my perfume bottles to the back of my vanity, out of range of Teddy's grasping hands. "I didn't think I'd like it, it being so different, and the language, and all. It wasn't easy."

"But you like it now?" Katie can be opaque; after several days of stifled tears on the trip over, she clearly decided to accept her fate, and from then on she was smooth-faced and uncomplaining.

"Yes, ma'am." A glimmer of her old spirit flickers in her eyes. "No one looks at me different here. I'm just a woman. It don't matter if I'm colored or not."

I had noticed the freedom she had here, but it hadn't occurred to me how it must have felt to her. Philadelphia isn't the south, but colored people are still definitely second class there. In France, it is less noticeable.

A battalion of colored soldiers had fought in France, and they were more highly regarded by the French than by their white American brethren. Some had remained after the war, finding a place in this beautiful city that would never be allowed at home. There are, I am sure, people here who think of Negros the way most Americans do, but they are in the minority.

Now, looking at Katie, my son's dearest friend and someone who I think of—realistically or not—as family, I understand for the first time why many of her people hadn't gone home.

"Do you want to stay?" I would hate to lose her, but I had always promised to pay for any future she chose, whether it was education or training for a different job. "We could—"

Her laughter stops me. "It don't matter what I want, Mrs. Claire. You come back without me, my mama will get on the next boat and fetch me back by the ear."

I smile, picturing small Esther Hedges striding through the streets of Paris in search of her errant child, and say, "You're right. I believe she would."

Pearl

April 27, 1935

They did it! They got married this time.

I don't have time to write about it now, and I'm not sure what I want to say anyway. Father Dennis came back with us from the wedding, after he gave Mama away. Thelma and I are going to cook supper for him tonight (pork roast and vegetables, heavy on the potatoes) and he's promised we can stay up as late as we want and he'll tell us stories about Mama and Aunt Claire when they were little, and all the things he can remember about Granny.

Ava

Our wedding supper takes place at a restaurant in South Philadelphia run by one of Max's innumerable friends. He parks Claire's roadster on Ninth Street and comes around to open the door. "My lady," he says, offering his arm. "Allow me to escort you to the best Italian dinner you've ever eaten."

"It'll be the only Italian dinner I've ever eaten," I tell him, once again reminded of my ignorance of the city. "Will I like it?"

The door opens as we approach and a trio of older men, all speaking loudly in what I assume is Italian, spill past us. They hold the door and I catch one glancing appreciatively at my legs.

Inside is a modestly sized restaurant with perhaps twenty-five tables scattered over a floor tiled with a snowflake-like pattern. Every table is occupied save one, and as Max leads me toward it, a man comes through a door in the back and blocks our path.

"Dr. Byrne!" he shouts. "You do not seat yourself in my restaurant, I don't care is your wedding day."

"Ralph!" He drops my arm to pound our host on the back. "Ralph, meet my wife! Ava, this is Ralph Dispigno, and this is his restaurant."

"My father's restaurant," he says, kissing my hand and leading me toward the empty table. "I'm the second generation. My kids, they'll be the third."

I let him tuck the chair in for me. The tables are covered with snowy cloths, some liberally spattered with the bright tomato gravy which covers nearly every dish. The air is heavy with the smell of garlic, and I realize how little lunch I ate, and how hungry I am.

"How are the kids?" Max asks, unfurling his napkin and tucking it into his collar. "And Mary?"

A waiter brings menus while the men talk, and I study it as seriously as Pearl studies her textbooks. Everything sounds appetizing; every plate that passes our table looks appetizing; none of it sounds familiar.

"What do I get?" I ask, when our host retreats to bring the wine.

"It's all good," he says, as if that's any help at all. "I'm getting the spaghetti. Ralph's meatballs are the best I've ever had."

I sigh; that was what I had been considering. "I'll get something else, then, and try yours."

Glasses of red wine arrive on the table, along with a plate of greens—spinach, I think—fried with oil and garlic. The smell makes my nose twitch.

"What's the hunter's style chicken?" I point at the menu.

"Amazing," he says with confidence. "You can't go wrong with anything in here."

We place our order and eat the spinach, which is delicious. The wine is sharp and too heavy, but I know little about wine and don't want to criticize. It may well be excellent and just not to my taste.

When our plates arrive, I lean over mine and inhale deeply. "I think you might be right."

"I usually am, where food is concerned." He cuts a piece of meatball with his fork, dredges it in the red sauce, and holds it out. "Try this."

The meatball is smooth and velvety—not just ground beef, then—and the sauce is bright and tastes of summer. I regret my choice until I begin to eat and understand that he is right: everything is that good.

This is a different world. I can count on one hand the number of times I've eaten in restaurants, and other than Claire's wedding lunch, Max has always been involved. It weighs on me sometimes in the same way that my lack of education weighs on me; my life has been so limited up until this point. How am I supposed to conduct myself as a doctor's wife when a simple restaurant meal can throw me into a tizzy?

What is it, anyway, to be a doctor's wife? Thankfully he's not the kind of doctor who leads a high profile life; he has friends like that, whom I'm certainly going to meet at some point, but they probably won't be very different from Claire's friends. They may even be the same people, for all I know. But it will be drastically different than being a miner's wife, or a widowed seamstress. I am Mrs. Dr. Max Byrne, whoever that may be.

"You're awfully quiet." Max twirls his spaghetti expertly on his fork. "Everything okay over there?"

With the part of my brain that's still functioning, I'm trying to figure out how to replicate the sauce, which has peppers, onions, carrots, and, surprisingly, olives. I stop in the middle of cutting my chicken to consider his question. The meat considerately falls off the bone. "I'm good," I say finally.

I am more than good, but I don't know how to explain that happiness like this is unfamiliar and somewhat frightening. It's not that I haven't been happy before; my work makes me happy, and my kids fill me with a deep joy. This is different, as if a knot had been untied somewhere deep inside me and I can relax for the first time in years.

It is not only happiness, but *safety*. I can count on Max to watch over us, and my vigilance can take a break. Having someone by my side who I can rely on utterly gives me a feeling so far beyond happy that I don't have words for it.

When I look up again, he is still watching. I'm pretty sure he knows everything I don't have words to say, and if he doesn't, I'll show him—wordlessly—when we get back to the house.

"I'm so tired of being afraid," I say before I can stop myself.

His glass stops halfway to his lips. "Afraid of what?"

He isn't surprised by my fear; I love him even more for that.

"Everything. Nothing." I wave my fork vaguely. "So many things." I bite my lip and continue, though I wanted to keep my two husbands separate on this day. "Daniel would have died to keep us safe, but it never stopped me being afraid."

Max reaches across the table to take my hand. "Daniel *did* die to keep you safe," he says quietly. "As would I, though I don't believe our current situation will require it." He gives me an uncertain smile, as if unsure how I will respond to his use of Daniel's name. "And certainly not so soon. I'd like to be married a few years at least."

"At least," I agree, my heart swelling with love for the unexpected blessing of this man. "Can we start being married soon, or is your friend going to insist we stay for dessert?"

The alarm jerks us from sleep entirely too soon. "It's not fair," Max grumbles, reaching out to slam the button and knocking the clock to the floor. "We shouldn't have to get out of bed until we're weak from hunger."

I disentangle my limbs from his. "You're the one who decided to have Sunday hours at the clinic," I remind him, retrieving the clock. "And I need to get back to the house. We're going to mass with Father Dennis before he goes home. Which means"—I lean over and kiss him—"you get to have breakfast with those poor people and make up for the impression we made last night."

We had left the car out front for Hedges. Linking hands, not quite running, we fell into the front hall, laughing at our adolescent eagerness. Max pinned me against the living room door frame and began to kiss my neck.

Then someone coughed. It was a soft and tactful sound, but in a house that should have been empty, it froze us in place. Sitting on the couch were two total strangers holding cups of tea. We stared at each other for a long moment before Max lifted his head from my neck, a smile quivering on his lips. I block him from their sight. "Who are you?"

"Josef and Renate Adler," the man said, standing and offering his hand. "We have come to stay."

I pull on my robe and retrieve my change of clothes from the chair. "I can't believe Claire didn't send a telegram to warn us. Do you mind if I have the bathroom first?"

"You forget where you are," he says. "We have a plethora of bathrooms. Choose whichever one you like."

"Just so long as I don't surprise the Adlers in one of them." I lean against him, amusement overtaking me at thought of their mortified expressions. "I don't think they could stand it."

"No." Max slides out of bed, yawning and stretching. "You know," he says, breaking into delighted laughter, "this is what we get for not telling Claire."

I laugh with him, the strange looseness of the night before still with me. Is this how normal people feel all the time—so light and unworried? I could get used to it.

"Max," I whisper, dropping my things and putting my arms around his waist. "I forgot to give you your wedding present last night."

I hadn't forgotten. Not exactly. But between the wine and the shock of my sister's guests, followed by champagne and the most leisurely lovemaking since our first time in Atlantic City, my brain was in no state for serious conversation.

One arm goes around me. "No, you didn't." The other hand slips into my robe, cups my breast. "It was perfect. Exactly what I wanted."

I squirm. I can't have this conversation while he's touching me. "Not that."

"What else could you give me?" he asks softly. "You're all I want."

Warmth fills me; he is as artless in his affection as a child. There is no wondering where I stand with him. "I thought you'd like to adopt Grace." When he doesn't speak, I go on. "You've said before that my kids are your kids, and I love you for that, but they *had* a father. Grace will never know Daniel, but she's known you since she was born. I thought maybe it would make her...more yours."

"Really?" His voice is tight. "What will the kids say?"

"We already talked about it. They agreed."

"Your priest called her Daniel's last gift." His cheek is pressed to mine; I can feel his jaw working.

"He wouldn't want her to grow up without a father." I say that—to Max, to the kids—but am I right? Or am I putting words in his mouth that I need to hear? Daniel could be jealous. He never had reason to be, but he was fiercely protective of what was his. Would he accept my choice of Max, my giving over of his baby girl to a man we have all come to love?

He would. Eventually. For all his fierceness, his heart was as big as the sun, and he would want his children happy and well cared for. His wife, too, for that matter, but I am not as sure of his grace on my behalf.

"And maybe she's not just a gift for us," I tell Max, moving away to look him in the face. "Maybe she's also a gift for the man who came after, who took up his work and is willing to raise children not his own."

For once, Max has no words. I hold him while he cries against my neck.

10

Claire

My sadness at going home has been allayed because Harry has miraculously found for us a first-class passage on the new French Line ship, *Normandie*, leaving for New York on May 29. We both adore the French line; Cunard is very nice, but if we have to return to Philadelphia, I want our French idyll to last as long as possible.

"How did you ever manage?" I ask again over breakfast. "Those tickets have been sold out for months, haven't they?"

He nods, taking a sip of his coffee. "Pure luck," he answers. "I was in the shipping office, about to book our return—slightly sooner—when they told me that there had been a cancellation. Someone's baby born early and not wanting to travel, I believe that's what it was."

"Lucky them, and lucky us."

Normandie had been in the news ever since the departure was officially scheduled. Its construction had been delayed by the Depression, with newspapers openly questioning whether a luxury vessel should even be built in perilous economic times, but the French government had eventually subsidized it. The ship had launched three years ago, and in that time it had been fitted out and decorated to the level expected by its passengers, most of whom would undoubtedly be wealthy Americans.

Like us. I have grown accustomed to living in a certain way over the last year. Reentering our more modest life in Philadelphia is going to be difficult, but not doing it will be worse. I try to imagine Ava's reaction to our life, and then I try not to, because it horrifies me that she is undoubtedly stitching herself blind while I have filled, at a minimum, three more trunks with clothing purchased in Paris and London. It's not fair, but I don't know how to make it fair, especially with a sister like mine.

In the midst of my packing and organizing, we receive a visit from Leo, back in Paris to assist another friend on his path to New

York. We had recently received word of the Adlers' arrival, sooner than expected, and I am eager to share the news with him once he has joined us in the living room.

"I have heard already," he says, accepting a glass of whiskey from Harry. "They were most apologetic about interrupting your sister's wedding."

"What?" It must be a translation error. "My sister is a widow."

Leo shakes his head slowly, gazing into the amber liquid. "Josef said plainly that she and the doctor had come in from their wedding dinner."

I try to process the information that my sister has gotten married without my involvement. I meet Harry's eyes, note the repressed laughter in their depths, and give in to my own. Ava has outwitted me again, married Max in her own fashion, and is probably happier for my not being there. It would hurt, if I didn't know her so well.

"I'll have to buy them a wedding gift."

"Didn't you already buy them a painting?" Harry is curious, not criticizing my spending.

"Yes, but that was when I thought I'd be there for the ceremony. Now I need to find something special, so Ava feels bad for doing it without us there."

A quiet knock heralds Teddy's arrival. Katie stands back as he bounds into the room, chattering in a mixture of French and English. When he sees us sitting apart, he stops, looking from one to the other, trying to decide who to approach. Then he glimpses Leo, and his smile broadens. "Lion!"

Leo kneels on the carpet and holds his arms out to my son. "Mein schatz, how I have missed you."

He loves children, it is obvious from the way he treats Teddy—and the way our boy has taken to him. Children can detect falsity in a way adults no longer can, the clarity of our vision muddied by self-interest or ambition or lust.

"I just happen," he says, reaching into his pocket, "to have something for you."

Teddy's eyes widen as Leo unfolds long fingers to reveal a small metal car, bright red with flashing silver wheels. He reaches out to touch one wheel and it spins, making him gasp.

"Me?" he asks, as if he doesn't already have a half dozen similar cars in a rainbow of colors.

"Who else?" Leo sits on the floor with a thump and puts the car on the carpet in front of him. "Let us see how well you drive."

Teddy buckles at the knees, folding until his nose is down and his bottom up. He makes small, earnest noises as he runs the toy along a wavering line in the oriental carpet.

"He's yours for life," Harry says. "He's got a car-mad cousin at home. He'll be old enough to play with him when we get back."

I doubt Toby will consider playing cars with a three-year-old a worthwhile activity, but I leave Harry his illusions.

Leo gets up with effort, rubbing his left knee. "I would be glad to call him mine," he says, and there is a note in his voice that is something like sadness. "I failed my son."

"I'm sure that's not true." I don't want it to be; Leo has endeared himself rapidly, even without his care for my boy.

He smiles gently. "I wish it was not, my dear lady. But I was not there when Manfred needed me, and he has replaced family with a system of beliefs that will never let him down." His expression turns serious. "A system of beliefs that will tear Europe apart before too long."

Such talk is chilling. When Teddy runs his car, and then his head, into the wall and begins to wail, I use his distress as an excuse to absent myself. After my son has been placated with kisses and pastry, I return to the living room to find they have moved their conversation to the small table by the window, where we often have late supper after the theater.

They look up, startled by my reappearance.

"I am sorry," Leo says graciously. "I am not a good houseguest, talking only of sadness. Please, tell me of something cheerful."

"These are not cheerful times." I sit on the couch near them, my hands in my lap. "Go on with your discussion."

After a moment, they do; Leo explains the nature of his latest rescue, and his hopes for two other people whom he has not yet been able to locate. "I have left word with mutual friends that I can help. I hope the message reaches them."

Harry looks up from the papers spread across the table's gleaming surface. "If there is anything I can do to assist, once we are at home…"

"This is not your battle." Leo stubs out his cigarette and looks at Harry plainly. "You are American."

"It's not yours, either. You're not a Jew." Harry's cigarette trembles in his fingers. "You're putting yourself at risk. Your business. Your family."

"Because my country is going mad." His eyes close as if in pain. "I cannot bear it, but I cannot stop it. The most I can do is to get some people out, people I know and who will trust me to help them." He sighs. "It is not enough."

"I wish there was more I could do." Harry takes off his glasses and passes a hand over his eyes. "I had no idea it was this bad."

"Go home, my friend," Leo tells him. "Go home and send money, if you mean it. Find sponsors and jobs. Help me get these people to safety."

His voice is weary, but I sense a steely determination in him that reminds me of Ava.

"Whatever I can do," Harry says hoarsely. "You can trust me."

"You can trust us." Harry has his contacts, Leo, but so do I. My husband is not on letter-writing terms with the First Lady of the United States. "We will do what we can."

When Leo has gone, my husband turns to me. "Did you mean what you said? Will you help?"

I clasp his hand. "Whither you goest, I will go. Your cause is my cause, your people are my people."

Something in him relaxes. "What about the clinic?"

I let out a breath. "Max has been in charge for the last year. I don't think he'll give me any trouble if I ask him to continue to run it."

He sends me regular updates, listing the number of patients treated, unusual expenses, and suggested improvements—of which there are many. He is very involved, which I appreciate as I am thousands of miles away and equally distant in my focus on the project. I spent a year coming up with the clinic and making it a reality, and yet I was perfectly content to hand it to him when we left for France. Even now, I can't bring myself to think about going back to caring about every detail, not when he is dealing so capably with it all.

And I don't want to, not really. If I'd been thinking clearly at the time, I would have seen that what I wanted was a purpose—something larger than myself. When I turned our lives upside down and almost destroyed my marriage, the clinic was the most important thing I could imagine. Now, Harry and my son are in that position, as they should be, but I have a lot of energy remaining to direct at a worthy cause. All the better if it is my husband's.

Ava

We return for Friday supper the week after our wedding, having sent a note with the boys to inquire whether our presence would be too much. Esther returns a message that my sister's guests are settling in well and looking forward to meeting us properly.

They are waiting in the living room when we arrive, their eyes widening as the kids spread around the room. Did Claire not warn them how many of us there were? I send them down to help Esther get supper ready, and join Mrs. Adler on the sofa. She is a petite woman, her black hair dressed in a neat chignon. Her dark, fitted suit has a touch of Claire about it, a scent of moneyed taste. She wears no jewelry, but seems no less adorned for the lack.

"I'm sorry if we disturbed you the other night." I can't imagine what they must have thought, the two of us tumbling into the house, acting no more than Dan's age.

"It is we who disturbed you." Her voice is low, powerful. "Or at least surprised."

"Definitely surprised." I venture a smile. Renate Adler is alarmingly self-possessed, but I have dealt with women like her before. If she doesn't realize I am intimidated, we'll be able to find a level where we can talk to each other. If she's going to live in this house for any length of time, we have no choice.

Her return smile is tight but genuine. "This is a very big change for us, you understand. Your sister and her husband, they took great risks to help us come here."

"Indeed," chips in Mr. Adler, breaking away from his conversation with Max. "Mr. Warriner moved mountains on our behalf. We are so very grateful."

Neither of them appear inclined to expand on this, leaving me wondering what possible risks Claire and Harry could have taken to send this perfectly average couple to stay in their home. Perhaps there was something, but Claire's letters, long as they are, are often short on information.

"Are you friends of Harry's, then?" Max asks, curious as I am. "From his previous travels?"

"No." Renate looks down at her hands, nails polished the color of blood. "We met only recently."

Even more mysterious. I exchange a glance with Max. He will find a way to winkle the information out of them; my husband's charm will always succeed where my plain-faced questions fail.

"Mrs. Warriner told us you are a physician." Mr. Adler fidgets with his cufflink, turning it round and round. "Of what specialty?"

"General practice." Max leans forward, in his element, all questions forgotten. He explains that his original background had been in research, but his interests had changed over the years. By the time Claire formed the clinic, his work was varied and took place all over the city.

"So you have no actual office?" Renate tilts her head. The heavy mass of her hair makes her neck look fragile.

"Only the clinic," he says. "But I've been known to make the occasional house call."

"Or two." He is often late because he's stopped off at a patient's house, or popped in to visit the orphanage in West Philadelphia. Having access to Harry's Packard has broadened the scope of his work, and I wonder what will happen when Harry returns and expects his car at his disposal again.

The supper conversation is wide-ranging: Pearl wants to hear all about Paris; Thelma asks after Teddy, whom the Adlers proclaim to be a darling boy; Toby wants to know about German cars. George is quiet, mechanically cleaning his plate. Then he looks up and asks, "So what are you going to do here?"

Everyone falls silent. Dan glares at his younger brother, and even Toby looks surprised by his rudeness.

"I'm sorry—" I begin.

"It is no matter," Mr. Adler says, his tone easy if his words are not. "Mr. Warriner has contacted an acquaintance at Princeton inquiring about a teaching position for me. As for my wife, she will no doubt go back to work very soon."

"What do you do, Mrs. Adler?" Pearl asks politely. She is fascinated by the woman, I can tell; otherness is like catnip to my eldest daughter.

Renate places her silver precisely across her plate. She has scarcely eaten anything, and drunk only a little water with her meal. "I am a performer."

Thelma's head snaps up. "I'm a dancer! Want to see?"

I stop her before she pushes her chair back. "After we eat, baby." I turn to Mrs. Adler. "What kind of performer?"

She draws herself up, a tiny woman somehow looking statuesque, even in a chair. "I am a singer." Glancing at Max, she says, "Mrs. Warriner has some of my recordings, she told me. You may play them for the children, if you wish, but I will go to my room first."

"Why?" Thelma can't imagine not wanting an audience.

"Because that was my old life, liebchen," she says gently. "What I do from here is all new."

The Adlers retire after supper, disappointing Thelma, who wanted them to watch her Shirley Temple dance routine. Before they go up, Mrs. Adler goes into the living room, kneeling before the cabinet of records beneath Harry's portable phonograph. She flicks rapidly through the albums, pulling several and putting them to one side. Rising gracefully, she brushes her skirt and hands the records to Pearl.

"You may listen to these," she says. "Please wait until my door is closed."

She says goodnight and departs, Mr. Adler on her heels. We settle on the sofa and various chairs, while Dan winds the phonograph and Pearl sorts through the records. "There are four," she says, holding them out. "*La Traviata, Tannhäuser*, and *The Marriage of Figaro*. Plus one called *Popular Puccini*, which looks like it has a bunch of different singers. I don't know which to pick."

Max looks up from the newspaper. "Puccini," he says. "Puccini is best if you don't know what you're listening to. Look out for her name—she sings under Renate Steiner."

Pearl slides the heavy record out of its paper sleeve and hands it to Dan, holding it by the edges as she's been taught. He places it on the turntable, checks the needle, and slowly lowers it to the correct place.

For a moment there is silence, only the record's pops and fuzzy beginning, then the room is filled with a voice that cannot belong to that impossibly tiny woman. It swoops and rises, turns in on itself, then spins out and draws us all in. I look around at my kids. Even the boys are sitting rapt, though it is by no means the kind of music they would normally listen to. Pearl's eyes are brimming. Thelma's feet are still, a miracle in itself.

I reach for Max. His hand meets mine halfway and clasps it just as Renate's voice spirals upward, taking my breath. I squeeze his fingers, having no other way to show what this music is doing to me.

When the song—is it a song?—ends, Dan lifts the needle. "Un bel di vedremo," he reads haltingly from the album cover. "What does that mean?"

Max speaks, surprising us all. "It's something like 'one fine day'," he says. "Don't quote me on that. My exposure to opera is minimal, at best."

"Can we go home?" Toby asks, hauling himself off the floor. "I'm tired."

"That's because you spent all day in a car, you dope." George kicks his ankle.

"Enough." Pearl grabs them each by the shoulder. "I don't want to hear another word out of you until we're home. You're not spoiling that music for me."

We go downstairs to say goodnight to Esther and Mason, having a last cup of tea in the kitchen. When we return through the dining room, Max is at the foot of the stairs with Renate Adler one step above him. Despite that, she seems even smaller. She speaks rapidly, her voice low, arms folded across her chest.

"Dr. Max!" Thelma plows forward, throwing her arms around his waist.

Startled, Renate turns to face us. "I hope you enjoyed the music."

"We did," I assure her. "It wasn't too loud?"

She shakes her head. "No. I was saying goodnight to Dr. Byrne."

Pearl gives her brothers one last shake and comes forward. "Thank you, Mrs. Adler," she says. Her voice is shaky. "We listened to the Butterfly song. It was beautiful."

"Thank you." Renate nods graciously. "I must find an accompanist so that I can practice again. It has been too long." She turns back to Max. "I don't suppose you know anyone, Dr. Byrne?"

Max considers, leaning back against the light wallpaper. It is brighter since Claire removed all traces of her mother-in-law's dreary personality from the house. "I might," he says. "Used to know someone at the Curtis Institute. Let me make some inquiries. If I find out anything, I'll stop in one day around lunchtime."

"Thank you." Her smile is brighter than any we've seen from her all evening. "That would be a great help."

Pearl

May 8, 1935

Progress has come to Ringgold Place! Mama is fussing like the world is about to end, because Dr. Max has had a telephone installed. She says it's unnecessary, but he pointed out, very reasonably I think, that as a doctor, he needs to be available. Especially since Aunt isn't back yet and he's lost access to her phone because Mama doesn't want us to live in Aunt's house. That's fine by me, I'd rather live here, and besides, with the Adlers now taking over Dr. Max's old rooms, it would be even more crowded and none of us want that.

The Adlers are nice enough, a little stiff, but in a foreign way, not a rude way. Both of them speak very good English. As a performer, I guess she would have opportunity to learn. She can speak multiple languages, or at least that's what she's told Thelma, who is completely starstruck, even though Mrs. Adler's a singer, not a dancer.

And what a singer! We listened to one of her recordings on Friday night, and I stopped at the house after school today to see if I could listen to more. Mrs. Adler was out, but her husband was there, sitting in the living room. I told him what I wanted and he took out one of the records, the one called *La Traviata*, and played the whole thing through for me. I'm embarrassed that I cried in front of a stranger, but he had tears in his eyes, too. I can't imagine having a gift like that. I hope Dr. Max can find someone to play for her. If he does, maybe she'll be nice enough to let me listen.

When I go to school tomorrow, I can give Hazel our phone number so she can call me up when she wants to go to the movies. I'll feel like someone out of the movies myself, being able to pick up the phone and make plans. When no one else was around today, I practiced answering. "Byrne residence, Miss Kimber speaking."

It felt silly and grown up at the same time.

11

Claire

Leo has come and gone with another refugee—a chemist from Bonn—spirited through Paris and onto a boat, bound this time for England. I marvel at his ingenuity and the network of friends and acquaintances he must have throughout Europe; meeting Harry was convenient, but he would have certainly managed without us.

Harry is away overnight, accompanying them to the boat. His interest in Leo's business has grown since the Adlers' departure. I will not be at all surprised if I come home one afternoon to find another set of strangers in the guest room.

On my own, I have become better acquainted with Mary Jayne Gold, listening to her tales of what was, according to her parents, several misspent years in France and other places, and allowing her to introduce me to people in Paris who might prove useful going forward. I have no idea if Harry can be of further help to Leo, but I have learned that you can never have too many useful acquaintances.

Also, I enjoy spending afternoons with Mary Jayne; they end either in wine or a shopping spree which requires that I leave some of my parcels downstairs with the concierge, who expects a large tip for concealing them from my husband. Harry doesn't care about my spending, but I am ashamed to bring too much up at one time.

This trip has brought home to me how fortunate we are, and how lightly, despite the damage to some of Harry's businesses, we have been affected by the Depression. Even among the wealthy of Philadelphia, there are few people who could comfortably spend a year in France; of course, because well-bred people do not often speak of money, there may be more than I realize. But even so.

We are fortunate, and I understand Harry's desire to do more with what he has: it is the same impulse that involved me first with the orphans and then in the creation of the clinic.

Pearl

May 13, 1935

The Peace Club talked about Germany today. Not for the first time. But they announced rearmament, which could be as scary as it sounds. Everyone thought after the last war that there wouldn't be any more wars, but people don't learn. At least that was the conclusion we came to.

It's hard to have an exchange of ideas when we're all a little spooked by the news, even the teacher, who lost her brother in the war.

We got a letter from Aunt yesterday. They'll be on their way home soon. Apparently old Mrs. Warriner is kicking up a fuss and Uncle needs to deal with her. I should try to be kind and not think uncharitable things, but she's an awful old woman and I'm pretty sure Mama and Aunt would agree with me.

Aunt's going to hit the roof when she finds out that Mama is Mrs. Max Byrne and they managed to do it without her help.

Ava

"Mrs. Byrne." Mr. Mendel gets down from his stool with some difficulty. "My nephew will wrap your purchase. Do you have a moment?"

Still unaccustomed to my new name, I follow him through a narrow door, half blocked with standing bolts of muslin and canvas, and find myself in what must be his office, though it is no bigger than the storage closet my son uses as a bedroom.

"Have you ever noticed the tailor's shop around the corner? Goldman's?" He leans against his desk but does not sit, as there is no second chair to offer me.

"I know it's there," I say, wondering where this is going. "But I've never been inside. Why?"

"Lev Goldman died two days ago," he says flatly, staring at his hands. "May his memory be a blessing."

"I'm sorry to hear that." When he asked to speak with me, I assumed it had something to do with his niece, whose arrival was delayed but who should be here any day now. This conversation about a tailor's shop makes no sense.

Mr. Mendel scratches his chin through his straggling beard. "He was my tenant," he explains. "I rented that back portion of the shop to him twenty years ago."

"You'll miss him."

He inclines his head. "I'll miss him, yes, but I'll also miss his rent. Mrs. Byrne, would you like to take over the lease?"

"Me? I don't need a shop. I have a perfectly good space in my house," I begin.

"In your house," he interrupts. "With your children coming and going and meals being cooked on the other side of the door." He nods, looking like a judgmental old owl. "No privacy for your customers, or for your family. No separation. You sew until you sleep, am I right?"

I look down at my shoes. "Only sometimes."

He cackles. "And your doctor, he likes a wife who is always working? Never paying attention to him?"

I shift my weight, wishing there was a place to sit. "Dr. Byrne understands about my work, Mr. Mendel. I'm not going to stop because we're married."

"Of course not." He rummages in a drawer and produces a ring of keys. "But a man expects certain things, such as a wife who maybe has a nice shop where she meets her customers during business hours and does a little handwork in the evenings." He straightens up, coming around the desk. I back up until I hit the wall. "That's why you should look at Goldman's shop."

I take the streetcar home. My head is spinning from the experiences of the last hour, and my feet ache on top of it.

We left Mendel's by the front door, turning onto the narrow side street. Perhaps thirty feet from the corner was a faded green awning, beneath which was a green-painted door and a narrow window crowded with two male torsos, one wearing a formal pin-tucked shirt and a bow tie, the other a striped shirt with a trim jacket on top. The jacket had basting stitches holding the pockets closed.

Lev Goldman, Men's Fine Tailoring was neatly painted on the door's glass pane.

Mr. Mendel fussed with the keys, muttering under his breath until the lock gave way. The door opened onto a cramped, dim space—a narrow span of floor divided by a wooden counter cluttered with the tools of Mr. Goldman's trade, tools not so different from the ones I use.

"It needs dusting," he said, switching on the light and looking around. "But is not bad."

I followed him behind the counter as he opened the next door. Another click, but this time the light was brighter. The interior room was larger than the shop front, with space for a long cutting table and two machines—the same setup I had at home, but with room to move. A counter to one side of the door held spools of thread, looped measuring tapes, chalk, dishes of pins. Piled papers and invoices on a spike showed Mr. Goldman's record-keeping abilities. A ramshackle screen and a wooden chair served as an area for customers to be fitted, and the wall beyond displayed several garments on hangers, waiting for a hand that would never finish them.

"What do you think?" he piped up, almost in my ear. "It would work, yes?"

"Well, yes," I said. "But Mr. Mendel, I don't need a shop. My customers don't mind coming to my house—this would be further for them to travel, anyway."

"Further, in their fancy cars." He pushes aside the gray wool left spread across the table. "I would rent it furnished, of course. Unless you bring your own things."

The cutting table is twice the size of the one I have; I could lay out patterns and work on more than one thing at once. I shook my head. I didn't need a shop.

"Maybe even one of the machines." His eyes narrowed, his fingers fiddling with the fringes that extended from beneath his black coat.

"It would need a good cleaning," I hear myself say. "And a coat of paint. My customers wouldn't come to a place that looked like an old man's tailor shop."

Dan could help. He'd worked wonders with my basement workroom. Which, I realized, could be turned into a dining room if I accepted Mr. Mendel's insane suggestion. We could have enough space to cook and serve supper without worrying about tripping over each other. We could have eight people at the table, maybe more, and all we would have to worry about would be having enough chairs.

I turned to him. "I need to talk this over with my family. It's a lot to take on."

"It is," he agreed. "But I believe in what you are doing, Mrs. Byrne. I would not make such an offer to just anyone."

I assumed he meant anyone outside his faith, which made his trust in me even more remarkable.

Was he correct? Would it be better to move into an actual storefront, to set myself up as a businesswoman? I had the customers—and he was right, they all came by car. A few blocks more or less wouldn't bother them in the slightest.

It would take more effort for me to get there, but the streetcars ran regularly. In fine weather I could walk. In the more than two years since I had begun sewing for Claire's friends, there had been no separation between my work and my home life. The kids understood; I had always worked. But now, with Max, it feels like we're bulging at the seams. Two adults, two near-adults, and four children was a lot for one small house. Having a portion of that space earmarked for a business, when we couldn't even eat supper comfortably, had begun to feel like selfishness on my part.

But was it? I had worked so hard to build this business from nothing, sewing at all hours, missing out on so much in my quest to succeed and prove my independence. And while I had done that, now I had a man who would support me utterly, whether I decided to take the shop or give up sewing entirely to stay home and keep his house.

I thank the driver and step down from the car, the bulky package of fabric under my arm. It's nearly time to eat; I'll put all this aside and think about it later.

Max fails to appear for supper. When I comment, Toby's eyes open wide. "Oh. He called on the telephone. I forgot to tell you."

"What have I told you about answering the phone?" I give him a pointed motherly gaze.

"Not to answer it unless there's nobody older around." His lip juts out. "There wasn't."

I sigh. "And?" The question merits no more than a shrug. "And to write any message on the pad by the telephone. Do you remember that part?"

"Yes!" His face brightens, and he digs in his pocket, producing a dirty square of paper. "I did write it down, I just forgot to give it to you."

I unfold the message, wondering how he managed to get the paper so grubby in the short distance between the telephone and the kitchen. Puzzling out his near illegible pencil scrawl, I decipher, "Pop late sorry home later."

"That's very helpful." I cuff the back of his stubbly head. "Next time try to actually give me the message."

After we finish eating, Toby and George go outside to play catch and Pearl and Thelma do the dishes. I sit out back and keep Dan company while he smokes, lost in a tug of war of conflicting thoughts.

"Okay, what is it?" He leans forward, elbows on knees, looking back at me over his shoulder. "Something's on your mind."

I want to keep thinking about it, to discuss it with Max before I involve the kids, but Dan and Pearl are nearly grown and Max is not here. "Wait. Thelma," I call from the back door. "Will you get Grace ready for bed? I'll be up, but I need to talk to Pearl and Dan."

"Yes, Mama." Her voice floats toward me and before I am back outside, a howl of protest rises from Grace.

Pearl joins us a few minutes later. "That girl does not like bedtime," she says, settling herself on a chair. She has not sat, hip to hip, on the step with me since Claire left for Paris.

"You were the same way," I remind her. "Every single one of you. Always afraid you were going to miss something."

Dan stretches out his legs, and I note in surprise that he's grown again. "Ma's got something she wants to talk about," he tells his sister. "You ready, Ma?"

I take a deep breath. "As I'll ever be. I was down on Fourth Street today," I say. "Mr. Mendel offered to rent me the tailor shop behind his store."

"What would you do with a shop?" Pearl asks. "You're a dressmaker."

"And Mr. Goldman was a tailor," I say. "People come to me here, Mr. Mendel's thought was they could as easily come to me there." I look from one to the other. "It would mean taking the business out of the house, at least mostly." I smile at Dan. "Which would be a shame, after all the work you did on that space."

He pushes up from the step. "What's it going to be, if it's not your workroom? Do you want me to turn it into a bedroom for the girls, so we all have some privacy?"

Privacy would be wonderful, but my idea for the space would serve us all, and our family comes first.

"I don't want to sleep next to the kitchen," Pearl protests before I can speak up. "I'm the first one up half the time anyway."

"Well, then, that would make it easier."

I interrupt before an argument breaks out. "I haven't decided to do it yet. It's a risk, expanding like that."

"It was a risk," Pearl says, her voice trembling a little, "to take this house and not live with Aunt forever. And you've made it work."

Support from an unexpected quarter. "That's true," I say. "With all of your help. I'm sure my customers wouldn't mind going there, as opposed to here. There'd be more space and more privacy for them to get fitted."

Pearl nods in agreement. "And maybe Dan could convert your workroom into a dining room."

My smart girl. "That's what I was thinking," I say. "We're too squashed in that kitchen, and it would be nice to have your aunt and uncle and Teddy over for supper, when they finally come home. The way it is now, at least two of you would have to sit in the backyard and talk to us through the window."

They go silent, thinking about the luxury of space. This house felt so big when we first moved in; it is shocking how quickly we've gotten used to not bumping into each other constantly. Before, they all shared a bedroom, or slept in the same room with me and Daniel if we had boarders in the second room. But this life is not that life.

"Remember when we first came to look at this house?" I ask Dan. "You told me we weren't small people, that we just had small lives. Are we ready to grow again?"

He puts his hand over mine—the left one, with its little finger missing from his childhood work on the breaker. "We're ready."

Pearl puts her hand on his, careful not to touch me. "I think so, too. Have you talked to Dr. Max?"

"Not yet." I put my other hand on top of hers. She freezes at my touch, then visibly forces herself to relax. "I was going to talk to him tonight, but I was going to talk to you, as well. It didn't matter which order—I need all the help I can get, making this decision."

"It sounds like you've already made it." Dan squeezes my shoulder. "I'm going to go drag those two inside."

Pearl shifts uncomfortably on the bench once he is gone. I pat the step with my hand. "Come sit with me."

"I'm fine here," she says, crossing and uncrossing her legs.

"But I'm not." I pat the step again. "I miss you."

Brushing off her skirt, she comes to sit beside me, keeping as much distance as possible between us without falling off the step. "I'm here," she says.

"Barely." I keep the reproof from my voice. "I know how busy you are with school, and that's wonderful. I don't want you to worry about having to help me in the shop, the way you've had to at home."

"How else will you manage?" The question is challenging but her tone is merely curious.

"I'll find a way. Mr. Mendel's niece is apparently a seamstress, so I'll give her some work. And I might"— I glance over at her—"I might bring home the rolled hems if you're willing to do them."

She laughs, knowing that I hate rolled hems and that she is far better at them. "I can do that."

"Good." I bump her with my shoulder. "You're growing up so fast, but I don't want you to grow away from me entirely. I know it's been hard this past year."

We've never spoken about her disappointment over not going to Paris. We've shouted about it, and she's cried and slammed doors and frozen me out, but we've never spoken. I hold my breath, waiting to see if she'll flounce off this time.

"I don't want to leave home for good," Pearl says. "But I do want to go somewhere else. Paris was important. I need to see other places. I need to be"—she hesitates, and I can see how hard this is for her—"I need to be someone other than your daughter, their sister."

I put my arm around her and she rests her head on my shoulder. "I know, baby," I tell her. "And you will. We'll make sure of it."

12

Pearl

When Dr. Max comes in, I go up to bed so they can talk. My feet drag on the stairs. I'm worn out from the long day and the conversation with Mama. Honestly, I could kill Dandy. Abandoning me when she needed to talk could have been a disaster.

She had big news, though. Mama has a chance to open a shop down on Fourth Street, instead of sewing in the house the way she always has. Even though I made more of a big deal out of getting a dining room, I'm impressed with her bravery for even considering it. A woman like her, with a business.

Their voices come, muffled, through the bathroom floorboards. I use the toilet, wash my face and hands, and dampen my hair so I can put it in pins. Thelma is already asleep, but I don't need light to do pin curls.

The boys' snores come easily through the wall. When Dandy comes up and adds his to the chorus, it will be unbearable if I'm not already asleep. How did we ever manage in Scovill Run? Are we so spoiled, so soon? Or is it just me?

I stand by the window with my small ceramic dish of bobby pins, mindlessly coiling my hair around my finger and anchoring it with crossed pins.

It won't leave my mind, how brave she is. If she can do something so different from what she knows, there's no excuse for me not to do the same, or more. There will be no limitation for me except ones I set myself. I have to be as brave as she is.

It scares me, just to think about it.

I want to put my pins away and run back downstairs and tell her how proud I am, but then I hear soft laughter and the squeak of the stairs. She's not just ours; it's Dr. Max's time now.

After I finish my hair, I put the dish on the dresser and slide in beside Thelma, careful not to wake her. She makes a kittenish noise and rolls over, but she stays asleep. I settle my head on the pillow, prepared to stare at the ceiling for the next hour as I wait for Dan to come home and try not to listen too closely to whatever might be happening downstairs.

I wanted to tell her I was proud of her, but instead I agreed to continue helping with hems. It's been so long since we had a real conversation that I don't remember how we used to talk. But she just wanted me to sit with her. And she mentioned Paris. She didn't apologize, but she brought it up, so it's out in the open now, so I said something and didn't apologize either. Can we get past it, just like that?

I'm afraid if I act like nothing's happened she'll ask why I've been a brat for the last year, and I don't know what to tell her that wouldn't cast me as a big, whiny baby, sulking like Jo March in *Little Women* because I was excluded from a trip I had counted on. At least Jo was somewhat to blame; her rudeness to her aunt made it obvious to everyone but Jo that she wouldn't be a good traveling companion.

In my case, there was no such reason. Aunt wanted me with them. So did Uncle Harry. And Katie didn't want to go, she was afraid of losing her job, or her whole family's jobs, if she said no.

A flush of renewed anger prickles my chest. It's all well and good for Mama to have her dreams! I'll be stuck in this house taking care of my little brothers and sisters until I'm a gray old lady. I flop over onto my side, bumping Thelma, who sits up right and loudly says, "What?"

"Nothing," I tell her, curling myself into a tight ball of misery. "Go to sleep."

Ava

Max's input into my dilemma is helpful, if helpful means telling me how excited he is and that any decision is ultimately mine.

"Come downstairs," I say. "Let me warm up some soup for you."

He follows obediently, telling me, as I stand at the stove, about his last patients of the day, a homeless mother and child. "The boy had nearly gotten clipped by a car on Washington Avenue," he explains. "Thankfully he jumped clear, but he landed badly."

"Was anything broken?" I cut two thick slices of bread and hand them to him on a napkin. The butter is already on the table, along with a knife that escaped the supper dishes.

"No." He energetically spreads the butter. "But he dislocated his shoulder, so that had to be put right. Then I had to give the mother tea, because she was more upset than he was."

"I'm sure." I ladle thick barley soup, flavored with a beef bone, into a brown crockery bowl, remembering when Dan had suffered the same injury, in the accident which killed his father.

When I place the bowl in front of him, he puts a hand on my arm. "That's enough of my day," he says. "Let me eat this delicious soup and you tell me all about the shop."

I drop into the chair next to his, and toe off my shoes. My feet are aching up to the ankles.

"Give one here." I put a foot on his lap, and he rubs with one hand while continuing to eat. "Tell me."

"Mr. Mendel's tenant, a tailor, recently passed away and he suggested that I take over the shop." I stop for a moment, to let the pleasure of his touch sink in. "He thought it would be good to get the business out of the house."

"Do you want the business out of the house?" Max puts down his spoon and crooks his finger. "Other foot."

I slide down in the chair to rest both feet on his lap, savoring his strong fingers on my sore feet. "It's not a bad idea," I say carefully. "It might make me look more legitimate."

He runs his knuckles up and down the sole of my foot. "I'd say you're pretty legitimate right now. You've got a constant parade of women in and out of that room."

"That's another thing. If I move the business, we could use that room to eat in." I retrieve my feet before he turns me to jelly, and tuck them under my chair. "When I told the kids earlier, that was the part they were most excited about."

"Pearl especially?" He loosens his tie and undoes his top button.

"Pearl especially. We actually had something close to a conversation about it." I don't tell him how excited I was by that momentary softening; it may or may not last, and I don't want to get our hopes up.

He picks up his bowl, spoon, and the butter knife and takes them to the sink, washing and rinsing them without a second thought. I keep hoping his example will sink into the boys, but so far they watch his domesticity with wide-eyed wonder and continue to ignore their messes.

"It sounds like a good idea," he says over his shoulder. "So long as you're willing. It'll give you a longer day, leaving the house. Will you like that?"

"I don't know," I say honestly. "I've never worked outside, other than a few cleaning jobs before I married Daniel. It might be good for us. When I lock the door and leave the shop, I'd be done for the day."

Max laughs, not unkindly. "You're no more likely to stop working at the end of the day than I am."

In that we are alike. "Maybe not," I agree. "But it would be small things. Hand work. Buttons and hems, not cutting or sitting at the machine." I raise an eyebrow. "Mr. Mendel thought it would be good for us. He believes I don't pay enough attention to you."

"Then come pay attention to me now." He catches me around the waist, his arm sliding upward. "I'm tired, but I'm not that tired."

Claire

As the packing goes forward, I sit at the gold-trimmed desk in the living room and write a raft of letters: to Prue Foster, Helen Dawes, Eleanor Roosevelt. Anyone I think might be able to help Harry in his future endeavors. Perhaps some sort of fund-raising activity once I return home—we raised thousands for the clinic, and a similar amount is taken in at each Christmas gala for the city's orphanages.

Why not a similar party to raise awareness—and money—which can be transmitted to Leo to assist in his activities. Possibly not; people might not want their money sent overseas, and although donors should have no say once the money leaves their hands, I don't want to reduce their potential numbers by something as off-putting as sending money to Germany. The funds can be used to cover the costs of visas, permits, and travel, in addition to providing the basis for a new arrival to set up life in America.

Teddy plays at my feet as I make notes, running his cars along the carpet and making motor noises under his breath. It is raining, which has spoiled his trip to the park with Katie, but it is a spring rain, the sort that comes down hard and passes quickly. I have errands to do once it clears, but most of all I want to walk through this city I love so much.

It is easier for me to get around when it is overcast; on a bright day, it is harder to sense the location of the Seine by its reflection on the clouds and I stray outside the familiar boundaries of the central arrondissements. While being lost in Paris is no bad thing—I've found some wonderful shops and galleries and tiny, jewel-like churches that way—I no longer have the luxury of getting lost for an entire afternoon. Teddy practices his counting by how many days are left until we depart, and while I don't count on my fingers, the number is always hovering at the front of my mind.

Where should I go? What else do I need to buy, or see, before we return home? Should I make one last trip to the Louvre for the Greek and Roman statues or should I take the Metro to Montmartre and visit Sacré-Coeur? The basilica was completed before the start of the 1914 war, but it feels older. On a bright day, its elongated white domes gleam like something from an illustrated book of fairy tales; the interior is beautiful and Byzantine.

With a sigh which is not really sad, I choose the Louvre. Montmartre has too many tempting cafés and shops, including fabric stores which would surely cause my sister to lose her tight grip on her purse. If I finish my museum wandering early, I can walk back along the Seine and be home before Harry is done with his correspondence.

"Katie, I'm going out," I call, and hear her immediate footsteps. "It looks like the rain has stopped, so you can take Teddy to the park when it dries a little."

"Yes, ma'am." She kneels down next to him. "You hear that, Mr. Teddy. Finish up your game and we'll go see the ducks in a little bit."

The cobbles of rue Balzac shine with moisture, but the swirling gray clouds have dissipated and the sky is the color of my oyster satin gown. I walk briskly to the Champs-Élysées and board the Metro at George V. When the train glides into the Louvre-Rivoli station, I follow the signs and emerge on the corner facing the museum. The sidewalks here have already begun to dry, and the pavements, as I move toward the entrance, are packed with humanity: Parisians, going about their business; groups of tourists, chattering in a variety of languages; and people like myself, caught between the two.

I pay the admission and walk slowly through the grand, marble-floored halls, allowing the scent of history seep into my pores. I let the ancient palace do its best to calm the worry about Harry that has infected my every waking moment.

It is that, more than anything, which makes me glad we are going home. In Paris, he would continue to avoid medical treatment, but there, he will have no choice. If I can't make him take care of himself, Max will certainly step in and drag him off to a specialist. It's not that I don't understand how my husband feels; often the unknown is less frightening than a certainty, especially when it has to do with something as personal as health. I ignored many signs from my body that my pregnancies weren't going well, hoping that if I refused to see them, the symptoms would go away. Instead, my pregnancies went away, although that would have happened whether or not I'd seen a doctor sooner.

Enough!

I shove my worries into a drawer in my mind and turn the key, then concentrate on the sound of my footsteps on the polished marble, echoing those of countless other art lovers who had walked these rooms before me. Following the signs and arrows through the labyrinthine galleries, I pass by paintings which are windows into different worlds, each canvas telling its own unique story of human creativity.

Each room is filled with masterpieces, yet today, the museum's usual magic is absent. My mind is as unruly as the crowds in the galleries, and by the time I reach my destination, I am ready to leave. I hesitate, then continue on, following the trail of visitors, each of us moving in a sort of choreographed dance through the space. I turn a final corner and there she is—the Venus de Milo. Bathed in the soft glow of strategically placed lights, her white marble form pulses with life. To me, her missing arms heighten her mystique, and I wonder, each time I visit, what she looked like before her full form was lost to history.

As I gaze at the statue, letting the others pass around me, I marvel that someone centuries in the past was able to create a work of art that touches souls in a future which would have been unimaginable to him. This train of thought is something I can often dwell upon for happy hours, but today the connection to the past does not hold, and I bid the statue an abrupt farewell before my worries spoil her for me.

Making my way out into the dull afternoon light, I walk along the river, avoiding the dangers of the Samaritaine department store, and cross over the Pont Neuf to the Île de la Cité. Art is not the religion I seek; today, I need God.

As I pass through the open doors of Notre-Dame, something loosens in my chest. I make the sign of the cross, dipping respectfully, and slide into a pew. The cathedral isn't empty, but the enormous space draws sound up and away from me; I feel as though I am alone in the colored light that leaks in through the clerestory windows.

I close my eyes and, instead of putting my worries aside, I present them to God, and ask that if he cannot make my husband well, that he at least make him see sense—and a doctor.

13

Ava

Two weeks later, the shop became mine. As soon as the lease was signed, Mr. Mendel had the place emptied of Lev Goldman's possessions. He was as good as his word, leaving the long cutting table and one sewing machine for my use, and sweeping up the worst of the dust. The dark green awning had been cleaned, but the rest of the shop needed work; I couldn't welcome customers into such a sad, neglected space.

On the day of the move, Max borrowed Harry's car. After he was done at the clinic, he would go home and load it up with my electric sewing machine, the dress form, and my boxed-up patterns, fabric and thread, and deliver it all to the shop. I had packed several dresses-in-progress myself and given him specific instructions as to how they should be transported.

"I should have swapped shifts with Spencer," he said that morning, as he dressed. "You've gotten stuck with all the work."

"You helped me pack," I reminded him, wrapping my hair in a scarf and anchoring it with pins. "And I won't be by myself. Pearl and Dan are coming, and Dan says Tommy will join us by lunchtime."

"Good." He kissed me soundly. "I'll be there by three at the latest. What about the other kids?"

"Grace is staying with Esther for the day," I say. "Bring the rest with you, if they'll fit in the car. And if you can find them."

My original plan had been to have all the kids help with the cleaning and preparations, but George and Toby require as much supervision as they did when they were six. It's not worth the aggravation it would cause me and Pearl. Thelma would behave, but she has a morning dance lesson and can go to Claire's house afterward and help Esther until Max appears.

While Dan, and later Tommy, patch and paint the smoke-stained walls, Pearl and I scrub floors and wash windows. Later I stand, hands on hips, as Dan proposes a small separate dressing area in the rear corner of the shop.

"Isn't it too much?" I ask. "We could use a screen."

He shakes his head. "Do it right, Ma. Plasterboard don't cost much, and you can make a curtain for the door."

Pearl jumps in. "Dan's right. And we could cover the bench with the same fabric, something pretty."

"Why don't you look for a remnant?" I suggest. "There's a store on the next block that sells curtain and upholstery fabric. Three yards should be enough for both."

"Me?" Her eyes widen. "Why not you? It's your shop."

"Because I trust you." Her surprise is touching; I will get my girl back yet.

We discuss ideas and colors, and I give her two dollars, telling her to spend as little of it as possible. After she leaves, I walk slowly around the cutting table, picturing the room filled with partly-sewn dresses on hangers and on the form, patterns in neat boxes along the counter where Mr. Goldman kept his invoices, bolts of muslin standing to one side, waiting to be used.

"It will work," I say softly, and start as Dan's arm comes around me.

"It will." White paint freckles his face; Tommy has paint in his hair. "You won't mind not working at home?"

"Sometimes," I acknowledge. "But I have your granny's treadle machine if I need it, so I think I'll survive." I tell him the truth. "I've spent all this time with my head down, trying to succeed. Now I can breathe a little."

"Because of Dr. Max." He dabs his brush along the window frame, cutting a sharp edge where it meets the glass.

"Yes." I wet my finger and rub a spot of paint from his chin. "I don't know how you can paint so neatly when there's so much of it on you."

"I'm glad you're accepting help." He waves the brush at me. "It's getting late. Go look out for Pearl and Dr. Max so we can get you unpacked and get out of here in time for supper."

Max soon arrives with my things, plus the younger kids all crammed into the Packard. They stream out, running in circles around the table while we carry in boxes and bolts of fabric.

"They call this thing a Featherweight?" Max hefts the black and gold machine from its resting place in the back seat. "It's at least ten pounds."

"Just you wait," I say, taking it from him. "You'll be carrying the treadle upstairs to our bedroom next. Now that's heavy."

Once we get everything inside, I call it a day. Pearl and I are weary and more than a little dirty, and Max has put in a full day at the clinic. Only Dan and Tommy show no signs of being tired.

"You two." Max beckons them over while I corral the younger boys and Pearl drags Thelma off the table, where she's been tap dancing to an invisible audience.

"Where are they off to?" I ask as my son and his friend sprint out the door without saying goodbye.

Max shrugs. "They've put in a long day. I gave them a couple of bucks and told them to go to the ballgame."

Toby immediately protests that he needs to go to the game. I point out that he hasn't done anything to earn it.

"Well, I would have," he grumbles, "if I'd known Pop was going to do that."

I pull the key out of my pocket. "Let's go, everyone. We still have to think about food."

"No, we don't." My husband beams at me. "I put in an order at the delicatessen on the way here. We can have ourselves a backyard picnic when we get home. What do you say to that?"

The boys perk up at the thought of deli sandwiches. I'm not unenthused myself; right now, any meal I don't have to cook is a good meal. I link my arm through his. "Home, James, and don't spare the horses."

Pearl

Smoke drifts in the window, ticking my nose as I try to read. I pick at the chipped paint on the sill, looking down at the small glowing light in the yard. Dan is on the back step, waiting, I think, for George and Toby to go to sleep so he doesn't have to answer any more questions.

Mama held back pretty well, considering the face she had when Dan came in, his eye swollen shut and dried blood all over his shirt. It was nothing, he tried to say, but his nose was bleeding a little even then. I sent Toby to get some ice, but by the time he got back it had stopped. He said it helped with his eye, though.

He's going to be black and blue tomorrow. Good thing the wedding already happened or that would have made quite a picture.

I look up from *Wuthering Heights*, disgusted with Catherine Earnshaw and the turnings of my mind. Mama is on the couch with Dr. Max, her sewing on her lap. She hasn't touched it in the last fifteen minutes.

"I'm going out to talk to him." Emily Bronte can't hold up against my worry for Dan. "Unless you want to?"

She shakes her head, her mouth a straight line. Wanting to mother him so bad, knowing he won't accept it.

Dr. Max looks up. "I'll stay out of it," he says. "That's probably what he wants. If I'm wrong, tell him to come talk to me."

I appreciate that he doesn't barge in where Dan is concerned. Mama's probably told him how things were between Dan and Daddy and he'd rather stay distant than put a foot wrong.

The door clicks as I let myself out. Dan shifts to one side to make room for me on the wooden step.

"You okay?" I whisper, settling myself by the faint light of the window above us.

"Yeah." He puts his cigarette out, knowing I don't like the smell. "Are they asking questions?"

"What can they ask?" I lean against him and he pulls away. "You haven't said what happened."

Crickets chirp along the wall as he sits, quiet, considering what to tell me. "I got in a fight," he says finally. "It was nothing."

"Were you still out with Tommy?" Lightning bugs blink in and around Mama's potted tomatoes and greens. "At the ball game?"

He nods.

"And was Mama right? Were you drinking?" She was more upset by the smell of liquor on his breath than she was at the sight of blood.

"Just a beer at the game." He moves away, stretches tentatively. "I got jumped, that's all. It happens."

"What about Tommy?"

Dan snorts. "You're more concerned about him than me."

Do men grow out of stupidity, or are they like boys forever? "I asked because you were together," I say. "Did he get hurt? Did he try to break it up?"

Did he defend you, I meant. They're so close, I can't imagine Dan into a fight without Tommy jumping in.

He gets up. "I'm going in."

"They're in the living room." I grab his arm, drag him through the empty workroom and out to the street. "We can talk out here with no one listening. Now what happened?"

"Nothing." He scuffs his feet, kicking a stone so it bounces over the curb and strikes the next set of steps. "Leave off, Pearl."

I follow doggedly as he walks up the street. "Slow down, I don't have shoes on."

"Then go in." He stops. "There's nothing to tell."

Crossing my arms, I say, "There is, or you'd have made a tale out of it for the littles and distracted Mama from worrying. Now spill it."

He looks around, chooses an unoccupied house and sits on the second step. "Fine. You want to know who did this?"

"Yes." I sit next to him, rubbing the grit from my soles.

"Tommy did it," he says, and fumbles in his pocket for his cigarettes again. Striking a match against the brick, he lights it and leans forward, elbows on his knees. "Your darling Tommy did his best to bash my face in."

"But...you're friends." I don't want to believe Tommy is capable of violence, but my brother doesn't lie. It's written all over his face, pain not just from the beating but the boy who administered it. "Why would he do that? He likes you."

Dan exhales. The smoke stays in the still air until I fan it away. "And I like him," he says quietly. "Problem is, I like him like you like him. And after the beer we drank, I guess I slipped and let him know."

I grasp his meaning: that he likes boys in the way he should like girls. It's something the priests would call unnatural, but like Mama, I have a hard time believing anything my brother does can be wrong. I concentrate on the part I don't understand. "How does that even work, boys together?"

"I'm not sure." He hangs his head. "But I've never thought about girls. It's just not in me, I guess."

"Poor you." I lean against him again.

"Don't feel sorry for me," he says roughly, not pulling away this time. "I'm the same person."

My eyes burn and I wipe them with my sleeve. "I can feel sorry about what happened, can't I? And that your friend did that to you." My voice trembles. "And that you've kept a secret from us all this time, so it's like I don't know you."

"It's not about you." He stubs out the cigarette. "I'm the same person, Pearl. Jeez, what do I have to do here?"

I look down at my feet, pale in the darkness, and think that being a child was easier than this in-between phase where nothing feels right. "I don't know. I just—I love you no matter who you like."

Dan puts his arm carefully around me. "I know that," he says. "But I thought he liked me, too, even if he didn't feel the same way. So I was afraid."

"What about Mama?" I ask against his shoulder. "You have to tell her."

He stiffens. "I don't have to do anything. What if she hates me?"

I draw back, laughing a little. "The sun rises and sets because of you, and you know it. The most she'll be is a little mad because you hid a part of yourself and kept something important from her." I squeeze his hand. "Trust her, Dan. She deserves it."

Claire

It does not seem possible that after nearly a year, our Parisian life can come so quickly to a close. We say farewell to Madame LeClerc and the other servants, along with our building's over-attentive concierge; I have one last rosé-soaked lunch with Mary Jayne Gold, who promises to make herself available to Leo Vollmer if he has need of her particular talents and contacts; and Harry and I say a personal goodbye to Paris, walking along the Seine and sitting at a café in the Place Dauphine, the very first spot we visited together on our honeymoon trip.

It will be a long time before we return, I am certain. War is coming; the best and safest place for us to be is Philadelphia. I regret that my niece will not visit Paris anytime soon. On my last shopping excursion, I purchase a guide to the city, with beautiful color photographs and maps.

"Perhaps this will make up for missing out," I say to Harry, showing him the book before tucking it into one of my trunks.

"Or it will make it worse." Harry has cheered up in the last several days; he is looking forward to going home, if not to the scheduled meeting with his mother. Before Leo returned to Berlin, they worked out a plan for their future efforts, including how to move forward should anything happen to Leo.

"Surely not?" I asked, when Harry told me the night before in bed. "They wouldn't arrest him?"

"They would," he said. "He's not only spiriting away people that the Nazis have forbidden to leave, he's doing it under their very noses. Embarrassing them is perhaps the bigger crime."

14

Pearl

Why is it, when you try to fix things they inevitably backfire?

Dan has been down in the dumps since he and Tommy fought, and since I couldn't cheer him up, I decided to try the other side of the problem.

I told Mama I had to stay late at school and to not hold supper for me. I did stay for a while, but after that I took the streetcar to South Philadelphia, and waited on the Marinellis' front step until Tommy came home from work. His sisters kept me company for a while, but they had schoolwork to do. Mrs. Marinelli asked me to come in, but I told her I needed to talk to Tommy and then get back for supper.

Since he and Dan are no longer goofing off on the way home, he was right on time, and he was surprised to see me sitting there. He said hey, and stayed on the other side of the step from me. "What are you doing here?"

I told him that we all missed him, Dan especially. Wasn't there any way they could make up the fight, whatever it was about?

"No," he said. And that's all he said. He's as bad as Dan.

"Whatever happened," I said again, "you two are good friends. Isn't there any way to get past it?"

Tommy shook his head. It hurts to look at him, because of how long I've liked him, and because he's even more important to Dan than he is to me.

"Why?" I asked. "You're his best friend. You two are so much alike—"

"We're not alike," Tommy said, and he sounded as angry with me as he was with Dan. He came around the steps then and grabbed me by the arms, pushing me back against the bricks. And then he kissed me.

It wasn't what I expected kissing to be like. It was both more and less, because it was so good that I could feel it in my stomach and my knees, but it also didn't feel like it was about me at all. When he was done, he let go and stepped back. His breath came hard, like the time we'd been chased for sneaking into a Phillies game.

"I'm nothing like your brother," he said. "Nothing."

Ava

Mendel's long-awaited niece arrives less than a week after the shop is complete. It is nearly suppertime; Dan showed up an hour before to paint my name on the window and we are preparing to walk home when Mr. Friedmann bursts in, causing the bell to clang madly. "Mrs. Byrne!"

I pick up my bag and slip out from behind the counter. "Good afternoon, Mr. Friedmann."

"Do you have a moment?" He blots his face with his handkerchief. "My uncle is asking for you."

"I'll be right there." I glance at Dan. "You can head home if you want. I'll be along soon."

"I can wait." He lounges against the counter, retrieving a crumpled pack of cigarettes from his pocket. "I go home, Pearl will find something for me to do."

The stool behind the register is unoccupied; the overhead lights are off. As we enter, the door to the tiny office swings wide, casting a golden stripe across the worn floorboards. "Did you find her?" comes Mr. Mendel's cracked voice.

"She is here, uncle." Mr. Friedmann and I wait at the counter for the old man to join us.

He shuffles forward, followed closely by a slight figure in a brown sweater, her hair covered by a scarf. "Mrs. Byrne," he wheezes. "This is my niece. Not Sonia, who we expected, but her sister, Hanne. Hanne Mendelssohn."

Hanne sidles around her uncle and nods to me. "Mrs. Byrne."

She is pale, dark-eyed. The hair under the headscarf is also dark. She appears to be in her mid-twenties, though her wardrobe is that of an elderly woman.

"I'm glad to meet you," I say. "Welcome to Philadelphia."

"Thank you." Her accent reminds me of my friend Trudy back in Scovill Run. "I am fortunate to be here."

"I do not understand why Sonia did not come," Mr. Mendel says querulously. "The papers were in her name. Avram wrote that he had chosen her."

Her eyes drift to the floor. "My sister did not wish to leave her family," she says. "And they could not afford to come together." She looks at me. "Sonia has two young children."

I could not imagine leaving my children behind. "I'm sure your uncle is happy to have you here."

Mr. Mendel's chin jerks up. He puts a hand on Hanne's upper arm, the only time I've ever seen him touch a woman. "You are very welcome, Hanne. You must know that."

"Yes, uncle." Her gaze darts to my face. "My sister and I, neither of us are trained seamstresses, but I can sew. I appreciate the opportunity you have offered, Mrs. Byrne."

The shop is in exchange for this young woman's employment; I knew it, but meeting her makes it real. I hold out my hand. "I'm looking forward to working with you. Why don't you come in tomorrow at nine and we'll see how we get on?"

After supper, Dan suggests another walk. He'd been quiet on the way home, different than his usual quiet, which makes me suspect something is on his mind. I agree, and we walk with no destination, enjoying the balmy warmth and the rare absence of the other kids. When we reach the entrance to Fitler Square, he inclines his head. "In here?"

"Sure." I've liked this little park since I found it, not long after Grace's birth. The benches at the far end are deserted. We choose one under a tree and make ourselves comfortable. "Was there something you wanted to tell me?"

There are some things I've been curious about—the fight, and what happened with Tommy, for starters—but I don't push, letting him order his thoughts.

"I want to go away for a while." His gaze is fixed on a building across the street, looking anywhere but at me.

My hands clench. I had half-expected this, but it still hurts. It's too soon for one of my babies to be leaving the nest. "Are you sure?"

He turns dark eyes to me. "Yes."

"But you have a job," I protest. "You're not one of these boys standing idle on corners, not even bothering to look for work. You're secure."

"And now so are you," he says. "Dr. Max brings in more than I ever could, and he'll take care of you besides." His head lowers for a second, suddenly old. "I need to go, Ma. For a while, at least."

I've felt it coming, this restlessness, even before my failed first attempt at remarriage. He's held back all this time for me, for the other kids. "Must you?"

"Yes." His expression clears, understanding I won't fight his decision. "I won't stay away forever, Ma. Don't worry."

"And you'll write." I'll give him stamps, the way I did when he and his father went to Washington. "Not often, but just to let me know you're...alive."

"Of course." He takes my hands. "The boys are growing up. Let them help more—they won't step up if I'm there to do things for them."

I nod, unable to speak. The thought of my son—my baby—taking to the rails like a hobo sends a chill through me. The trains are full of rough men, the sort that Max treats at the clinic. Men who could eat my boy for lunch without a second thought. My eyes burn and I squeeze them shut. Immediately every bad thing that could befall him begins to play on the insides of my eyelids, like an obscene movie.

"Don't cry." Dan pulls me against him. "It scares me when you cry."

"It scares *me* when I cry." I laugh against his chest. "You won't go alone, will you?"

A momentary stiffening of his arm tells me there is something I don't know. But it is best not to push him; my boy can go as silent as his father. I don't want that between us before he leaves.

"Tommy can't go," he says at last. "And I don't have another friend I'd want to travel with."

His words remind me that Tommy hasn't come by for him in the mornings recently, and I wonder what's gone wrong between them. "Will you see him before you leave?"

"I don't know." He lets go of me abruptly. It strikes me that I will have to do without his stalwart comfort for months, perhaps longer. "I want to go soon. This weekend, if I can."

"What does Mr. Howe say?" His employer has been good to us from the beginning. He rented the house to us on the basis of his friendship with Harry, but he didn't have to hire Dan, nor keep him on all this time when older, more skilled men were looking for work.

"That a boy needs adventure." Dan's mouth turns up. "He's even willing to take me back when I come home."

"That's good." I don't want him burning bridges, even though I understand that urge for adventure.

Dan crushes me to him, so hard that I squeak. "I'll come back, Ma. I promise."

Claire

The train takes us north and then west to Le Havre, where we spend our last night in a hotel near the port. In the morning we go to the pier and stand, awed, with thousands of other people who have come to gawk at the ship.

"What do you think, Teddy?" I bend to whisper in his ear. He wears a navy sailor suit with white braid and an adorable matching cap, and looks like a child out of a movie.

He clings tightly to Katie's hand, his eyes wide. "Big."

"That's right, Mr. Teddy, it is big," she says, glancing at me. "I didn't think a boat could be bigger than the first one."

But it is. Rising above the pier like a shining black-and-white sea creature, *Normandie* seems almost unreal. Three oval-shaped funnels, slightly raked to give the impression of speed, already show the first wisps of smoke, though we will not get under way for some hours.

Our luggage—an absolute mountain, most of it mine—had been sent on ahead and is already stowed in the bowels of the ship. Only a few pieces traveled with us, and at Harry's raised hand, several boys with abundant gold buttons on their red uniform jackets appear to carry them to our cabin. Katie and Teddy follow, while Harry and I set out to do some last-minute errands.

The ship will not depart until late afternoon, unusual but calculated, Harry tells me, so that when we arrive in New York, all the world will be there to witness it. Perhaps not all the world, but reporters and photographers and celebrities, all eager to attach their names to the world's fastest ship.

If we do it. If *Normandie* beats the record and achieves the Blue Riband.

I don't truly care, but it adds an extra layer of excitement in the city. Every restaurant and cafe is packed with humanity, and our brief shopping trip turns into a quest of epic proportions.

"I'm done in," Harry says, as we hesitate before a café, waiting for a table to open. The aroma of mussels and frites reaches the sidewalk, pulling me in. "Do you mind if we board early?"

"Aren't you hungry?" My gaze lingers on a couple who appear to be ready to leave.

He turns away. "Not really. I'd like to lie down."

I catch up and slip my arm through his. "Is it your stomach again?"

"I'm just tired." His hand lifts towards his chest then drops away, giving the lie to his words. "It will be good to have a few days of peace before we get home."

Considering that the ship has multiple dining rooms and restaurants, a tennis court, a swimming pool, and a theater, not to mention a beauty parlor, smoking room, and full facilities for watching over Teddy so Katie can also have some time to herself, I'm at a loss as to how my husband plans to find peace. But I let it pass.

"Then that's what we'll do."

Boarding early is no hardship. As I step from the embarkation hall onto *Normandie*'s grand deck, a surge of anticipation courses through my veins. The air is charged with elegance and sophistication, befitting a vessel hailed as the epitome of luxury. I expected to be impressed, but the sight before me surpasses even my lofty expectations.

I look up at Harry. His jaw is tight, his eyes seeking the quickest route to our stateroom. Following, I allow my gaze to sweep across the expansive deck, scattered with immaculate deck chairs. Polished woodwork gleams under the warm sunlight, inviting me to indulge in a leisurely stroll along its length.

Once I have left Harry napping with Teddy on the enormous bed in our cabin, an Art Deco masterpiece in shades of blue and silver—a room after my own heart—I borrow a copy of *Good-bye, Mr. Chips* from the library and find my way to the wide-open deck, choosing a spot far away from the crowded rails. If there are this many people milling about already, what sort of bedlam will transpire when the ship departs?

The book claims my attention for an hour, then I put it aside and lose myself in meandering thoughts of returning home. It is more than time; I miss my family and my friends, and I don't want Teddy to forget where he comes from, but this past year in France has been a gift, showing me—somehow, for the first time—the true value of the life I've been given. Despite the unlikeliness of my marriage and elevation, I took Harry for granted; despite my years of yearning for a child, Teddy's arrival in my life did not turn me into the mother I should have been.

I am different now. At least I hope I am. Having nothing to distract me and no mother-in-law to make me question my every move and decision, I feel, at the ridiculous age of thirty-three, like an adult. I am fortunate that I do not have to work, and from this point out, I will throw my energy into things that will benefit my marriage and my family. That will be enough.

"Madame."

My eyes open; I've been drifting. "Yes?"

"You are Madame Warriner, yes?" One of those red-jacketed young men stands beside my deck chair, hands clasped behind his back.

"Yes," I say again. "What is it?"

He offers me his arm. "Your maid sent me to locate you. The ship's physician is with your husband."

Ava

Dan's first postcard is from New Orleans, which I had to look up in Pearl's geography book. Louisiana! Washington had seemed like a long journey, and yet here was my son in the deep south, in a town where he says half the people spoke French.

"I could maybe talk to them," Pearl says when I hand her the card. "If they speak French."

I bite my lip. France is still a sore point, though Pearl has mostly returned to her sweet-natured self. "I'm sure you could," I say neutrally. "But why do they speak French and not English?"

Diverted, she tells me of Louisiana's history, that many of the French speakers there are called Creoles, and that the French they speak might not be the same as that spoken in Paris.

Later, I see her bent over the same geography book, showing the younger kids where their brother is. I listen as they speculate about this exotic place, reading his words again and again.

"He's washing dishes," Toby says, scrutinizing the card. "At least he won't go hungry."

After they go to bed, I take up the book and find the world map, looking for Paris and then some place called Le Havre, where Claire said the ship would leave. It is astonishing that they have gone so far away, and so casually. The furthest I've ever been from home is Atlantic City, and that was enough; Europe holds no attractions.

Neither does Louisiana, except my son is there. Like Claire, he will tell us of his travels when he returns. And like Claire, I hope that when he returns, he is content to think of Philadelphia as home.

Hanne Mendelssohn was correct in saying that she was no trained seamstress, but she is a pleasant young woman, eager to please and quick to learn. Since I have lost access to Pearl, I enjoy having her in the shop to do simple tasks—pinning and basting, sewing on buttons, tidying up at the end of the day. For the first week, she took an hour each afternoon and practiced on the sewing machine with remnants brought from her uncle's shop, and before long she showed herself capable of straight seams and clean finishes.

Perhaps it won't be so bad after all to have an assistant. And I do like having company, though she rarely speaks unless spoken to, a far cry from my chattering daughter who was always willing to tell me the plot of the latest book she was reading or an interesting fact picked up at school.

"Are you settling in well with your relatives?" I ask one afternoon. She has come back from Mendel's with cups of tea for us, and I have brought out a packet of cookies from home.

"Yes." Her head dips over the cup, inhaling the fragrant steam. "Everyone has been so very kind."

I'm glad. It must be a wrench, to have been sent across the ocean on a decision reached by the men of her family—and then to be introduced as the wrong niece. "I always get hungry at this time of the afternoon." I push the cookies along the counter. "Would you like one?"

She leans back, shaking her head. "No, thank you."

"My daughter made them." Under Esther's tutelage, Thelma has become a good baker.

"I cannot," she says softly. "We keep kosher in my uncle's house. To eat with a gentile—a non-Jew—is not permitted."

"Oh." I don't know how to respond.

"That means we follow dietary restrictions set out in the Torah," Hanne explains. "It has nothing to do with you as a person. Please don't be insulted."

Though I know little about their religion, I understand Mr. Mendel is very devout. "Is it all right to share tea?"

When she smiles, she looks like a whole different person. "My uncle has given his permission. He says you are an exception, but I must keep a separate cup and plate here, and wash them in his shop."

I don't know if it's simply because he likes me or because I gave his niece a job. Either way, it is an honor. "I'm glad he thinks so."

Another shy smile. "You have made America seem not so frightening."

15

Claire

Harry is resting comfortably, for which I am so profoundly grateful that I visit the ship's chapel to say a prayer—after he has fallen asleep, with Katie listening from the next room in case of need. Because *Normandie* is a French ship, it is a Catholic chapel, with the stations of the cross on the marble walls. I try to find peace in my faith, but worry rises to the top like cream.

When the steward found me, I ran back to our cabin far ahead of him to discover the doctor in a near-argument with my husband. From Harry's belligerent expression, my appearance was far from welcome.

"What's wrong?" I tried to quiet my breathing so I didn't sound as panicky as I felt.

"Nothing." Harry was propped up on pillows, his skin waxy and damp. There were smudges under his eyes that were not there earlier.

"That is not quite true, monsieur," the physician responded. "Madame, your husband is suffering from—"

"Ça suffit!" He sat up, pain flickering across his face. "Thank you for coming so promptly, doctor. Your services are no longer required."

Turning to me, the physician bowed neatly. "Pardon, madame. Should your husband have any further need for me, please call."

When he had gone, I sat on the bed, taking Harry's hand in mine. "Now what was all that about?"

"Nothing." He turned his face away. "Katie overreacted and called for him. I would have been fine."

There was a sound from the sitting room, where Katie and Teddy were playing quietly when I came in. "Katie?" I called.

"Ma'am." She appeared in the door, disapproval in every slender line.

"Mr. Warriner says he was fine."

"Hmm."

I looked between them, knowing already who was telling the truth. "Why did you call the doctor?"

She sighed heavily. "Because that poor man was in the bathroom bringing up and it was scaring Mr. Teddy." With a swish of skirts that somehow sounded like judgment, she returned to the other room.

"Harry?" I squeezed his fingers. "I won't pester you about it now, but when we get home, you're going to the doctor."

"Fine." His tone was cranky, but there was gratitude beneath it, that I would make him do the right thing and keep him from ignoring these frightening symptoms, whatever they were. "I'm going back to sleep. We should be leaving soon. Why don't you go back out on deck so you can tell me about it later?"

When I leave the chapel, another steward is going up and down the passage, beating a gong, warning visitors to go ashore. I follow the trickle of departing men and women, but instead of going to the embarkation hall, I return to the deck and watch from the rail as they venture down the gangplank, waving madly back at the lucky travelers.

Beneath my feet, the engines throb. I grip the rail and wonder what lies ahead. Despite his assurances to the contrary, it is clear that Harry is not well, and has not been for some time. If only I'd paid more attention instead of gadding about Paris like a shopping-obsessed marionette.

The race to New York acquires more urgency. For the first time, beating the record becomes important. The sooner we are back in the United States, the sooner he will get better. Max at first, I think. Harry trusts him, so he is the logical choice.

Slowly, the ship begins to pull away from the dock. *Normandie* is different, straight away; there is less vibration, and the wave that streams from the bow is negligible, where other ships have almost appeared to plunge through the water.

I want to go back to the cabin, but I should give Harry more time to reassemble his dignity before we venture to the grand dining room for our evening meal. I leave the crowd at the rail and walk toward the stern, pulling up a deck chair to watch France fall away until it is nothing more than a frail line of unevenly blinking lights. I lay back under the blue sky, in the wind, until my head clears and I can see the way forward.

Ava

We have returned from another Friday night supper at my sister's—the last before her return. At first I thought we would have to change the schedule, but it is easy for me to leave the shop early on Fridays because most of the fabric sellers close in the late afternoon to observe their Sabbath.

After we eat, the kids clear the table. Pearl pauses in the door of the dining room. "Mrs. Adler, would you pick out another record for us to listen to?"

Renate Adler looks disoriented, putting a light hand on her midsection, though Pearl asked the same question last week. "Of course. But you know—"

"Yes, but please come back after and talk to us." My daughters always have questions about the operas, where they were recorded, what cities she has performed in. I am happy to listen, but her talk does no more to convince me of the merits of travel than my sister's abundant letters.

Thelma and the boys lie on the carpet like a litter of puppies, while Max and I sit on the sofa with Mr. Adler. With Dan gone, Pearl has taken charge of cranking the phonograph and placing the needle on the record. Renate chooses one and hands it to her.

"I will take my leave," she says. "Dr. Byrne, do you have a moment?"

He follows her out, closing the door firmly behind them so she does not have to suffer the sound of her own voice.

"What was all that about?" I ask later, when Max and I are alone in our basement kitchen. The kettle hums, not yet boiling. "Mrs. Adler wanting to speak to you."

Max's head comes up. "Are you jealous so soon?" He pulls me onto his lap. "Let me show you how silly that is."

He finds the spot on my neck that makes my brain go cloudy and I lean into him. "Is she pregnant?"

His lips stop moving. "What makes you think that?"

The kettle shrieks and I slide free. There's something in his gaze that I don't understand and I don't want to be distracted by how he makes me feel. "After this many kids, I can practically smell it. Is she?"

"Yes," he says. "But there's a problem."

"What's the problem?" I move around the table and pour the tea, noting that my hands are shaking.

He puts his palms flat on the table. "She doesn't want to be," he says plainly. "And she's asked me for help."

"Help how? With what?"

"What do you think?"

There is conflict on his face. I can't tell if it's because of what she has asked of him or my questions. "That's illegal."

Max turns the cup in his hands. "It is," he acknowledges. "But it's also far from uncommon. Rich women go to doctors, poor women find other ways. She happens to be a momentarily poor woman who has the good fortune to know a doctor."

"But she's married!" She's also nearly forty: old for a first child, but not unreasonably so. Max could recommend a physician who would shepherd her through a risky pregnancy, if it came to that.

"So are a lot of women who do this," he tells me. "They have their reasons. This isn't a good time for her."

With the memory of that amazing voice in my ears, I understand why she wants to rebuild her career. She's left everything behind; a pregnancy would get in the way of that pursuit. I open my mouth to tell him that it's selfishness, pure and simple, and then shut it again.

Max is funny where Germany is concerned, as if there could ever be another war.

"They've only just arrived," he continues. "Josef, especially, is uncomfortable with charity and staying in the home of near strangers. If Renate has a baby, they'll never get their feet under them."

Such things happen, but I can't wrap my head around wanting to rid myself of a baby—especially if I had a husband. Our kids came too quickly, but Daniel and I wouldn't have had it any other way.

"There are more important things than getting their feet under them. She's asking you to do murder." As the words leave my mouth I know it's the wrong thing to say.

"How is it murder?" he snaps back. "It's not a baby yet."

"The church says it's a baby," I counter.

"*Your* church. Renate and her husband are Jewish. In their religion, it isn't a baby until it's outside the mother's body."

"Convenient." Disagreeing with Max twists something deep inside, but everything I've ever believed tells me this is wrong. "It has a soul."

"And so does Renate." He rubs his face wearily. "Whose life is more important?"

I don't know if that's a question that can be answered. "Every life is important."

Max swallows hard, tamping down what seems to me an irrationally strong reaction. "Why should her life be ruined because she got pregnant?"

"Maybe she shouldn't have gotten pregnant," I say steadily. "It's not as if we don't know how it happens."

He pushes away from the table, disgust curling his mouth. "Claire told me what happened to her as a girl, and how you helped her after. Would you have wanted her to bear the child of that rape, knowing what it would do to her—and to the child?"

For all her later attempts with Harry, the last thing Claire would have wanted at fifteen was a baby.

"No."

Max stares at me evenly. "The baby isn't Josef's. And she can't bear for him to find that out."

He has already agreed to do it, it turns out. On Sunday, while we are at church, he and Mrs. Adler will meet with someone from the Curtis Institute, so that she will not in fact be lying to her husband—at least not entirely. After that, Max will escort her to Dr. Spencer's office, borrowed for the day, and perform the procedure. The subterfuge was assembled in the time it took us to listen to the first side of *La Traviata.*

It stuns me that Max, who I thought I knew so well, is willing to turn a blind eye to morality and accommodate this woman's qualms about bearing a child while trying to begin a new life. Every child begets new life in its parents, I want to tell him, but he will not listen to me.

Pearl

June 2, 1935

Sunday suppers are light, because Dr. Max has taken it on himself to make lunch after church, and it's always enormous. I'm still surprised by a man volunteering to make a meal, even if it is just sandwiches, but Mama just smiles and says thank you and eats her roast beef at our new dining table, which is actually an eight-foot-long door that Dan and Tommy dragged back from a building he saw being demolished.

I like having a dining room. It's one of the better changes, unlike all of us kids sharing the third floor. Dan did a nice job with the divider, taking apart what he'd done on the second floor and carting it upstairs, but still, one room divided in half, with me and Thelma on one side, Toby and George on the other, and Dan (when he gets back) in his closet space looking over the back yard. It's as cramped as Scovill Run. And things are supposed to be better now.

Anyway, I was helping Thelma get supper on the table when someone knocked at the downstairs door. I still want to call it the workroom, but Mama's workroom is over a mile away now. It was Tommy! I didn't think he'd ever talk to me again after what happened, and honestly, I wasn't sure if I wanted him to. Except when I saw him, my heart started pounding and I had to hide my hands behind my back so I could wipe my palms on my skirt.

He apologized for interrupting and asked if I had a few minutes to sit on the step with him and talk. I wanted to. Oh, how I wanted to, but Thelma was behind me yelling at the boys, and I knew how that would end if I didn't break it up before Mama came down. So I said no, but in a way that I hoped didn't sound rude.

And I guess it didn't, because he asked me to the movies next Saturday.

!!!!

Claire

This morning, Harry claims to feel himself again. I look at him doubtfully, but his color is better and when breakfast is delivered, he eats heartily and shows no sign of distress after. The skies are bright blue outside our windows, so we go on deck after breakfast and spend some time exploring the ship. I look with envy at the tiled outdoor pool, but my swimsuit is buried deep in one of the trunks. Anyway, I don't want to waste time in the beauty salon having my hair restored after a swim. Teddy would love it, but he won't understand that he can't sail his boat—which is in our cabin, because he would not be parted from it—on the turquoise waters of *Normandie*'s piscine, so it is an area best left unexplored when he is with us.

We settle on chairs overlooking the tennis courts and let the sun toast our upturned faces. "Part of me is glad to go home," I say.

Harry's hand comes to rest over mine on the arm of the chair. "And the other part?"

I turn to him. "Would love to live in Paris for the rest of my life, but it's not practical." Thinking of Leo and the Adlers, I add, "And it may not be safe, come to that."

"No," he agrees. "It may not." One corner of his mouth turns up. "I'm glad Teddy is so young."

It hadn't occurred to me that America might be pulled into another European war. "Do you think we'll end up in it, if it happens?"

"More than likely, though not right off the bat." He shades his eyes, following a particularly ferocious volley on the court. "No doubt it'll be the same as last time. We'll wait until it looks like all is lost, then sweep in and claim credit for victory. The government will stall, the same as they're stalling on the refugee visas, and people will die." Squeezing my hand, he concludes, "I don't see us getting into the war until absolutely necessary—or until we're attacked, which is unlikely."

The morning air is balmy but a chill descends at his words. I don't want to think about war; I don't want to think about anything unpleasant in this time-out-of-time we have been given. So long as Harry stays well, I want to do nothing but enjoy myself until we dock in New York.

He accepts my change of mood without question and suggests that we continue our explorations. "You might enjoy the winter garden."

"If you say so." I try to shrug off my disquiet but do not succeed until we pass through the double doors into a quiet sanctuary amidst the splendors of the ship. As we wander into this lush oasis, calm washes over me, and I find myself transported to a place far removed from the vast expanse of the ocean outside—or the dark threat of war in my mind.

The scent of flowers perfumes the air, their colors adding a touch of vibrancy to the ferns and tropical foliage. Delicate orchids trail from hanging baskets, their petals gently swaying with the rhythmic motion of the ship. Amazingly, finches and canaries flit from branch to branch, flashes of color against the backdrop of greenery.

I am drawn to a rustic bench tucked away amidst the foliage. As we make ourselves comfortable, a sense of tranquility envelopes me, enhanced by the gentle trickle of a nearby fountain. Its waters form a shimmering pool, reflecting the sunlight that filters through the glass ceiling above. Patterns of light and shadow dance over the tiled floor beyond our bench.

In this haven of serenity, I can almost forget the bustling excitement of life onboard; my worries over the future; whatever stresses and strains await us in Philadelphia. The winter garden is a testament to the French Line's commitment to opulence in every detail, a harmonious blend of man-made luxury and the enchantments of nature. It will be forever entwined with my memories of this remarkable voyage.

Ava

I wake to silence, the other pillow untouched by my husband's head. When I turned in past midnight, Max had not come back, though according to Esther Hedges, Mrs. Adler had returned from her outing with him around three and gone straight upstairs with a headache. I thought about calling the clinic or around to the hospitals, but then wondered what I would say if I reached him—that I was sorry for picking at him until he blew up? I didn't regret my words, only their consequences. I fell into a restless sleep, waking at every creak and mutter, understanding only that he wasn't there.

It had been an early day, and a long one. Sunday is no day of rest when you have five kids to get ready for church. As we dressed, Max reminded me that he wouldn't be home to prepare his usual lunch. Remembering the reason, I let my temper get the better of me. I've always had a short fuse, but usually it was impatience that set me off. It turned out that Max's steady, placid disagreement was more than adequate fuel. The more he persisted in his explanation that he was doing nothing more than what a good doctor must, the more I defended beliefs as important to me as his oath was to him.

"You offered to quit the clinic if I wanted you to. How is this any different?"

"For all that I love it," he said, "the clinic is a job. Medicine is who I am, Ava. I won't change that, not even for you."

"I thought the kids and I were the most important things in your life." I didn't mean to sound like a sulky child, but the heat of his anger was unexpected.

He paced the length of the bedroom, crackling with energy. "You are important. But medicine came first, and I don't know how to change that. Or if I want to. I'm not hurting you by helping people."

"You call that *helping*."

"I do." There is a dangerous edge to his voice. "Who are you to tell another woman what to do with her life? You've had seven children."

"What does that have to do with anything?" Even as I wanted to shriek at him to prove my point, I appreciated that he counted Teddy as mine. "I've always managed."

"And that's all you've done." It was almost a sneer. "You've managed. You've gone hungry, your kids have gone hungry. Your husband took a job that killed him so you could *manage*. What would your lives have been like if you'd had less kids or spaced them out a little better?"

I had never seen the point of theoretical conversations. My life was what it was, and looking backward, wondering how it could have been different, was a waste of time that could be better used elsewhere. It's not that I hadn't thought about it, but I would never give him the satisfaction of knowing, especially after that remark about Daniel. Max had no idea how much I regretted Daniel taking that job, how I blamed myself for not forcing him to accept Harry's repeated offers of employment.

"But you're talking about preventing babies, not disposing of one because it's inconvenient."

"To some people it's not that different." His troubled gaze met mine. "It's not like I enjoy performing the procedure, but sometimes it's necessary."

I couldn't acknowledge his admission. "How often have you been asked to do...that?"

"Three times in my entire career. Two of them had been raped. One was just a child."

I swallowed, shutting my mind to thoughts of my girls, my sister. "And the third?"

"Is it impossible for you to back down?" He took a deep breath, held it for a moment. "She knew that carrying a baby to term might very well kill her, and she had a husband and three kids already at home. She chose to live for them, and mourn the loss with her family."

I felt for the woman, but I wouldn't say it.

"You've stopped talking." Max smiled, delighted. "Does that mean I'm right?"

"You're supposed to love me," I said. "That means agreeing, doesn't it?"

"Not necessarily. Not all the time." He came up behind me and drew me against him. "Not if you're wrong. Renate is in a bad place, and I can help her. So I will."

"That goes against everything I believe."

"But it doesn't go against her beliefs." His voice was far from his usual light tone. "I don't expect you to approve what Renate has decided. Just understand that it was her choice to make, and that she had a conversation with her own god on the way to making it."

I slipped my green dress over my head and ran hasty fingers through my hair. "If you say so."

Max sighed. "Maybe it was a difficult decision. Maybe not. But my job, as her doctor, is to provide her with the best care and the best outcome I can. Nothing more."

"The best outcome would be a baby." I looked at my reflection, saw the old stubborn look on my face.

"Not always." He turned away, pulling clean underwear and socks out of the drawer. "You're thinking of unwanted pregnancies, but what about pregnancies that are wanted? What about women like that patient I mentioned, or like Claire, who can't carry a child to term? When it comes to a choice between a woman and an unborn child, I'll always come down on the side of the living." He pulled his shirt on and buttoned it without looking. "It's tragic that Claire couldn't have a child of her own, but look at all the good she's done with that thwarted love—not to mention the good she's done for Teddy."

I resist the urge to slap him for reminding me of what my sister has done for my son, choosing instead to concentrate on the argument at hand.

"It's a sin." Since childhood, the church's teachings have come to me in Father Dennis's rich voice. All human beings are created in the image of God. Those same human beings are worthy of love and respect and compassion—and forgiveness—no matter the sin.

"Don't judge her by your God, Ava." Max's breath was warm on my neck. He nipped my earlobe. "They're not the same."

"I can't stop you," I said. The warmth of his body behind me—and the things his hands were doing—was enough to make me forget, at least briefly. "But please don't talk about this in front of Claire."

Claire adored Max; she must also like the Adlers, if they're living in her house. But I knew her best. She would be on my side in this argument.

"I wouldn't presume to upset her." His hazel eyes meet mine; the disappointment I see there makes me shrink. "Not everyone is as strong as you are, but some people are more compassionate."

I pressed my lips together so I wouldn't say something that would make this quarrel worse. I didn't like being told I was more unbending than my sister. Even if I was.

Max left without eating breakfast. I herded the kids to St. Pat's, so far from a state of grace that I refrained from taking communion, risking curious glances from Pearl and the others. If a small voice asked whether holding a non-Catholic to the rules of my faith was entirely fair, I didn't want to hear it.

The clock, which Max needs—I still wake unaided—reads just past five. There is no sound from the upstairs rooms, the kids sleeping like the innocents they are, unaware that their mother may have upended their lives again.

I throw the covers back and swing my legs out of bed. The gray flowered carpet is rough beneath my feet. Once I would have been grateful. I use the toilet, put a robe over my nightgown, and go carefully down the twisting stairs. Grace will be awake soon, and I need a cup of coffee before I face her demands.

As I round the curve to the living room, I see a pair of shoes, not recently polished, sticking out over the arm of the sofa. Something loosens in my chest and I creep quietly over. Max is asleep, a sofa pillow clutched to his chest, covering his face. A faint snore emerges from beneath the prickly fabric. His jacket is lying over the chair, but he is otherwise fully dressed. His bag lies on its side, under the table.

For a moment I can't move, all the tension draining from my muscles so abruptly that I cling to the back of the sofa. I stand over him until my legs decide to function, then continue downstairs and put the coffee on. When it is done, I fill two mugs and carry them to the living room. Sitting on the edge of the couch, I put the mugs on the table and nudge his leg. "Max."

He snuffles and hugs the pillow tighter.

"Max." I peel his hands away from the pillow. "It's morning. I have coffee."

"Oomph." He blinks owlishly at me. "Coffee. Good."

"What time did you get in?" Most mornings, he's not this incoherent.

Sitting up, he looks at his watch. "Three? Maybe a little later. I didn't want to wake you."

I understand this to mean that he didn't want to continue our quarrel in the middle of the night. Nor would I have wanted him to crawl in bed with me, looking for comfort after our harsh words. One night on the sofa will not hurt our marriage, but it's not something that can be repeated. Nor do I want it repeated; this must be settled between us.

"Drink this," I tell him, pushing the mug closer. It won't keep him up; Max could sleep standing up, like a horse, if he chose. "Then you can go back to bed while the kids get ready for school."

He downs half the mug in one swallow. "I have to be at the clinic by eight."

"You do not." I bump him with my hip, then stand so he will be forced to follow. "Lucille is perfectly able to cope without you. I'll call and tell her you'll be there at noon."

"Eleven." He finishes his coffee. "After a nap. And a bath."

"Deal." I pick up his jacket, shake out the wrinkles, and nudge his bag under the chair where he won't trip over it. "Upstairs, before they all come down."

"Yes, ma'am." Instead of moving, he puts his arms around me and leans his head against my ribcage. "I'm sorry about yesterday."

"So am I."

"I shouldn't have shouted."

His head is warm. I scrub my fingers through his curly hair, feel the movement of his cheek against me; he is smiling. "Neither should I. You know how I feel. I know how you feel. We just need to not talk about it."

He sighs, and tugs me back down again. "That's the thing, Ava. We shouldn't have things we can't talk about. Especially medical things, because I never know what's going to happen in my job and I can't be afraid to talk to you."

It makes sense, but it's like he's trying to convince me all over again. "I'll never be able to see what she's done as a good thing. I can't help it."

"A baby doesn't ask to be born." Max's expression is troubled. "It's on the parents to give that child the best life they can."

I listen as he speaks, thinking of the hardships Daniel and I endured to keep the kids fed and clothed when the mine was barely paying enough to keep the roof over our heads. It was on us, and we had done it, but at what cost? Until last year, all the kids had been scrawny and underweight. Thelma had been crippled. Our best hadn't been good enough for her, or her twin, born dead. It is through luck—and my sister's interference—that Thelma is healthy now.

Max cannot know the direction of my thoughts. "What life could Renate offer—cut off from everything she's ever known, living under Harry's obligation, worried over her husband, not even sure if she can resurrect her career." He pauses. "Not to mention the baby's father."

"Who am I to judge?" I murmur, exhausted by the whole topic and unwilling to think any more about how Renate became pregnant. My faith and my marriage are at odds; I know what I feel, but Max will do the right thing, by his patients and by me. "Enough. It's not my life or my choice."

"That's all I've ever wanted you to realize." Max wraps both arms around me and pulls me close. "I don't want to fight with you."

"Me either."

"Not even"—he slides his hand inside my robe—"if you let me make it up to you. How soon did you say the kids are leaving?"

16

Claire

Whatever I expected of *Normandie*'s arrival—given our departure from Le Havre—those expectations are shattered to glittering bits by the madness of New York's welcome. The speed record, as shattered as my expectations, grants us permission to steam into the harbor with a brilliant blue pennon flying, and each passenger has been given a commemorative medallion.

Teddy clutches it to his chest as Harry holds him. Beyond the rail, the sparkling waters of the harbor are filled with boats: tugs, to guide us in; pleasure boats with sails like sheets snapping on a line; fire boats spraying festive diamonds of water.

"Look, Teddy." I point to the Statue of Liberty, tall and impassive on her island, weighted with meaning that my son is too young to understand. I think of the words engraved on her base and hope that America will continue to offer a haven to the world's huddled masses.

"Lady!" He waves to her, knocking Harry's hat sideways. "Look, lady, I got a medal!"

Music plays on board, and yet more music reaches us from the Hudson Piers, where a seething crowd of humanity waits with admirable patience. I turn my back on the towers of Manhattan to meet my husband's eyes.

"How soon do you think we'll be able to get away?" Now that home is in sight, I want to be there as soon as possible. Although it is early, it's unlikely we'll be able to disembark, collect our luggage, and take the train to Philadelphia before tomorrow.

He confirms my suspicions. "Not soon enough. I cabled ahead and we have a suite at the Waldorf tonight. Our things will be sent on ahead. Once we're at the hotel, we can call and tell Hedges when to collect them."

The thought of surrendering our existence into the competent hands of Katie's parents brings a smile to my lips. "And when to collect us."

"That, too." He kisses Teddy's cheek and deposits our wriggling son on the deck. "We're almost home, Teddy. Do you remember home?"

Teddy's face screws up and for a moment he looks near tears. I've been coaching him, making his bedtime stories about Pixie and his cousins. Never Ava, though; even after all this time I am afraid he will realize she's his mother and turn from me. He will remember her when he sees her, or he won't. All in good time, as our eventual revelation of his adoption will be.

"The children will be enormous," Harry says. "I hope they haven't outgrown their gifts."

"I doubt it." For Pearl, it's books, including Colette in the original French after she told me she was studying it at school. Possibly it's too racy for her age, but I will trust her to figure that out. Because she is growing up, I also bought her a Bakelite dresser set.

Thelma will receive a small red suitcase with a miniature can-can costume I found at a street market, along with a few other bits and pieces—enough to make any budding performer happy.

The boys were more difficult. Toby and George have entered that difficult age of no-longer-young-but-not-young-adult. Toy cars and cowboy suits are too childish now. At Harry's instigation, we purchased model airplane kits with motors and an illustrated magazine about Lindbergh's 1927 flight to Paris.

Dan is nearly an adult, and as enigmatic as his father. I love my nephew dearly but I do not know him; he is good-looking, kind, handy with tools, and willing to do anything for his family. Admirable qualities, but it is not the sort of resume that leads to deep personal connection. Finally, remembering his enjoyment of the camera we'd sent him for Christmas years ago, I spent entirely too much on a new Leica rangefinder, in the hope that he will turn his attention from construction to photography. Harry doubts my plot will succeed, but he had no better ideas, and pointed out that a man who works with his hands can still have a hobby.

For Ava, the Cortes painting, a bottle of Guerlain scent, and several pairs of stockings, including sheer black ones with embroidered seams, which I hope Max will also enjoy. Max's gift is a joyously hideous Hermes paisley tie in shades of green, orange, and purple. It shocks me that they even make something so unattractive, but he will love it. And my sister will hate it.

Thoughts of Ava remind me of her covert marriage, and I am annoyed all over again. How could she get married without me, especially after what she put everyone through last June—not being ready, whatever that meant. As if marrying Max could be difficult when it was clear they were in love.

"Stop." Harry's calm voice cuts through the noise in my head, as well as the music and excited chatter surrounding us.

"What?"

"You *snorted*." He tilts his head. "You're thinking about Ava."

I consider denying it, but there's no point. "Yes."

He puts an arm around me, trapping Teddy between the railing and our legs. "Let her live her life, Claire. We've lived ours this past year, haven't we?"

I tip my head back and catch sight of a small plane flying low over the harbor. No doubt there is a photographer strapped into the cockpit, hoping to get a shot of *Normandie* like no other.

"We have, but I'm ready to go back to real life now. It's been rather like living in a floating museum," I confess to Harry. "I worry that I'm not dressed up enough when we're alone in our cabin. I wouldn't want to live like this forever."

Ava

Trust my sister to make such a splash with her homecoming that it's covered by all the radio stations at once!

The *Normandie* landed today, with apparently every movie star not in Hollywood making a picture there to greet it, with music and celebrations because the ship broke some kind of speed record getting from France to New York. They're gone for a year, almost, and then they have to come home on a boat going so fast that it sets records.

I hope Teddy enjoyed it.

There are times over the last months where I've missed my sister deeply, but it's different than the gap left by our shared son. Teddy, for all that I keep my distance and treat him as Harry and Claire's boy, is *my child*, and having been this long without him—Claire's photographs notwithstanding—has been painful.

Max knows, and I appreciate his tact in not mentioning it. The radio is burbling nonsense about blue ribbons and a slew of movie actors who I've never heard of but who have apparently dropped everything to see a boat dock. As if boats don't do that every day.

I need my sister to be home—not that I'll tell her so when we're face-to-face. We've been apart for much of our lives, and this past few years, before they went to France, has felt like our happiest childhood days combined with an adult appreciation of each other. Recent events have battered the sense of myself that I have painfully built and I need Claire's presence to see if I am on the right track. Her reactions are as opposite to mine as her looks, but we come from the same root. Separated from my sister plant, I am, even with Max, adrift.

Too many of the thoughts plaguing my brain are because of him: the thing Renate Adler has done, to which he was a willing accomplice; my discomfort at the alien position of doctor's wife. Motherhood is easier than all this, and motherhood is never easy. Neither is survival, but both are instincts, whereas marriage is like a complicated board game whose rules change with every couple.

Their train arrives at three; Hedges will pick them up at Broad Street Station and carry them home to Delancey Place, where we are waiting. I had planned to stay home until Claire called to say they were ready for company, but the kids wanted to be there and I allowed myself to be convinced.

The Adlers will be there, of course. I don't know how I will face Renate. Max is little help in that regard. We are still tentative with each other, though our making up on Monday morning had been vigorous enough to knock a slat from the bed. But the thought of being in the same space with both him and Renate, much less her husband, unaware of all that has transpired, makes me twitch. When Thelma touches my arm to get my attention, I nearly jump out of my skin.

We settle in the living room, the whole family except Dan. Josef Adler is there, but his wife is upstairs. Renate has a headache, he explains. She has not been well these last two days.

"Should I go and check on her?" Max does not have his bag, but appears ready to bound up the stairs regardless.

Mr. Adler rises on stalk-like legs. "I asked already if she would see you. She says it is a headache. I believe the heat is bothering her."

Philadelphia can be stifling in the summer, the air wet and unpleasant as a blanket, but it is the fourth of June. If the weather is truly bothering her at this stage, she'll melt into a puddle come August.

Max nods. "If she feels worse, please give me a call."

The unspoken reason for Renate's absence presses on me to the point where I can no longer look at Max. I reach for Grace, taking her onto my lap despite her squirms and objections. Better to occupy myself with her than to have my thoughts show on my face, raising questions with everyone. If only Harry and Claire would get here—I need my sister, and their arrival will distract everyone, including me.

It is no more than twenty minutes when the sound of a car draws everyone to the front windows. "They're here!" Pearl shouts, forgetting the maturity of her fifteen years in her excitement.

We hang in the doorway as Hedges opens the doors to the Packard. Claire is the first to emerge, wearing a stunning dark blue dress with a matching fedora. Behind me, Pearl gasps. "Mama, look at her."

Claire turns, reaching into the back seat for Teddy. She sets him on the sidewalk and he comes toward us on sturdy legs, a proper little boy now, not the toddler who left last June. He looks uncertainly at the crowd of faces in the doorway, then back at Claire. She beams at him and waves him forward. "Go on, Teddy, it's your cousins!"

Thelma pushes past, dropping to her knees on the front step and gathering him to her. She is crying. Teddy blinks in recognition and opens his mouth in a wail.

Over their heads, my eyes meet Claire's. A world of information is exchanged in a glance; she is there, my sister. I may not be able to talk to her properly today in the midst of the madness of welcome, but she is there, and we will be all right.

Another door slams and Harry emerges. He stands with Claire, slightly stooped. "This is quite a welcome."

Max comes forward to shake his hand. "Welcome back." He looks Harry up and down. "What's wrong, man? You look like hell."

Claire

It is an hour before we have the house to ourselves again. I want Ava to stay, so I can pour out my worries about Harry, but it is better to wait until everyone has settled back into a routine.

Harry has gone to make phone calls, informing his lawyer and the office of his return. I climb the stairs to our bedroom and shut the door. The room, usually spacious and uncluttered, is filled to the bursting with luggage. I step around it—Katie and I will handle it soon enough—and sit on the bed, letting the peace of my house close in around me.

Our sojourn in France and the *Normandie* voyage were unforgettable, but it is good to be home, surrounded by things of my own choosing, by light and air and pale colors. Aboard the ship, every surface was either gold, marble, glass, or fine wood; there was no place for my eyes to rest, and in an agitated state, I have discovered that I need at least visual calm.

My agitation subsided because Max's exclamation—*you look like hell*—confirmed all my fears; I can take a breath, knowing it is easier to fight City Hall than Max Byrne on a mission. Harry has already agreed to meet with him tomorrow morning to discuss his symptoms, which is more progress than I'd been able to achieve in months.

Teddy's shrieks echo from the nursery. He's a sweet boy, wanting to befriend everyone, so the abrupt introduction of five cousins, whether or not he remembered them, was overwhelming. Once he wiggled out of Thelma's grasp, Pearl hauled him into her arms and kissed him until he squealed.

Ava stayed well back. It was clear she had missed him—I had hoped, guiltily, that she would have come to think of him as her nephew after all this time, but her hastily wiped tears told me otherwise.

She looks good, my sister. The tightness of worry that has always marked her is mostly gone, and when Max took her arm she leaned against him with an expression so fond that I forgave them instantly for not waiting for me to come home. He is good for her, and the children have always adored him.

Dan was missing. I asked if he was at work, and Ava said that he was away. She will tell me more when we have time for a proper conversation. I can't imagine where he's gone, nor why she would allow it. The timing is suspicious: I hope he did not object to the wedding and go off somewhere in protest.

I said I would come over one morning later in the week and she informed me that she wouldn't be home. During my absence, she moved her business down to Fourth Street to be near the fabric sellers. Things must be going very well if she's acquired a shop. I'd been afraid my friends would abandon her when I was no longer around to model her creations, but it appears they have remained loyal and that she has acquired other customers.

"When, then?" I asked as she gathered the children. "We need to catch up, Ava. Letters aren't enough."

"Don't criticize my letter-writing," she said, smiling to take the sting from her words. "I'll come home early on Friday. We can talk before supper."

Ava

"What do you think is wrong with Harry?" I ask, before we've reached the end of the street.

Max stops. "Not sure," he replies. "My best guess, from what little he's told me, is a peptic ulcer."

"What's that?" Pearl tags close behind, pushing Grace's coach.

"It's a sore that develops in the stomach lining or the small intestine." Max's eyes light up at the opportunity to impart knowledge; Pearl looks equally interested. "It usually manifests as stomach pain, which your uncle has been having, off and on, for at least the past year."

Her mouth drops open. "Why didn't he go to the doctor before now?"

"You're assuming he's gone to a doctor now." He starts walking again. "We've spoken, but he hasn't agreed to anything beyond another conversation tomorrow."

"But you'll make him do it?" Toby has caught up. "Is Uncle Harry very sick?"

"Not *sick*," Max qualifies. "Just not well. If it's an ulcer, there are treatments—changes to his diet, antacids—that will help to heal it."

"He won't like that," I say drily. "I'm assuming by changes you mean a bland diet?"

Max grins. "Yep. And a decrease in his alcohol intake and fewer cigarettes."

"Why fewer cigarettes?" Harry doesn't have a smoker's cough despite the number of Chesterfields he smokes each day.

We reach the house. I stand back while Max rummages in his pocket for the key.

"They're an irritant," he says. "Not every doctor is of the same opinion, but if he does have an ulcer, I'd recommend that he stop, at least while he's recovering."

Following him up the steps, I murmur, "Good luck with that," and am gratified by his laughter.

17

Claire

The next day, Max arrives bright and early, joining us for breakfast. The Adlers are not yet down; Katie informs me they keep the same hours here that they did in Paris, rarely appearing before nine.

"Doesn't Ava mind that you're out and about so early?" I am embarrassed at being caught in my nightclothes, even if they are covered by a lilac satin peignoir, but Max notices neither my discomfort nor my wardrobe. It had felt so good to lie side by side in our bed that I resisted dressing, pretending, as a child might, that we could go back to bed at any time. Harry, however, is fully dressed in a suit and tie, even though he'd made no mention of going into the office.

"She might," Max says, entirely too cheerful for this hour of the morning, "but this isn't a social call. I'm here to take your husband off to be evaluated."

Harry's newspaper comes down abruptly. "You can't possibly have made an appointment this quickly," he says. "I'm sure I'll be fine with some home cooking and my bed. Come back in a week."

"Nope. I called in a favor." Max helps himself to a plate of Mrs. Hedges' delicious shirred eggs and snags two slices of toast, buttering them liberally while never taking his eyes off my husband. "You're coming with me. I don't think you want to worry Claire any further, do you?"

I look up, my coffee cup halfway to my lips. "I'm coming along, too," I say. "Harry?"

"So much for getting back into a routine," he grumbles. He folds the newspaper and puts it to the side. "Fine, Max, I'll come with you." He turns his gaze on me, and I notice that his eyes are puffy and the creases at their corners are deeper than they used to be. "You, however, are staying home."

"But—" If I'm not there, how will I know what the doctor says?

"No buts." He tempers his severity with a smile. "I'd like to go to bed tonight and not think that I'm walking into *Normandie*'s baggage hold. See if you and Katie can dispense with at least half that luggage before I get back."

And so we do, emptying suitcases and trunks on the bed and the floor, hanging some things, putting others into storage, and filling several bags of laundry to be sent out. Katie holds up a silk slip.

"Ma'am, I know you had someone else do this in Paris, but these don't look right to me. I don't know if it's that Paulette or the French soap, but I'm going to do a special wash here myself."

I let her do what she wants. She is also glad to be home, back with her parents and her duties as housemaid, rather than as Teddy's exclusive companion. I will have to check if Pearl is available to look after him—though I'm not sure how often I will need her, as I am no longer up to my ears in meetings and activities related to the clinic. Still, I do have friends and it would be nice to see them all again—and not wear out the good nature of the Hedges family with requests for babysitting.

The phone rings in the early afternoon. Harry advises me curtly that he is heading into his office and will be home in time for dinner.

"How did your examination go?" I ask, twisting the telephone cord around my hand. "What did the doctor say?"

A pause. "I'll tell you tonight," he promises. "Don't worry."

But naturally I worry, as any wife would worry about her husband when she realizes that he has been unwell for some time and keeping that information from her. Perhaps I should have noticed—perhaps our sojourn in Paris had not changed me after all and I was an empty-headed, oblivious woman whose husband might have a serious malady which could have been treated earlier but for my inattention.

"Don't be blaming yourself," Katie says softly, turning from the trunk with an armload of Harry's crisply folded shirts. "Dr. Byrne will take good care of Mr. Warriner, whatever his problem is."

I open my train case, smile involuntarily at the glittering cluster of perfume bottles within. "But Dr. Byrne won't be treating him."

"Maybe not." She slides the drawer shut and returns to the trunk. "But he knows just about everybody. He'll know the right doctor, you wait and see."

I wish for my maid's simple faith in Max Byrne. While I am at it, I wish for my sister. I can't believe we have to wait until Friday to spend time together.

But still, how splendid that she's been able to open a shop. Maybe, if things are well with Harry, I'll find out the address and surprise her on Friday afternoon, admire everything, place an unnecessary dress order, and then bring her home in the roadster to have a proper chat before dinner.

Would she allow it? Has marriage to Max dulled some of my sister's sharp edges? I doubt it; he always rather admired their gleam.

While Pearl does not appear after school, Thelma does. She must be nearly nine, I realize, and has a striking combination of the Kimber height and our father's pale Polish coloring. When I ask her if she'd like to spend time with Teddy, up from a nap and careening around the nursery, getting reacquainted with his toys, she bolts for the stairs, her long legs moving as gracefully as any dancer's—which, of course, she is.

I inquire after her sister, and she tells me that Pearl stays after school most days for clubs or to do homework with her friends. "Now that Mama has the shop," she volunteers, "I come here and help Mrs. Hedges with the baking most afternoons so I'm not by myself."

"Well, there will be more of that now that we're home," I tell her. "But since Pearl isn't available the way she used to be, maybe you'd like to spend a couple afternoons a week with Teddy?"

She stops and leans over the railing, her curls tumbling. "For money?"

"Yes, of course," I say. "What will you spend it on?"

Her eyes widen. "Movies! Have you ever seen Shirley Temple?"

I admit that I have not, although I have seen photographs. There is more than a passing resemblance between the two children, although Thelma never had Shirley's round, cherubic face, even as a smaller child; none of Ava's kids ever had an extra ounce of flesh on them. It made me happy last night that they all look so healthy.

"By the way," I ask, before she disappears into the nursery. "Where's Dan?"

Harry is preoccupied during dinner, paying little attention to his salad and picking at his favorite chicken with cream sauce.

"Not hungry?" I ask, wondering if his stomach is paining him again.

He glances up. His color is better than earlier, I think, but he looks deeply tired. "No," he says. "Having spent most of the day talking about my gut, I can't get excited about putting food into it."

I place my knife and fork across the plate, and focus on him, choosing to ignore that the Adlers are still eating. "Will you tell me what the doctor said?"

He takes a sip of white wine and I see the familiar tightening of his jaw. "They did tests. They won't know anything conclusive until the end of the week, but they believe it's an ulcer." Done with the unpleasant topic of his health, he turns to Josef Adler. "I made some calls today to a few acquaintances at Princeton. They may be interested in adding you to their faculty, once you've had time to meet."

"Princeton?" he says. "How far is that?"

"An easy train ride," Harry tells him. "I doubt you'd want to remain in Philadelphia—"

Renate's fork clatters to the plate. "We will be staying in Philadelphia," she announces. "Just last Sunday, Dr. Byrne introduced me to someone at the Curtis Institute who has promised to find an accompanist for me."

Josef sighs. "I'm afraid Princeton is out of the question."

Ava

When Claire walks into the shop at three in the afternoon, in what is obviously a French-made dress of dusty lavender silk spattered with loosely-printed white flowers, I am torn between annoyance at having to stop and a desire to throw my arms around her and sob with relief. I choose a middle ground, standing and brushing thread from my lap before offering a smile. "Well, this is unexpected."

"I'm happy to see you, too." She grins at me, unfazed by my lack of enthusiasm. "I knew if I waited for you to knock off early and come to me, you'd arrive at six with everyone else, and I wanted us to have some time alone."

I come out from behind the counter to embrace her, then step back to take in her outfit. "You look like something out of a magazine."

Her blue eyes sparkle. "I shopped like a drunken sailor on shore leave," she confesses. "You must see everything—it'll give you so many ideas!"

"How can I resist an invitation like that?" I call back through the open door. "Hanne, my sister is here. Come and let me introduce you." I explain rapidly her relationship to Mr. Mendel. "Hanne Mendelssohn, this is my sister, Claire Warriner."

Claire greets Hanne politely. She takes in the girl's furtive air and shabby clothes, which I have not been able to convince her to give up. "You've come from Germany?"

"Yes." Hanne lights up. "How did you know?"

"We have friends staying with us who recently got out of Berlin."

I do not want her speaking of the Adlers in the same breath as Hanne and her family, who are obviously good, plain people. "They're not the same, Claire."

My sister gives me a sharp-eyed glance. "Don't be too sure." She takes Hanne's arm and leads her over to the bench by the front window, talking quietly.

I leave them to get my bag and turn off the lights in the back room. "Hanne, don't worry about whatever you were working on. We don't have any rush jobs, so we can pick up Monday."

"All right." Her cheeks are flushed. What has Claire been asking her? "Thank you, Mrs. Warriner," she says. "It was not easy—my uncle bought the ticket and paid for the visa—but it was Sonia, my sister, who should have come."

Claire puts down her purse, ready to listen to whatever tale my assistant has to tell, a tale she has not yet seen fit to tell me. "Then why are you here?"

"I was in danger," Hanne says bluntly. "Sonia has our mother's blue eyes and light hair. She can pass. And her husband is gentile. My brother and I, there was no mistaking what we were."

"What about your parents? Your grandparents?" I ask, wondering also about the brother, never mentioned before. "Where are they?"

"In Königsberg." There is infinite weariness in her eyes. "The synagogue is closed, but my grandfather will not leave his congregation. Or his books. Or his home." A tiny shrug. "And my grandmother will not leave him. I have told Uncle Aaron this." She sighs. "My parents and my brother are...gone."

"Gone?" I repeat, hoping the truth is not as dire as I fear. "Gone where?"

Hanne shrugs again, her shoulders drooping beneath the baggy sweater. "I know not. My brother works—worked—on an underground newspaper at the university. He did not come home one night. I went looking, but they said he was gone. When I came back, my parents were also gone." She blinks away tears. "I went to Sonia. She said I must use her papers. Take her name and her ticket and come to America before I disappeared, too."

Claire exhales, for a moment looking as weary as poor Hanne. Then she gathers the girl into her arms and lets her cry, stroking her back and murmuring words of comfort. When her sobs slow, she leads her to the bench and takes her hands. "You must write down your family's names for me, their addresses, and any information you think may be helpful. My husband has friends in Germany who may be able to locate them."

"I know where they are." Hanne sniffs, fishing a handkerchief from the sleeve of her sweater. "They are gone. Dead."

My sister puts an arm around her. "Then wouldn't it be best to know for certain?"

Claire's conversation with Hanne has taken the wind out of my sails. It shook me, listening to how her family had been torn apart for no reason other than their religion. It is, I suppose, the same reason the Adlers fled, but they don't strike me as Jewish in the same way as Mr. Mendel and his family. Are there different kinds of Jews, I wonder, as there are so many varieties of Christianity?

The house on Delancey Place feels different now that Harry and Claire have returned. The windows are open, and the light scent of my sister's perfume lingers in the air. When we drop our things and settle on opposite ends of the sofa, it almost feels as if she'd never been gone. Then the air is filled with pounding footsteps and Teddy plunges into the room.

"Mama!" He stops short when he sees me, then smiles. My heart stops, and I smile in return. My baby.

"What is it, Teddy?" Claire swings him onto her lap in total disregard of her fragile dress. "What's the matter?"

He holds out a chubby hand. "I hurt my finger."

"Oh, poor boy." She kisses it, then slides him off her lap, pushing him toward me. "Let both of us kiss it better, and it will be like it never happened."

Teddy considers for a moment, then pokes his finger in my face. I cup his head with one hand and give the injured finger a loud kiss. "There. All better?"

"Maybe." He looks back to Claire. "Can I have a cookie?"

"When your cousin gets here." She looks at her watch. "Which should be any minute. Go on down and wait for her with Mrs. Hedges, so your aunt and I can talk."

He patters away, and I turn to face Claire, hoping my face doesn't show how that brief contact with my son made me feel. "How did you get Hanne to tell you all that? I've worked with her for weeks and she's barely said two words about her family in Germany."

Claire sighs. "You don't invite confidences, Ava."

I sit with that thought for a long moment. "You haven't yelled at me yet for getting married."

"If you'd had a telephone then, you would have gotten an earful," she says cheerfully. "I admit that when Harry's friend Leo told me—"

"His friend?" I assumed that Esther told her when they got home.

"He had a letter from Josef, saying how embarrassed they were to have intruded on your wedding night."

I laugh helplessly, thinking of their stunned faces. "We felt bad, later."

"Why later?" Claire's smile is broad, thinking no doubt of her houseguests' reaction.

"We were...busy." I let my smile tell her the rest.

"That's all right, then."

We stop talking when Katie brings in a tray with frosted glasses of lemonade. "Hot out there today," she says. "My mama made it this morning."

"It's perfect." It is: sweet and tart and cold, it washes away the lingering clouds from Hanne's story and the story I haven't yet told.

The door closes quietly and Claire returns to her interrupted thought. "I was mad, for about ten minutes," she says. "I wanted to be there for you, the way I was the first time. The way you were there for me."

Something twists in my middle; I had been so set on getting married without her interference that I'd also done it without her support.

"I'm sorry." I cross my legs, turning toward her. "When we finally decided, we wanted to do it as soon as we could." I hesitate. "And we didn't know when—if—you were coming home."

Claire's smile fades. "I will always come home." Her eyes brim and a single tear mars her smooth cheek. "After last year, after what she did, I was afraid...I wanted to get away and pretend none of it happened."

After Irene Warriner tried to break up her marriage. A year later, she still can't bring herself to talk about it. A betrayal like that is hard to get past.

She shakes herself, willing the memories away. "We're not talking about me, though. How are you and Max doing?"

"We're good," I say. "Mostly. We have a telephone now, as you pointed out. And he's mentioned getting a used car, now that he's lost access to yours."

"I knew he'd been in my car! There were candy wrappers under the seat."

"He's no older than George sometimes." Discovering my husband's boyish side has been an unexpected joy. His laughter is frequent and comes from deep inside; he can almost always find humor in a situation, which I find surprising, considering that his work can expose him to the worst of people.

Sometimes Max says things in bed, shocking things that make me want him more. I'm not capable of responding, but he doesn't seem to require it. I am enough, as I am. These are not images to think of now; I fold them away and work around to the source of the stress in my young marriage.

"How long do you expect the Adlers to stay?"

"I'm not sure." Claire toys with her bracelet, a sure sign she is worried about something. Harry probably. "Josef had some interest from Princeton but Renate won't leave the city. She's agreed to take on a few students at Curtis in exchange for an accompanist."

"I'm sure she's a perfectly nice person," I say, wishing I had a bracelet to play with, "but I'm not sure I want her around the girls anymore."

"Because of the abortion?" She says the word without fear that the sky will fall on her head.

"She told you?" I'm shocked; what Renate has done is not something I would tell a near stranger.

Claire rises gracefully from the sofa and crosses to the liquor cart. She pours two small glasses of sherry and hands one to me.

"She did," she says quietly, once I have knocked back my drink. "And who performed the procedure." Raising an eyebrow, she asks, "I assume you don't approve of Max helping her?"

"How can I?" How can *she*? We were raised by the same woman, in the same faith.

"You don't trust him to do the right thing?"

I close my eyes. "Maybe I don't trust her to ask for the right thing."

"She's a perfectly ordinary woman," Claire says. "With an extraordinary talent, perhaps, but no different than you or me."

"How did you meet them?"

Her expression clears, becomes focused. "We met them through Harry's friend, the one I mentioned. He was trying to get visas for them once they got out of Germany. When he couldn't, Harry stepped in."

"They had to leave?" I'm following the news more now, but what's happening in Germany makes very little sense to me: a government turning on a portion of its own people. "Why? She's famous. I would think they'd have wanted her to stay."

"You don't understand what it's like to be a Jew in Germany," Claire says. "I didn't either, until I spoke to Leo, and then Renate. What she went through"—she shakes her head—"it terrifies me to think that people are capable of such behavior."

"What did she go through?" I have my suspicions, but I would like confirmation. Not that it will change my feelings for Renate, but I would understand *her* feelings a bit more.

Claire inhales sharply through her nose. "She and Josef were arrested," she says shortly. "Renate did what she had to do to ensure their freedom—and her husband's safety."

"And that's how she got pregnant?"

"Yes."

I look at my empty glass, wishing I hadn't drunk the sherry so quickly. "Still. I can't imagine doing that."

She tops off both our glasses. "Putting aside what happened, some women would have very different lives—lives that suited them better—if they had no children. What would your life have been like?"

"Max asked the same question."

"Did he?"

"Among many others." I let the hurt show in my voice.

"You haven't fought, have you?"

"We have." My mouth twists, thinking of his enthusiastic response on Monday morning. "But he seems unable to hold a grudge."

"Whereas you..."

"Whereas I can't let go of anything." I remember every painful word we hurled at each other, even as I know we didn't mean them. "I don't know how we'll ever talk about this."

"Maybe you shouldn't," she says. "Let it go. He's a good man, Ava. Trust him to do what's right."

I let that uncomfortable thought settle. "So how is Harry?"

Her face clouds, my problems forgotten. "Better," she says. "But if you ask him, it's the end of the world to be told to eat bland food and drink less."

"Why didn't he see a doctor before this?" I help myself to another one of Esther's chocolate chip cookies.

Claire sits back in her chair. "He thought if he ignored it, it would go away." Turning her wedding rings, she says, "My suspicion is he assumed it was related to the stress of dealing with Irene, and it would fade. And maybe it would have..."

"But a year of high living didn't help." When I first came to Philadelphia, I noticed how particular Harry was about food, and he and Claire had failed spectacularly to observe Prohibition. Claire has described French cuisine to me and all that rich food sounds like an accident waiting to happen for a man with an ulcer.

"It did not." Her eyes cloud over. "And he does drink too much. Not in the way Tata did," she assures me hastily, as if I would be silly enough to worry about Teddy's safety with the two of them. "Because that's what he's always seen as civilized, or as a way to be social. And we did a lot of socializing in Paris."

"What about socializing in Philadelphia?" We are about to sit down to a meal, after all, and Esther has been anticipating their return and practicing new recipes.

"We're embarking on a diet of fish, chicken, and steamed vegetables," she responds. "Harry insists he will die of boredom, but

I pointed out that the doctor told him if he didn't change his ways, he might end up in the hospital on a liquid diet, so he's agreed that boredom might not be the worst thing to happen."

Pearl

June 7, 1935

They're finally back!

Really, they came home on Tuesday but other than us being there for less than an hour to say welcome home, we haven't seen anyone at all. Mama said to give them time to unpack and get themselves to rights and Dr. Max said Uncle had to go to the doctor on the hop.

But today was Friday, and we always eat supper there on Fridays. Even when they were away, we did that. It was my job to round up the kids and Pixie and meet Mama and Dr. Max there when they got in from work.

Thelma was crying buckets over Pixie. I knew she wouldn't want to give up the dog. It's why Mama didn't want us to take Pixie to begin with. But I got the leash and Pixie was excited to go out so we all walked over.

Turns out Mama was already there. Aunt fetched her early from the shop so they could have some time alone. They're sisters, so I understand, I just hate missing out on things. I dropped Pixie's leash and when Aunt went to her knees and called, that little dog might as well have been shot from a cannon. Even Thelma couldn't protest.

Dr. Max and Uncle came out of the living room with hard faces. Uncle doesn't like doctors except socially and Dr. Max was ribbing him pretty bad about letting himself go.

Supper was good, of course. Mrs. Hedges is an even better cook than Mama. But it was fairly plain chicken and vegetables, which made Uncle grumpy because apparently that's how Dr. Max wants him to eat.

After we all went back to the living room and Aunt brought out presents for everyone. She gave me the most beautiful dresser set with lace and dried flowers pressed between layers of glass for the tray. I'll bet even Hazel doesn't have anything like it.

The boys got model airplane kits with real motors and practically had to be tied down not to start building them on the dining table.

Thelma's gift was a sweet little red case, which I thought was nice enough but when she opened it, ruffles spilled out all over. It's some kind of French dance costume, Aunt said, a satin skirt with all the ruffles on the underneath, like a petticoat in reverse. Aunt promised to teach her how to kick and show them off, and Mama got a face on her.

There's a box for Dan, too. That was an uncomfortable conversation, Aunt not having known he took off and Mama having to not-exactly-explain things. Anyway, Aunt's keeping his present until he comes back. She says it's a new camera, a German one better than the one he's got. (Which he took with him, and I hope he's managed not to lose).

There were small gifts for Mama and Dr. Max, but their wedding present was a painting of Paris. It's the most beautiful thing I've ever seen, one of those paintings that Aunt likes with no hard edges or straight lines. I don't always understand them even though I think they're pretty, but this one is different. The smeariness felt more like looking at the city through a rain-streaked window. The sidewalks were wet, with street lights reflecting off them. I want to sit in front of it and wish myself inside the frame.

Aunt knows, because she made them promise to put it over the fireplace, which means I can look at it every day.

And I will see the real Paris. I don't care if I have to wait until I'm an old woman. I'll get there.

18

Ava

Over the next days, I cook for and sleep with and talk to Max, but some part of me stays distant, hearing Claire's words again and again. "He's a good man. Trust him to do what's right."

And that's the problem. I do trust him. I wouldn't have tied my future, and that of my kids, to a man I didn't trust. So why am I having a hard time accepting that in this case he might know best?

It has nothing to do with medicine. It comes down to God and my mother. I've always followed Mama's path; if she survived raising seven kids with no husband to help, then so could I; if her kids left school young, that was hard, but life was hard. I didn't fight for Dan, not the way I would now. Not the way I fought for Pearl to stay in school. She won't repeat my life, my mama's life. Let her marry when she's ready, but I won't encourage her to do it young, same as I've already told her not to start a family too young.

But that's different from a pregnant woman choosing not to be pregnant anymore. Mama would have called that seven different kinds of sin, and I'm not sure she'd have been wrong.

That's where God comes in. I was baptized into the church a week after my birth. The church doesn't approve of any method of trying not to catch a baby, whether it's rubbers or pulling out or counting on your fingers and praying to the Virgin Mary for a few months' recovery time. Children are a gift from God. I've heard it over and over. I believe it with every fiber of my being.

And yet—is a child of rape a gift from God? Would the mother be able to see it that way, or would the child always remind her of its violent conception? And what happens when the child finds out—as would inevitably happen—who its father was?

I think of fifteen-year-old Claire, sobbing in my arms, pleading with me not to tell Mama, and how the two of us prayed on our knees until her curse saved her from the shame of early motherhood.

Max has done it three times before, he says. One a child. What if Pearl—what if Thelma—

A sob forces its way past the thickness in my throat when I consider that horror. Would I feel this way if it were my daughter?

Perhaps the Jewish God is more merciful than mine. Max said that until a baby is born, it is considered to be a part of a woman's body. As a woman who has borne many babies, I can hardly disagree. They were a part of me, and their first cry outside my body was a different sort of pain than labor, a pain that said they were now a new person, no longer truly mine.

I know the pain of loss as well: miscarriage, stillbirth. They are not the same as the raw terror when I thought Dan had perished in the mine. I loved my lost babies for the children they might have been; Dan was my living son and to lose him would have been unbearable.

I lower my forehead to my crossed arms and sob.

Pearl

For our first date, Tommy takes me to a matinee at the Boyd, a film called *Break of Hearts* about a famous conductor and a composer. The music and all its talk of Europe reminds me a bit of Mr. and Mrs. Adler, though I find Charles Boyer more attractive. The most interesting part, aside from the boy sitting next to me, was the newsreel, which showed the arrival of the *Normandie* in New York. As the camera pans over the famous faces waiting on the pier to greet the ship—Clark Gable, Greta Garbo, Jean Harlow—I lean over and whisper, "My aunt came home on that ship."

He lets out a low whistle; his breath on my cheek sends me into goosebumps. "That's some fancy."

I turned down Tommy's offer of candy at the theater, knowing he helps to support his family, but after the movie is over, he insists we go for ice cream. When he won't give in, I suggest Woolworths rather than an ice cream parlor, thinking it will be less expensive.

"You want to walk all the way down there?"

"It's not that far." And I like the idea of walking through the city, being seen with him, having people think what a fine-looking boy he is. Like Dan, Tommy's not a talker, so I find myself filling the silence as we walk. I tell him about my brother's latest postcard. "He's in Florida, can you imagine? He says he's camping on a beach somewhere, and goes in the ocean every day."

"I went to the shore once." He looks down at the sidewalk, nearly bumping into a man crossing in front of him. "It was years ago."

"Mama's been to Atlantic City," I tell him. "I've never been. At least not yet." I hope he doesn't think I'm angling for him to invite me! "Dan's always wanted to travel."

"He talked about it a lot."

"I know." We follow a crowd of people into Woolworths and make our way toward the counter. "He told me you two talked about it."

We find stools side by side and Tommy orders two ice cream sundaes. "I miss talking to him."

"You should tell him," I say. "When he gets home."

Tommy pokes the ice cream with his spoon, dislodging the cherry on top. "Last time I saw him, I wasn't so nice."

"Dan's not always nice." He is, at least to us, but I don't want Tommy to feel worse about hitting him than he already does. Friendship is winning out over anger, and that is what I hoped for. "He didn't mean to upset you."

"I know." His hands are flat against the counter. Long-fingered, short-nailed, scraped and nicked like my brother's hands. At least he has all his fingers. "But we are brought up—the church says that he is wrong. Evil."

I suddenly want to push his face into his ice cream, even though—or because—I had briefly had those same thoughts before understanding that it didn't matter. "My brother is not evil, Tommy Marinelli. You take that back."

He takes my hand. "I take it back," he says. "It is what I was taught. It's hard to believe it about someone I know so well."

Claire

Although I would like to have my family there as moral support, Irene will likely resent even my presence during her birthday dinner. With an apology and a brief explanation, I make reservations elsewhere for the Adlers for that evening and sit down with Mrs. Hedges to plan the menu.

"Mr. Warriner doesn't want his mother to know about his ulcer," I tell her. "So we need to come up with a menu that follows his restrictions without being too obvious about them."

She shakes her head dubiously. "He came down early this morning and told me he wants a menu like the old days, so she doesn't suspect."

"Well, wanting doesn't always make it yours," I say impatiently. "I'm not having him end up in the hospital because of Irene Warriner."

Between us, we come up with a menu which should satisfy everyone: a chilled asparagus soup to start, followed by roast chicken with herbed stuffing; glazed carrots, green beans with almonds, and duchess potatoes for sides. Dessert will be a pineapple upside-down cake and fresh berries with cream.

"He'll want the upside-down cake," she cautions. "Don't matter what kind of berries I find at the market or how fluffy I whip the cream."

I consider this and decide. "I'll offer both. And you can send the cake up already sliced, so he can't overdo it."

We smile, this much of the evening managed, and I make my way upstairs to stare into my closet to choose an outfit so devastatingly French that even Irene Warriner will be cowed into submission.

Ava

A horn blows incessantly in the street. "Go see what it is," I direct Toby. "Maybe someone's trying to get past one of Mr. Howe's trucks."

He scampers off, and comes back almost immediately, smiling fit to burst. "It's Pop!"

"And?" I look up, thinking Max is on his way in. "Who's making all the noise?"

"He is!" Toby grabs my wrist and drags me to the window. Below, my husband leans against a battered Model T. He reaches through the window and presses the horn. The resulting blare bounces off the brick walls.

I shove the window open wider and stick my head out. "What are you doing with that rattletrap?"

He sags against the car, clutching his chest as if mortally wounded. "You have insulted my new girl," he says, winking at me. "Once the boys and I clean her up, she'll look plenty good for her age."

Toby gallops past me, out the front door and down the steps. "Is it ours, Pop? Is it really ours?"

"It is." Max puts him in a genial headlock. "Her name is Petunia. Maybe by the time you're old enough to drive I'll be able to afford a better one. But in the meantime, you can help keep it clean."

"Max." I beckon him over to the foot of the steps. "Did you buy a car?"

He grins sheepishly. "Well, you keep making the point that I can't use Claire's car now that she's home."

"I thought that meant you'd go back to your bicycle." He can't have purchased a car. I may not be as aware of his financial situation as I am of my own, but cars are enormously expensive. He doesn't—we don't—have that kind of money.

"I let Dan have the bike. Even though he's away, I'm not going to be an Indian giver." He snakes an arm around my waist. "And if my best girl ever lets me take her out for dinner again, I'd like to do it in style."

I walk in a slow, deliberate circle around the car. "What style would this be?" I ask. "Pre-war? Prehistoric?"

"She's not that old." Max pats the hood affectionately. "Matter of fact, I think she's rather handsome for a ten-year-old car."

"Hmm." I look at the vehicle skeptically. Its dark green paint is dusty, except where it's missing entirely, showing dull gray metal. The roof folds back, but there are splits in the canvas which tell me that the driver and his unfortunate passengers will get plenty of fresh air whether or not the top is up. "Does it run, or is it only the horn that works?"

"I'm glad you asked." Max leaps into action, opening the door and leaning inside to engage the handbrake. He pulls a lever and turns the key. "Toby, will you do the honors?"

My son is only too happy to turn the crank until the engine chokes to life. Max releases the lever and turns something, and the engine dies.

"Again," he calls, and repeats the process. Toby cranks several more times, leaning into it, and this time the engine catches with a roar. The entire car vibrates. Toby jumps away and comes to the passenger side. "Can I have a ride?"

Max looks from him to me. "Why don't you let me take your mama for a spin first? She's the one I've got to soften up here."

Taking two steps back, I tell him, "It sounds like my sewing machine."

"The mechanicals probably aren't that different." He gives me a melting smile. "Come on, Ava, take a chance."

I shake my head. "I have something to finish. Let Toby have the honor—he'll tell me about it in enough detail I'll feel like I was there." I try not to notice his expression, as disappointed as my son's is jubilant. Toby jumps in and slams the door, and they rattle off down the street, leaving me on the sidewalk with no actual work to do and a creeping suspicion that I have been unkind to my husband.

By the time they return, I have worked my way back around to being annoyed. He should have discussed it with me first. A car is an unnecessary expense. If he's purchased it for cash, he paid too much, and if he's bought it on time, he'll be overpaying in the end. I resolve to have a talk with him later about the fact that we don't borrow money. I've been poor all my life; I've never been in debt.

The other kids have since come home and insist on going out to inspect the car. Toby hops out and goes over its features and functions as if he is both owner and driver. Max stays in his seat, his hand resting on the door frame. "Change your mind yet?"

I don't want to have this conversation now. "First the telephone and now this." I keep my voice low. "Did we need a car?"

"Do you take pleasure in being contrary?"

Pearl stops admiring herself in the side mirror and cackles. "Dr. Max, have you met my mother?"

"I thought she could be swayed by a fancy car," he says wryly. "Or at least a functioning car."

The kids shove in, seeing how many of them fit on the back bench seat. It takes some squashing and lap sitting but they manage to do it. Max pats the seat beside him. "Just around the block?" he asks. "For me?"

"Fine." I get in and shut the door. The seats are in better condition than the top canvas, a single strip of tape mending a split under Max's thigh.

Toby gets back out to crank again. This time it starts more quickly. We cruise shakily up the block, turn onto Twentieth Street, then Pine, and then back up Nineteenth to Ringgold Place.

"That's it?" George asks. "Toby got a better ride than that."

"And you'll get a better one next time," Max says smoothly. "Now, all of you out. I need to convince your mother this was a good idea."

They vanish, more amenable to his mild direction than if I had shouted at them. This also irritates me.

"I'm not sure I can be convinced," I say straight out. "You borrowed Claire's car out of convenience, but can we afford an expense like this? Do you need it to get around?"

"I borrowed Claire and Harry's cars," he says patiently, "because they told me to. And for the convenience, because it got me to the clinic and home to you all that much faster. Also because you worry about me riding my bike everywhere." He covers my hand with his. "And we can afford it. You won't let me pay for anything except my living expenses—what do you think I do with the salary your sister pays me?"

"What *does* she pay you?" I've never known.

"Nowhere near what I'm worth to her." He turns the wheel idly with one hand. "This will make my life easier. And it'll be a tight squeeze, but we'll be able to do family outings in this. I'd love to be able to take you and the kids to the shore."

Mention of the shore softens me, as it was intended to. "We could borrow—"

"The Packard?" Max asks. "Because we'll never fit the whole tribe into Claire's little two-seater. And I thought you wanted to be less beholden to your sister."

I do, and he knows it.

"Fine." Giving in is the first step on a slippery slope, where I'm about to plunge headlong with nothing to stop me before I reach the unfamiliar territory at the bottom.

Pearl

June 17, 1935

I caught Hazel throwing up in the girls' washroom this morning. She said she must have some kind of bug, because she's been throwing up every day for the past week and everything tastes and smells funny.

When she said that, I almost threw up, because I knew what it meant. I'd seen Mama turn green and run for the basin when she was carrying Teddy, and Thelma before that, though she wasn't quite so bad with Grace.

I can't believe she doesn't know. But she's an only child, so I guess it's possible, if her mother hasn't explained where babies come from. I don't know what to do. I don't want to be the one to tell her. But she's my friend. I owe her the truth, so she's prepared to face it.

"Meeting on the roof garden at lunch," I say to Lenny between first and second period. "Tell the others."

She nods, waving me past. She is on the traffic squad, responsible for maintaining order in the crowded halls, and will likely encounter our friends before I do.

My last class before lunch is in the gym, and when I arrive on the roof, sweaty and rushing, the other girls are already there, sitting on the corner benches that look out over the city. Peggy and Lenny are eating, while Hazel pokes at her lunch.

"How are you feeling?" I sit down beside her and open my bag, which contains one of Dr. Max's smelly liverwurst sandwiches.

She gags. "Better before you waved that under my nose."

Lenny takes an appreciative sniff. "I love liverwurst."

"So do I." I keep my sandwich on my lap. "You used to like liverwurst. What's wrong?"

"I don't know." She looks down at her hands. "I told you, I've got this stomach thing, I keep throwing up."

The three of us exchange glances. I'm not alone in my suspicions, but I'm the one willing to speak. "Hazel, could you be pregnant?"

She looks up, appalled. "No!"

"Are you sure?" Lenny asks, dropping her voice as two girls walk past, arm-in-arm, to work on the flower beds. "You and Charlie have been walking out for months now. You haven't let him…"

Her voice is indignant. "Babies are for married ladies."

Peggy takes a deep breath. "Honey, have you let him touch you, down there? With his"— she looks at us for an appropriate word— "pecker?"

Lenny squawks, then sobers abruptly as Hazel's eyes fill with tears.

"Yes? He said it was a way to prove we loved each other." She blushes so deeply that her freckles disappear. "It was nice, after the first time."

"Oh, honey." Peggy takes her hand. "That's how you make babies."

Her mouth drops open. "He didn't tell me—"

"He wouldn't." Lenny folds her arms across her chest. "Men are like that."

"Not Charlie. Maybe he didn't understand?" Hazel knows this is false; I can see it on her face as the truth sinks in. "Why didn't he tell me?"

"Why didn't your mother tell you?" I take a bite of my sandwich. "Mama explained it to me years ago."

Hazel looks between us. "You mean…you all know about it?"

"We're crammed into one or two rooms," Lenny tells her. "We all know where babies come from. It's hard to be poor and stay ignorant." She shakes off her judgment of Hazel's innocence. "The question is, what are you going to do about it? Do you want a baby?"

She shakes her head so hard it almost comes off her neck. "No! I'm supposed to work in my daddy's law office this summer, I can't do that if I'm pregnant."

"You could." I think of all the things Mama accomplished while carrying a baby. "You'd be fine until the last month or so. How far along are you?"

"I don't know." She bursts into noisy tears and we circle around her to hide her from the others on the roof. "How can you even tell?"

Lenny explains about the curse and its connection to how our bodies work. Hazel listens with the expression of a girl whose mother has told her absolutely nothing, and I find myself angry on her behalf—and grateful to Mama, for telling me things *before* I needed to know.

"It's been two months, I guess," she says. "I'm not very regular."

"A doctor could take care of your problem," Peggy says suddenly. "There's something they can do."

Hazel turns to me, hope lighting her face. "Isn't your stepfather a doctor?"

"He is," I say, "but I don't see how I could ask him about something like that. I'm not even sure what Peggy's talking about is legal."

"Neither am I." Peggy shakes her head. "Or more people would do it, I guess. My cousin Lorraine—one of my uncle's girls—got in the family way two years ago, but they sent her to a home to have it and told everybody she was visiting her aunt."

"What happened to the baby?" I've heard similar stories of girls visiting relatives.

She shrugs. "Adopted, I guess. Lorraine came home skinny again. And sad."

Hazel is sitting curled into herself, absorbing the fact that her world has monumentally changed. "I'll call Charlie this evening," she says, looking determined. "He'll know what to do."

"What about your parents?" Lenny asks. "Aren't you going to tell them?"

"I couldn't embarrass them like that. Even if I wanted to get married, they'd say no. It's not Charlie, it's boys in general. Daddy warned me not to get serious about anyone until I've graduated college," she says matter-of-factly. "It would ruin my prospects."

19

Claire

Having Irene back in the house immediately makes me feel small. Harry has visited her since our return, but I have limited my exposure, knowing that, even now, she has the ability to cut me down. The fact that I got one over on her, by failing to fall for her plot to destroy my marriage, has caused our relationship to break down almost entirely. Other than the effect that our hostilities have on my husband, I don't care.

When I come downstairs, he is already in the living room, lingering around the liquor cart. "I haven't," he says, at my curious glance. "But it's the first thing I'll do when she enters the room."

"It is not." I kiss him on both cheeks and on the mouth, so he knows I mean it. "You will greet her politely, to distract from any bad impression I may make."

He looks me up and down. "How can you make a bad impression looking like that?"

My dress is a straight column of crepe with a narrow belt, discreet rhinestones picking out the buckle. Red was a color totally lacking in my wardrobe until one of my shopping trips with Mary Jayne. I told her about my fraught relationship with Irene, and she convinced me to buy it, saying it was the perfect thing to wear if I wanted to tell my mother-in-law to go to hell without saying a word.

I convince him to take a seat, rather than stare at the forbidden martini fixings. We wait quietly, my hand resting on Harry's thigh; he is as tense as a racehorse at the post. When the bell rings promptly at seven, he nearly springs up, but I do not lift my hand. When Katie announces Irene, we rise from the sofa united to greet her.

"Harry, darling." She stands with her face tilted up, waiting for his kiss. Which he gives, as he is a good son who truly hates the position she has put him in. "You look well, considering."

"Considering what?" he asks quickly, as if fearing she's learned of his condition.

"France, of course!" she titters and turns to me. "And Claire."

"Irene." I kiss her powdery cheek, smell her faint violet perfume. The red dress gives me courage. "You haven't changed."

"Well, I hope not." She sits on the edge of the chair that had been hers—a new chair, actually, as she had taken her favorite pieces of furniture when she moved out. This one is simply in the same spot on the carpet, and the habits of a lifetime are strong. "Isn't anyone going to offer me a drink?"

Harry returns to the liquor cart before I can offer. "What'll it be, Mother?" He picks up the gleaming shaker. "Martini?"

She appears shocked to her core. "I never drink hard liquor." She purses her lips. "I'll have a sherry."

He pours her drink, and looks over at me. "Claire—martini?"

Gin makes Irene more palatable, but I do not want to let the genie out of the bottle, not this early in the evening. "I'll have sherry, too," I tell him. "I'm looking forward to wine with dinner and don't want to spoil the taste."

Disappointed at being deprived of his martini, he pours two more sherries and we resume our positions on the couch.

The sherry is sweet, Irene's favorite; I prefer dry if I'm going to drink it at all.

"That's a lovely dress, Irene." It's one of her peignoir affairs, all filmy peach ruffles with a diamond brooch on her left breast. I wouldn't wear such an outfit to sleep in, but Irene's closets are crammed with clothes better suited to an ingénue.

"Thank you, dear." She straightens the flounce at her neckline. "Yours is rather…vivid."

I smile broadly, my lipstick the same scarlet as the dress. "Isn't it?"

Conversation is stilted, and when Katie comes to the door a half hour later to announce dinner, I could hug her.

The asparagus soup is a success, and while Irene raises a brow at the chicken, it is too delicious for even her to disparage for long. "Your cook is improving," she says grudgingly. "Or perhaps you hired a new one? Though the girl is still here."

"Katie will be here until she finds something better." I take a healthy swallow of my wine, crisp and white and worth the wait. "As will her parents."

She finishes the last of her green beans, then places her knife and fork across the plate. "I thought perhaps we'd be a larger party this evening."

Damn. I should have invited Max and Ava, at least. "I thought you'd prefer to celebrate your birthday with us, and not include my family."

"That's very considerate of you," she says with a regal lowering of her chin. "I meant your houseguests, naturally. They are not here?"

How has she learned about the Adlers? My gaze flicks to Harry. "They're out for the evening," I end up saying. "I'm not sure what time they'll be back."

Irene takes a precise sip of wine. "They've been here for some time, I understand. Before you even returned."

"Yes." Harry has rejoined the conversation. "They are close friends of my college friend, Leo Vollmer, from Berlin. He asked if we'd house them while they sort themselves out in this country."

She is quiet for a moment, staring at her plate. When Katie comes to remove them, she springs back, as if our maid would strike her, or drop food in her lap. "Harry, I can't believe you've let strangers stay in this house—your father's house—without being here to keep an eye on them. It's not like you, it's very irresponsible."

Harry pauses, then exhales an infinitely patient breath. "They're very nice people, Mother. Friends, as I said, of a friend. I have no expectation that they will be anything other than the pleasant guests they were when they first stayed with us in Paris."

There is a pause between courses, and the silence stretches out. I wait for Irene to say something foolish or infuriating, and she does not disappoint.

"I heard they were"—she lowers her voice—"Jews. Is that true?"

"Yes." He nods enthusiastically, as if the Adlers' faith was the specific reason we invited them into our home, rather than the reason they were chased out of their own. "It's a very dangerous time for their people right now, in Germany, so Leo suggested they come here."

Irene inhales sharply. "Why didn't this Leo keep them himself?"

"Because he is *in* Germany." Harry's tone has changed; his patience is running thin. "And Josef and Renate Adler are none of your concern, Mother, if you want the absolute truth."

"Well! I'm very glad they're out, because I have no interest in meeting those people. Nor do I appreciate your tone, Harry."

Her tantrum is forestalled by Katie's arrival. "Ma'am, are you ready for coffee and dessert?"

"Yes, I think we are." I blink at her, happy to have her sane presence to counteract Irene's awfulness. "I forget what your mother and I decided on."

"Pineapple upside down cake or berries and cream," she says. "Blackberries and raspberries, ma'am, picked fresh this morning."

I spread my hands across the smooth white cloth. "Berries for me, thank you. Irene?"

"Cake." Her mouth is puckered with disappointment. Had she actually expected a birthday cake? "And I take cream in my coffee, not milk."

Katie turns an impassive face to her. "I remember, ma'am." Then, with her usual smile, "Mr. Warriner? Which should I bring for you?"

"What?" he asks, brought from his thoughts. "Berries, Katie. Thank you."

One good thing comes out of the painful dinner. Returning from a trip to the bathroom, I hear Irene regaling Harry with her thoughts for the upcoming orchestra season, along with the annual outdoor concert series. "The summer season is already open at the Robin Hood Dell," she says, "but I've never cared for 'music under the stars,' or whatever they choose to call it."

I've always enjoyed the outdoor concerts, and whenever Harry and I were out walking in Paris and came across a group of musicians playing—under the stars, as it were—I always insisted that we stop and listen.

"What about a little music?" I interrupt. "Summer nights seem to call for it, and we are all safely indoors."

"If you like." Irene turns back to Harry. "Honora has a box, but our agreement says…"

I kneel before the cabinet and slide out a record, loading it onto the turntable as they continue their conversation. If the children have been using the phonograph during our absence, they have been good about replacing the needle. Winding the handle, I place the needle onto the record, listen to the comforting hiss that announces the arrival of the music, and take my seat again beside Harry.

When the opening of *La Bohème* flows into the room, Harry stops talking. I press his fingers and nod for him to continue on.

It strikes me, out of the blue, that, if he does not know already, Leopold Stokowski would be very interested to learn of Renate's presence in the city. I listen to my mother-in-law's chatter with half my brain as I try to work out a way to introduce our guest to the orchestra's celebrated conductor, a man as legendary for his effect on Philadelphia's ladies as for his musical prowess.

Though he is very attractive, I've never felt the pull of Stokie's magnetism. His height, his pale hair and penetrating gaze, remind me of my father. But he has brought more than one woman to a new appreciation for classical music, and he loves to make headlines. Securing Renate Steiner for the upcoming season would definitely make a splash in the papers—and it would devastate Irene Warriner to boot.

One song turns into another, and then I hold my breath as Renate's voice enters the room, pure and sinuous as a silken scarf, weaving through the flow of words until we fall silent.

"Ah." Irene's hands are clasped to the ruffles trembling on her breast. "*Sì, mi chiamano Mimì.* Puccini is hackneyed, but I will never tire of this piece. Especially when Renate Steiner sings it. She is a true artist."

I count to five before I allow myself to speak. "I'm so sorry that our inconvenient houseguests are out, then."

She turns, birdlike, to face me. "Whatever for?"

"Because Renate Adler is Renate Steiner. What a shame you made it clear that you had no wish to meet her."

Pearl

July 6, 1935

Hazel called today. She started to tell me something but then her voice changed and she said she and Charlie are having lunch downtown one day this week. I think one of her parents walked into the room, but also that Charlie finally got an appointment with a doctor to have everything taken care of. He's been dragging his feet like Hazel isn't at risk of being found out if he delays. It's not like she can do this by herself.

Last time we talked, before school let out, she told me he'd promised to go to the appointment with her. I think she would have rather had one of us, but he's the one who knows the doctor. And I'm not sure how I'd feel about going.

She has to do it. She's sixteen, she can't have a baby and finish school and have any kind of life. I mean, she could. Lots of girls have probably done it, but they've ended up with lives like Mama's, and even Mama wouldn't wish that on someone. It's not legal, that's why Charlie has to pay extra to have it done, and why they couldn't do it right away. Apparently even a boy like that doesn't have enough pocket money to pay for an illegal operation.

Last time I went to confession, I tried to talk to the priest about it, but these city priests aren't like Father Dennis. Or maybe he's unusual. But I don't think he'd talk about sin in this case, except maybe the sin of keeping a girl in ignorance so that she gets in trouble.

Claire

Prue Foster, it turns out, is friendly with Stokowski and offers to connect us. "When he finds out about Mrs. Adler, he'll move heaven and earth to get her on his stage."

"That's what I'm hoping." I like Renate and Josef, but he's drooping around the house like a sick plant from lack of occupation and worry over his wife, while she's become snappish about the quality of her student accompanist at the Curtis. A bit of good news would go a long way to improving both their moods.

We set a meeting for a weekday afternoon, with Prue promising that she won't tell Stokowski the identity of the fourth member of our party. For all that she likes to be at the center of things, agreeing to leave the introductions to me is a big step.

When I told Renate of our plan, her eyes lit up in a way quite unfamiliar. "I have, of course, heard of Stokowski," she says. "His recordings are played even in Berlin, though I have never myself seen him conduct."

"There are rumors that this may be his last season in Philadelphia." I have watched Stokowski conduct the orchestra for over fifteen years. In all that time, his hold over the music lovers of Philadelphia has never lapsed.

"All the better, then, that we meet now."

I pace the living room, my eyes flickering from the tasteful ornaments on the mantel to the new Renoir between the front windows. Why am I nervous about how my home will be perceived? This meeting is not about me, but Renate. Who is an island of elegance on the sofa, legs tucked neatly to one side, black skirt in graceful folds around her calves. Waiting with a stillness that is beyond me.

"Your friend, she has promised to bring him?" she asks quietly, and I understand that her anxiety is the same as mine, under her smooth, professional demeanor.

"She called this morning." Prue is generally late; I don't bother to mention that because I'm trying to forget it myself.

The bell rings and Katie is right there to open the door; knowing the importance of this meeting, she was undoubtedly sitting on the stairs. Voices—one male, one female—reach our ears, and then Katie opens the door. "Ma'am, Mr. Stokowski and Mrs. Foster."

Stokowski enters the room ahead of Prue, his hands already outstretched. "Mrs. Warriner! So good to see you again."

"Thank you for coming, Mr. Stokowski." A surge of anticipation fills me. If I can get him to agree to work with Renate, it will solve all their problems. "I'm so pleased you could join us."

"Ahem." Over his shoulder, Prue pulls a face. *What about me?* Her exaggerated expression is made more comical by her dramatic, oversized hat. Ava would say it balanced her bottom. I hide a smile.

"And you, Prue, of course. Thank you for all your hard work—I know how difficult you find social functions." Katie slips in behind them and pours four small glasses of sherry, sliding the tray onto the table next to the couch. "Won't you please sit down and have a drink?"

Stokowski takes a glass, which looks absurdly tiny in his large hands. "Very nice. Now, Mrs. Warriner"—he turns his penetrating gaze on me—"Mrs. Foster said that you wished to introduce me to someone."

"Well, yes." I put down my drink. "My friend, Renate Adler."

Renate smiles graciously. "Thank you, Claire. I'm honored to meet you, maestro."

"The pleasure is mine, dear lady." His words are genuine; he has been compelled to undergo similar introductions many times before in the name of his career. "Wait—" His expression changes, eyes widening. A smile spreads across his face and he begins speaking to Renate in rapid German. "Frau Steiner! Ist das wirklich du?"

Confusion washes over me as I am unable to comprehend the sudden shift in the conversation. Prue, beside him on the couch, pantomimes her bewilderment. It hadn't occurred to either of us that he spoke German.

Under the flood of words, Renate leans close, her voice low. "He has recognized me."

"Ah." That is logical; I remember the sense of unreality when I first comprehended her identity, and Mary Jayne Gold's shock when she learned Renate Steiner was staying with us.

As I endeavor to sort all this out, Stokowski continues his uneven conversation in a mixture of German and English. "Frau Steiner, I saw you perform in London, it must be five years ago. His voice is a blend of nostalgia and enthusiasm. "You are a remarkable talent. It is wonderful to see you here, and safe."

Renate nods appreciatively, her ringed hands clasped over one knee. "Ihr talent ist das wahre, maestro. Ich hatte keine ahnung, als ich nach Philadelphia kam, dass ich die ehre haben würde, sie zu treffen."

I glance between them, trying to grasp what is going on. Prue, more straightforward and always willing to speak her mind, sets her empty glass back on the tray. "Would someone please tell me what the hell you're saying?"

He breaks into hearty laughter. "I'm sorry to be so rude. I do not often have the chance to practice my German beyond shouting 'Achtung!' at a disobedient first violin. The sight of Renate Steiner—here!—is quite tremendous." He smiles broadly. "In plain English, I am trying to think how I can ask her to perform with us this season. The schedule is set, but it can be unset, for such a performer."

Pride swells within me. "That's exactly what I was hoping for, Mr. Stokowski. And Renate deserves this opportunity, after everything that she and her husband went through to get here."

"Now, Claire." Renate rises smoothly, moving to the liquor cabinet and retrieving the bottle of sherry. "Let us not trouble the maestro with stories of struggle. This day is about the future."

Prue holds out her glass, rolling her eyes at me.

"And what a future it will be," Stokowski says, raising his glass. "To beautiful ladies and even more beautiful music."

By the time they depart, Stokowski still speaking German even though Renate has begun answering him in English, it has been agreed that she will make three guest appearances with the orchestra before the holiday season, but not in the written-in-stone first weeks of October. "It will more than make up for the Metropolitan Opera's failure to return to Philadelphia," Stokowski said severely.

The details weren't entirely clear, but rumor had it that New York's opera company had lost money for years in coming to Philadelphia, and as the Depression wore on, they pulled back, and last year decided not to offer any performances in the city at all.

"I must discipline myself and rehearse more frequently," Renate says, almost submissively. She is glowing with restrained joy. "How I wish you had a piano."

"If I had a piano, your accompanist would be living in my guest room and there would never be a moment in this house without music." She sings now, in their rooms, and while I am glad she is happy enough to do that, even the venerated Renate Steiner is not permitted to shatter my peaceful afternoons.

She gives a rueful smile. "That is true."

Stokowski kisses her on both cheeks, then turns to me. I offer my hand and he brings it to his lips. "I cannot thank you enough, Mrs. Warriner, for bringing Renate Steiner into your home. You have done a great service to music." To Renate, he says, "Frau Steiner, ich freue mich darauf, mit Ihnen zusammenzuarbeiten. Wir werden bald sprechen, um ein programm zu besprechen."

Prue hugs me and shakes hands with Renate. "We must have lunch soon, Claire—I've seen your sister more often than you."

"I'll call and we'll set something up for next week," I promise. When they are gone, Renate and I drop simultaneously onto the sofa and contemplate the sherry. "What was all that at the end?"

"He said he is looking forward to our collaboration, and will call soon to discuss a program." She closes her eyes and looks for all the world as though she has just run a mile. "Such drama, these conductors. This one, waving his hands about like birds, no baton—but he will give me work. That is what matters."

20

Ava

I should have been at the shop an hour ago, but with one thing and another it is after ten and I haven't left the house. Pearl comes down to the living room, one finger holding a place in her book. "Do you have plans today?"

"No," she responds. "What do you need me to do?"

"Nothing much." I gauge how long it will take to get to the shop, finish altering the dress that no longer suits Mrs. Fishwick, and come home again. "Get supper started if I'm not back by four."

She nods, and passes me to reach the couch. "There's a car out front, I can hear it." She drops her book and goes to the window. "It's Hazel."

I open the door. A yellow taxi is pulling away from the curb. On the sidewalk, leaning on the railing, is Pearl's friend. She is dead white, freckles standing out all over her face. "Are you all right?"

The girl looks up at me, her chin trembling. Then she bursts into tears and sits down hard on the bottom step.

Pearl shoves past me, running down the steps to squat in front of her. Hazel sobs more than she speaks, her face buried against my daughter's shoulder.

"What is it?"

Pearl looks up, stricken. "Can she come in, Mama? She's sick."

"Of course!"

Between the two of us, we get her up the steps and into the living room, where she collapses stiffly onto the couch and hides her face in her hands, still crying. Pearl sits beside her, rubbing her back and whispering fiercely into her ear. Hazel nods once and then wails, a sound of fear or pain that sends a chill through me. What is wrong with the girl?

"I'd like to put her to bed in my room." Pearl stands, hauling Hazel to her feet. "Do you mind?"

Why would I mind? "Can you get her up there yourself? I'll put on some tea."

"Thank you, Mrs. Kimber," Hazel says faintly. "Mrs. Byrne. I'm sorry for the inconvenience."

I put the kettle on, then go up to the telephone and call Mendel's shop. "It's Ava, Mr. Friedmann. Could you go next door and tell Hanne I might not be there? Something has come up." I listen to his excited questions. "No, we're all fine—it's my daughter's friend, but I may have to stay home." I wonder if she should come here, but change my mind. "Tell her to take apart the yellow dress and leave it on the table, we'll work on it tomorrow."

When the tea is ready, I put three mugs on a tray with a handful of cookies and carry it carefully up the curving stairs to the third floor. Hazel is in Pearl's bed, wearing her nightgown. Her eyes are red-rimmed and swollen, but she has stopped crying.

"Better?" I ask, setting the tray on the dresser. "How do you take your tea, Hazel?"

She bites her lip, as if it is the most difficult question she's ever been asked. A quick glance at my daughter, then she says, "A little sugar, please."

I catch the look on Pearl's face. There is something happening here which I do not understand. "Pearl? Is there something I need to know?"

"No, Mama." She shakes her head. "Hazel came over dizzy on her way home from an appointment, and she took a taxi here because it was closest. She was afraid to go home on the train feeling sick."

That makes sense, but instinct tells me there is more to the story. "Where were you, Hazel?"

"A doctor—" She breaks off, chewing her lip again. "I was going out with my fellow, but he had to go home. And then I got dizzy."

So there was a doctor involved. A suspicion grows. "Is it your monthlies, Hazel?"

She nods, but tears well up and track down her cheeks. "You said she'd figure everything out." The sheet is pulled over her head and she curls into a shaking ball under the covers.

"Pearl?"

My daughter sighs. "Let's talk in the hall, Mama." She puts a hand on Hazel's knee. "We'll be right outside. Come out from under there before you melt and drink your tea."

Closing the door, we stand on the landing by the open window. "Have you figured out everything?" she asks. "You always do."

"I don't want to be right about this." Hazel's behavior—the tears, the shame—tells me everything I need. "Was she in the family way?"

Pearl blanches. "Yes." She leans against the wall, rubbing her face with one hand. "She didn't even know. Her mother never explained anything to her, and neither did Charlie." Her pale eyes are bright with tears. "When the girls and I explained to her what was going on, I was scared for her. She was so upset."

"As she would be." I am appalled that Hazel has got herself into such a situation, but I reserve some anger for the mother who kept her in the dark and for the young man who put his pleasure over her safety. "What happened this morning? Did she go to a doctor?"

"Yes." She sits abruptly, as if the strength has gone out of her legs. "Charlie found someone and they went together, but when she came out, he was gone." She sniffs and backhands tears from her eyes. "She was in pain and afraid to go home, so she came to us."

Pearl comes slowly down to the kitchen, her feet dragging on the stairs. I sit at the table, a cooling cup of tea in my hands.

"She's asleep," she says quietly. "I gave her a hot water bottle for her stomach. It seems to help."

"Will she be all right?" I can't bring myself to look at my daughter.

She sits in the chair nearest the stove and drops her head into her hands. "I think so. She's bleeding, she says, but no worse than a bad monthly. The doctor told her that was normal, that it would last for a day or two."

I close my eyes, grateful we will not have to involve Max. "Did you know about this?"

An indrawn breath. "Not this," she says. "But about the baby, and that he was going to have it taken care of."

The cold tea is bitter in my mouth. "This was taking care of it?"

Pearl rubs her eyes, looking tired and very young. And yet, after this, I know she will never be truly young again.

"The doctor told her she was bad. He took Charlie's money and he did what was asked of him, but he told Hazel she was filthy and that no one would want her after this." Her voice rises, indignant. "As if she got that way by herself. Why is it never the man's fault?"

"I don't know," I say, "but it never is." This realization makes me feel a bit kindlier toward Hazel. "Do you want Max to check her when he gets in?"

She presses hard against her temples. "Only if she's worse, I guess. I don't want him to think badly of her because of what she's done."

I close my fingers around her wrist. "You don't have to worry about that," I say. "He would never."

Pearl

July 17, 1935

Hazel was crying so hard when she arrived I thought she was dying. Upstairs, once she calmed down, I realized that while she was hurting some, the worst pain was that Charlie had abandoned her at the doctor's office. She wanted to know how he could have done that, and what she was going to have to do to make him not mad at her.

I wanted to call Mama, so she could explain that a boy who truly cared wouldn't have left her to find her own way home. Matter of fact, a boy who cared wouldn't have gotten her into that situation knowing she didn't understand what they were doing. Accidents happen, but that was no accident. Charlie may be handsome, and he may be rich, but he's not a nice boy.

I think the shock of what they did also scared her. She said she didn't think of it as a baby until the doctor put his hand on her bare leg and said she could get up off the table. She was so worried about losing Charlie and her future that it never occurred to her, and now she's scared she's going to hell. I don't know what to tell her there, either, because it doesn't say anywhere that God is kind and won't send innocent girls to hell for making dumb mistakes, but that's how I want to believe He is. Hazel doesn't deserve eternal suffering because a boy convinced her to take her pants down.

And isn't her life worth more than a life that doesn't exist yet? Maybe I'm being selfish on her behalf or I'm not as good a person as I think I am, but Hazel's just a scared kid. She wants to go back to school in the fall, not go away to some place and have her baby taken away or be shunned by her family. She thinks badly enough of herself without everyone else jumping on that bandwagon.

Mama suggested that Hazel call her parents and tell them we'd been out and to ask permission to stay the night with us. I don't know if I'm more surprised that Mama made up a lie or that she was all right with this whole thing. Sort of all right.

Not completely, though. I saw her face when she realized, and she wasn't happy. But she also didn't judge Hazel. That was what the doctor did. Now I'm almost sorry I didn't get Dr. Max involved from the beginning, because even though I don't imagine it's something he approves of, either, he wouldn't be a hypocrite and take money to do something and then make a girl feel dirty.

I wish I could talk—really talk—to Mama about this, but I don't know where to start, or if she'd even want to. She didn't judge Hazel, but is she judging me because of my friend?

Claire

A few days later, Renate returns from the Curtis almost vibrating with excitement. "The maestro came to watch rehearsal today," she says, skidding to a stop in the hall. "We are to have lunch tomorrow to plan the program."

"That's wonderful!" I knew he would follow up, but this is faster than I expected. On the other hand, he has to present a revised concert schedule to the Academy of Music, so I suppose the sooner the better.

She pauses with one hand on the rail. "Would your sister make two performance gowns for me? Her work is very beautiful, and I would like to give her the commission as a thank you for all that you've done for me."

"I'm sure she'd be happy to help you," I say, not at all sure that Ava will even accept Renate as a customer. Now that she has Max, she can pick and choose, and she might choose not to work with a woman whose behavior she has judged so severely.

The next day I meet my sister and the children on the steps of St. Patrick's and agree to go back to the house after mass for Max's special Sunday lunch.

"Do you know how lucky you are to have a man who's willing to prepare meals?"

Her eyebrows lift. "Says the woman who has someone to prepare *all* her meals, not one lunch each week." She shakes her head, then puts her arm through mine. "Well, then, come along and eat my food. Is Harry joining us?"

"No. He's got a headache and he's staying in with a book." And probably an illicit cigarette or two, but I won't think about that. I can nag the poor man only so much.

"Our house is no place to be if you've got a headache," she says cheerfully. "There are quieter madhouses."

We bring up the end of a ragged parade led by Pearl with the coach, then George and Toby, and finally Thelma, leading Teddy by the hand.

"How's business?" As we turn onto Ringgold Place, I notice that the street has undergone some repairs; the holes left by George Howe's construction vehicles have been filled with gravel. With any luck, paving will follow.

"Busy. Hanne's been a godsend." Ava briskly strips off her gloves. "She'll never be a fine seamstress but she's able to take a lot of the burden from me, especially now that Pearl's busier."

"Do you have time for another commission?" I ask lightly, hoping she will say no so I don't have to try to persuade her. "Or are you too busy?"

We go in, and she closes the door behind us. The kitchen smells of deli meat and onions and fresh coffee. Max is at the table, swaddled in an oversized apron, slicing pickles.

"Never too busy," she says. "What do you need?"

"It's not for me." This is possibly the best time to broach the idea; she can't explode in front of the entire family. "It's for Renate."

"No." She slips past, kisses Max on the cheek, and starts herding the children to their seats. "Sit down, all of you."

I try to sit beside her but end up between Pearl and George, with Teddy thrashing on my lap. George tells me an incomprehensible story about a fireman marrying a girl he rescued from a burning building, while Toby gets up twice to sneak pickles off the plate at the other end of the table.

"Sit down." Max grabs him by the waistband and propels him to his chair. "Eat your turkey sandwich before someone else does."

I bide my time. When lunch is over, Max and the boys go out to play ball in the street. Pearl starts to clear and I head her off. "Why don't you take the little ones upstairs?" I suggest. "Your mama and I will clean up."

Ava bangs dishes into the sink. "Thanks. I was looking forward to putting my feet up."

"Go ahead." I nod toward her seat. "I'm capable of washing the dishes."

To my surprise, she sits, swinging her legs up and putting her feet on an empty chair. "Get started, then. I'll dry when you're ready."

Eight plates, eight cups, knives and forks and spoons. Bowls sticky with the remains of egg and potato salads. How has Max made such a mess from one meal, most of which was picked up from the delicatessen and assembled at home?

"Had enough yet?" Ava pushes herself up and grabs a towel. "You're not used to dishpan hands."

I thought of that, but I have a special hand lotion acquired in Paris that will repair the damage before it has time to show. My manicure, on the other hand, is doomed.

"I'll let you dry, if you'll consider making something for Renate."

"I said no." Her expression is as obstinate as George's as she rapidly dries plates, stacking them on the table like pancakes. "Why would I do that?"

"Because she needs two gowns to wear onstage at the Academy of Music," I say baldly. "You'll probably get your name in the paper. Certainly there will be photographs of her in your dresses." I cut a glance in her direction to see if that convinces her. "And as a favor to me."

"Damn it." She turns from the sink. Her shoulders are squared; she's holding back for fear the children will overhear us. "Why, Claire? You know how I feel about her."

I dump the water from the basin, listen as it gurgles loudly down the drain. "I'm sorry," I tell her. "But she's the only famous opera singer I know who can get you that kind of exposure." I play my trump card. "And she asked for you, because you're my sister and she wants to thank me for helping them."

"So she should thank you," she grumbles, "and leave me out of it."

Her tone is unchanged but I've reached her. Even though her marriage to Max means she doesn't have to work as hard, my sister is who she is. She will work, because that's what she's always done. The kind of clients who might hire her on the basis of an association with Renate Steiner are different from my well-heeled friends and the nouveau riche she's had up to this point, and they've got the money to prove it.

Ava

When we are alone, I share with Max my frustration about Claire's request. "I know you don't like my feelings about Renate, but put that aside for a moment. Am I being selfish, to even consider doing this?"

"Why would that make you selfish?" he asks, dropping his shirt on the chair and stretching his arms toward the ceiling. His shoulder audibly pops. "It's your job."

That is part of it, I think: I am putting my job over my beliefs, as I have sometimes put my job ahead of the kids. "It doesn't make me any less of a mother if I have a job," I say, expecting him to follow my unspoken train of thought. "I've always worked, only I did at home. But now that we have less space, the shop is a logical solution."

"I'm not debating that." He finishes his undressing and comes to sit on the bed. "Do you want to make the dress or not?"

"No." I puff out an exasperated breath. "Yes. I can see it already, what it could be. I'm just irritated."

He pushes the sheet down to the foot of the bed and sprawls full length, one hand resting lightly on my stomach. "What irritates you?"

"Everything." I put my hand over his, letting the weight and warmth of his palm take some of the pressure off my brain. "I feel like I should be at home with the kids, and then something like this happens. It's not like I don't want to be home with them, but I have to work. And I want to."

Max turns his face toward my ear. "You might want to work," he says. "But you don't have to. We can make do perfectly well on my salary."

"I don't want to make do," I respond. "I've worked too hard for too long to not do better than making do." I tilt my head so our foreheads touch. "And I don't want to live on your salary. You married me, and you took on the kids, but you shouldn't have to pay for everything. You went from a single man to a father of six. It's a little bit of a stretch."

"It's a stretch I can manage," he says, leaning in to kiss me lightly. "And I'm due for a raise. Your sister set my salary when I was a full-time doctor, but now I'm all but running the clinic in her name. That costs more."

I have trouble accepting that Max's salary comes from my sister. Or her clinic. It's close enough to the same thing. "Asking for more, so I can stop working, would be unbearable. I wouldn't be able to look her in the face."

"Understood." Max rarely argues. "But I wanted you to know it was an option, if you change your mind. Or if you want to cut back—not take every job that comes along or work for women you don't like." He smiles, and I can tell he is about to change the subject. "Make yourself exclusive. Play hard to get. Look how well it worked with me."

We make stealthy love while the kids argue upstairs. Max drops into sleep quickly afterwards and I lie beside him, my mind turning, unwillingly, to the question of what sort of dress Renate Adler would want me to make for her. I haven't agreed to anything, but Claire went home as if I'd said yes.

It would be an interesting challenge to come up with a design for someone so petite. She appears tall, but it is all attitude and stage training; she barely reaches my chin.

Bare shoulders, I think, for one of them. She's so dark that vivid colors would be more flattering, but she will likely want one of them to be black. I'm not sure why I think that, but it seems obvious. Claire told me she left her entire concert wardrobe behind and got out of Germany with no more than a small suitcase for the two of them.

I would be a hypocrite if I gave in. It's not as if I disliked Renate personally and decided that making money off her back was a proper revenge; I've judged her, and tying myself to her thus taints my own actions. But I want to succeed even more than I want the moral high ground. I think Claire would understand—it's most likely how she felt last year when she took on a man Harry disliked to help her organize the clinic. She nearly burned her marriage to the ground in the name of that clinic, but to this day I doubt she has any regrets.

21

Pearl

Now that Aunt is home, I can go back to watching Teddy some afternoons and earning a little spending money. I missed that as much as I missed them. If Thelma thinks she's taking my place, she can think again.

When I get there, Teddy is asleep. "He ran himself so hard earlier," Mrs. Hedges tells me, "that he just fell down."

Those are the best days, when he's asleep and I can work my way through Aunt's bookshelves uninterrupted or talk to Katie. "Where is Katie?"

"Out running an errand for Mrs. Claire," her mother says. "She'll be back soon enough."

We haven't had time to talk since they came back. I wrote to her three times and she never answered me. What little I've seen of her, she was friendly, but I want to ask if she's mad because I was quiet for so long, or if I said something thoughtless in one of my letters. I don't think I did, but people can be touchy.

I should know that. I live with one of the touchiest people in the world.

When Katie's step sounds on the stairs, I'm curled in the rocker in Teddy's nursery. He's asleep, but if he's anything like his brothers, he'll wake up soon and bolt straight upright in the bed and then run downstairs and find something to get into.

"Katie!" I call, placing my finger in *Tender Is the Night* to hold my place. "In here."

She comes to the doorway. "You got lucky," she says. "Mr. Teddy's snoring away."

"It won't last." I get up, putting the book aside. "How are you? We haven't had time to catch up."

She takes a step back. "Busy," she says. "Mr. and Mrs. Adler, they don't make much mess, but it's another room to keep up."

"At least you don't have Dr. Max anymore." Though I'm not sure he was any trouble at all—he brought so little with him that it scarcely makes a difference in their room. And he's tidy! I hope that's contagious and the boys learn how to fold their clothes and put things away.

"Dr. Byrne, he was all right." Katie's voice is wistful. "Always a smile on his face."

She starts up the steps to the third floor and I follow, leaving the nursery door open so I can hear Teddy when he wakes up.

"I missed you," I tell her. "You didn't write."

Katie opens the Adlers' door, revealing an unmade bed and a vase of drooping flowers on the dresser.

"I didn't know what to say." She throws the bedspread over a chair and rapidly strips the sheets. "I'm taking a load of whites to the laundry, you don't mind if I keep working?"

"Let me help." I grab the pillows, yank the cases off. "How did you not know what to say? You were in Paris—the place I wanted to be more than anything." I catch her wrist as she turns, her arms full of linens. "If I couldn't go, I wanted to see it through your eyes."

She stoops to pick up the pillowcases. "I didn't know how to write back to you," she says. "You use all these book words, and I don't know how to write like that."

That stops me. I had never considered that, like Mama, she might be sensitive about her lack of education. When I first came to Philadelphia, we used to talk over my lessons, but by the time they left, we'd stopped. Was it my fault?

"I'd have been happy with anything you wrote," I tell her truthfully. "I missed you. And you were seeing everything I wanted to." I make a face like Thelma would, if she'd been caught in a scrape. "For a while there, I was mad at everybody."

Katie skins past, reaches into the bathroom and retrieves a handful of towels. "I wish you could have gone," she says. "I didn't want to."

"But you did like it?" I ask. "In the end?"

I can't conceive of not liking the City of Light, the most beautiful, romantic place on earth. I've already worn creases in the book Aunt brought back, imagining myself walking those narrow medieval streets, buying fresh bread from a bakery, looking at the book stalls where she bought my copy of *Great Expectations*.

She nods. "I did. Once I got used to how funny they talked." Her laugh lets me know she's at least partly joking. "Turns out it's easier to be colored there than it is here."

"Really?"

She drops the laundry into a large wicker basket and hauls it up onto her hip. "I don't know why, but I got a lot less funny looks when I was out with Mr. Teddy, and nobody treated me like I was trash if I was on my own."

I open my mouth to ask how often that's happened here, but before I get the words out there is a crash from downstairs, followed by Teddy's delighted laughter.

"I'm not the only one gotta get to work," she says. "That sounds like he rode his horse into the wall."

Ava

From the window, I watch the Packard pull away. Renate Adler remains for a moment on the narrow sidewalk outside the shop, looking after the car. Then she straightens her hat, takes a deep breath, and opens the door.

"Hedges dropped you off?" I ask, after the briefest of pleasantries are exchanged; I am uncomfortable in her presence though I am doing my best to mask it.

"He did. He has errands for your sister and will come for me in an hour, if that is enough time." She removes her gloves and hat, places them on the counter beside her bag. "Shall we begin?"

I put the closed sign on the door so we can work undisturbed. It would look very unprofessional if someone came in and she had to dive behind the screen. Taking up my measuring tape, I turn to find her already half undressed. "Do you want to discuss your ideas first?"

Her skirt drops to the floor. "I can speak and be measured at the same time." She offers a tight smile. "I have had many dresses made for me. I am not shy, Mrs. Byrne."

By the time Mason Hedges returns, Renate is dressed and waiting by the door. I have taken all possible measurements and we have had a profitable discussion about the style of gowns she wants, selected colors—one black, one red—and I have offered to bring fabric samples to Claire's on Friday for her to select from. When she leaves, I sag into my chair and without being asked, Hanne brings me a cup of tea.

When I come in from work, Thelma has the table set and Pearl is slicing cold ham for supper. Grace is playing quietly in the corner with an old stuffed bear.

"Where are the boys?" I take off my hat and lay my bag and gloves to one side, wishing it wasn't necessary to wear so many layers of clothing in hot weather. "For that matter, where's Max?"

"The phone rang a little bit ago," Pearl says. "Dr. Max answered, and he went right out and took George with him. He said they should be back soon, but not to hold supper."

"Okay." I smooth my hair away from my hot forehead and fan myself with a napkin. "No clues as to where they were going?"

She shakes her head, and I scoot around her to the sink, where I run a glass of cold water and drink it down.

"Do you want the puffy, mama?" Thelma reaches for a tied handkerchief filled with cornstarch, and I blot the back of my neck and the insides of my elbows gratefully. All my daughters bear the powdery marks of the puff; we look like we've been floured prior to baking, but it cools and absorbs the sweat, and in a Philadelphia summer, that is what matters.

We wait for thirty minutes, but when they don't come back, we eat without them. It is a quiet, uncomfortable meal, Pearl apologizing several times for not getting more information from Max.

"You didn't know," I tell her, wondering what could possibly have happened, and if it involves Toby, since he is also missing.

Finally, the door opens upstairs. George plunges down the steps and into the kitchen. "Toby got arrested!"

"What?" My napkin drops to the floor. "Max!"

Further footsteps, slower, come down the steps. Toby appears first, Max's hand on his shoulder.

"Did you save us anything?" Max asks, breaking into an easy smile, as if George hadn't come down shouting about the police.

Pearl fills three plates and slides them into the table. "You must be hungry."

Toby sits and begins shoveling food into his mouth. George drops down beside him. He ignores his plate, which tells me how serious it is. "We went to the precinct, Ma, and they had Toby locked up in a cell like a bank robber!"

I stop Max before he can join them. "What on earth happened?"

"Nothing." He looks up with a smile that tells me he's concealing something. "Well, not nothing. But nothing we want to discuss before supper." He wraps warm fingers around my wrist. "Everything is better on a full stomach. Trust me, I'm a doctor."

We sit and watch as they eat, George and Toby like they've never seen food and Max not much better, though he does look up once to inquire about my day.

"It was work," I tell him. "I met with Mrs. Adler and Celia Fishwick. This time she brought a friend—not for a dress, mind you, only to watch her fitting."

"More effort than she's worth," he says, spearing a slice of ham. "What did I tell you about being more selective?"

"Don't change the subject." I stare at the boys until they finish, and then at Max until his plate is cleared. When they are done, Pearl reaches to collect the dishes to add to the others in the sink.

"Sit down," Max says. "You all need to hear what happened."

"Not everybody," Toby says in a miserable tone. "It's enough Ma has to find out."

"I already know." George is gloating. "You can tell her or I will."

Toby drops his head on the table with an audible thunk and crosses his arms, doing his best to become invisible. "Pop will tell her, not you, you dope."

"Don't call your brother names," I say absently. "George, don't tease your brother." I look at Max. "Well?"

He folds his hands, his expression earnest. "Pearl told you we got a call?"

"Yes." He is figuring out what—and how much—to tell me, I realize.

"It was the police station." He tilts his head towards Toby. "That one there was walking down Market Street, saw a Wanamakers delivery truck idling at the curb, and decided to take it for a ride."

George snickers. Pearl slaps the back of his head.

"You stole a car." I enunciate each word, trying to wrap my brain around what Max said. "*You stole a car.*"

"A truck," comes his muffled voice. "Not a car."

My hand encounters Pearl's on the back of Toby's head. Our eyes meet and we silently agree not to hit him.

"That's even worse." I shake his shoulder, none too gently. "Sit up. Tell me what happened."

He obeys, a little too slowly. I fix him with a glare and he quickly straightens.

"I was on Market Street, like Pop said. Doing an errand for Mr. Jack at the garage. I came up behind the store on Thirteenth Street and there was a whole line of trucks getting loaded for deliveries." He takes a deep breath, then continues. "I started talking to one of the drivers. He had to go back in to get more boxes and I said I'd watch the truck.

"And I did." Toby's voice rises. "I watched it, and when he didn't come back right away, I sat in the seat and turned the wheel and thought about where I'd go if I was old enough to drive." He licks his lips. "And then I was driving. I don't even remember starting it, but all of a sudden I was at Tenth Street and there was a cop climbing in the door and pulling me out by the ear."

George hoots. Max's lips are twitching with the struggle not to laugh. Pearl turns away to tend to Grace. Only Thelma and I remain straight-faced, listening intently to my criminal son's tale.

"And that's all I know," he concludes. "They took me to the station and locked me up until Pop came to get me." He sneaks a glance at Max. "Thanks, Pop."

"My pleasure." Max reaches for a scrap of bread abandoned on my plate and munches it contentedly. "Never thought I'd have the privilege of rescuing a kid of mine from the pokey, so we're square."

I push away from the table. "Well, you're not square with me." Yanking Toby out of his seat, I push him toward the steps. "Go to your room. I'll be up in a few minutes."

"Ooh, you're gonna get the belt!" George calls after him, and I whip around.

"You should go outside before you get it, too."

He scuttles away, snickering. Pearl and Thelma start the dishes, leaving me at the table with Max.

"It's not a big deal," he says. "It was stupid and dangerous, but boys do stupid, dangerous things all the time."

"Not my boys." What should I do? Having grown up with fathers who used their hands too frequently, Daniel and I didn't spank the kids, but he would have made an exception for this. I remember his reaction when he discovered Dan had been bootlegging coal, and compare it to Max's blasé response.

"What do you call what Dan's doing?" he asks softly. "Going off hoboing for the summer? It's not his brightest moment, but you didn't object."

"He's older. And more responsible than his brothers will ever be."

"And he's your pet, so he'd probably have to shoot someone before you acknowledged he did anything wrong." He puts a hand over mine. "I'm saying you don't give the younger boys that same grace."

Toby and George have run wild since we moved to the city; they ran wild in Scovill Run, too, but there was less to get into, so long as they stayed away from the mines. I should have known what they were up to, though. I thought I did. Toby at the garage, George at the firehouse. Pearl and I had visited the firehouse, once, but when was the last time I checked on Toby?

"I should have kept a better track of them. It's just...I'm always busy, and as long as they make it home for supper, I know they're safe." I'm making excuses for my own shabby mothering. I should never be too busy to pay attention to my kids. It's easier with the girls; they're at home, helping me and not ranging loose around the city the way boys do. Maybe boys leave home because they don't feel seen in the way their sisters are.

Max is talking. "He got lucky. The desk sergeant is a buddy—I stitched up one of his guys a few years back, and we run into each other every so often. He recognized my name and called me himself, and after I got there and we had a chat, he settled things with Wanamakers. They won't press charges."

"That's very good of him." I close my eyes, embarrassed at the thought of facing a policeman because of my child. But also knowing it could have been worse without him. "We should have him to supper to say thank you."

"And use this new dining room!" Max looks as excited as a boy. "I think that's a fine idea. He and his wife don't live too far from here."

"You should ask him." I don't even know what I'm saying, my mind is in a hundred places trying to figure out how to handle Toby's actions. I'm shocked and angry and even frightened that he would do such a thing—opening the door to worse behavior in his future—but it's at least partly my fault. I have been so mired in grief and building a business and falling in love that my two younger boys have gotten lost.

"Anyway," he says, "Sarge could tell Toby was scared, and since he knew I was coming, he put him in a group cell for an hour." Max shakes his head. "I don't think he'll do anything to land himself in jail again anytime soon. They put the fear of God into him."

Now my head is full of images of my boy, all knees and elbows, small for his age, sitting in a cell with drunks and criminals. "How awful."

"One of the men kept a close eye on him." He pushes his chair back, leans over to kiss my neck. "Why don't you let me deal with Toby? He's not a bad kid, he just did something stupid."

The girls file quietly past, Pearl tugging Thelma by the hand. They will no doubt settle in the living room overhead and eavesdrop through the floorboards.

I close my eyes, dreading what comes next. "I should do it. I'm his mother."

"And you claim I'm his father." Max drops his hands on my shoulders. "Let me do this. It might be because of me, anyway—he might be pushing, to see what we'll let him get away with. Let him realize he has a father again. Or at least a stepfather."

Pearl

I came up to get a book, and so I wouldn't overhear Mama's conversation with Dr. Max, but then he came upstairs and went into the boys' room and now I'm stuck here because I don't want them to think I'm listening.

I don't want to hear it. It's Dr. Max, not Mama, so I don't know what to expect. She was so mad, she'd take the strap to him, even if it would make her go quiet later. The boys get away with a lot because she's not home and they won't listen to me, but Toby can't steal a truck and expect to be able to sit down for the next few days.

A murmur of conversation comes through the wall. Toby's voice rises and falls, explanatory, but I can't catch the words. In spite of myself, I move closer.

"Hit me and get it over with, will you? My dad would have whipped me by now."

There is a long silence. I wonder if Dr. Max's feelings are hurt that Toby referred to Daddy, when he's doing his best to fill that role.

"I don't believe in hitting kids." His tone sounds friendly; he's trying to reach my hard-headed brother. "Would a whipping change anything?"

"I dunno. But it would hurt."

"Well," Dr. Max says, "I don't want to hurt you. There's been enough hurt in this family."

My fingers are tight around the spine of my book. This is a different kind of conversation than I'm used to hearing between a father and son. He's speaking to Toby like an adult, pointing out what we've all been through, that he and George may have felt adrift without a man to look after them.

"We had Dandy," Toby says. I can almost see his lip jutting out. That boy disagrees on principle sometimes.

Boards creak as Dr. Max walks back and forth. "That's true enough. But for all that he acts grown up, Dan's not that much older than you. He's had to assume a man's duties. That's why he needs this break."

"And we've got Ma," he says stubbornly. "When she remembers."

"Come here, Toby." The springs squeak as they sit on the bed. "I'm sure you probably feel like she doesn't pay enough attention to you sometimes. But she's had a lot on her plate, especially since you've moved here. But even before. You and George, you get to run a little wild because she trusts you not to go too far."

Toby says nothing for a long time. "You think I went too far?"

"I do."

There is a smile in his voice, and my lips curve in response. Dr. Max is good with him.

"I'll say sorry, then." He sounds chipper, as if apologizing to Mama will make everything better.

"That's a good start, but I want you to think about something, Toby." He stretches the words. "Hasn't your mom been through enough without you worrying her like this?"

There is a hiccuping sound which I understand is my brother and the bed creaks again as Dr. Max hugs him and lets him cry. I take advantage of the moment, removing my shoes and slipping past the door to return to the living room.

Mama is on the sofa, a bit of mending neglected on her lap. Thelma is reading to Grace on the window seat. George is folded into the chair with the funnies. They all look up as I come around the bend in the stairs.

"Did Pop whip him?" George's grin is a little too gloating considering he is capable of the same level of behavior. "Did he cry?"

"I didn't hear anything." Sitting beside Mama with my book, I mouth the words, "It's okay," and we settle in to wait.

Eventually they come down. Dr. Max looks serious, and Toby's eyes are red, but he's not walking like he'd been spanked. He stops before the sofa, twisting his hands together. "I'm sorry, Mama," he says. "I didn't mean to disappoint you. I'll do better."

"I hope you will." Mama looks at him for a long moment, and then hugs him. "You worry me, sometimes, Toby." She looks over. "And you too, George."

"I don't steal cars," George says.

Toby makes a face over Mama's shoulder. "You'd probably steal the fire engine, you got a chance."

Leaning against the fireplace mantle, Dr. Max says, "The apology is the first half of it. Toby's lost his right to go to the garage for the rest of the summer."

"Is he going to stay home?" If we leave him in the house alone, he'll be back at the garage like a shot, and I don't want to have to watch him, not when Uncle has finally agreed to let me help in his office.

"No." Dr. Max gives Toby a nod that holds an entire conversation. "He's coming to work with me."

22

Claire

The letters I mailed from France begin to show results. I receive a note from Eleanor Roosevelt talking about a proposed Emergency Rescue Committee, but warning that, as with all things political, it is coming together slowly. "Continue on with your work," she advised, "and persuade everyone in your circle to do the same, or to assist in whatever way is in their power. I fear that Mr. Warriner's friend is correct and that we are facing perilous times. Germany is hostile not only to those of the Jewish faith, but to intellectuals, politicians, and anyone whose opinions dare to oppose Mr. Hitler's."

I know that already. Obscurely worded cables cross the Atlantic on a regular basis, and Harry has pulled strings to find sponsors and funding for several of Leo's refugees. On two occasions, they stayed briefly with us before moving on to Chicago and Washington.

Helen Dawes is more skeptical than the First Lady, but she and her husband sponsored a quiet man named Zimmer, who spent a single night under our roof before taking the train to the capital. More importantly for the long term, she provided the names of several people at the state department who might be contacted in case of emergency.

I wonder if, once she's done her concerts with the orchestra, Renate can be persuaded to give a charity recital. Sooner would be better, but even though she is well known, people would be more prone to donate for a concert in a smaller venue—perhaps at the Curtis, where she is rehearsing—after having seen her perform at the Academy. Maybe even a premium charged for a small drinks party afterward? I make some notes and resolve to talk to Prue about it at our next luncheon.

Despite my sister's many reservations, her first meeting with Renate appears to have gone well enough. I have decided not to involve myself in their encounters. If they are uncomfortable, nothing can be done about it now and much good will come from it in the end. Ava will get exposure on an undreamed-of level, while Renate will get exactly what—miracle of miracles—Leopold Stokowski has offered to pay for: performance dresses of excellent quality and superb fit.

She has done her homework, my sister. One morning, she even came over without being invited to look at the photos of Renate on my records and then invited herself upstairs to inspect the clothes I bought in France. Her restraint when confronted with my extravagance is admirable, but while Lanvin and Hartnell and Chanel impressed her into silence, my prized Fortuny Delphos gown returned her to speech.

"What's this?" She took a round white box off the shelf in my closet. "You keep your hats in here now?"

"It's not a hat, it's a dress." I removed the lid and the tissue paper and lifted out the dark blue pleated silk coiled inside. "It's meant to be stored this way so the pleats don't loosen."

Ava took it from me and placed it carefully on the bed. I could see her mind working, trying to figure out the construction.

"It's a simple shape," she said, chewing her bottom lip. "But this pleating—how do they do it?"

"I have no idea." The dress came that way, and all I knew was that it must be twisted and coiled into its box after wearing to retain the shape. "It doesn't look like anything, laid out flat like that, but it's beautiful on. So light and comfortable."

She looked from the dress to me. "Do you have time to play dress-up?"

"Are you going to make something like this for Renate?" I asked.

"Never." A tiny shake of her head. "I wouldn't know where to start, or where to find such light silk." Curiosity overtook her and she smiled. "But that doesn't mean I don't want to see what it looks like on."

Ava

Toby's punishment begins the next day. By seven, he is up and scrubbed, waiting at the table for Max to come down.

"You're down early," I comment, putting together sandwiches for their lunch. I tuck an extra into the bag because he is bottomless.

"Pop said to be ready to leave by eight." He smiles brightly, last night's tears forgotten. "I've always wanted to see where he worked, so this will be fun."

He did? It never occurred to me that the kids would be interested in the clinic. "It's not all fun," I warn him. "There's sick people and blood and all kinds of mess."

"I know." He regards me solemnly, his freckles almost invisible on his tanned cheeks. "He told me I'm in charge of cleaning up the mess."

"And you don't mind?" I put a bowl of oatmeal in front of him, then dish up Max's when he bounds down the stairs.

"I figure I'm lucky I can sit," he says. "I'll do what he asks."

They leave before eight, walking to the forbidden garage to pick up Petunia. Toby has to confess his crime to his friends there, as part of his penance, and he agreed to that, as well.

When they are gone, Pearl turns to me. "Was that Toby?"

"I don't know what Max said to him." I shake my head. "It must have been something."

She scoops up the sticky bowls and stacks them by the sink. "I heard part of it," she confesses.

"And?" I knew she'd been listening, but we hadn't had time to talk.

"Dr. Max asked if he didn't think you'd been through enough, and that was what started him crying." She turns on the water, stepping back as it splashes into the basin. "It almost made *me* cry."

"Why?" I hadn't expected Max to use guilt, but it was more effective than a beating.

Pearl wraps an apron around her middle to protect her dress. "Because of how I was this last year," she says. "I was disappointed about France, and I took it out on you. Dr. Max is right. You've been through enough."

I wrap my arms around her. "It's forgotten," I say. "You've been a huge help to me for so many years, you were overdue to have a few bad days."

"A few bad months." Her laughter is genuine. "I love you, Mama."

By the end of the week, George comes down for breakfast with Toby. "I'm going, too," he says. "Toby don't get to have all the fun."

"Fun?" Pearl asks. "He's helping at the clinic. How is that fun?"

Toby turns a bright face to her. "I got to fix the faucet yesterday and today Pop promised I could watch him take an x-ray!"

I look from him to our kitchen tap, which has been dripping for a month. "So I don't have to wait for Dan to come home to get this fixed?"

He beams up at me. "Can it wait until my day off tomorrow? That way if Dan's toolbox don't have the right washer, I can go to the hardware store."

"I'll go!" George elbows him. "She'd sooner I do it. I ain't no car thief."

"Enough!" Pearl shoves them apart. "One of you can do the faucet, the other one can fix the knob on the back door. It keeps coming loose."

I leave it to Max to make arrangements with the sergeant as to when he and his wife will come for supper. His charity toward my son is because of his friendship with Max; I'm sure not every boy dragged into that precinct would have left having only had the bejesus frightened out of him. But I must thank him, nonetheless, as must Toby.

"Friday evening," he says when as we prepare for bed. "That give you enough time?"

It is four days from now. "How long do you think it takes to organize a meal?"

"No idea." He nuzzles my neck, blowing on the curls at my nape until I threaten him with the hairbrush.

"How do you think I'd look in trousers?" I ask abruptly. One of the many glorious outfits Claire brought back from France was a set of linen beach pajamas. Pants. On a woman. I've seen women in movies wearing pants, disguised as men or portraying particularly unfeminine characters, but my sister? There is no one more feminine than Claire

Max sprawls on the quilt wearing nothing but his boxers. "Better than me," he says, smile lines radiating from his eyes. "Why?"

"Claire brought some home with her," I tell him. "I would have never considered pants, but I can see times when they'd be very practical."

"And warm," he points out. "I don't know how you ladies do stockings in cold weather. The draft would kill me."

"I'll have to see if there's a pattern." I put the brush aside, returning to our original conversation. "Why Friday?"

"Because we can send the kids to Claire's and have a quiet evening of adult conversation until they get home."

Sergeant O'Donnell is of middling height, with Max's stocky build. His rusty hair is a vivid contrast to his wide, pink Irish face, which instantly reminds me of Father Dennis. His wife is plump and heavily freckled, with a sweet smile. They greet me as if we've known each other forever, something I've come to understand is a side effect of being married to Max.

"It's kind of you to be having us." Sergeant O'Donnell is still in uniform. He unbuttons his stiff dark blue jacket and removes his hat.

"It's the least we could do." I take his hat and hang it on the rack. "I hope Max has told you how grateful I am for what you did."

"Boys will be boys," Mrs. O'Donnell says. "We've got two, and their daddy being in the police is all that's kept them out of the same trouble."

"You've gotten them off the hook?" Max asks, coming up from the kitchen, a dish towel over his shoulder. He pumps the sergeant's hand vigorously. "Or is it fear of the consequences?"

"That's it exactly," she says. "How is your boy, Mrs. Byrne? Has he recovered from his adventure?"

I don't like that she knows what happened with Toby, but I also can't fault a man who tells his wife about his work day. "He has," I say. "At least for the moment."

"He'll think twice about doing that again," Max agrees. "He's been coming to the clinic with me the last week or so." He grins at the sergeant. "Could I offer you a beer, Pat?"

"Wouldn't say no." At Max's nod, he sits on the sofa.

"Rosaleen?"

"Thank you, no." Her hand darts to her belly, and I understand that she is expecting. "If Mrs. Byrne is going downstairs, I'd be happy to keep company in the kitchen."

"I am, and please, call me Ava."

Rosaleen has a cup of tea while I finish supper preparations. "Usually my daughter helps," I tell her, "but the kids are eating at my sister's tonight. We didn't want to hit you with all of them at once."

"How nice that you've got a sister close by." Her expression turns momentarily sad. "My people are all back in Sligo. We write letters, but it's not the same."

"No, it's not," I agree, taking plates from the cupboard and stacking them on the table. "My sister and I spent many years apart, even though I only lived upstate. She came home when our mother passed, and then, after I lost my husband, we moved here to be closer to her."

"I'm sorry about your man." She lays the plates and nods her head toward the cutlery on the counter. "You found a fine one in the doctor. I hope you're very happy."

"We are," I say, and I mean it. Even our disagreements pale in comparison to how happy he makes me. Something in Rosaleen O'Donnell's open face makes me add, "I don't just love him. I respect him. He's taken on another man's children without a blink. He's healed me in a way I didn't believe possible."

Sitting down to eat without the kids is a strange experience. The O'Donnells seem to feel the same strangeness, their own brood being absent.

"No one's poking each other," I say to Max.

"Or complaining that their brother got more than they did," he responds.

Rosaleen O'Donnell chips in. "Or that they've got the growing pains and need an extra helping."

There is laughter and conversation, and it is strangely wonderful. The O'Donnells met in Philadelphia, but their families in Ireland live less than five miles apart.

"We might have never met in Ireland," the sergeant says. "My people never went far from home until the landlord put them out."

"Mine moved to Sligo in the famine," she says. "But that was as bad, or worse. I came here when I was seventeen."

"And I wish I'd been there to meet the boat." Her husband gives her a look that goes a long way toward explaining their number of children and the one in her belly. "I didn't find her until three years later."

"And a fine husband you'd have been back then," she teases. "Just another Irish brickie."

"A brickie with ambitions," he protests. "It wasn't long after that I joined the force."

Max offers another bottle of beer, which the sergeant accepts. "How is the job? Did I hear right that you're looking to move to the northeast?"

"Looking to." He tips the bottle back. "But who knows if I'll get a transfer or a promotion. There's a lot more open land up there. It'd be good for the kiddies."

"And for me." Rosaleen exhales. "I love where we live, but I'd take a smaller house with green out the window any day."

I tell her that the kids and I came from a rural area, but that the city is a wonderland to us. "In a mining town, there's not much green out the window, and if there is, there's black dust on it."

Feet pass the front window as the kids climb the steps to the living room. When the door bangs, I call, "Down here!"

They troop down, and when Toby is presented with Sergeant O'Donnell, he blanches and his eyes go round. "I didn't do nothing."

"Anything." Pearl shoves him. "Speak English."

He ignores her, focusing on the surprising fact of a policeman at the family table. "Honest, I didn't do"—a glance at Pearl—"anything. Officer. Sergeant."

"Don't I know that?" Sergeant O'Donnell gets up and lays a slablike hand on his shoulder. "Your ma and dad invited us for supper to say thanks for not throwing you in the clink." He winks at me. "You're lucky your ma's a good cook."

Claire

"You're late. Do you need to go upstairs before dinner?" I take Harry's case and kiss his cheek.

"I'm not hungry." His face has that grayish cast I haven't seen since we returned from Paris. "I think I'll go upstairs."

"I'll be right there." I pop down to tell Mrs. Hedges we won't be eating after all, and that I'll pick at something later if she and Hedges want to call it a night.

"Is Mr. Warriner all right?" she asks, shifting the poached fish from its platter into a glass refrigerator dish.

"I hope so." When I kissed him, I caught a whiff of cigarette smoke. "He had a lunch meeting at the Union League today. I hope he hasn't overdone it."

"Men." She empties another dish. "They do that."

The sound of running water tells me that Harry has decided to take a shower. I return to the kitchen, where the dishes are drying in the drainer, and make a quick sandwich; if he's unwell, I don't want to eat in front of him.

"That's better," he says, emerging in sky-blue pajamas. He gestures vaguely. "The heat today..."

"It was warm," I agree. "How was your lunch? Burt, wasn't it?"

"Burt," he says, "and an associate he's bringing in on my account. Nice young fellow. Mitchell."

"At the Union League?" I follow him to the bedroom, peeking into the nursery to see Teddy sound asleep. "What did you eat?"

"Why?" His expression turns chilly.

It is only eight, but we are obviously in for the evening. I bring out my silk pajamas, shaking the creases from the delicate fabric.

"Because the Union League does heavy food, and you're on a restricted diet." I remove the clips from my hair and run a brush through it. My set will get me through another day, but I should put a scarf over it if I want it to look decent come morning. "What did you eat?"

Harry sits on the edge of the bed. His eyes drift shut. "Shrimp cocktail," he recites. "Filet and lobster tail with asparagus and potato gratin. A bottle of very nice red. Port. Chocolate cake. Cigars in the lounge after." He falls back on the bed. "It was goddamn delicious."

"Harry!" Every item on that list, with the possible exception of the asparagus, is something he shouldn't eat. "How do you feel?"

One hand comes to rest on his abdomen. "Like there's something in there with fangs and claws, trying to get out." He lifts his head, opens one eye. "And I don't care. If I can't occasionally feel like myself, I might as well be dead."

That makes me slam the brush down on the dresser. Might as well be dead! As if food and drink and cigars are worth more than a wife and child. I snatch up my pajamas and head for the bathroom to soak in a cool tub until I'm less likely to shout at my husband.

He is in bed with an Agatha Christie novel when I return, cooler and somewhat calmer. "Better?" he asks, slipping a bookmark between the pages.

"Maybe." I take the book—*Murder on the Orient Express*—out of his hands. "How are you feeling now? Aside from being victorious over medical advice?"

"Like hell," he says honestly. "Heartburn and pain in my gut and a headache to beat the band. And"—he catches my wrist in his hand—"it was worth every moment of discomfort tonight. I'll resume the straight and narrow path tomorrow."

He appears genuinely contrite. This has been hard on him; food and drink are his chief pleasures, and I can't remember a time when he didn't smoke.

I put Agatha Christie aside and climb in next to him. "You do that," I say. "None of us are doing this to be unkind, Harry. I for one would like to keep you around as long as possible."

Cupping my cheek with his hand, he kisses my mouth and says, "If I felt better, I'd put some effort into showing you how I feel about those Japanese pajamas." He shrugs. "As it is, and with this heat, I'll settle for lying beside you, trying not to be sick, and plotting my approach for the morning."

"Ma'am."

I swim up from a dream of an unfamiliar and frightening Paris, where darkness curled and twisted like smoke through the streets. Katie's soft hand is on my shoulder. "What time is it?"

"Just past six," she says. "Mr. Warriner's shut himself in the bathroom, ma'am. It sounds like he's being sick again."

"I'm not surprised." That meal would have given indigestion to a healthy man, much less someone with a fragile peptic ulcer. I throw on a silk kimono and stand outside the closed door. "Harry?"

Silence. Then, "Go away, Claire. I'm fine."

"You're not fine," I say steadily, though the weakness in his voice is alarming. "If you don't open the door, I'm calling Max."

"Perhaps you'd better." His words are more frightening than anything that occurred in my amorphous dream.

Ava answers the phone with suspicion in her voice. "Oh, it's you. I hate this thing. The few times it's rung this early it's scared me out of my skin."

"Sorry," I say. "Could you send Max over before he goes to the clinic? Harry's had a rough night and he's asking for him."

"He's getting dressed." Her tone changes completely. "He'll be there as soon as he can. Call me later and let me know what you need from me."

Harry lets Max into the bathroom. I listen to the rise and fall of their voices from the hallway. Infuriatingly, I can't make out the words. Within fifteen minutes, Max comes out, his expression serious.

"Is Mason available?"

"I'm sure he is." It strikes me that both Max and Ava are on a first name basis with Katie's parents, while I would never consider calling them Esther and Mason. "What do you need?"

"He needs to drive Harry to the hospital," he says bluntly. "He doesn't want an ambulance, and I'll allow that, so long as he gets there within the hour."

"The hospital!" My fingernails dig painfully into my palms. "Is it that bad?"

Max tips his head back against the door frame. "Ava's told you what Toby did recently?"

"Yes." What does Harry's illness have to do with my nephew stealing a car?

"This is the adult version of that level of stupid." He rubs his face, and I note that he hasn't taken time to shave. "I told him he could cheat occasionally, not have a meal that would put Henry VIII to shame." An exasperated sigh. "Now he's going to be on a liquid diet until this gets sorted out."

"Oh, no." That is Harry's worst fear, Max's threat of being tethered to a feeding tube in the hospital. "Is that necessary?"

"He's brought it on himself," he says, with some sympathy. "Now you go downstairs, Claire. I'll help Harry get dressed. He doesn't want you to see him until he's himself again."

"But—"

From the other side of the door comes my husband's voice. "Just go, Claire. Please."

I put clothes on, and Katie brings me tea and stays to keep me company. Foolishly, I want to hold her hand. She would let me, but what sort of adult needs to hold the hand of a twenty-year-old girl to keep from falling apart?

The front door opens. "Ma'am," Hedges calls. "I have the car out front. Do you need my help with Mr. Warriner?"

"Start the car." Max's voice comes over the rail. "I can manage him. We'll be down in a moment."

"I don't need to be managed," Harry says testily. "I can walk perfectly well."

They start down the steps, Max behind him. "That's good to know," he says. "Considering your earlier position on the bathroom tile, I wasn't sure we could get you vertical."

Harry stops, turns his head. "Shut up, Max."

I put my hand on the rail, swallowing a horrified gasp. He looks far more ill than he did at bedtime. Before I can take a step toward him, Harry's expression stops me. He wants no assistance, not from Max, and certainly not from his wife.

"You're not coming with us," he says, before I can ask. "I'll call from the hospital to let you know how I'm doing."

Behind him, Max shakes his head, and mouths that he will be the one to call.

"I love you, darling." I stand on my toes to kiss his cheek.

He stops and pulls me close to his chest. "And I love you, Claire." He looks embarrassed. "I'm sorry about all this. I'll be home soon."

23

Ava

As soon as Mendel's is open, I call the shop and leave instructions for Hanne to clean up from yesterday and to take my fitting with Prue Foster if I'm not there by the time she arrives. Hanne isn't a seamstress by any stretch, but Prue's dress will likely need very little adjustment and I'll be able to manage from Hanne's notes.

Then I take Grace and walk over to Claire's house. Max said it would take some time after Harry is admitted for them to run the necessary tests. Results could take days. I don't want my sister sitting and worrying alone.

We negotiate the few blocks quickly, Grace hardly even having time to object to her routine being broken. Having her there will be a distraction for Teddy.

My sister answers the door. I am surprised to see no signs of tears on her face. "Are you all right?" I ask, letting Grace slide to the floor. She immediately takes off into the living room.

Claire goes after her. "I'm fine. Waiting to hear from the hospital."

"That could take some time, Max told me."

"He told me the same." She sounds remarkably calm for my emotional sister. "Would you like some tea? Coffee?"

"Coffee, if you're having some." I can't imagine she needs anything to add to her jitters, but she smiles placidly and calls for Katie, giving her a request for coffee and a plate of cookies.

"I've just had breakfast," I protest, patting my stomach. "And I hardly need cookies."

"You look fine." She sits easily on the couch and studies her manicure: freshly pink and shining. "I'll have one with you, if that makes you feel better."

I corral Grace as she heads for the shining objects on the liquor cart. "How about if I take this one up to Teddy, before she figures out how to mix herself a martini?"

"He's out," she tells me. "Renate and Josef took him to the park."

"Oh." It seems everything is under control. "I brought Grace along to keep him company, in case you needed to run to the hospital."

"Mrs. Hedges or Katie will keep him company." The door opens and she gestures for Katie to put the tray on the table. "I'm sure they'd be happy to watch Grace, too, if you need to get to work."

There will be time to drop Grace back at home, I think; Pearl and Thelma are both there, one working on a new school dress and the other baking cookies very similar to the ones on the plate in front of me. "Hanne is handling Prue's fitting this morning," I tell her. "I'll head down to the shop once I know you're all right."

She pours the coffee, gazing at me with wide blue eyes. "I'm fine, Ava. Why do you persist in treating me as if I'm no older than Thelma?"

"Because your husband's in the hospital," I say, wondering where my sister has gone. "And on a normal day, you would be in pieces all over this room."

"Well, perhaps I've grown up and learned how to handle myself." She smiles at me, showing nothing, and I wonder if my inability to show my feelings is this frustrating to others. "Cream and sugar, or would you prefer it black this morning?"

Claire

Not long after Ava departs in a huff, Max calls to give me an update on Harry. As I was afraid, his ulcer has been inflamed by his recent excesses. He will have to stay in the hospital for the next few days.

"Can I see him?"

Max hesitates. "You can," he says, "but you might not want to."

"Why?" All I want is to see that he's okay.

His voice drops. "Because they had to insert a naso-gastric tube to remove fluid from his stomach," he says. "It looks nasty, it felt worse going in, and even though he's not my patient I won't have you upsetting him by falling to pieces."

I lick my lips, pushing down angry words that Max doesn't deserve. "No matter how distressing I might find his condition, I can be trusted not to upset my husband," I say crisply. "Would you give Ava that same warning?"

"No." I can hear him smiling. "But I think she'd have to see internal organs before she cracked."

"We are sisters." I take a deep breath. "I'll be there within the hour."

I track down Teddy, kiss him all over his protesting face, and tell him that Daddy had to go away on business before he woke up and so he won't be home for dinner, but he left all his love behind.

"He bring me a present?" Teddy believes the lie; Katie smiles sympathetically behind him. "I got no toys."

"You have a million toys, Mr. Teddy," she says, turning him toward the train track set out on the floor. "Let's count them and practice your numbers."

I leave them slowly counting and duck into our room to change into something appropriate for a hospital visit. I want to look pretty for Harry, provide what little distraction I can considering the horrid tube—did naso mean nose, I wonder?

Ten minutes later, clad in a blue print dress with matching gloves and white t-straps, I dash down the stairs and skid to a stop on the black and white marble tiles when the doorbell shrills.

"I've got it," I call before Katie interrupts herself.

On the step is a small man in a dark suit, too heavy for the weather, with a homburg set squarely on his head. Three suitcases are lined up in size order on the sidewalk behind him. A taxi glides off down the street.

"Yes?" Whatever he is selling, I don't even have time to be intrigued, not even if it's one of those new compact Hoovers I've seen advertised in the papers.

"Frau Warriner?" His accent is thick, turning the W to a V. "I am Gittings, Wilhelm Gittings." At my blank look, he adds, "I am sent by Herr Vollmer?"

"Of course." Remembering, I push the door open. "Mr. Gittings, welcome." Backing into the hall, I look around. No one is there. "Katie! Mrs. Hedges!" I smile at Mr. Gittings, knowing I must look quite wild-eyed. "I'm sorry, you've caught us at sixes and sevens. My husband is in the hospital. Katie!"

"Claire, may I be of help?" Josef Adler looms in the living room doorway, a newspaper dangling from one hand.

I look from him to the confused Mr. Gittings, who has brought his luggage into the hall. "This is Wilhelm Gittings, another friend of Leo's."

But that information is unnecessary, as the men are embracing and crying and talking over each other. I am forgotten and begin to creep away.

"Ma'am?" Katie is on the landing. "Is that—"

"Another one," I say, resigned but near laughter. "Who we weren't expecting until next week." The men disappear into the living room, talking excitedly in German. "Please put him in the guest room and make my apologies. I'm going to the hospital."

Katie skips down and attempts to pick up the suitcases. They resist, and she glares at them. "They're full of rocks. Or books." She shakes her head. "You go on to the hospital, Mrs. Claire. I'll make up the room and my daddy will bring up his bags. Tell Mr. Warriner we're praying for him."

By the time I park the roadster outside the hospital, the hour is almost up. I snap open my compact, dust my nose with powder, and reapply my lipstick. I may be flustered but I won't let my husband see me at anything but my best.

I stop at the reception desk and a pleasant young woman directs me upstairs. Riding in the elevator, I try to slow my heartbeat; Max is right, Harry doesn't need to see me fall to pieces. But I can fall to pieces all I want once the visit is done. I take a deep breath and promise myself a proper breakdown in the car afterward.

He is in a private room with a card outside reading "Mr. Warriner." The door is ajar, and I push it further. The bed is hidden behind a long curtain on rings, but I feel my husband's presence.

"Harry?"

A strangled sound. "I told Max not to let you come." His voice is hoarse. "Damn it, Claire."

I move the curtain aside and busy myself with dragging a chair over to give myself a moment to recover from the sight of the tube, which is indeed in his nose. Another tube, connected to a needle in the back of his hand, is fed from a glass bottle suspended from a pole.

"How are you, darling?" I bend over the bed to kiss his cheek, careful not to brush the tube or the surgical tape holding out in place. "Or should I not ask?"

I can do this. It's alarming, seeing him this way, but he's in the best place, being looked after by the best doctors. Max would soften bad news, but he wouldn't lie to me.

"Like hell," he says scratchily. "What do you think?"

"You don't look like yourself," I say, before I think better of it.

"Of course I don't." His free hand gestures at the tape across his nose.

"I meant your glasses." Harry hardly ever removes them except to polish them. "Where are they?"

His mouth twitches beneath his mustache. "Can't reach them."

I find them on a nearby table and put them on for him. His eyes focus on me, and he smiles faintly. His free hand reaches out and I slide mine beneath it.

"Does it hurt?" I lean down to pick up my bag. "I brought your pajamas, but I guess you can't change into them with that." I nod at his arm. I do not mention the wreckage of his sky blue pajamas, stained with blood and vomit; they have gone directly into the garbage.

"Gown is fine."

It is the same gown I was put into when I was hospitalized, before Harry brought me something better. I lift the edge of the sheet. "A bit drafty, though."

"Don't make me laugh." His words are slow and deliberate around the tube. "It hurts."

I sit back. "I'm sorry."

He raises his fingers, wanting my hand back. "Just no laughing."

We sit in silence, listening to the bustle of the hospital outside the door: soft-footed nurses and rolling carts and the authoritative leather soles of doctors, whose voices are rarely lowered.

"I've never found hospitals to be restful places." I remember my admissions after several miscarriages and for my tubal ligation surgery. "It's always noisy and someone is constantly waking you up to ask how you feel."

He makes an affirmative sound. His eyes are closed, but he's not sleeping; probably he can't bear to watch me look at him.

"A visitor arrived just before I left," I tell him. "A Herr Gittings."

"Damn!" His eyes fly open. "I should have been there."

I weave my fingers between his. "Well, you're not there, and he and Josef are apparently acquainted, so he's in good hands for the moment. We'll take good care of him, I promise."

He sinks back against the pillow. "What choice do I have, trapped in this place?" His eyes meet mine. "And before you say it, yes, I know I brought this on myself."

"I would never say that." Harry feels bad enough about the situation; I'm hardly going to point fingers.

"Max had no problem saying it." He groans with frustration. "I should be there. I promised Leo I would take care of his people."

"*We* promised Leo," I say. "And we will take care of Herr Gittings. He will be fed and housed and provided with anything else he needs. He's not supposed to stay long, is he?"

"A few days," Harry says. "He's expected in Washington. Dawes found a sponsor for him. We're just a way station between New York and Washington."

It pleases me that Helen's husband is more persuaded by Harry's project than she is.

"When I get home, I'll put in a call to let them know he's arrived. Unless he wants him immediately, I suggest we give him some time to recover before putting him on another train."

Harry nods. The conversation has exhausted him. "And maybe I'll be home by then."

"In the meantime," I say, "are there any other parcels I should expect? I don't mind running a hotel, only we're beginning to run out of rooms."

He smiles at that. "Not for a month at least." He raises my hand to his lips. "Now, I would like you to go home, call Ty, and then send a cable to Leo reassuring him of the arrival of his parcel."

I should have thought of that before I left. "I don't want to leave yet," I protest. "You'll be all by yourself."

"I'm sure there will be a flotilla of nurses in here before long, and someone will be kind enough to bring me a newspaper to pass the time. At least I don't have to try to eat hospital food, since I'm being fed through this thing." He waggles the hand with the needle in it. "Besides, I need time to contemplate my new, flavorless future."

Perhaps he does need time alone. I'm not used to Harry being self-pitying, but this situation would bring it out in the strongest of men.

This time I kiss him on the lips, and let him know that I see more than a man in a gown with a tube down his throat. "The fact that you have a future is enough for me."

I discover more about Wilhelm Gittings from Leo's letters and a brief conversation on the stairs with Josef Adler, who thanks me profusely for rescuing him.

"It wasn't me," I say, edging past him. I need to check on Teddy and change for a late dinner with our guests. "Leo and Harry did it all."

"You too are a part of it," he insists. "They made our journeys possible, but you have given us a place and a kind welcome—in two countries, no less."

"I'm glad you were in when Herr Gittings arrived. How do you know each other?"

His brows lift but his voice does not show his surprise. "You do not know who he is?"

"No." I continue up the steps, letting him follow. I don't even care if we've somehow ended up with another famous houseguest; if I don't get these shoes off soon I will scream.

"He is a journalist," he says, "a very prominent one. Until 1933, he worked for Vorwärts, the newspaper of the Social Democratic Party, which was obviously critical of the Nazis. He also taught a class in journalism at the university, which is how we met."

"I'm very glad you had a prior acquaintance. I felt terrible about running out, but I needed to get to the hospital."

"Ach, yes." His expression turns serious. "How is Mr. Warriner?"

"Somewhat better." I haven't shared with our guests the severity of Harry's condition; there is no need to worry them, or bring on unnecessary questions when he gets home. "They expect him to remain in the hospital for the next few days, so I would appreciate if you could take on more of a host's role with Herr Gittings."

"It would be my honor!" He gives a short bow and continues upstairs to collect his wife. I turn into my room first, sitting on the edge of the bed to remove my shoes, and padding in my stocking feet to the nursery door.

"Mama!" Teddy is already in his pajamas, sitting on the floor in front of Katie while she reads to him. He pushes up and shoots across the room, wrapping his arms around my legs. "You were gone."

I squat down to hug him. "But I came back. Have you eaten?"

He nods.

"You've had your bath?" I ask, though the answer is obvious from his damp hair and the scent of soap.

"With my boat." He grins broadly. "It sunk."

Ruffling his hair, I tap my cheek and he kisses me on both sides. "It's a good thing the *Normandie* didn't sink."

Teddy pulls out of my arms and retrieves the Blue Riband medal, which he insists on hanging on his bed post. "It was fast!"

"It was," I agree. "Mama has to change for dinner. Why don't you let Katie finish reading to you, and then go to bed? Before you know it, it will be morning."

Closing the door partway, so I can hear the rise and fall of their voices, I step out of my dress, which has, to my nose, acquired a slightly antiseptic scent which clashes with my perfume. There is no time for a bath, but I wash my face, neck, and hands and run a comb through my hair before choosing a fresh dress.

I take a few minutes to myself before changing, sitting on the vanity bench and touching up my makeup. There are lavender shadows under my eyes, and what had been faint lines at the corners seem suddenly more noticeable, as do the lines on my neck. I dab on lotion and mist myself with Shalimar, closing my eyes and letting the fragrance take me far from this difficult day.

When I reach the living room, the Adlers are chatting away with Herr Gittings. I understand not a word, but greet them breezily and pour myself a brimming martini from the pitcher Josef has considerately mixed. The first mouthful goes down like cleansing fire. After the second, I am fit once again for conversation.

The question of Harry's health is dealt with first—a minor setback, a few days in the hospital, nothing to worry about—and then Herr Gittings begins what I have come to think of unkindly as the refugee's gratitude presentation.

"It is so kind of you and Herr Warriner to offer me the hospitality of your very comfortable home." He has removed his homburg, but is still clad in the dark, ill-fitting suit of his arrival. When he raises his arm to gesture, I get a whiff of old sweat, and understand that this is yet another person who has made it out of

Germany with the clothes on his back, despite the volume of his luggage.

"Mr. Adler," I interrupt, "could I presume upon you to take Herr Gittings shopping tomorrow? We cannot send him to Washington appearing as though we have not provided a decent welcome."

"I am fine, I am fine," he protests. "A man is more than his clothes. He is more than his body, for that matter, but I need my body to continue my work."

I settle on the sofa next to Renate, hopefully out of sniffing distance. "What is your work, Herr Gittings? Herr Adler told me that you worked for a newspaper."

"I did," he says, taking a delicate sip of his drink. "But I am currently writing a history—a modern history—of the Weimar Republic and the roots of the Nazi party in Germany."

"He has brought his work with him," Josef Adler explains eagerly. "All his notes and references, even his typewriter."

That explains the suitcases full of rocks, as Katie no doubt discovered if he permitted her to unpack for him.

"And the transcription of my interviews with several high ranking party officials," Herr Gittings says. "Those interviews were not sanctioned by Herr Goebbels, the minister of propaganda." He smiles modestly. "I am a very wanted man, for a gentile."

I hadn't realized he wasn't, or that Leo was also working to rescue non-Jews. With all the people currently at risk—Jews and intellectuals and political opponents, among others—I wonder how he even begins to choose. Then I realize they are simply people in his orbit at the most obvious risk. There are so many. Harry told me the Adlers were the fourth group of people he got out of Paris, and there have been others in Belgium and Marseille.

The next day I regale Harry with the story of a rollicking meal, with both men getting drunk and sentimental and Renate translating until she got bored with them and went to bed.

"Herr Gittings brought nothing with him but a typewriter and a manuscript," I tell him. "Josef is taking him out shopping today. I can't bear the smell of a wool suit that's been lived in for more than a month. He smells like a bear just out of hibernation."

"Makes me almost glad I'm not there." His voice is stronger today and some kind nurse or orderly has changed him into his wine colored pajamas. "I'd have to light a cigarette to cut the stench."

"Now, none of that." It is easier to look at him today; the tube, despite its appearance, is doing its job, according to Max, as is the intravenous feeding. I am grateful for Max, as Harry's official physician has not deigned to give me any information on my husband's condition.

"I should be there. This is too much for you."

He is growing agitated again, and I stroke his hand. "It is not," I assure him. "If you weren't in the hospital, I wouldn't even have a reason to leave the house, so I'd be the lucky one to take Herr Gittings to buy a new suit. Maybe you've done me a favor."

"Stop trying to distract me. I'm not Teddy."

I can count on one hand the times Harry has raised his voice to me, but I have the same reaction each time. Growing up with a father who shouted and hit, it doesn't matter that Harry's words are mild in comparison; my body reacts as if it's in danger. The hair prickles on my neck and I have a sudden urge to urinate.

I sit with that for a moment, and then say, with a steadiness I don't feel, "That's not fair. This isn't something that happened out of the blue. You're in here partly because you get yourself so worked up. You need to remain calm—and you need to not take it out on me."

His eyes close. "I'm sorry," he murmurs. "I'm ashamed of myself. All this is because I offered to help Leo. You shouldn't have to deal with any of this. Or me, for that matter."

I let go of his hand abruptly, wait for him to look at me. "I can handle this, Harry. One small, smelly journalist is nothing—remember, I've dealt with your mother."

Pearl

August 16, 1935

After lunch, when I'd done as much sewing on my new dress as I could stand, I crammed Grace into her coach and took her to Aunt's. She's getting too big for it, but she's such a hardhead, it's impossible to get her to walk anywhere. I thought if I took her and Teddy up to Fitler Square they could run around on the grass and maybe she'd be a little easier later on. More fool me, because she was no better at all.

Aunt was at the hospital with Uncle, but Katie said things were stable, whatever that means. I'll have to ask Dr. Max later. And Aunt might not have been there, but there was another German in the living room with Mr. Adler. This one's name is Gibbing or Getting, something like that. He's small, no more than my height, and he wears thick, horn-rimmed spectacles that magnify his eyes so they're very blue and swimmy. He bowed and said something polite-sounding, but it doesn't seem like he has very much English at all.

I can't wait to tell Mama when she gets home. She was already a little grumpy when she came back yesterday with Grace, but I can't imagine this Mr. Gibble-Gabble was there then, or she'd have said something. She already has strong opinions about the Adlers, which I think are unjustified since they're both very nice people and Mrs. Adler is a world-famous singer, for Pete's sake. What more does Mama want to make her acceptable?

Claire

Early the next morning, the phone rings downstairs. I bolt upright, worrying that it's the hospital with bad news. Though Max has allayed my fears, I can't help but worry, and I've barely had any sleep. While Harry and I have slept apart before, it's been because he was traveling, not because he's in the hospital.

"Ma'am." A soft knock and Katie pops her head in. "The other Mrs. Warriner is on the line."

Irene? I breathe a sigh of relief, then think: at this hour? It's six-thirty. "What does she want?"

Katie's eyes turn skyward. "Like she would tell me. She barely acknowledges that I've answered the telephone."

The Katie I hired would never have spoken this way about her employer's mother. I blame Paris, and yet I am grateful, too. I don't want her to feel constrained with me, and Irene has always treated her badly.

"I'll call her after I've eaten." I sit up and throw off the sheet. "I need coffee before I speak to her."

"Yes, ma'am." Katie vanishes and I debate delaying my conversation with my mother-in-law further by taking a bath, but I hid in the bathroom last evening to avoid spending time with the Adlers and Herr Gittings, so it is unnecessary. I use the toilet, wash my face and apply light makeup, and stand before my closet unable to choose an outfit.

"Mama!" Teddy's voice trails from the nursery.

I throw on a robe and go to him. "Hello, darling."

"It's early," he says, blinking at me like a young owl. "Why I awake?"

"Maybe because you wanted this?" I sit on the bed beside him and tickle him under the arms. "Or this?" He rolls into a giggling ball and my fingers find the tender skin under his ear.

"Stop! Stop!" He wraps his arms around me and buries his face in my stomach. I scrub my fingers through his blond curls, grateful for his early waking as it has done more to calm me than anything else.

Eventually he falls away to his pillow, pulling a stuffed bear to his chest. It has recently replaced Pearl's stuffed dog as his favorite animal to sleep with.

"Go back to sleep," I suggest, pulling the sheet over him. "Katie will be up with breakfast in two shakes."

An enormous yawn is his only response, and I slip back to my room to dress. A fan is pulling warm air in through the window, and I put aside the dress I'd chosen and instead pull on a pair of mint green linen beach pajamas—perhaps not the most appropriate costume for a hospital visit, but they will make Harry smile. I add a stack of Bakelite bangles to show off my tan and a broad-brimmed white hat to keep the sun from my face, catch up a pair of white slingbacks by their straps and skin downstairs ahead of everyone.

Harry is the early riser, dealing with his newspapers and correspondence before heading to the office. I've never been a morning person, perhaps because my childhood was controlled by whistles and sirens. At thirteen, when I started high school, I had to leave the house before seven to get to school on time. Often I'd arrive half asleep, with no memory of the walk along the tracks between the Scovill Run and Henderson.

That would be Pearl's lot, if Ava hadn't brought her family to the city. I wonder how often she thinks of that: not just Max and their level of relative comfort now, but the difference in her children's lives, and their eventual families. She has broken the pattern of poverty which was so deeply ingrained in us. I did, too, but my sister did it through honest labor, not by marrying money. Her life was already changed when she allowed Max in.

And there it is. I understand, finally, why Max stopped their first wedding. He understood, where I did not, how important it was for her to succeed on her own before hitching her future to someone else.

Katie brings in coffee and the newspapers on a tray. "It's habit," she says. "Unless you want them?"

"Leave them here." I'll never have Harry's interest in the news, but current events, and our involvement with them, have made the papers more interesting. I skim the headlines while I drink my coffee.

When the Adlers appear, with Herr Gittings on their heels, I put the papers aside and paste on a smile. "Good morning, everyone."

Seated at Harry's desk to give myself privacy, I dial Irene's number. It's past nine, a far more civilized hour for a stressful conversation.

She picks up immediately. "Claire?"

"Good morning," I say smoothly. "You're up early today."

"Della Frayne is in the hospital," she says, her voice shaking. "Her sister called last night and said she saw Harry there. I told her she was wrong."

The last thing Harry needs is for his mother to find out about all this. "He's in New York," I say, deciding quickly. "Another refugee case. When he checks in later, I'll tell him to give you a call. It probably won't be until tonight."

A pause, and I hear Aunt Nora's voice in the background. "Is he all right, Irene? I told you it was nonsense. Judith Frayne is a booby."

"Thank you," she says at last. "I'll wait for his call."

Harry had made me promise not to come back until afternoon—to have a normal day, to play with Teddy and make sure our guest is settling in properly, and I think, to have some time to adjust to the fact that he can't bend a peptic ulcer to his will, or negotiate with it like the opposing party in a business deal.

When I arrive, he is sleeping lightly but his eyes open as soon as I sit down. "You missed Mother," he says.

"What?" I blanch. "Judith Frayne told her you were here, but I gave her the same story I told Teddy, that you were out of town and would call her tonight."

"She didn't believe you," he says. "She showed up just after ten, guns blazing."

That damned woman. I knew she would. "That's why I didn't tell her."

"No." He laughs. "She's mad at you. And me, on the assumption that I told you to lie."

Well, that's all right. I don't care if Irene is mad at me, or Harry. It will make our lives easier. "How did she manage"—I wave my hand vaguely—"with all this?"

Harry shakes his head. "She behaved as if we were sitting across a lunch table from each other. If she saw the tubes, and there's no way she couldn't, she didn't mention them."

Now that is surprising. Irene has always been known for her extreme reactions to anything involving her precious son. Seeing him confined to a bed with a tube up his nose should have had her raving in the hallways. "Are you sure she didn't check into Byberry on her way home?"

"I wouldn't be surprised." He takes my hand. "Now, tell me about life at the Hotel Warriner. I want to know everything."

24

Ava

With Harry in the hospital, all Claire's attention is focused on him and the eternal parade of Germans traipsing through their house—otherwise she would find an excuse to tag along for Renate's fittings. She would not be the best buffer; Hanne is better, should conversation become difficult. She doesn't need to know why Renate makes me uncomfortable, but I have told her that if she senses any awkwardness, she should distract Renate by speaking to her in German.

The black dress is coming along well. It is not strapless, as I had originally wanted, but has narrow banded sleeves and a bias-cut train dropping from her bare shoulders. Dramatic in its simplicity, it will be kept up by an intricate interior structure and Renate's natural authority.

"This reminds me of a gown I wore in Budapest," she says, turning before the mirror, tilting her chin up and stretching her neck.

"Was it also black?" I make a minute adjustment to mark the train's fastening, then remove the pins and hand the train to Hanne.

"Aubergine." At my blank look, she explains, "Dark purple."

She has mentioned this last tour several times, always with a touch of nostalgia and something else. "You were on tour for a long time?"

"A year," she says. "We thought to stay away from Berlin until the political situation improved."

Hanne speaks up unexpectedly. "But it never did."

"No."

I glance at Hanne, hoping she will take up more of the conversation, but she is staring at the wall, her lip caught in her teeth. She is seeing something from her past; Renate's troubles must seem very strange in comparison to hers.

"Mr. Adler traveled with you on this tour," I say, and put my hand on her hip. "To the left, please. Was it just the two of you, or did you have a manager?"

She turns obediently. "The two of us and my accompanist, Georg. My manager would come to certain shows, but frequently it was the three of us, traveling together." She takes a deep breath, and I watch how the bodice flexes and recovers. "I traveled many miles with George over the years. More even than with my husband."

"He did not come with you?" Hanne has returned to the present. "You must miss him."

Renate goes very still. "I need a moment," she says, stepping down from the stool. "I grow dizzy."

"Would you like a cup of tea? Water?" Hanne is poised to dash next door.

"Water, please."

When the door closes, Renate leans against the table. "I am sorry, Mrs. Byrne. It becomes wearying."

I move the pincushion before she rests her hand on it. "Fittings can be exhausting, but they're the best way to get the result you want."

"I know that." An upward glance from dark eyes. "I did not mean the fitting, but talking of my past. Of Georg."

"We do not have to speak." I would prefer, quite often, that she did not, but she was the one to refer back to her previous gown, and then the tour. "If you would rather not."

"It is Georg, you see," she says, as if I had not spoken.

"How long had you worked together?"

"Work?" Renate's face goes blank. "It was never work. He had heard my mother play when he was a boy, and he became a pianist because of her. When we were introduced, at school, he told me that and asked if he could accompany me." She bows her head when I touch her shoulder. The knot of hair at the back of her head seems to weigh her down. "He played for me for fifteen years, and then, in Krakow, in the middle of the tour, he left."

"What happened?" I am intrigued, in spite of myself, by this woman whose life is so different. Who has made choices so different from mine.

Renate sighs. "He had...changed. Begun to listen to what was being said about the Jews."

She speaks of Jews as if they are other people, not herself or her husband. "So Georg wasn't Jewish?" I am careful with the pronunciation of his name, my son's but not.

"No. He was Aryan, almost comically so. Blond hair, blue eyes. The Nazi ideal. In our photographs together, we looked ridiculous. I came to his shoulder. He was taller than my husband, and he had the energy of three men. He would play for hours, until a mortal man's hands would have cramped and pained him." Her lips twitch at a private memory. "He would never stop until I couldn't sing another note. I had to give in first."

I can't imagine a relationship like that shattering overnight. Talking to Renate—listening to her, really—is different from my other clients. Her clear, almost accentless voice tells of things new to me, and a world outside of books. It is difficult sometimes to remember that I don't like her.

"What happened in Krakow?" My father came from a village outside of Krakow, I want to tell her, but my past has no place here; this is her story.

"I knew, before the first piece was over, that something was wrong." At my look, she says, somewhat impatiently, "We were as close as lovers; I spent more time in his company than my husband."

"How did you know something was wrong?"

Her brow creases. "I'm not certain. He was behind me, but I could feel...something."

"What was it?" I smooth the velvet over her ribs, make a light mark with tailor's chalk to tell me where to move the seam. Renate's bust is minimal, but her ribcage makes up for it. Even so, she is the smallest adult woman I've ever sewn for, not much bigger than Thelma, who will have her father's height someday.

"I am not certain." She takes a breath. "There was a break, a moment where his mind was elsewhere. And"—she turns to face me, careful of the line of pins studding her bodice—"and that was not Georg's way. He was always with me, his entire attention."

"And then?" Hanne returns with a glass of water and I step back.

She takes a sip and closes her eyes. "And then he returned to the piece and played flawlessly for the rest of the evening. After the concert, we had champagne with several government officials and returned to our hotel. In the morning, he was gone."

Claire

Harry comes home in time to bid farewell to Herr Gittings, who, with his three leaden suitcases, is off to Washington and a bright future of writing and talking about politics. Helen Dawes has arranged for him to speak with Dorothy Thompson, the reporter who was expelled from Berlin by the Gestapo last year. According to Helen, she is as interested in his story as she is in his book about the rise of the Nazis.

When Herr Gittings has departed for the station, Harry stands in the hall as if uncertain what to do with himself. "I should make phone calls," he says. "But I can't be bothered."

"Phone calls can wait." I take his hand. "Would you like something to drink? Some soup?" The tube came out yesterday, but his dietary restrictions will persist for a while. Mrs. Hedges says she likes a challenge; I assume that his dinner will be both liquid and delicious.

He shakes his head. "What I'd like, if I'm being honest, is to take off all this"—he waves a hand at jacket, shirt, and tie—"and climb into my own bed and sleep for a week. At least an hour or two."

"Then that's what you'll do. I can keep Teddy occupied and quiet while you nap." I pause at the bedroom door. "He'll be so excited to see you later. He's missed you."

"I've missed him. You didn't tell him about the hospital?" His forehead, taut and almost without lines despite his age, creases with concern. "I don't want him worrying."

"No." I thought he was too young for a truth that I could barely handle myself. "You've been away on business."

Harry walks into the bedroom and immediately drops his jacket and tie on the chair. "A shower, too," he says. "To get the hospital stink off me."

I come close, winding my arms around his neck, and take a healthy sniff. "You smell like yourself," I tell him. Minus the smell of cigarettes, which his doctors have told him to quit because they, like alcohol and coffee and rich foods, will aggravate his stomach lining. "I've missed that. But take your shower, I'll be here when you come out."

He pulls me so tightly against him that I can feel the buttons on his shirt. "I was afraid I wasn't coming home," he says hoarsely. "I was so afraid."

I return his embrace, wrapping my arms around him as if I could pull him inside myself for protection. "You're home now. You're safe, and we're going to keep you that way."

While he showers, I go to the nursery to let Teddy know his daddy has returned. "He's very tired," I tell him. "He needs to take a nap, like you take naps, and then we'll play a game or go to the park before dinner."

Teddy is surrounded by the detritus of some elaborate game, cars and trucks and pieces of his train set strewn everywhere on the carpet. "Did he bring presents?"

"I don't know." I squat down and he comes to me and puts his arms around my neck. "You can't get a present every time he goes away. You have so many toys already."

He shakes his head, his lip sticking out, and I am suddenly struck by his resemblance to Ava's boys. "No!"

"Yes," I say firmly. This incipient George behavior must be nipped in the bud. "You have enough toys, but if you're good and let Papa sleep, we'll go to the park before dinner." I hold out my hand. "Deal?"

"No." He slaps my hand instead of shaking it and then points to the rubble of vehicles on the floor. "Was an earthquake."

"You better tidy up from that earthquake," I tell him. "I'd like to see the floor before we go out."

"Katie do." He smiles at me with the sunshiny confidence of a child who's never been told no.

I debate trying that, but I hear the bathroom door close. "We'll be in later," I promise. "You play quietly."

He's already lining up his cars, aiming them at a stuffed bear on the floor. "Bye," he says absently, pushing the first car at top speed and giggling as it bounces off the animal's soft fur.

Harry's hair is damp, his glasses fogged with moisture. He wears his blue pajama bottoms but no top. The puffiness in his abdomen has decreased, I notice, but I swear there is more gray in his chest hair than last week.

"Better?" I lay my head against his chest, listening to his heartbeat.

"I smell better, anyway." He puts an arm loosely around me and rubs my back. "And you're better medicine than a raft of doctors."

"Only if you don't pay attention to the doctors." I draw away to look into his wry, tired eyes. "Please, Harry."

He sinks onto the edge of the bed and reaches out, capturing my wrists in both hands. "I promise." Drawing me down beside him, he says, "This scared the hell out of me, Claire. I never want to find myself in one of those beds again, with or without tubes up my nose." He sighs heavily. "Even if that means bland food and no alcohol."

It's not as if Harry is a heavy drinker, but he's a social drinker in the way of most of the men in our set. Dinners are meat-heavy with rich sauces and the expectation of a hearty appetite. Business meetings don't start with drinks, but a successful deal or the signing of a contract almost always ends with a round or two at the Union League or the Vesper Club.

"It's not for long." I lean my head against his shoulder. "Let your body heal, and you'll be able to eat everything in moderation again, isn't that what the doctors said?"

He sighs again, and his body sags beneath my cheek. "And I want to believe them."

"Then do." I push myself up, then drop to my knees in front of him like he's Teddy. "Behave yourself for a few months." I put my hands on his knees. "I was so worried about you. About us."

This was the longest week of my life, and I want to make sure he understands that. Also that I will not permit him to abuse his body and risk his life for no reason other than that it's easier to fit in than stand up for his health.

He leans forward and kisses my forehead. "You and Teddy would be taken care of, Claire, even without me. I had Burt come into the hospital and I updated my will."

"That's not the point." Tears prick at the thought of him making plans for a future without him. "You are not negotiable. I understood when we married that because of the difference in our ages, I might end up a widow at some point." I fall forward, rest my head on his knee so that my words come out muffled. "I'd prefer it not to happen until I'm in my seventies, at least."

His hand comes to rest on my hair. "Darling Claire."

"I mean it." I slide from beneath his hand and get to my feet. "I'd rather have them put a tube up my nose than go through another week like that."

Harry rises, touches my cheek. "I will be more careful," he says. "And now, I must lie down before I fall down."

Two hours later, he emerges from our room fully dressed and carrying Teddy on his shoulders. "This little highwayman woke me up, demanding toys."

"Teddy!" I tweak his bare knee. "What did we talk about earlier?"

He turns wide and guileless eyes on me. "Dunno."

We take him to the park and let him run across the grass, wearing himself out, while we remain on a bench. Harry looks refreshed, but I don't want him to push himself too hard—as I well know, time in the hospital can be as depleting as illness.

"I assume Mrs. Hedges has learned how to make baby food?" The words are joking enough, but there is an edge of worry in his voice.

"Summer soups, for the most part," I tell him. "But I did have Wanamakers deliver a blender, to give her more options."

"Pureed beef?" He looks aghast. "I'll stick to the soup."

I slide my hand into the space between us, where my fingers tangle with his. Harry is not often affectionate in public, but he clasps them and keeps his hand there. "It's only soft food until your throat is better," I remind him. "Don't knock it until you've tried it. She's an excellent cook."

"True enough." He pats his breast pocket for the Chesterfields which are not there. "In Mother's day, this would have been more difficult."

That's because Mrs. Fell was as adept a cook as Irene is kind. I let the topic go, and point to Teddy, now kicking a ball with two other small boys. "He'll sleep tonight."

"And with any luck," Harry says, "he'll forget that I didn't bring him a gift from the hospital."

I shift so that I can lean against him on the bench. "I'm sorry he woke you up this afternoon. I would move him upstairs, except that means the Adlers would have to listen to him rampaging around. But they won't be with us forever."

He leans over and kisses my lips. "Sometimes it feels like it."

Does he regret what he's done for them or is it the exhaustion of a man who's been through too much lately? I decide to interpret it as the latter. "Josef was a great help with Herr Gittings."

"I'm glad of that. You had enough to deal with."

I tap a finger hard on the back of his hand so he looks at me. "I am capable of dealing with things. I'd prefer not to—I'd prefer that you remain healthy—but I'm not incapable."

"I know that, darling." He stops, then calls to Teddy, "Too far, Ted. Come back!" Once he sees that our son has listened, he continues, "But you have your own occupations. Teddy, your committees. The clinic."

"Of those things, Teddy is the only one that counts," I tell him. "There are women fighting to get on those committees. They wouldn't notice if I went missing for the rest of my life. And as far as the clinic"—I debate a moment whether to tell him the truth, and then do—"these days it feels like something I made to give to Max. He runs it, he's in charge of the staff, the budget. He chaired the board meetings while we were gone, even if he did gripe about it in his letters."

"But you created it."

Teddy returns, shooting between Harry's knees and burying his head against his chest. There is an involuntary stiffening as he absorbs the impact of our sturdy son against his stomach, and then Harry's arms come around him.

I gaze at the two of them, both so dear, and so unexpected, even after all these years. Harry, older, wealthy, certainly not the kind of man I was brought up to expect; and Teddy, my miracle baby by way of my sister, from whom I had been so long estranged. Nothing matters more than them.

"I think I created the clinic to prove to myself that I was capable," I say carefully. "After our trip to Washington, meeting Mrs. Roosevelt and Helen Dawes and all those accomplished women, I felt like I needed to do something."

"And you did. You created that clinic by sheer force of will."

And I nearly destroyed my marriage in the pursuit of it. "Maybe the creation was enough. It exists, it will continue to be funded, and I couldn't ask for anyone better than Max to run it."

Teddy shifts and grabs a handful of my skirt. "Hungry."

"Are you?" I stand, brushing the creases out of my dress and taking his hand. "Then let's go home and get you fed."

Harry takes his other hand. Over Teddy's head, he asks, "But what will you do without it?"

What will I do? The answer is clear. "Be a wife and mother," I tell him. "It's all I ever wanted to begin with."

Pearl

Almost from the time we sat down, Tommy's arm has been on the back of my seat. As Garbo turns her soulful gaze on Fredric March and the audience gasps in anticipation, his hand slides down and cups my shoulder. His fingers are warm through my sleeve. I lean a little toward him so he can pull me in closer, and he does. It's like a dance, I realize. When he put his arm around me, I could have stiffened and he would have moved away; when he touched my shoulder, I could have stayed still or shrugged or leaned in. I'm leading, whereas if we were really dancing, he would lead.

For a long while I stay tucked under his arm, getting used to him being so close to me. When he turns his head and reaches for my chin with his other hand, I'm curious what he'll do, and what my next move will be.

He tips my head up and leans down a little to kiss me. His lips are chapped. I hope my lipstick isn't getting all over him. Then I forget about my lipstick and the bits of Greta Garbo I can see over his shoulder as he pulls me close. It's not like the time before, when he kissed me because he was angry at Dan. This is about me. His fingers are in my hair, and there is a small clatter as my barrette hits the floor. I don't tell him to stop. I'm afraid to, because then the world will go back to normal and we'll be in a dark theater that smells like popcorn and feet and I'll have to figure out how to look him in the eye when he's made me feel like Jell-O all over.

I don't have that worry, as Tommy is unwilling—or unable—to look at me when the movie is over. Without discussion, we head for the lunch counter at Woolworths to get ice cream, not speaking until we are seated on high revolving stools and our order for two root beers and one vanilla ice cream has been placed before us.

Tommy pushes the dish of ice cream toward me. "You've been quiet all night. You okay?"

"We were at a movie," I say around a spoonful of vanilla with chocolate sauce. "How was I supposed to talk?"

"You probably knew everything that was going to happen." His smile shows he is teasing. "Who knew I'd end up with a girl who read so many books."

A part of me thrills to the word *end up with a girl*, but even *Anna Karenina* isn't enough to distract me from my worry over Hazel, who, despite working in her father's law office as planned, hasn't recovered her pep since the operation.

"I've just got something on my mind."

Tommy's dark eyes narrow with concern. "Have you heard from Dan?"

I put the spoon down. "Not recently. Mama's getting worried. So am I."

The muted sounds of the lunch counter rise around us as he goes quiet. I listen to the soft conversation, the clink of silverware on china and glass, and watch his face as he decides what to say.

"Your brother can take care of himself," is what he finally comes up with.

"I'd be happier if you were with him." That had been Dan's original plan, for the two of them to have an adventure together. Not separate, hurting.

His rough hand covers mine. "Isn't this good?"

There is a girl from my class at school at the end of the counter. She's sitting with a boy, their heads almost touching.

For a moment, Hazel's freckled face swims before me, splotched with tears and pain, betrayed by a boy she thought was in love with her.

I remove my hand, gently but firmly. "It's not Dan," I tell him. "I'm thinking about a friend. She got herself in trouble with a boy."

"I'm sorry for her," he says with all sincerity. "Is she all right?"

Something releases in me at his lack of judgment. "She's better now. But it scared me."

"Don't be scared." He takes my hand again, weaving his fingers through mine. "You're safe with me, Pearl. I promise."

How I want that—that promise of safety and care. But I also want that flush I felt when he kissed me in the theater, the knowledge that this is the beginning of such feelings. That it would be entirely too easy to end up in the same boat as poor dumb innocent Hazel, without the excuse of ignorance to save me.

25

Ava

For a while now, ever since our wedding and the move to the shop, the days have raced past in a blur. I reach out, trying to catch hold of one and slow the time down, but I fail, over and over. More quickly than I would have expected, getting up and leaving the house has become an ordinary part of my existence. I would have liked more time to become accustomed to it—the achievement of it all, and the changes it has wrought upon us, even Grace, who spends the day with Mrs. Malloy if I have clients scheduled in the afternoons—but there is no time.

It doesn't take long for the streetcar to convey me to Fourth Street, but standing on the corner and waiting makes me impatient, so unless I am laden with a dress or a heavy bag of fabric, I save my money and walk both ways. Max laughs, but it's fine for him: he never stops moving. Most of my waking hours are spent seated at the machine; the walk is often the only time I get to be alone.

Because Hanne comes in with Mr. Mendel, she frequently opens up and either cleans from the day before or sets out our work for the day. She leaves at four, so the responsibility for locking up falls on me.

It reminds me that work is over, and that it is time to go home to my husband and my kids. A separate part of my life. Is this how men have always felt, with their lives in tidy compartments? I think I could grow to like it, if I could rid myself of the guilt over leaving Grace.

I've never not been wholly available for my kids. I might have been doing three things at once, but I was there, in the house with them. There are other benefits to our new life which are good for Grace, but I can't help thinking that I'm doing a disservice to my youngest by not being with her all the time.

To my surprise, my clients, even Prue, have questioned moving my business out of my house. I would have expected them to prefer a less chaotic, more professional environment, but while they do appreciate the dressing room and the larger space, to a one they have asked how I can work outside the home and leave my children to be cared for by others

"It's just until she's a little older," Pearl says, when I mention it. "She can't be expected to play quietly at her age, and the ladies can only handle so much screaming."

"True." And she does have a tendency to howl when thwarted. "But Mrs. Malloy has so many kids."

Pearl bursts into laughter. "She has one less than you do, Mama!"

I subside. I shouldn't have expected my daughter to understand; despite what she's experienced this summer, she doesn't know the pull of motherhood. And I don't want her to, not this soon.

Pearl

For the first day of school, I am up before anyone, and out of the house by seven. It's been a strange summer. I'm even happier than usual to go back. And I've missed the girls—despite all our good intentions, we never managed to meet up to go to the movies because we've all been working and Hazel's kept to herself since July.

The four of us meet on the front steps of the school, like we'd agreed in June, and for a moment I'm completely happy, hugging and kissing my friends, chattering like a bunch of magpies, Mama would say. All of us happy to be back together again.

"How's Charlie?" Lenny asks, and Hazel's face closes.

"We broke up." She doesn't look at me, knowing I'll keep her secret. "And the other problem solved itself."

"What about you, Pearl? Got a boyfriend yet?"

Peggy is wearing the same tired white blouse from last year. It's beginning to pull over her bust, and she's not a big girl. I'm glad Mama and I found time to make me a new one, plus my dress. Clothes may not make me smarter, but I feel better when I fit in.

I shake my head. I'm not sure what to call Tommy and I'm afraid to jinx our relationship by calling him my boyfriend. "Too busy," I fib. "What about you?"

"No time," she says. "My uncle got me a job, so I barely saw the house during the day." She holds out her hands, revealing chipped nails. "He could have found something a little easier on me, but I can't say anything. My brothers all needed shoes this fall."

"Did you end up working at your uncle's office?" Lenny remembers every conversation we've ever had, and I sometimes think she uses them to deflect our questions. "That was the plan, wasn't it?"

"It was," I confirm. "But he hasn't been well, so I've mostly been helping my mother and watching my nephew. What did you get up to?"

"I worked in the taproom." Lenny grins, not at all embarrassed by her family's business. "Since it's right off Front Street, the customers are mainly longshoremen."

"Aren't they rough?" I think of the drunken men I'd occasionally seen back in Scovill Run, and of one in particular who had lodged with us for a while.

"Not when I'm there." Her eyebrows lift; she's very close to laughter. "My father would throw out any man who used foul language around his daughter."

The bell rings before we can say anything further. We link arms and march into the auditorium, sitting with the other juniors. I glow with pride to be sitting in this place, with so many other smart girls. When Dr. Hart speaks, it's a variation on the speech she gave last year: welcoming us back and reminding us of the importance of being a graduate of Girls High. It will follow us all our lives.

Which means I need to start thinking properly about my future. My roster for this semester is scary but I can do the work. I might skip one club, unless I can get into the Service Club. According to the school counselor, that's the one that looks good on college applications.

As we sit through more speeches, I look around the auditorium. The seniors, seated ahead of us, look like women already in their suits and nice dresses, their hair permed or pinned up in adult styles. I've got one more year before that will be me. Somehow. It's not all clothes, but that's as good a place to start as any. On the inside I can still be Pearl Kimber from Scovill Run, so long as my outside looks like what it should. I need to learn how to be that new Pearl before anyone finds out I'm a fraud.

Claire

Max arrives for dinner straight from the clinic, his tie loosened and a smudge of dirt on one cheek. "You're early," I tell him, wanting to take a damp rag to his face as if he were Teddy. "Ava and the children won't be here for half an hour."

"Good." He drops his hat on the hall table. "I wonder if we could have a word before they get here."

"Of course." We retreat to my sitting room and I settle into my favorite armchair. "Is it about Harry? Should I call Katie for tea?"

"Harry's fine." Max paces back and forth until I tell him to sit down. "Well, not fine, but so long as he behaves himself. I need to talk to you without everyone else around."

"What's the problem?" He rarely admits to needing anything.

His pacing ceases. "I want a raise."

"You agreed to that salary when the clinic was set up." I am not averse to giving Max a raise, only surprised that he would ask. Money has never been important—he never used it for anything but his projects anyway, and now the clinic has given him all the projects he has time for. He and Ava can't be hurting for cash.

"I was a single man then." He balances on the edge of a too-small chair, looking like a boy sent to the principal's office. "Last month, Ava brought in more than I did."

"Last month was the Academy ball," I remind him. "She sewed nonstop, and that doesn't even take Renate's gowns into account."

"I'd like her to take it easy, if she's capable of it. My salary covers a portion of the rent and the light and telephone bills, but that's it." A tiny shake of his head. "I'm not downplaying the skill involved in her work, not at all, but I went to medical school. I should be able to support my family. If she won't accept that support now, I'd like to put money away for the kids."

He has me there, knowing I will do almost anything to help my nieces and nephews—at least within the boundaries of what my sister will allow.

"I think I can authorize another ten percent," I say carefully, "without having to call the entire board."

"That'll do," he says cheerfully. "I've got some cash put aside for a rainy day, but I've got my eye on a house, so I need to know what I can offer."

"A house? To purchase?" I am excited for them. It will make all the difference for Ava to own her home. Perhaps she'll feel settled enough to finally relax.

He makes a sound between laughter and choking. "To rent. Even with that ten percent, I won't have the funds to go out and buy property. But it's okay," he assures me. "We don't need to buy it."

"What about Ava?" She's so attached to the Ringgold Place house, which I can understand—it's not just her home, but shelter in the very hardest time of their lives. "She loves that house."

"She does." For a moment, he looks troubled. "Let me handle your sister. All I need from you is the money. You're sure you have it?"

"We have it." Harry's arrangement with Irene means that the clinic is fully funded until her death, and then a portion of her estate will be invested to keep it running.

"Good. Because I could fundraise, but that would take time."

"Do you think you'd make enough? We already had a fundraising gala."

"Some rich people are burdened by their money," he says, laughter in his eyes. "I'm helping them to feel better about themselves." His grin makes him look like George. "And that includes you and Harry."

Pearl

September 6, 1935

First Friday supper at Aunt's since school started. We're supposed to meet there and do homework in the kitchen with Katie and Mrs. Hedges until Mama or Dr. Max appear. Usually they show up together. Mama comes home early on Fridays, so I think we're not supposed to be there so they can have some time alone. But not this week, apparently, because when I came upstairs, he was talking to Aunt in the living room.

I went up to get Teddy and bumped into Mrs. Adler. She's so nice. She asked about school and what I want to do when I graduate. I told her college, and then probably teaching. Then I took a deep breath and told her the secret I've only shared with Mama, that I want to be a writer.

Because she's an artist, she understood. She said it will be hard, but that I should keep my dream alive even if I have to teach for years, and to never stop writing.

I was too embarrassed to tell her that most of my stories only exist in my head because I'm afraid to write them down and find out they're not as good as I think.

I carted Teddy down to the kitchen and he threw himself on Thelma like he hasn't seen her in weeks, but she comes here every day after school, so it was yesterday. She loves third grade. I thought she'd be nervous about walking alone, since my classes start earlier this year, but she was fine. Better than walking with the boys, she says. I can believe that.

They might be growing up, but I can't see them as any older than six because they haven't changed except to get taller. They kicked up a fuss about wearing shoes to school, so bad that Dr. Max had to speak to them. Mama said the way they run barefoot was helpful when we couldn't afford shoes. Now, though, they look like hobos and she won't stand for that.

I was going to suggest they stay barefoot and she let me have a second pair, but I didn't want a clip around the ear and that was the mood she's been in lately.

Ava

It is not long before the O'Donnells return the favor and ask us to supper. When Max tells me where they live, I can't picture it, though it is apparently close to my route to the shop each day.

Max parks on Spruce just below Thirteenth. "Camac is as narrow as our street, so I'll leave the car here."

It's an easy six blocks from home, it turns out; we could have walked but for him getting in late from work. Also, there's a threat of rain later, though right now the sky is a bright porcelain blue, without a cloud in sight.

We turn onto the street. A dozen kids race back and forth, playing some sort of game; one holds up a hand in greeting as we approach.

"I've never noticed this little street before," I say, "and I walk down Pine Street all the time."

"It's easy to miss."

Like Ringgold Place, these houses are solidly attached to their neighbors, but there is more to differentiate them than a number and the presence or absence of shutters; some have center doors, while others are located to one side. A few have three stories, but most are only two, with a single attic dormer protruding from a slate roof. Window and door frames vary wildly in their design and paint colors. Several have wooden access doors to the cellar, but others have nothing more than a slotted window at ground level. The brick sidewalk comes right up to the houses; there are no gardens, but most homes have plants or window boxes out front.

He leads me to a neat brick two-story house with large windows on one side of a blue door. Pots of bright geraniums and other flowers are arranged on either side of the shallow front step, where an iron boot scraper is anchored to the marble. The whole construction is so clean it's obvious that Rosaleen or one of her daughters has recently scrubbed the step.

Max raps lightly with the brass knocker, a series of taps that echo back through the open windows.

"This is nice," I whisper as we wait. "They can afford this on a police officer's salary?"

"Apparently." The door opens and Max breaks off to greet our hostess with a broad smile. "Rosaleen, you're absolutely blooming."

"Well, thank you, Dr. Byrne." She is blooming, her belly already more apparent beneath a loose pink flowered dress. "And Mrs. Byrne—Ava—how are you this evening?"

"Not as blooming as you, but not complaining." We exchange kisses and I look around quickly as the narrow entry hall leads into the living room. Despite showing the occupation of children, it is a clean and cheerful room with the evening light flooding through the west-facing front windows. "You have a beautiful home."

"Thank you, Ava." She brushes a wisp of hair from her face. "Pat's in the back, doctor, if you want to go on through." Turning to me, she says, "Would you like to see the rest of the house?"

"I would love to." I'm far more curious than is appropriate, but the street has charmed me and the interior looks to be even better.

She waves me toward a small table where I can leave my hat and bag. "I wouldn't be so forward about showing it off except the girls and I turned the whole place over this week and it looks far better than usual."

"I doubt that." It smells of polish; all the wood surfaces, from the floors to the furniture, are gleaming.

The house is a good size: big enough for a family but not extravagantly so. The living room ceiling feels like a cathedral after our den-like trinity house, but it is probably no more than eight feet. Lower than Claire's but surprising in a modest home like this.

"How old is the house?" I follow her up the stairs, which have strips of flowered carpet tacked to each step.

"Eighteen-twenties," she tells me as we reach the landing. "Two bedrooms on this floor, ours and the girls. Plus a bathroom."

A peek into the front bedroom reveals a full-size metal-framed bed with a light quilt on top, net curtains and not much else. The girls' room is similarly plain, with the addition of bright hair ribbons and a doll on the dresser.

The bathroom is a marvel—a deep claw foot tub, porcelain sink and toilet set on a black and white floor in a basket-weave pattern. Narrow white tile covers the walls halfway up.

"That's lovely," I say, tracing a finger over the roll-edged border.

"Easy to keep clean," she says briskly. "Even with boys, though they have a smaller second bathroom upstairs—only a sink and toilet."

Two bathrooms! I revise my estimate of a police sergeant's salary upward.

The stairs to the attic are narrower, leading to two smaller bedrooms and a closet-sized bathroom.

"It's bigger than it looks from outside," I offer. The bedroom windows look out not to the street but a flat section of roof at the back of the house. Max's voice reaches us faintly from downstairs.

"That it is." She nods toward the untidy second bedroom. "We rent this to one of the young patrolmen in Pat's precinct. He's just out from home and needs some looking after." She looks at me plainly. "And the money doesn't hurt either."

"It never does."

We troop back down, pass through an archway into the dining room, where the table is already laid for supper, and she pushes open the last door with her hip. "And here's where I spend most of my days."

I expect to find the men there, but the room is empty except for a pot bubbling companionably on the stovetop. It is the centerpiece of the room, as stoves always are, but my eyes go immediately to the shining white enamel sink and the built-in cabinets that line one wall. Drawers on the bottom, glass-doored shelves above—it is a more workmanlike version of Claire's kitchen, and my heart yearns unreasonably to call it my own.

Rosaleen follows my gaze. "More storage than we have things to store," she says. "Same as the rest of the place. Every time we plan to buy something for the house, I end up in the family way and we have to put it off."

I understand that too well, except that Daniel and I rarely purchased anything because even without constant babies there was no money. All the furnishings we brought with us from Scovill Run had existed in my childhood home; nearly everything acquired since has come from Dan's scavenging or from Claire, either a gift or something her treasure trove of an attic. New things...

"Can I help with supper?" Thoughts of those dark days don't belong in this sunny, happy house.

"Not a bit." She gives me a light shove. "Go out back with the men. I'll dish up as soon as the kids come in. They'll eat in the kitchen, and we can eat in peace in the dining room."

The back door leads directly to a bricked seating area. Max and the sergeant welcome me, and I accept a sweating bottle of beer, pressing its cold surface against my wrists.

"Rosie showing off, was she?" The sergeant tips his chair onto its back legs.

"It's a beautiful house," I tell him. "Worth showing off." Looking at Max, I add, "You're lucky I like where we're living, because I could be very happy in a house like this."

26

Pearl

Throughout the summer, further cards have trickled in from Dan, but none have mentioned when he might return. "He's going to use up all his stamps," Toby complains. "And then where will he be?"

"Maybe he'll come home when he runs out." Thelma turns over the card, with a photo of a Texas steer, and pushes it back to her brother. "I miss him."

I miss him, too. And I can't imagine how Mama feels. She talks to Dr. Max about him at night. While I try not to listen, sometimes I can't help it.

"He's almost grown," he said the other night, and I knew what they were talking about, though I couldn't hear Mama's response. "Is grown, with all he's been through. Maybe he needs to cut loose a little."

It's that, and more than that, as I well know. Tommy has never told me exactly what happened between them on the night they fought, but I think I understand. I also know he cares about Dan, and the longer my brother stays away, the happier Tommy will be to see him when he gets back.

Selfishly, I want Dan to come home *now*, because I miss him, but I also want him to stay away. Because once he's back, I'll be alone again—if he and Tommy make up. I've gotten used to going with Tommy every weekend; I'm not so nervous now as I was, scared that he was seeing me only because he couldn't have Dan.

Sometimes we go out on Friday or Saturday, and sometimes he comes to Dr. Max's Sunday lunch and then we go out afterward. It's almost always to the movies, which is fine. It's not expensive and there's always something good playing, especially if we're willing to walk a ways to one of the cheaper neighborhood theaters.

I go with Mama and Thelma every so often, but we've lost the boys. Toby is back at the garage after school. He's on his best behavior, as is George, who still goes to the firehouse. On Saturdays, they spend the day with Dr. Max at the clinic. The house is so nice and quiet when they're gone, it's almost a shame to go out. And yet, when Tommy knocks at the kitchen door, I'm always there, wearing something warm from the iron and my hair just brushed from spending the day in pins.

Ava

The O'Donnell house draws me like a magnet. I leave the shop a little early and decide to walk home by way of Pine Street, using as an excuse a hankering for corn which Max had voiced over breakfast. I could as easily go to our local shop, but Rosaleen had mentioned there was a good grocer around the corner from her, so I decide to stop in. Corn will be heavy, but it's not that long a walk; I can fit a good number of ears in my bag.

Coming up on Eleventh Street, I move into the cool shadow of the Gladstone, a fancy ten-story apartment building that takes up most of the block. A luxury building like this existing a short distance away from the row of little colonial houses seems strange, but I have come to understand that Philadelphia is a city of contrasts—poverty and wealth, simplicity and modernity—all blended together.

I turn onto Camac, walking tentatively, as if I have no right to be there. I stop short of the house, standing in the middle of the street to better look at it. It gives me the same feeling I had when I first saw our house, that it is both perfect and too much. Shaking myself, I hitch my bag into my shoulder and continue on, listening to the odd sound my heels make on the wooden blocks that make up the street.

I asked Max about them, and he said it was a method of paving no longer used, which made for a lower level of noise with hooves and carriage wheels. It is an interesting look, but like brick and cobblestone streets, which are abundant in Philadelphia, opportunities abound to catch a heel or turn an ankle.

"Ava!"

Turning the sound of my name, I see Rosaleen waving from her front step and squash an urge to flee. But why should I feel guilty?

It's a free country. I can walk down her street and admire the houses if I want.

"Hello! I was going to check that grocer you told me." I gesture to my bag. "I meant to stop at the one near my shop, but this was easier as it's on the way home."

"Wait a moment, I'll come along with you." She closes the door and catches up, one hand on her burgeoning belly. "We're almost out of tea and none of the kids have come in yet to send to the shop."

People are coming home from work, men and women walking west from Spruce and Walnut Streets, where the streetcars run. Rosaleen has a word for most of them. "It's a nice street," she says. "If Pat's transfer comes through, I'll miss it."

"I thought you wanted a different place?" I'd be perfectly content on a street like this.

She acknowledges the contradictory nature of her statements with a smile. "I won't miss the city, its dirt and its noise," she says. "I'll miss the neighbors."

Good neighbors don't just happen. I also know it takes effort to befriend this many people. It's a skill Max has in abundance but I am sorely lacking.

"It's as much you as them," I tell her. "We've lived in our house since January of '33, and I barely know anyone."

"But you're so busy." She turns abruptly toward a green-painted shop front. "All the kids, and working away from home. I don't think I could do it."

There is no judgment in her voice, but it stings anyway, the same as it does when my wealthy clients ask who's watching my children as I kneel at their feet, pinning a hem.

"I haven't had a lot of choice," I say shortly. "And having the shop gives us more room in the house."

She moves toward the back of the store and I turn towards the display of vegetables—fat red tomatoes, sacks of potatoes, green beans, apples. And baskets of corn. I select a dozen ears and carry them to the counter with difficulty.

Rosaleen joins me, clutching a box of tea. "I didn't mean to sound rude," she says as I pay for my purchase. "I speak out of turn sometimes. Pat is always on me about it."

"It's all right. I'm sensitive about it is all." I don't want to hold a grudge against this nice woman, with her nice husband and nice family. "Do you have plans on Sunday after church?"

"Going home and putting my feet up, that's all. Pat's off, so we'll be eating as a family."

Husbands with unpredictable schedules mean that a meal together can be a special thing. "I wouldn't want to interrupt that," I say, "but Max always makes a big lunch on Sundays and I thought it would be nice for the kids to meet."

"The doctor cooks?" There's no judgment this time, only surprise.

"I wouldn't call it cooking." I shift the heavy bag higher onto my shoulder. "He goes out and buys sandwich fixings. It's his way of apologizing for not coming to church."

She nods understanding. "He's not Catholic then?"

"No," I say, "but my first husband was and he didn't go to mass either. He always said that God rested on Sunday and so would he."

Claire

Despite Max's request for a raise and the reasons behind it, I've heard nothing from either him or my sister about a potential move. But that may not mean a thing. Knowing Ava, she would invite me to a housewarming without ever having let me see her pack a dish.

And that's assuming Max can even convince her to move. She's always lived a certain way and she's resistant to change. I understand; her life hasn't left room for her to consider other ways, but they do exist. When I came to live in Philadelphia, the sheer size of the Delancey Place house was unsettling. Why did people need so many rooms? I certainly didn't want to be in Irene's pocket, but that she had an entire suite of rooms to herself, and that I was expected to have my own sitting room, felt extravagant and unnecessary.

But with a half dozen children, Ava and Max need the space. Also, while I'm not clear on his family's financial situation when he was growing up, Max was an only child. The lack of privacy in Ava's house must drive him mad, as the silence and loneliness in the Warriner house frequently drove me to tears that first year.

If they can afford something that will make their lives easier and more pleasant, Ava shouldn't dig her heels in and refuse to go along. I know how she feels about that house; her independence is all tied up in her ability to care for her family after Daniel's death. But now she has Max, and while she'll never stop working, I hope she will at least cut back and spend more time with the children. The little boys, especially—not so little now, they need a firm hand and at least some of the focus she gave to Dan when he was that age.

"How are you managing with the bigger kitchen?" I ask, sitting at the table and glancing around. She has repurposed her old work space into a dining room, yet somehow it's more like a basement than it was before.

She shrugs. "It's better, of course, but we're still falling all over each other." Quirking an eyebrow, she says, "At least we've got the dog out from under foot."

"Not today you don't." Pixie's silken head is atop my foot; we detoured to Ava's on our walk.

"I'll make an exception, since he's with you and Thelma's not here to beg to keep him again."

I knew when I left Pixie behind that Thelma wouldn't want to give him back. "Would you ever consider getting the children a dog?"

"No." The reply comes promptly. "We have enough mouths to feed."

"But surely you're making enough now, between you and Max." Stokowski is going to pay handsomely for Renate's dresses. I'm not sure she realizes how much, but he didn't blink an eye at the amount I named.

"That has nothing to do with it." Ava sits down with a thump, addressing herself to her coffee with the same energy she throws at everything. "I have more than enough to take care of in this house."

It is an oblique criticism: do I have enough to do? Ava's constant, simmering anger and Max's many projects make me embarrassed of my languor. Even Pearl has more occupation than I do. "Harry's refugee work has gotten busier," I tell her. "His friend in Berlin is sending someone else through this month, but he's going to Boston."

"It's like you're running a hotel over there." She takes a sip of coffee, shaking her head. "I don't understand what he's doing, exactly."

I explain Leo's efforts first, trying to get Jews and other prominent targets out from under the noses of the Nazi government. "We often do provide a bed for a few days, depending on their destination," I say, "but Harry's work is mostly financial. He's convinced several friends to assist with funding visas and the other necessary paperwork, and depending on the skills of the refugees, he helps find them work and sponsors in America."

She listens intently. "Not all of them are as easy as the Adlers, I assume?"

"Not all." I think how fortunate we are to have been able to help them. "I'm so grateful to Max."

"Why?" Ava's brow wrinkles; it must have seemed like an odd change of topic.

"Because of the way he stepped up and took over the clinic when we went away last year."

Her expression clears. "And has kept firm hold of it ever since. You'll be lucky if you ever get it back."

"I don't want it back," I tell her. "All I ever wanted was to be a wife and mother. I started the clinic because I thought I needed to be more. I looked at my friends"—I glance at her—"and even you, Ava, and I felt like I wasn't doing enough. The clinic was to prove to myself that I was capable of creating something." My cheeks grow warm. "But I never was interested, not the way Max is. And I should be, if I'm in charge." I fold my hands. "I'll stay on the board, of course. Our name will always be a help, but the clinic won't need much in the way of outside money, because of Irene."

I have already explained Harry's deal with the devil, and while Ava respects him for it, she rightfully doesn't trust Irene Warriner enough to ask her the time of day.

"What will you do?" she asks, unable to imagine a life of anything less than constant effort—though that has never been my life, and she knows it.

"I'll assist Harry. He has this now, and I want to do everything I can to help him."

Ava

We've no sooner returned from mass than a voice calls through the open door to the basement. "I heard a rumor that a man can get a free lunch in this house."

"Sarge!" Max looks up from building sandwiches. "Come on in and bring the tribe."

Rosaleen files in with four kids in size order: a boy Thelma's age, two girls of around six and seven, and a small, sturdy boy who is the mirror image of his father. My formerly shy daughter immediately sweeps the girls aside. Toby and George look skeptically at the older boy, then beckon him into their corner. Only the littlest one remains, but rather than stay with his mother or go to Pearl, who offers her lap, he stomps determinedly after the boys.

"There's no telling that one," Rosaleen says. "He's his own man, and he's not yet four."

"Some of them are like that." Toby and George were always like that, but they had each other, which made them even more dangerous.

Max distributes sandwiches and bottles of cold root beer. The usual bowls of salads line the center of the table. There are too many of us to sit down together, so the boys take their lunches to the yard and Thelma and the girls sit on the landing near the open door.

The men are talking about work and I'm telling Rosaleen about the challenge of making stage dresses for Renate when she interrupts.

"I'm sorry, but we've had some news." She glances shyly at her husband. "Pat's got his transfer."

"Congratulations!" Max slaps him on the back. "You're a man who gets what he wants, Pat."

His naturally high color increases until he's glowing like a ham. "I'll miss the boys at the station," he says, "but it's better for Rose and the kiddies. And I can't say I'll mind a bit of green space myself."

"So you'll be moving." Max looks at Rosaleen. "Are you waiting until after the little one is born?"

"We want to do it as soon as possible," she says, "so Pat doesn't have to travel back and forth. And I'd like to get the new place in order before I get any bigger."

Max nods and I can tell from his suddenly gleeful face that he's about to turn everything upside down. "So you'll be giving up the house, then. Do you know if the landlord's started looking for new tenants?"

"You promised you wouldn't try to change us."

My words drop into the silence of our darkened bedroom; from upstairs, I hear the boys' soft snores and hope that sharp-eared Pearl is also asleep.

"I'm not trying to change anything." Max's voice is right in my ear. "I only suggested—"

"That we give up this house." I thump onto my side to face him, and the mattress groans at such furious movement. I freeze until I'm sure we haven't woken anyone. "First a telephone and then you needed a car. This is our *home*."

"It's a house." His breath tickles. "A small house. And you said—"

"That I liked someone else's house. It doesn't mean I want to live in it. This is *ours*." I will not have this conversation; if I do, he will somehow make me agree with him. "We belong here."

Beneath the covers, his hand comes to rest on my hip. "Do I belong here?"

"Of course." I tilt back out of range; serious discussion is impossible when he's touching me.

The hand follows, the fingers curving around my bottom. "Because it's damned inconvenient to have to wait to touch you until a half-dozen other people are fast asleep." He kisses my nose. "I'm staggering tired by morning. Have pity."

I roll to the edge of the bed, holding fast to the mattress to keep from falling. "Then go to sleep. I'm not talking about this."

27

Claire

"Can you come over?"

The shock of my sister's voice on the telephone at eight in the morning is enough to send me back to bed. "Of course," I say, when I am able. "What's wrong?"

"I need to talk," she says curtly and puts down the phone.

Katie is running the sweeper and has other chores, so I wrangle Teddy into suitable clothes and we are there within the hour. The children are at school, but Teddy will play nicely in the backyard while we sit and talk. Or at least I hope he will.

Ava is in the kitchen with fabric spread all over the table, her mouth bristling with pins and an equal amount of bristle emanating from her.

"I thought you weren't working at home anymore?" I kiss her cheek and carry Teddy past, opening the back door. "Play out here for a few minutes, okay?"

"Why?" He stands with his legs wide apart, a metal car in each hand. "Want the floor."

"Yard, Teddy."

"Let him," comes Ava's voice. "It's easier than checking on him."

Victorious, Teddy goes to the far end of the room to play with his cars, and I pour two cups of coffee and join her at the table. "Now, what is it?"

She spits pins into her palm, her lips a narrow line. "Max wants to move."

Oh. This has been coming since he asked for a raise, and I've known she would react this way. "I'm sure you can put him off," I say. "It's just a suggestion."

"It's not." She takes a sip of coffee, wrinkles her nose. "He's found a house."

"What?" I hadn't expected him to move this quickly; he knows as well as I do that Ava is a mule when it comes to change. "How did he manage that?"

My sister explains about the police officer involved in Toby's near-arrest, the courtesy dinner, and their return invitation. "I didn't say I wanted to move, though," she protests. "And now the sergeant's been transferred and they'll be giving up this perfectly wonderful house."

I curl my hands around my cup; though the stove was lit to make the coffee, the room is chilly. "If it's perfectly wonderful, why not take it?"

Her face crumples for a moment, then she gets control of herself. "Because it's too soon," she says firmly. "We've only been here a few years. We're fine. We don't *need* a bigger house."

They are tripping over each other in this house is what I want to tell her—even with Dan away, it's too crowded. Then it hits me. "When was the last time you heard from Dan?"

"A week or so ago, from Texas." She pushes her cup away and goes back to pinning the scarlet satin bodice pieces. Her hands are shaking. "That's a long ways away."

Ava may have wanted me to come over to talk, but she's never one to start a sensitive conversation, or even to participate once it's started. I know why she's resistant to the move, aside from her natural contrariness: she doesn't want Dan to return and find them gone.

"He would come to us if you weren't here," I tell her. "Or even to George Howe's office, if it was daytime. He'd have no problem finding you."

She shakes her head. "I won't have my son return to an empty house. Max should understand that."

So should I, apparently. But it hadn't occurred to me that it would be so important: Dan is a level-headed boy—a man, really—whose mind wouldn't assume disaster if he found his family not at home. He would walk the few blocks to my house and I, or whoever answered the door, would give him the new address and that would be that.

"Did he say when he'd be back?" I want to hug her or take her hand, but I don't dare—Ava accepts affection on her own terms and only on her own terms.

"No." She worries her lower lip between her teeth. "Claire…it's silly, I know, but what if he doesn't *come* back?"

Pins scatter as I reach over and embrace her, whether she likes it or not. *This* is what she's been worrying about? "Of course, he'll come back!" I tell her. "He's your son."

She is stiff in my arms. "Jake was Mama's son, too."

Understanding dawns.

"Jake was mad at Mama when he left, for insisting he go back underground." Our brother had run away, leaving Mama alone with her daughters to support. For two decades, we'd assumed he was lost or dead, until he reappeared last year and wreaked havoc on our lives. "He had his reasons, whether they were good or not. Dan would never do that."

"And Margit disappeared, too." Her voice is almost inaudible. "People leave this family, Claire. What if my son is one of them?"

Our sister Margit had joined the church, a closed order of nuns, and other than a few letters before she took her final vows, she might as well have vanished off the face of the earth. I wrote to her when Mama died, and again after Daniel, to give her Ava's address in the city, but I never got a response.

"He won't be," is all I can tell her, because I am certain, as I am certain of very few things, that Dan will return.

Ava

I don't go to the shop after Claire leaves; I am too shaken by the events of the last two days to allow myself to be seen. When Rosaleen said they were moving, my immediate thought was that their house would be available, but I hadn't expected Max to come out with it and get all the kids excited about the prospect of moving.

We can't move. Dan's absence is the most important part of my refusal, but it's not only that. We can't possibly have the money for a house, and even if Max scrapes it together from somewhere—though I can't imagine how he'd manage, after buying that car in the spring—we'd need to borrow a truck or cart from Harry, and pay the drivers. There wouldn't be enough furniture, and Claire's attic has very little left that wouldn't look ridiculous in our home.

It's too much. Marrying Max has brought far more changes to our lives than I had anticipated; if I'd known how stressful it would be, I might have kept our relationship as it was, and made do with the occasional afternoon and more yearning than is probably healthy for people our age.

Claire had been surprisingly comforting. I often think of her as my little sister, or the flighty woman she seemed to be when we reconnected at Mama's funeral, but she's become a woman of substance over the last few years, able to give not just Harry's money, but herself. I will probably never be able to tell her how I appreciate the soft landing she's given us in this still-strange world.

"Changing our lives like this—going along with all these changes Max wants—it's like a betrayal," I told her. "Daniel couldn't give us any of those things." He sacrificed himself for his family, I wanted to add, but Claire knew that.

"Do you think he'd want you no better off than you were?" Claire took my hand, absently stroking it. "Daniel wanted the best for you and the children. The world just wasn't in a place where he could give it to you."

"But Max..." I didn't know how to articulate the stranded emotions knotted in my chest.

She laced her fingers with mine. "Max also wants the best for you. His best is simply different, because he is different." Her head tilted, soft blonde hair falling smoothly along the curve of her jawline. "Do you think Daniel wouldn't want you to be happy?"

"I don't even know if I *am* happy." I wanted to avoid discussion of my dead husband's feelings. "Everything is so raw, all the time. I'm angry and impatient with everyone—I don't know what's going on."

Claire laughed softly. "You've been angry and impatient since the cradle, sister mine. You relaxed your guard for a while and change crept in and you're mad because you didn't see it coming."

I push the scarlet fabric to one side before I spoil it. Marriage is a close-fitting garment, but unlike the satin bodice of Renate's gown, the seams are not tested until the garment is in use; there are no muslins or alterations for marriage. I pause, thinking of our overnight trip to Atlantic City. We'd had a fitting, anyway. That sorted out physical matters, but the emotional fit can take years. Daniel and I had known each other since we were babies and we struggled within its confines on a variety of matters, right up until the end.

But that hadn't mattered, either; we were buttoned into that snugly tailored garment, and we learned how to work together.

With Max it is different. If I think about it, I'm getting off easy. In a way completely opposite to Daniel, he allows me to have things my way most of the time. Not having been married before, living in rented rooms or with friends, he is less attached to structure than I am; when he digs in his heels, it is for what he considers good reason.

There's nothing wrong with his suggestion, only the timing is bad. The house on Camac Street is the stuff of dreams, as far as I'm concerned. And I love my house; I am happy here; it houses not just my family, but my independence. But it's not big enough for a family of eight, especially when Max will surely want to entertain beyond an informal dinner in the kitchen. And I will have to learn to deal with that. Learning to be a doctor's wife might be easier if the house looked a bit more appropriate to his circumstances.

But I will not consider moving again, no matter how often I think about that spacious kitchen, those sunny bedrooms, until Dan is home. Perhaps what I need to do is to sit Max down, when he gets in from work, and explain that to him.

Claire

Leo's most recent cable read, "*Please retrieve parcel, arriving 1 p.m., 28 September, NY pier 90.*" We had planned on making the trip together, possibly going up the evening before to take in a show before picking up his latest refugee, but one of us hadn't checked the engagement diary and Harry has an appointment on that date for a round of tests to confirm that his ulcer is improving.

"You can't reschedule your appointment," I tell him. "We need to know that you're doing better. And I'm perfectly capable of taking the train to New York without an escort."

His forehead creases. "But what about—"

"The parcel?" I interrupt. "We've had a half dozen people pass through here by now. I think I can be trusted to transport one home." Leo never explained why this one had to be picked up personally. It wasn't the sort of conversation to be carried out by cable; it is easier simply to do as he asks.

"I don't like it." Harry looks resigned. "You shouldn't have to do this."

My brows lift. "No one should have to do this. They shouldn't be having to flee their homes because a madman has taken over their government." I snuggle against him on the sofa. "If you behave nicely, I'll even let you drop me off at the station tomorrow before your appointment."

"All right," he grumbles. "But be sure to call if there are any complications."

"I will," I promise. "But I'm sure everything will be fine. Now give me a kiss and stop fussing, or I'll tell your mother you're being a bad patient."

He looks horrified. "Please, not that!"

The train was late, some obstruction on the tracks in northern New Jersey keeping us in place for almost an hour. When I alight in Penn Station, I have to rush through the crowds to the Thirty-Fourth Street doors. There was, as always, a rank of taxis at the curb, but there was also a line of people pushing to get into them.

Finally, a cab slews in to the curb and a station employee opens the door for me.

"Where to?" the cabbie asks around his cigar.

"Pier 90," I tell him. "As quickly as you can." Leo asked that we pick up the parcel at one, and it was already half past.

"You got it." The cab pulls into traffic, inching forward, turning west toward the Hudson.

The New York Passenger Ship Terminal extends from West Forty-Sixth to West Fifty-Fourth Streets. We came though there in June when we returned from France, but there was so much bedlam around *Normandie*'s arrival that I paid little attention to the changes made to the old Chelsea Piers by the U.S. Corps of Engineers.

People pass in and out so constantly that the enormous doors never quite close. Dodging an overloaded luggage cart pushed by a diminutive redcap, I enter the terminal and am greeted by a large, open space with a soaring ceiling. The walls are decorated with murals depicting scenes from the city's long history. The floor is marble, so everyone's steps are magnified. In the center of the space is a large clock with rows of benches around it. This is where I hope to find our parcel.

When a ship arrives, it docks at the pier, and the passengers disembark via gangplank. Once they reach the pier, they are met by immigration officials and customs agents. After they have cleared immigration and customs, they are free to leave or come to the waiting room.

I hurry over to the benches, looking for someone as obviously European as Herr Gittings or as hunted as the Adlers. No one matches either description, and I circle the area. How am I supposed to find this person without a name, or even a gender?

Perhaps the passenger is slow, or elderly. Perhaps they are dealing with their immigration paperwork, which in these cases is often complicated. If Leo sent a cable, they made it onto the ship; I will find them eventually, or they will find me.

My feet hurt. I take a seat near the end of a bench, and commence to wait.

It occurs to me, after a quarter hour, that perhaps they traveled first class. The first class waiting room is even more luxurious than the main waiting room, with plush carpets, comfortable chairs, and a refreshment bar. I explain my predicament to the porter at the door, and he allows me to take a quick circuit of the room. No one appears to be anxiously waiting, so I return to the main hall.

The moment I walk through the doors, I see an older woman, stocky and stern-faced, in a drab tweed suit. In one hand, she holds a square of cardboard with my last name.

I hurry to her. "I'm Claire Warriner."

Her face clears. Still stern but no longer worried, she folds the sign and tucks it into her bag. "I was afraid we had missed you," she says. "Immigration, it took so long."

"You're here now, I say, doing my best to comfort though this woman hardly seems the sort to need it. For that matter, she doesn't seem the sort to need an escort. "Welcome."

She stops a moment, blinks. "You are not here for me, Mrs. Warriner. It's my charge."

"Your charge?" My head is beginning to ache. I don't have the energy for guessing games.

The woman turns, gesturing for me to follow. "Mr. Vollmer did not explain?"

"He did not," I say. "His cable only said to meet someone here."

We stop at a bench. On it are seated a man and three children, luggage stacked at their feet. Another child, no more than four, rides a suitcase like a rocking horse.

"Sofie," she says. "I have found Mr. Vollmer's friend."

One of the older children stands and detaches herself from the others. She's small and fine-boned, with long brown braids and gold-rimmed spectacles. A stuffed bear is tucked under one arm. Her face is shuttered, closed off. She does not meet my eyes.

I know that expression. She is grieving something, and deeply.

"Sofie?" I repeat. So it's the girl, and not this woman and her family?

"She is Mr. Vollmer's niece," the woman says. "He entrusted her to us, to get her as far as New York. Now you are here, and she is your problem. We must take a train to Chicago to meet my brother." She bends down, puts a hand on the child's shoulder. "Sofie, you will go with Mrs. Warriner now. She is your uncle's friend. She will take care of you."

The girl nods silently. Her eyes brim with tears, but she blinks them back. Bending her knees, she picks up a small suitcase. "Danke, Frau Schiller. Herr Schiller."

A child. With no warning or preparation, Leo Vollmer has sent us a child. I take a deep breath. It is not the girl's fault.

"Hello, Sofie," I say gently. "Do you speak English?"

"Ja," she says, her quiet voice nearly inaudible in the echoing hall. "A little."

I squat before her, watching the Schiller family's departure from the corner of my eye. "Are you hungry?"

She shakes her head. "Nein."

"Well, I am." I also need to sit down and figure out my next move, which I can't do in this place. I had assumed I would be meeting an adult, not a ten-year-old girl. "Let's go somewhere close by. Maybe you would like some ice cream?"

She is silent, but she's a ten-year-old girl. She's not going to refuse ice cream.

I hold out my hand. "May I carry your bag?"

Another head shake.

"Well, then, hold on to me and let's get out of here." The welcome sensation of a child's hand in mine, and the even more welcome breeze on my flushed face. I look down. Behind her glasses, Sofie's blue eyes are wide, taking in the noise and furor of the city.

A taxi stops for us, and Sofie gets in, her eyes darting back as if to make certain I have not abandoned her. I slide onto the cushioned seat beside her, addressing the driver. "Louis Sherry, please."

As the cab makes its way through the crowded streets, Sofie's face is glued to the window. I am often disoriented by the scope of the city; I can't imagine how it feels to a child.

Inside Sherry's, I ask for a quiet table away from the boisterous families and courting couples, and we are placed along a wall toward the back of the restaurant, well away from the velvet booths and crystal chandeliers of the main seating area.

"That's better," I say, as the waitress presents us with menus. "A little quiet, so we can get acquainted."

Sofie glances at the menu and places it back on the table. "I am not hungry."

"Not even for ice cream?" I wheedle. "How about a root beer float?"

"Nein." The bear is on her lap, while the suitcase sits alongside her chair, partly hidden by the tablecloth; when I suggested checking it, she grew visibly upset.

I exhale through my nose. She's not making this easy. "Well, I'm having tea and a dish of ice cream, and unless you want something else, I'm going to order you a root beer float. You can eat it, or you can let it go to waste."

As the words leave my lips, I realize that I sound like my sister. And maybe I need to. Maybe Ava can help me get through to this child.

"What did your uncle tell you before you left?" I can't believe that Leo would send a child across the ocean with no warning.

Sofie shakes her head, a gesture I've already come to dislike. "Only that I had to go, and that you would keep me." She bites her lip. "Frau Schiller, she said I must be good or you would put me in a home for orphans."

Keep her! I put that alarming thought aside for a moment. "Frau Schiller is wrong," I tell her firmly. "I would prefer that you be good, but we won't put you out. Your uncle is a friend, and if he wants you to stay with us, then that is what we will do."

She visibly relaxes, and when our ice cream is delivered to the table—fresh strawberry with whipped cream for me, and a root beer float in a tall frosted glass for her—she immediately picks the maraschino cherry from the top and pops it in her mouth.

"Cherries are my favorite, too," I confide. When our waitress passes again, I hold up a discreet finger and mouth, "More cherries."

Her eyes light with comprehension, and she hurries away, returning with a cut glass bowl of maraschino cherries. "I'm sorry," she says. "I forgot to bring these to go with your root beer."

Sofie actually smiles, then presses her lips together as if alarmed by her loss of control. "You first."

"All right." I pick one up by the stem, pulling it loose with my teeth. The bright, artificial flavor fills my mouth. "Yum."

As the bowl of cherries diminishes, Sofie softens but becomes no more communicative. She looks around the restaurant, paying particular attention to the families. Does she have a family, other than Leo? I want to ask, but something in her tight little face makes me hold back. She will crack, at some point, but for her sake I do not want it to be in a public place.

"Would you like to stay the night in New York?" I ask. "I can get a hotel room for us. Otherwise we'll have to take the train to Philadelphia and we won't get in until after dark."

"Is that where you live?" She swallows the last cherry and licks her red-stained lips.

"It is." I would love to stay over, even though it would mean buying a few things. The thought of facing another train ride makes me wilt. Choosing to stay would mean spending the night with this strange, wordless child, which sways my mind in the other direction.

Sofie sucks up the last of her root beer through the straw. "Is that where I will stay?"

"Yes, of course." Has the poor thing been worrying about what we would do with her? What has she been told about us? Or worse—what hasn't she been told? The child probably spent the better part of a week worrying about where, and to whom, she's being sent.

"I would like the train, please." She stands, as if ready to leave now.

"Sit down, dear. I have to pay the check." I look at her frankly across the table. "Did Leo tell you anything about us?"

She shakes her head. "It was very sudden." Twisting her fingers together, she adds, "He came to get me at school and said I must go away."

Something must be very wrong. I hope there is a way for Harry to reach him—calling Berlin is difficult, and it is unlikely they would be able to discuss the situation with any clarity.

"I'm glad he chose to trust us with you," I tell her, and find that it's the truth. She will be an unexpected, possibly uncomfortable addition to the household, but that's happened before. No child in my orbit will ever be unsafe.

"If you like, you can call me Aunt Claire. My husband will be your Uncle Harry. He has known Leo since they were in college together." Her gaze is fixed on me, attentive. "We have a little boy named Teddy, who will be four on Christmas Day."

"Do you love him?"

"So very much! And you will love him too." It occurs to me that there will be other people who will help us care for her. "You'll have cousins, as well. My sister lives nearby, and she has six children. One is a girl very near your age."

"I'm ten," Sofie says. "Is she ten?"

"Thelma is nine," I say, rapidly calculating. "But that's close enough, and it will be good to have a friend your age when you start school."

I pay the check and we make our way back to Pennsylvania station. After purchasing our tickets, I leave the girl with her suitcase and slip into a telephone booth to call home.

"Mr. Warriner is out with Mr. Adler," Katie says. "Are you coming home, ma'am?"

I confirm that I am, and that the guest room is ready to receive another visitor.

"It's ready. I made up the bed this afternoon. Mr. Gittings, he left it tidy." She pauses. "Who is it this time?"

I've never looked at our strange situation from Katie's point of view: a constant stream of visitors, none of whose first language is English, usually arriving with next to no luggage.

"A little girl," I tell her. "And this one is staying."

28

Ava

The kids settle in the living room after supper, as requested. Seeing five kids instead of six hurts my heart and I almost reach out to tell Max that I've changed my mind, he shouldn't tell them.

"Is it *Gangbusters*?" Toby asks.

"I want *The Shadow*," his brother says, kicking the leg of the sofa until I glare at him to stop.

Instead of turning on the radio, Max comes to stand in front of the fireplace, hands locked behind his back. He's in shirt sleeves, his tie long discarded, and somehow his hair has become rumpled simply by walking up the stairs. I want to tidy him, the way I would Toby or George, but it wouldn't last, and I shouldn't treat him like one of my boys.

"Remember at Sunday lunch, when Sergeant O'Donnell talked about moving?" he begins. My chest tightens and I remind myself to breathe.

"When Mama got so mad?" George asks. Toby elbows him, sensitive about anything concerning the sergeant.

"Yes," I say. They deserve my honesty—as does my husband. "And I'm still a little upset, but it was mainly because I was surprised." I glance at Max; he knows better than to do that again. "We've talked about it since then and we want to know, what would you all think about moving?"

"Where?"

"When?"

"Would I have my own room?"

"Can we get a dog?"

The questions come thick and fast until Max holds up a hand to cut them off. "The sergeant's house is on Camac street," he says. "That's right on the other side of Broad. Nobody gets their own room, but the bedrooms will be bigger." He grins. "That means your Mama and I will finally get some privacy."

Thelma opens her mouth and I cut her off. "You can visit Pixie anytime you want, but we're not getting a dog."

"When would we move?" Pearl sits in a corner of the sofa. Grace is in her lap, chewing a stand of wooden beads that Esther gave me.

I join Max by the fireplace. "That's what I was upset about. I don't mind the idea of moving—I love this house, but even I can see that it's too small for us. But I don't want to move before your brother comes home."

There's more to it than that, but I choose not to think about it right now; Dan being gone is enough of a reason to push back against the biggest change Max has suggested to date.

"But he'd know to go to Aunt's." Toby shrugs, trusting his brother to figure it out. "If he came home on a Friday, he'd probably go there first."

"That's true." I take a deep breath and reveal the compromise that kept us up talking half the night. "What we've decided is that we'll do it after the Christmas holidays. If Dan comes home before then, we'll move it up."

Max cuts in. "We'll rent the house starting next month. The O'Donnells have been in there for six years. You all know what a house full of kids can do. This will give us plenty of time to clean and paint and make any changes we want before we move in and destroy it all over again."

They take in the news in relative silence until Pearl says, with a dreamlike smile, "No more dividers. Thelma, we can close our door and not hear the boys."

She claps her hands. "Will there be a place for me to dance?"

Max reaches forward and ruffles her hair. "Is there any place you *won't* dance, sweetheart?"

We tell them more about the house—four bedrooms, a real dining room, a kitchen large enough to eat in. Radiator heat. A small backyard, but big enough for a bit of a garden.

I think about the built-in dish cupboard, the white enamel sink with its attached drainboard. The window over the sink that looks out into the yard. *Two* bathrooms.

"Could I get chickens again?" Pearl asks. "I kind of miss them."

"I miss the fresh eggs." I didn't pay close enough attention to the yard, so I don't want to get her hopes up. "We'll see. We wouldn't want to get them until spring anyway."

The conversation goes more smoothly than I expected. Pearl is pleased with the prospect of having more space, and the boys only care that they will be in easy walking distance to the firehouse and the garage. I am the only sticking point, but when I came home from Claire's and dragged Max out for a walk to explain myself, he completely understood, making me wish I had trusted him enough to speak in the first place.

"Is that all?" Toby asks, when we fall silent. "Can we listen to *Gangbusters* now?"

"Go on, then." Max clicks on the radio, and he and I go out to the front step. "We'll be paying rent for two months before we move," he says. "That's not long, and it'll give us time to do the work without having to go flat out, like we did with the shop."

Or like we did before we moved into this house. Claire volunteered to help, along with Katie and Esther, and it took days to get the place in order.

"I can live with that," I say. "So long as it won't put us in a hole, paying two rents."

Max looks around the empty street, then back at the partly-open door before kissing me soundly. "You barely allow me to pay my way, woman. Let me do this." He gives me a sideways smile. "And if the prodigal son comes home before the new year, he can jump right in to help with the painting and we'll move all the sooner."

Claire

The rain began outside of Princeton and has kept up steadily ever since, streaking the glass and making the compartment feel chilly, although the heat, which fogs the windows on the inside, has kept us warm enough.

"There'll be a car," I tell Sofie. "So we won't get very wet."

She regards me silently, and I feel silly for worrying about the weather.

Harry meets us on the platform, and although Katie has warned him, he can't hide his shock at the sight of the girl at my side. "Darling." He kisses my cheek and quickly turns his attention to Sofie. "Guten tag, Sofie. That looks heavy. May I carry it for you?"

"I will manage," she says precisely, and shoves the bear at him. "You may carry this. It's for you anyway."

He takes the bear. "What do you mean it's for me?"

"It's for you," she repeats. "Uncle bought it to carry a letter. He said no one would look at a child's toy." She glances at it with disdain. "You have a little boy. Give it to him."

"I'll do that."

As we leave, Harry puts up his umbrella, holding it over our heads. Once Hedges sees us emerge from the station, he jumps out of the Packard with a second umbrella. Sofie walks past both of them, letting the rain soak her braids and her plaid dress.

I breathe a sigh of relief as I get into the car. It feels like days have elapsed since Hedges dropped me off this morning. I swallow a yawn and wonder how soon I can politely go to bed. I can't leave Harry alone with her, but the day—and Sofie, if I'm honest—has exhausted me.

When we reach the house, Katie is there to open the door and welcome us. There is a flicker of a reaction from Sofie when Pixie scrambles into the hall, but then the veil drops and she says, "I am very tired. Is there a place where I may sleep in this house?"

Katie takes in the situation. "I have a room made up for you, Miss Sofie. Why don't you follow me?" As they disappear up the stairs, she asks, "Would you like a glass of warm milk or a cookie before bed?"

"She's in good hands," Harry says.

I release the yawn I've been holding back. "I wish someone would offer me warm milk or a cookie."

"How about a martini?" He puts his arms loosely around me and I rest against his chest, thinking I could fall asleep standing up, given the opportunity.

"I can't." I yawn again. "But I'm not going to be able to sleep until I know what that bear has to say."

It is a perfectly normal Steiff teddy bear, its shaggy hair the color of wet sand. It wears a spotted bow around its neck. Harry turns it over in his hands, looking for something obvious, but the bear is relatively new and shows no sign of being tampered with.

"Wait," he says, removing the bow. "There. Do you have a pair of scissors?"

I fetch a pair from the desk in my sitting room, and he neatly slices open a repaired seam on the back of the bear's neck. "Ava will be able to fix that, won't she?"

"You did such a tidy job, even I can fix it."

I look over his shoulder as he reaches into the bear's kapok stuffing and retrieves a tightly folded square of paper. He opens it, lets out a hard breath, and looks at me. "Let's sit down for this. You might reconsider your martini after what he has to say."

My dear friend,

Let me first apologize for the secrecy surrounding this parcel, the most precious one I shall ever send into your capable hands.

Sofie is my sister's child. Etta and her husband, Hans Mehrle, were killed in a car accident over a year ago. At first she lived with Hans's parents, but they are elderly and in ill health and asked me to take her.

She is a wonderful girl, smart and funny and as loving as my sister. But my situation here is growing more tenuous by the day, and even if I gave up my work tomorrow, enough damage has been done that I could be arrested at any time. I will not have this child endangered because of me. She has been through enough in her short life.

Why am I sending her to you instead of asking one of my children to take her in? My daughters already have children and do not wish to add to their families. My son is now engaged, and while he and his soon-to-be wife have offered to adopt her, Manfred is not a suitable choice for reasons we have discussed.

Most importantly, I want her out of Germany before war is declared, as I fear is inevitable.

This journey across the ocean and into your lives will be a disruption for all concerned, but I have seen your love for your boy, and I know that you will give her the home she deserves. Perhaps things will change. Perhaps madness will recede like a tide and our world will become sane again, and safe for little girls. That time is not this time.

For our deep friendship, for the man I know you are, I trust you to do what is right for my Sofie.

Leo

P.S. I will write for as long as I am able. If you cease to hear from me, assume the worst, and comfort her.

Harry's voice trails off, and he drops the letter on the table. "Good God."

"That poor child." To lose her parents, and then her grandparents, and now Leo, in quick succession. No wonder she's so prickly. "Of course we'll give her a home."

"You don't mind?" Harry's eyes are damp; he is thinking either of his friend in danger, or Sofie's pitiable situation.

"Of course not." I turn his face toward me, feeling the roughness of stubble against my fingertips. "We wanted children. It seems to be our lot that we will get none of them by conventional means." Leaning over, I kiss him soundly. "That doesn't mean we love them any less."

"And it means I love you more." He draws me close and I take comfort from his even breathing, his return to health. From the life we have built together to the people whose lives we have touched and who have touched ours in return.

"Let's go to bed."

Pearl

We've seen all the nearby movies, so instead Tommy and I go out for ice cream and then a walk. We could have taken the trolley to one of the neighborhood theaters, but I'd rather be out in the air than packed in the streetcar; if we're going to be that close, I'd prefer a dark theater.

This, I think, will give us a chance to talk. My knowledge of Tommy has been filtered through Dan, so while I know about his family and what he likes and doesn't like about his job, I don't know him, not in the way I know my girlfriends.

Maybe boys don't share the same way. Daddy was quiet, but he and Mama knew each other for so long that maybe there was no need for conversation. I hope that's how it was, anyway, because if she was as frustrated by his silence as I am with Tommy's, marriage must have felt like a long haul sometimes.

Dr. Max is full of chat—purposeful if it's asked for, but otherwise just gentle teasing or questions about school or stories about things that happened at the clinic. I think about this as Tommy and I walk, hand in hand, in silence, through Rittenhouse Square.

He talked to Dan. They were always laughing and joshing and carrying on conversations that were like a secret language to the rest of us, because we weren't with them all the time. I wonder where that Tommy went? We walk, and inside my head I'm screaming, *Talk to me! Don't make me do all the work.* But I can't bring myself to say it.

"Nice evening," I finally offer.

He looks at me. His brown eyes are kind; there is someone in there, if I could reach him. "It is. Not too hot."

The weather dealt with, another canyon yawns before me. Since we have no fixed destination, I suggest one. "Do you know where Camac Street is?"

Stopping for a moment to think, he nods. "Yeah. It's right off Pine Street."

"Let's walk down there, then." I tell him that we will be moving there by the end of the year, and how Mama's been resisting because Dan isn't back yet.

"She doesn't want him to come home and find us gone." I understand why she's upset, but even Dandy would be in favor of this move. If he's enough of a grown man to go kiting around the country on his lonesome, then he's smart enough to go ask Aunt where we are.

"You get any cards from him recently?" His tone is casual, but I've come to understand that Dan's absence hurts him in almost the same way it hurts me.

"Not for a while." We pause at the corner of Broad Street, waiting for traffic to pass. I look left, up the street toward City Hall, to the clock tower that is the highest point in Philadelphia. The hour is visible, if I squint; it's too early for the clock to be lit.

"Not far now." Tommy takes my hand again, and something warms in my stomach. His hands are hard from work. They are men's hands, even though he is still a boy. But what happened to Hazel reminds me that boys and girls can do adult things and end up in adult messes.

I leave my hand in his, and quiet the fluttering in my middle. "There it is."

We turn onto the street, and I look around curiously at what will be our new home. It's almost as narrow as Ringgold Place, but it looks wider because there are no trucks and piles of building supplies. All these houses are finished, and lived in, by the look of them. Partway down, where the block is bisected by another tiny street, a cluster of girls is jumping rope. I recognize one of the O'Donnell daughters, and head for the group.

"Hey, Pearl!" Brigid doesn't stop jumping. The other girls count her steps aloud. "You moving into our house?"

"It looks like it," I say. "Which one is it?"

She turns in a circle, still skipping, and nods her head toward a house with a blue door. "That one. My mom's home, if you want to knock."

"No, that's okay. I just wanted to see it."

Brigid begins hopping on one foot. "That your boyfriend?"

I continue looking at the house. Then I look at the ground. I look at anything other than Tommy, who is standing there, with his hands in his pockets, apparently waiting for my reply along with Brigid.

"Well?" She trips over her rope. "Shoot. How many was that?"

"Three hundred and six," one of the girls says. "I beat you."

Brigid O'Donnell tosses her head. "It's not my fault. I was asking about Pearl's boyfriend."

"What are you, eight?" I ask. "You shouldn't be worrying about boyfriends yet."

"I'll want one sooner or later," she says, coiling her rope in one hand. "You're next, Nancy."

I drift away from them, going to study the house with the blue door. It has two big windows on the ground floor—wonderful light to read by. I want to stand on tiptoe and look in, but I restrain myself. I'll see inside soon enough, even if we don't move in until after Christmas.

"So this is where you'll be living?" Tommy catches up and tries to take my hand again, but I move away, pretending to look at the flowers planted in front of the house next door.

"Eventually." I keep walking, looking at the tidy stoops and pots of geraniums, until I come out on Pine Street. "Like I said, probably not until the new year."

"Tell your mother if she needs help with the move, or painting and stuff like that, I'm glad to do it."

His offer makes me feel more charitable. "Thanks, I will. Dr. Max said he wants to have it painted before we move in."

"Then I'm your man." He takes my hand again, firmly, and squeezes it. "What was that, back there?" he asks. "You couldn't say I was your boyfriend?"

I turn on him. "Why did you wait for me to say it? You could have just as easily said yes, instead of leaving it to me. I don't know if we're boyfriend and girlfriend or not."

He blinks, startled by my rush of words. "I thought we were."

"Well, maybe I'm not so sure." I start walking again, and he follows. "It's not like you've ever said it. Having a conversation with you is like pulling teeth."

All of my upset and confusion from the last months comes out, directed squarely at him.

"So I don't talk much." He shrugs, and kicks a stone into the gutter: a quick, boyish motion which reminds me that although he is supporting his family, he is only seventeen. "You know what I'm like."

"You talked to Dan." Again, I feel like a replacement for my brother, and I turn away. "All we have in common is him. I don't know why I'm wasting my time."

He stays where I left him, then runs after me, grabbing my shoulder and spinning me around. "Because I like you, Pearl." His eyes glisten—could they be tears? "I really do."

"It doesn't feel like it," I say, crossing my arms over my chest.

"What do you want?" Tommy's grip on my shoulders tightens. "Do I have to do this all the time for you to know I like you?"

He pulls me close and kisses me the way he does at the movies, during the love scenes or when it gets boring. This is definitely not boring. When his tongue slips between my lips, my knees go weak and my stomach fills with heat.

Hoots and clapping make us break apart. A bunch of boys stand on the opposite corner of Broad and Pine, grinning at us. To my horror, one of them is Toby.

"Tough it out," Tommy murmurs. "Come on."

Together we bow and curtsy to our jeering audience before turning toward home.

Softened by his kisses, I try again. "I sometimes feel like for all the time we spend together, we don't know each other very well." I swallow hard, continue. "Whenever we talk, it's usually me talking about my family or telling you what I've been reading. You never say anything in return."

"I don't read," he says. "Never saw the point. But I like listening to you talk about them." He ventures a smile. "You're cute when you're all worked up."

Never saw the point! The shock of that statement is tempered by his easy assumption that he *is* my boyfriend. Is it impossible to get everything you need from one person? Once upon a time, that's the kind of question I would have asked Mama, but these days I'm not that brave.

It's early yet. Maybe he'll come in for a while. I'm sure Toby is following us, preparing to make my life a misery. If he takes the boys to a field where they can fly their planes, that might convince Toby not to tell on me.

"You probably won't have to wait until the holidays," Tommy says suddenly.

"Why?"

"Because our boss will hold his job for six months." He swings my hand up in the air. "So he should be back before the end of October."

I'd forgotten that Dan had told me that, and I'm so happy to be reminded I reach up and kiss Tommy on the cheek. "I'm going to cross my fingers," I say, "but I'm also not going to tell my mother, just in case."

Claire

With some effort, I mend Sofie's bear and return it to her after breakfast.

"It is for your son," she says, holding it in her hands like it's a dead thing. "I do not want it."

"That's fine." I put a hand on her shoulder and steer her down the hall to the nursery. "I thought it would be nice if you gave it to Teddy."

Her expression is skeptical, but when we enter the nursery and I introduce them, he barely notices her because his eyes are fixed on the bear.

"Mine?" he asks, visibly restraining himself from reaching for it.

"Yes," she says. "I brought it for you."

He plunges forward, grabbing the bear and wrapping one arm around her legs. "Thank you!"

I sit on the carpet and pull him onto my lap. "Sofie is going to be living with us," I tell him. "She's your cousin, like Thelma."

His face crinkles. "But live here?" Thelma spent six months with us when Teddy first came, and their relationship has deep roots. I hope he learns to care as much for Sofie.

"Yes, silly boy." She folds herself neatly onto the floor. "I'll live with you."

Teddy struggles off my lap, clutching the bear, and goes to his bed, where his other animals are lined up. He chooses one—a skin pony I gave him last year—and brings it to her.

"This for you."

She takes the pony, holding it around the middle. "But it is yours."

He shakes his head. "Yours now."

When I envisioned having a daughter, I pictured someone like Thelma: blonde and sweet tempered, a living doll for me to dress up, who would grow up belonging to a life I had to marry into.

Sofie is quiet, and I know, from my own instincts and Leo's excruciating letter, that she is in mourning. Not only for her parents and her uncle, but for the life that she is likely never to have. Because of her age, she doesn't have the words to express those feelings, if she even knows what they are. I wouldn't have, at that age. I didn't realize until years later it was possible to mourn versions of your own life that did not come to pass.

"I don't know what to do with her," I say, explaining the matter to Ava in our morning telephone call.

Our newest house guest appeared promptly at half past seven that first morning, clean and neatly dressed in what appeared to be a school uniform. She greeted us, sat down at the table, thanked Katie with exquisite politeness, and dealt neatly with her eggs and toast. Offered milk, coffee, or tea, she poured herself a half cup of coffee, added milk, and stirred in two sugars.

Harry raised his eyebrows, but I shook my head behind Sofie's back. Let her have coffee if she wants it.

"Have you unpacked?" I asked.

She nodded stiffly. "Yes."

"Would you like to go out shopping later? I'm sure you'd like a few new dresses." Perhaps we could bond over shopping; that worked with most women and girls.

"Uncle purchased everything I need before I left." She took a sip of coffee.

I tried smiling. "Everything you need, but isn't there anything you want?"

She stared at me, unblinking. "Nein."

"You don't know what to do when your charm doesn't work," my sister says, laughing. "You'll have to find a different way in with this one."

"I'm grateful that she's taken to Katie, at least."

"Everyone takes to Katie." Ava's voice changes. "Max wants to know if Harry will lend us a truck for the move. Whenever it happens."

"Of course he will." I resist telling her again how happy about their new house. Although it will take her several inconvenient blocks further east, it is a bigger house, on a better block, and it's a fresh start for their marriage. Ringgold Place was right for the time, but times change, and lives change. I hope she understands this.

"That's one thing off the list, then." She pauses, uncomfortable with chatting on the telephone for what she calls no reason at all. "Thelma will stop at the house after school. Why don't you introduce her to your Sofie? Maybe they'll get along."

"That's what I'm hoping," I say. "I'm going to have to put her into school soon, and it would be nice if she had a friend."

29

Ava

When the bell jangles in the front room, I have already finished work for the day. There is little foot traffic on a Friday afternoon, when most of the Orthodox cloth merchants have closed for their Sabbath. At four, Hanne went home with Mr. Mendel, but I stayed to work on a different project, as the occasional customer has found their way to me in the off hours. I put the iron on to heat and edge around the cutting table and into the front room.

A young woman hesitates just inside the door. Her face is turned away, as if intending to leave again, but I recognize her immediately.

"Hazel."

"Mrs. Kimber." She blushes, stammering, "Mrs. Byrne, I mean. Hello."

I haven't laid eyes on Hazel since Max and Pearl drove her home, after she'd spent the night under our roof recovering from that abominable procedure. How young she seems, compared to the assured girl I'd met earlier this year. "What can I do for you?"

"I'm not certain." Her hands twist together and she sinks down on the padded bench, smoothing her skirt over her knees. Her shoes are very good quality, I notice, and she wears stockings, not ankle socks like the other girls. "I wanted to see you. To thank you."

"You did that already." I lean against the counter, watching.

"I don't think I did." Her voice is low. "I was ashamed."

And so she should be. When I realized what she'd done, my first instinct was to order Pearl never to speak to her again, but I came to my senses in time. That would have drawn them closer, and anyway, from her recent comments, Pearl is spending more time with that pretty girl named Peggy.

"I have work to do," I tell her, hoping it will make her go. Instead, her slow footsteps cross the floor and she appears in the workroom doorway.

"Can I watch?"

"Nothing to watch." I lick my finger and touch the iron. The sizzle tells me I've let it sit for too long. I switch it off again and turn my attention to the dress I plan to remake for Pearl, spreading it on the table. It is another castoff from Claire's attic. Slowly but surely, between the equipping of refugees and occasional raids for myself or my children, the bounty of that space is being emptied.

Pearl will appreciate this. Or perhaps she won't; while we have been easier, since she got Paris out of her system, there is a distance that was not there before. Whether it is ill feeling or just growing up, I can't be sure.

"What are you doing?" She comes around the table. "Why are you taking it apart?"

"I'm remaking it for Pearl," I say reluctantly. "It's as much effort or more as making one from scratch."

Claire was uncertain who this dress belonged to, but remade, it will suit my girl to a tee. Navy blue gabardine with a subtle, shadowy stripe, it has a long, paneled skirt and a bodice with leg-o-mutton sleeves. My plan is to cut it down, remake the sleeves with the excess skirt fabric, and construct several removable collars from remnants in my stash.

She strokes the fabric against the grain, then tries it the other way. "It's pretty, but why don't you buy a new dress?"

"Because we can't afford it." I assess her outfit: a short-sleeved blue silk blouse with a scalloped collar; gray and blue plaid wool skirt. Neat gold earrings and a locket on a chain. Those pricey leather shoes and seamed stockings, more suitable for a woman than a sixteen-year-old girl.

She tucks her chin. "That was thoughtless of me. I'm sorry."

"Your family's never had to skimp to give you anything." I snip a few stitches at the hem, then take hold of the skirt and rip it along the seam with a satisfying rending of cloth. The girl flinches at the sound.

"No." Her voice is soft.

I'm afraid to look at her, for fear she is crying. "If you're going to stand around, at least make yourself useful," I say roughly. "There's a broom over there. You can sweep up while I work on this."

Why am I being patient with this girl, who has done something I believe so abhorrent? Because she is in pain, and she doesn't have the skills to cope with it. She hates what she has done as much as I do, but she chose her life over the unborn life, and in a way I can't blame her.

She is a child. Pearl's age, but so sheltered that she didn't even understand the deed that got her with child. I blame her parents more than her, not to mention the boy. But boys—men—rarely pay for their transgressions.

I think of my daughter, whose first thought had been for her friend; if there been any judgment about what Hazel did, it was never visible on her face and she has never spoken to me about it. I think of Renate, and what happened to her. Rape. I will say it. Renate was raped in a German police station and forced to perform for those same men, the threat of her husband's life hanging over her head if she refused.

No wonder she wanted to end the pregnancy. Whether or not she should have told Josef is something I will not think about; no one knows a marriage better than the people inside it. Would they be able to push down the horror of what had been done to her for the sake of the child?

What Renate asked of Max—what Max did for her, because he is a doctor, and a good and caring man—I can no longer look at it in the same light, not after Hazel.

Pearl

Turning onto Ringgold Place, our shadows walk, long-legged, ahead of us in the fading light. The street is quiet, though the number of lighted windows shows how many more houses are occupied than when we moved in.

As we reach the house, I lean against the white marble step, careful not to catch my skirt on the rough brick. I'm not sure if I want him to kiss me or not.

"Movie was good," he says, leaning forward, his hand braced on the brickwork. "A little heavy on the dancing for me, but it was good."

We had seen *Top Hat* at the Stanley, with shared popcorn and a Baby Ruth bar.

"I liked it, too," I say. "Especially Ginger Rogers. Gosh she's pretty." She reminds me of a livelier, wisecracking version of Aunt.

Her singing voice isn't bad, but it's hard to listen to anyone sing after being exposed to Mrs. Adler.

"Fred Astaire is pretty slick." Tommy pretends to tap dance and almost falls backward off the curb. "But I'd hate to have to wear those monkey suits all the time."

"You'd look dashing in white tie and tails," I say, surprising myself. He would, but with his dark good looks he would be more Ramon Novarro than Fred Astaire.

He grins, returning to the step. "I'd like to see you in that feathery getup. You think your mother could knock that together?"

It is too much to hope that he'll say I'm pretty. I'll never be like Ginger Rogers, no matter what soap I use or how many lipsticks Aunt sneaks me.

Tommy shifts his weight from his left arm to his right, scrubbing his palm on his pants leg. "I guess you should get in."

"I guess." I don't move, hoping he will.

He does, but it's to look away from me at a figure coming up the street from the same direction we've just come.

The figure is tall, carrying a sack over one shoulder, a cap pushed far back on his head.

Dandy.

I duck under Tommy's arm, all thoughts of kissing forgotten. When he sees me, Dan drops the bag and I throw myself at him, crying like I'm no older than Thelma.

"Go on, now," he says, squeezing me and setting me back from him. "I'll get you all dirty. I stink like a polecat."

"I don't care." I wipe my eyes with the heel of my hand. He *does* stink.

"Me either."

Tommy has come up behind me.

Something flashes over my brother's face and he reaches out his hand, but instead Tommy pulls him into a big, thumping boys' hug. The two of them are laughing and near-crying at the same time and then they aren't—they're hugging as tightly as before, but neither of them are saying a word, and in that moment, I know two things.

My brother is home and I wouldn't change that for the world. And Tommy Marinelli will never kiss me again.

Ava

The door opens. "We're home," Pearl calls.

I don't look up from my magazine. "Does Tommy want to come in for something to eat?"

"I don't know about him," a familiar voice says, "but I'd sure like something to eat."

My chest tightens and all the blood drains from my head. Taking a shaky breath, I manage to turn my head toward the door, afraid that I'm hearing things.

Dan stands on the step, bracketed by Pearl and Tommy, grinning at me. "Hey, Ma. I'm home."

"Well, I can see that," I say shakily, and push myself off the sofa. "And it's about time."

Footsteps pound down the stairs when George and Toby hear their brother's voice, and I exhale with relief; their attentions will give me time to get myself together so I don't weep or do anything too embarrassing.

The boys hit Dan at full speed so that he staggers into the door frame. Over his shoulder, Pearl meets my eyes. I'm not hiding anything from her; tears shine on her cheeks and she's smiling so wide that her face must hurt.

"Dandy!" Thelma runs up from the kitchen and pushes her way into the fray, kicking George's ankle when he doesn't move to let her in.

"All right, all right." He makes it through the door, three children hanging off him. Max gets up and he offers his hand. "Could you peel them off?" he asks. "I need to hug Ma."

Max shepherds the kids to one side. I come around the sofa, smoothing my skirt to give my hands something to do, but before I can even raise them, Dan has swept me off the floor and into a tight hug. I bury my face on his shoulder, get an eye-watering whiff of unwashed boy, and hug him even harder.

He finally puts me off him, kissing my forehead and taking a step back. "You all look...clean."

"And you stink," Thelma says, giggling. "When did you last wash? Did you bring us anything?"

"It wasn't a shopping trip." Dan rummages in his bag and brings out the camera Claire gave him, battered and more than a little worse for wear. "Put this someplace safe, Ma? It's been through a lot." He adds two rolls of film, then leans against the sofa, one hand over his eyes, as if overcome.

"You need a bath," I tell him firmly. "Drop your clothes out the bathroom window, I'll wash them later."

"Better to burn them," Pearl says critically. "You'll never get them clean."

He's grown in the months he's been away—another inch to his already looming height—but he's thin enough that his ribs show against the thin cotton of his shirt. His cheeks are hollow, his eyes deep set, and a shadow of stubble lines his jaw.

"Are you hungry?" There is so much behind the question, but all I can think is to offer him food.

"Starving," he says with a brief grin. "I haven't eaten in two days."

A fading bruise streaks one forearm. My first instinct is to ask what happened, but I keep my mouth shut; it is healing and I won't badger him. It is more important that he is back under our roof. There will be time to feed him up and hear about his adventures—and to hope he's gotten that desire out of his system.

"You go on and wash up." The stench coming off him will make eating difficult. "I'll get something together for you by the time you're done."

The other kids follow me to the kitchen as if Max's Sunday lunch never happened. Tommy fits himself in with the rest, so whatever bother there was between the boys is past. I notice Pearl looking at him and smiling to herself, and wonder what was going on before Dan interrupted.

"There's not much that can be prepared quickly." She steps back to reveal the few cans on the pantry shelves. "Can I run over to Aunt's for something?"

"Go ahead." Ordinarily I wouldn't beg food from my sister, but this is a special occasion. "Ask if she's got a fatted calf in that icebox of hers. Your brother could probably eat it."

"I'll ask." She grins at me, then looks at Tommy. "You can come, too. Aunt will empty the kitchen and I'll need help carrying everything."

I fill the kettle and put it on the burner, take a loaf from the breadbox for slicing. "She'll probably run you home in the car."

"Maybe, but I don't want to disturb her if she's busy." Pearl folds her arms and looks at Tommy. "Come on."

He follows, and I gaze after them. She's usually more tentative, acting as if she were fortunate that he looked at her, but her brother's reappearance has changed something.

Claire comes through, sending a basket containing an entire cold roast chicken, potato salad, chocolates, and a bag of apples. The kids parcel it out on the table and I call up the stairs for Dan. He comes down slowly, Max just behind him. Max meets my eyes and gives a small nod: there is nothing to worry about.

It's like Thanksgiving, with food spread out along the table and everyone sitting and talking at once, and then falling back, silent, as Dan begins another portion of his tale.

"One town let us sleep at the jail."

"The jail!" Toby's mouth drops open. "What did you do?"

Dan laughs darkly. "In exchange for a week's labor, we got two meals a day and they locked us into a cell together at night." He presses his lips together. "I didn't like that, the being locked in. Second day, we were chopping wood and loading a truck for the sheriff and another truck stopped next to us. Woman driving. She looked out the window and said, real quiet, that she could take two of us if we got in back and hid ourselves in the bales she was carrying. I jumped in, but nobody else did."

"What happened next?" Thelma's plate is almost untouched; like the other kids, she is spellbound.

"She drove out of the town, to the rattiest old farm I'd ever seen. Looked like their last good days were before the war. Her father took one look at me and told me they had no work and no food, but the lady—Miss Susan, she told me to call her—she said they had enough to share. She gave me supper and let me have a bath. I slept in the barn. There was no lock on the door, so I didn't care."

He looks at the chicken remaining on the platter and I nod, cutting a warning glance at his brothers, who are listening raptly to his every word. "I stayed for a week, helped the old man fix the roof and did some heavy work in the garden. Miss Susan taught me to milk cows, but I didn't much like them." Grinning crookedly, he adds, "I liked the milk, though."

Getting up, I start to clean the table, and Pearl catches my wrist. "Let me do it," she says. "Go sit by Dan."

I obey, clasping my hands in my lap to keep from touching him. Max reaches across to take one hand, grounding me so I can listen to Dan's hardships and revel in the fact that he is home again.

"Why'd you come back?" George asks at last, as I remind everyone it's nearly time for bed. "It sounds like fun."

Dan stands and stretches. "It was, in the beginning. And when it wasn't fun, it was interesting. But then, one day, I came back to myself," he says. "I remembered where home was, and I missed it. I've had enough adventures." He wraps an arm around me and pulls me close. "At least for now."

30

Pearl

Dan slept in this morning. I'm not surprised. We kept him up late talking, and he didn't look like he'd rested or eaten lately. He's started making up for that already. He tore apart most of that roast chicken all by himself.

Mama and Dr. Max are already in the kitchen when I come down, their heads together over their coffee mugs. "Don't mind me," I say, pouring a cup. "I can take this upstairs if you want to talk."

"No secrets," Dr. Max says. "We're talking about accelerating our plans."

"To move?" Mama's face doesn't show much; I wonder how she feels. She agreed that we could move sooner if Dan came home early, but I'll bet she wasn't expecting to get hit with it the very next morning.

"Let's wait until after the concert," Mama bargains. "Just in case anything goes wrong. I can't be in two places at once, and it'll give Dan and Tommy some more time to work on the place."

"I'll hold you to that." He drains his coffee, swoops down to kiss her on the cheek, and clatters out the front door.

I slide into his still warm seat. "Are you okay?"

She laughs, but there's little humor in it. "In what way?"

"At least he's home." And he appears, for all her fretting, to be fine.

"At least he's home," she repeats. "I better get started on breakfast. He'll probably eat enough for three."

I leave for school before he comes down. It's good to get there and share the news with my friends and have them all be happy for us and hug me, but after that, the day gets a little bumpy. I fail my math test, despite Hazel's tutelage, but I make up for it by passing my history exam without having to think very hard. At the end of the day, I stop in at French club to let the teacher know I have to go home early.

"I'll let you go this one time," she says, smiling when I tell her the reason. "You got well ahead over the summer, so missing an afternoon of conversation won't hurt."

"Merci, mademoiselle!"

I waste money on the streetcar to get back quicker, but I don't go home right away. Before I left for school, I put Dan's two rolls of film in my pocket and I drop them at the Woolworths counter before I go home. I promise to pay extra for a quicker turnaround, and then hope that Aunt will have some babysitting time for me to make up for the money I'm spending on my brother's pictures.

He's gone when I get in. All the younger kids are home already, Toby and George not even complaining about missing out on their usual after school activities. When I ask where Dan is, Mama says, "Tommy came by for him at lunch. He went to see Mr. Howe about starting his job again next Monday."

That gives him a week to work on the house, with Tommy joining him in the evenings. I could come along, help paint trim or wash windows, but I think they'd rather be on their own. They have a lot to catch up on.

"We're going to aunt's for supper," Thelma tells me, pirouetting around the living room.

I thought we might. Let her help feed him up. And maybe, when we're done, if Mrs. Adler is upstairs or in a good mood, we can play one of her records for him.

Claire

I am thrilled, for my sister and for the rest of the family, that Dan has at last come home from his wanderings. That first dinner at our house after his return, he ate like one starved, but was reticent about his adventures. Ava told me later that he'd shared his stories easily enough when he got home, but like his father, he speaks only when necessary; apparently, repeating himself is unnecessary.

When we sat down to eat, Renate was still at rehearsal. Josef says that prior to a major performance, she disappears into her work, and it's true—I've barely seen her this past week. Ava says she was in for a fitting but disappeared immediately afterward. I'm glad they're managing to get along; my sister is difficult at the best of times, and when she levels a judgment on someone, as she has Renate, it is difficult to sway her. Max seems to have escaped her judgment, for which I am grateful. I didn't work as hard as I did to push them together for her to take against him simply for doing his job.

Dan's return means they will be moving into their new house sooner. Max speculates by Halloween, while Ava says after Thanksgiving is a more reasonable date. I thought that once Dan was home, they would move almost immediately, but my nephew says that he and his friend are going to do some painting and minor repairs first.

Pearl came to me before they left, asking if I would need her to watch Teddy over the next week.

"I don't think so," I told her. "I don't have a lot going on right now, and I'm trying to spend a lot of time with Sofie until she settles in."

"Oh." Her face fell. "That's good."

"What's wrong?"

She bit her lip, looking exactly like her mother in her internal debate of how much to tell me. "I need money," she admitted finally. "Dan took his camera with him and I put the pictures in to be developed but I don't have the money to pay for them."

I had given Dan the Leica we'd bought in France and was gratified by his obvious pleasure. Max's eyes widened when he saw it, but he, unlike my sister, has the sense not to lecture me about how I spend my money.

"I'm glad he's been using it," I said. "Get my purse from the table there and I'll give you the money for them. Consider it his welcome home present."

Pearl looked confused. "Wasn't that the new camera?"

"No," I told her. "That was *my* welcome home present." I hand her five dollars, not knowing offhand what the developing would cost. "If there's any left over, buy a treat for the rest of the children."

"I will." Her face lit up. "Thank you, Aunt Claire. Let's go back with the others and listen to Mrs. Adler sing. I could listen to *Butterfly* all day long."

"So could I."

A few days later, she comes to me in the late afternoon, dropping her books on the sofa with a thump. "I picked up Dan's pictures yesterday and he told me I could show them to you."

I clear space on the coffee table. "Have you seen them already?"

"Yes." Her voice is uncertain. "They're good, I think." Her pause stretches, and she says finally, "But they're hard to look at."

I see what she means immediately. Dan has documented his journey across the south in stark black-and-white. Male figures stand framed in the doors of boxcars; stooped men working in fields register nothing so much as defeat. There is a photo of a mining town, with a loose grouping of men in helmets, picks dangling exhausted from their hands. Several photos are from the Gulf, with men of every race hauling nets over the sides of boats whose best days were long before the Crash.

He has talent, my nephew. A sharp, incisive view. He sees, somehow, what's important in each scene and renders it explicable to someone who has never experienced it.

"Dan is wasted as a builder," I murmur, flipping through them again. I want Harry to see these.

"He might not do that forever," Pearl says. "He learned welding while he was away, and he says he might try that instead. He and Tommy are talking about applying at Baldwin Locomotive come spring."

That's not what I mean. Dan Kimber has an eye that isn't granted to everyone; it would be a shame, having been saved from his father's fate in the mines, if he isn't nurtured into developing it. "May I keep these to show Harry?" I ask. "I'll bring them back tomorrow."

She shrugs. "He won't mind. He likes to take pictures, but he hardly ever looks at them once they're developed. He's already on to the next thing, whatever that is."

I consider this. "Does the new house have a basement?"

"Not real big, but there's some room." Her head cocks to one side. "Why?"

"Because I think what your brother needs next is a darkroom, where he can learn to develop his photos." Ava will object, but when she realizes it's to give Dan a profession—at least an interest—she'll find her way around to accepting it. "Then maybe he'll be as interested in the result as he is in the process."

Pearl

I caught Peggy crying in the washroom today. At first I was afraid she was in trouble, but she doesn't have a boyfriend and Hazel's trouble has taught us all a lesson. She told me her aunt and uncle are moving to Delaware, to be near his family. They're willing to take Peggy and her brothers, but Peggy would have to leave school and go to work, to earn her keep.

Of course she doesn't want to do that. Who would? We've worked too hard to get here, and if she's allowed to finish school and go to college, she'll be able to do more than earn her keep. She said that, and even promised to pay them back for keeping her and her brothers all this time, but they said no. Her father hasn't written or sent money since the spring, so they can't count on him.

She doesn't know what to do, and I don't know what to tell her. She's not old enough to get a room somewhere, and she'd never be able to take care of her brothers and go to school. The boys are young enough that her aunt and uncle don't expect them to work, at least not yet, but being the oldest and a girl, Peggy has to pay her way.

I sat with her while she cried, and then ran a towel under the cold tap for her to put over her eyes. By the time we got out of the washroom, lunch was over and we went on to French class, where she answered all Mademoiselle's questions without even blinking. And they say girls aren't strong.

That night, and all through the weekend I kept thinking about her problem. It's selfish, but I don't want her to move away—I love all my friends, but Peggy is the most like me—and her situation reminds me how precarious our lives are. She's being completely turned upside down because her uncle needs to help take care of his mother. Good on him but Peggy has to think about her own life. We're almost grown up, we have to.

On Sunday, walking back from church, Mama asked what was on my mind, and I told her. Mama has been in worse spots than Peggy. Maybe she can think of a solution.

She didn't say anything at first, beyond wondering out loud what Dr. Max was making for lunch. That got Toby and George yammering and even I realized how hungry I was. We ran for home and when we got there, Dr. Max had a tray of sandwiches waiting for us—roast beef with mustard and cheese and sliced onions on wonderful chewy bread. I got so wrapped up in making sure I got my fair share that I didn't realize until later Mama had never answered my question.

Ava

My intention to not bring work home has been shattered by Renate's commissions. These dresses need to stand up to more than an evening of cocktails, conversation, and a bit of dancing, and the underpinnings are entirely different. I experiment with boning and a waist stay to give more structure to the gowns.

The first one, made of scarlet crepe-backed satin, is almost complete. With Renate's dark coloring, it needed no more than a molded bodice and an interesting drape to the skirt to show her at her best advantage. The bodice, however, required skills I didn't possess, and I had to take the entire thing apart multiple times. Once I figured out how to manipulate the fabric to take advantage of both sides, I constructed it directly on the boned undergarment and it stopped fighting me.

The black gown requires more thought than skill. I don't want it to turn into a blot of ink in photographs or onstage. The simplicity of the bodice will do well enough, along with the off-the-shoulder sleeves, but the narrow skirt and the train need work to not blend in. I'm still considering the dilemma when the bell rings and Hazel edges through the door.

"You again?" I have grown accustomed to her occasional appearances. "Doesn't anyone wonder where you are?"

"No." She drops her books on the counter. "Is there anything I can help with?"

"Possibly." I call into the back room, "Hanne, I'll be back in fifteen minutes." I look at Hazel. "Come with me. We're going shopping."

Despite being Mr. Mendel's tenant, and at least somewhat his friend, I patronize other shops when he does not have what I need. There are several stores further south that specialize in trimmings and which do a brisk business with the city's theatrical community. These shops are our destination.

The first is crowded and no one has time to talk to us. The shop across the street, however, has more staff than customers, and the female shop assistant who greets us is only too willing to answer questions.

"Black velvet is difficult," she says. You need something that will pick up the light."

"That's what I was thinking." I produce a scrap of the velvet and put it on the counter. "Silk velvet has a sheen, but I'm not sure how it will show from the stage. She's a small woman, with dark hair. I don't want her to completely disappear."

"What about sequins?" Hazel speaks up. "Do you have any?"

"Of course." The woman brushes the velvet against the grain, then flattens it again. "Have you done much sequin work?"

"Not a lot," I admit. "It's not what my customers usually want." Mostly because I have trained them to want simplicity, clean lines, and good fabrics.

She opens a drawer and takes out several small boxes. "There's plain black," she says, spilling a handful onto the velvet. "It's got a good shine. Then there's black iridescent, which is showy but would look very nice."

The iridescent sequins gleam like fish scales. I don't know if there is such a thing as too showy in this instance, but I know which I prefer. "I'll take the plain black."

"Are you anchoring with thread or beads?"

Either will take time, but beads will add a little extra glitter. "Seed beads," I say. "And not black. Silver." That will make up for using the plain sequins. Explaining that I will need enough for the hem and the train, and possibly for a bit of interest at the neckline, my purchase makes for a tidy package.

"It's going to be so pretty," Hazel says. "This is for the opera singer who's staying with your sister?" She smiles at my questioning look. "Pearl told me about listening to her recordings on Fridays and that you're making dresses for her."

"She'll be performing at the Academy of Music sometime later this fall." I don't yet know the dates, nor am I sure that I want to go. It appears to be another occasion where I will have to think about my clothes as much as Renate's.

"My family has season tickets for the orchestra," she says. "I'd love to take Pearl, if you're not going as a family."

I look at her approvingly. "Well, that's very nice. And I'm not sure we are, at least not yet." We return to the shop, which has been tidied in our absence. Hanne says goodnight and leaves, while I say to Hazel, "I'm going to spread out on the big table. Would you like to help me mark the design?"

Pearl, as it turns out, is happy to help with the embellishment of the gown. "I've missed doing this," she says, squinting to thread one of the slender beading needles, which are about half the size of regular needles. "Not all the time, but I do miss doing this together."

We spread out the train, marked every two inches with shining pins, and I show her the simple triangular design I began at the shop. "If you start at the other end, we should meet in the middle in almost no time."

31

Pearl

October 20, 1935

Dan's not had much to say since he got back. He told his stories, he showed his photos, and now he's gone back to work like none of it never happened. I see his ears prick up sometimes at night when we hear the train whistle and I know the urge to travel hasn't completely left him. But he's home for now, at least, and that's something to be grateful for because it means I don't have to worry about Mama as much. She can be his job, and Dr. Max's.

Girls High is having a dance next month. None of us—me, Hazel, Peggy, or Lenny—have dates. I'm so proud of Hazel. She's never forgiven Charlie. Lenny and Peggy don't have boyfriends. I don't know what I had, but I don't have him anymore.

I miss how special I felt when I was with Tommy, but it also makes me think of the time Thelma asked if I liked him for himself or because he was Dan's friend. Did Tommy ever like me for me, or did he just like me because I was Dan's sister, and that was easier to accept?

Mama is right. I'm too young to be thinking about boys like this. Two years ago, no boy would have looked at me. I guess I've improved some, or they still wouldn't, but I don't want a boyfriend because he thinks I'm okay to look at. I want somebody I can talk to in the same way that I talk to my girlfriends or Dan. And as much as I liked Tommy, he didn't know me that way.

It strikes me, though. Dan and Tommy. I don't know what's going on between them, and I'm not sure I want to know. But whatever it is, they're back to being inseparable. And my brother and his friend could take me and my friend to the dance.

I would have to talk to Peggy, so she understands there's no chance Dan's looking for a girlfriend, but I think she'll be okay with that. She wants what I want. She wants to go to the dance and have a good time and make some good memories before she has to leave.

Dan's not in yet. I'm going to listen for him and catch him on the steps, before he can go hide in his room and pretend he's not a full part of this family. Just because he disappeared for months doesn't mean he's off the hook. Actually, it means he owes me for leaving me alone with the younger kids all that time.

Taking Peggy to the dance will make up for—

Well. Mama just startled the life out of me to the point where I let Dan go past on the stairs and forgot I wanted to talk to him.

"What would you think about Peggy coming to live with us?" she asked.

I stared at her until she leaned against the window sill, her hands resting on her lap, still for once. "I thought you'd like having a girl your age in the house. She needs a place to live, and I need someone to look after the kids in the afternoon, when they get in from school. If she did that and helped out with chores, I wouldn't ask her for any rent."

I know Mama's been fretting about the younger kids fending for themselves in the afternoons in the new house, but she won't ask me to give up my school clubs. She's right to worry. If George wasn't so crazy about the firehouse, there's no knowing what he'd get up to, and we already know what Toby's capable of. Thelma doesn't mind going to Aunt's every afternoon, but I hate that it's her only option besides being alone. And once we're living further away, it will be harder on her.

I told her I would love it! Peggy is my best friend, even though I see her the least, because of where her family lives and having to take care of her brothers. I can tell her anything, and whenever we spend time together, we have so much fun.

Mama said she didn't want to interfere, that Peggy is my friend, and if I didn't want to see her outside of school, she would understand.

But I wouldn't see her outside of school. Or at school, for that matter, because her aunt and uncle want her to move with them. I'm sure they'd let her stay in the city if she could send a little money toward her brothers' upkeep. They wouldn't have the cost of feeding her, and because of her jobs, she's hardly ever home for the boys anyway.

I told Mama I'd talk to her tomorrow, and offered to bring her home from school with me, but she shook her head and said that if Peggy agreed, then she would talk to the aunt and uncle. Maybe have them over for supper, so they can meet us and see what kind of situation she'd be getting into.

I don't think they'd care. It's not that they're cruel, but they think she's old enough to take care of herself. Even so, Mama said, she wants to set their minds at ease, and then we can make a plan for Peggy to move in with us. If she wants to.

She will. She absolutely will.

Ava

Renate's gowns are done with only a few days to spare. I have gone over them again and again, but I cannot find a single hanging thread or loose bead. I leave a message at Claire's house that she can come down in the afternoon to try them on for a final time and then take them home. Katie is excited. "Mrs. Ava, Pearl told me how beautiful they are and how much work you've done. I can't wait to see them."

She won't be able to attend the performance, but at least she will see the gowns in the Adlers' rooms, and perhaps Renate will model them. I'm sorry that she will be excluded from the concert, but when I asked Claire, she seemed shocked I would think it possible for her colored maid to attend such an event.

"It's not done, Ava," she said. "And Katie would be so uncomfortable."

I don't see why. She's as good as anyone else. But Claire wasn't being unkind; perhaps she knows more about how the world works than I do, or more about Katie's feelings.

Renate arrives promptly at one, wearing an enviable dark red coat with a fur collar. Coming into the back room, she stops short at the sight of the gowns spread out on the table. "Oh." She takes a breath that makes her somehow larger. "It is good to see concert gowns again. It is my life back."

That throws me, a bit—that these dresses are not just income for my family, but a return to her old way of existence in this new country. "You should try them on one last time."

She nods. "Will you help me?"

"Hanne," I call. "Could you assist Mrs. Adler, please?"

I make a show of tidying up the space as Hanne comes scurrying from the front room to help Renate into the first gown. The process of sewing for her hasn't been as bad as I expected, but there is something about the sight of a woman in her underthings, vulnerable, that doesn't fit with my idea of Renate Adler.

She is vulnerable, obviously—no woman survives what happened to her untouched—but it is difficult for me to see her that way. Because of Hazel, I have stopped judging others for acts I don't understand. And it is a struggle, but I'm even learning that my beliefs are not the only valid ones in the universe; Renate believes differently than I do, but she is no worse for it, as I am no better.

It is because she dragged Max into her situation. Learning to live and let live would have been easier if my husband hadn't been involved, and if he hadn't come back at me with such force when I questioned his actions.

Chatter in German filters out from the dressing area. Judging by the tone, Renate is happy and Hanne is ecstatic. Hanne keeps backing out to give Renate room to move, smiling widely at me, and then going back in. At last they are done. Hanne comes to me with both gowns over her arm. "Is good," she says. "Is very good."

I breathe a sigh of relief, for all that I know the gowns are excellent. Mr. Stokowski's check arrived the day before, an amount that made my eyes water, and I do not, for any reason, want to give a cent of that money back.

Renate emerges from the dressing area in her own clothes, as Hanne and I swaddle her gowns in tissue and then bundle them into large white boxes. "They are perfect, Mrs. Byrne. Exactly right. You are a marvel."

"You were very clear in what you wanted." I do not take compliments well.

Renate says something in German, and Hanne backs out of the room. She turns to me. "I wish to thank you again, for everything." Her face tightens. "I know you do not like me."

Her words are like a dash of cold water to the face. "Of course I do."

"You do not." She sits, precisely, on the edge of a chair. "You judge me for what I asked of your husband." She holds up a hand. "I know that he told you—he said he would, if you asked, and you have too many children not to know the signs. So you think I am a terrible woman, but if I am honest, Mrs. Byrne, I do not care what you think. I did what was necessary for me, and I thank you now for doing the same."

I sit across the table from her. My old kitchen table from our house back in Scovill Run, now used as a cutting table because I couldn't let go. Despite its uneven leg, I can't discard it because Daniel repaired it; because we ate our meals around it, as a family, my entire life. "I do understand," I say carefully. "I don't approve, but our lives are very different." I exhale, and it feels like years' worth of held-back emotion. "It isn't my place to judge you."

She nods slowly. "Your husband is a good man. I like him."

"He is," I agree, though I don't like her liking. But our lives are entwined now, because of what he did for her, and because of her connection to my sister.

Renate smiles, a little sadly. "He would make a good Jew."

That was not what I was expecting. "Why do you think that?"

She takes black kid gloves from her bag, pulls them on with great care, straightening the seams on the backs of her hands. "There is a concept in my religion called tikkun," she says at last. "To repair the world, to struggle for justice. Some men avoid it, some work at it, but he...he seems to have been born to it."

This reminds me of a conversation I had with Max, a few days ago, when he received a call from the orphanage after ten at night. "If you try to right all the wrongs in the world, you'll exhaust yourself in a day," I told him, as he put on his coat and hat.

He cupped my cheek with one hand and kissed me thoroughly enough to last until morning. "That's no reason not to try."

Pearl

The repeated clanging of the bell cuts through the noisy conversation around me and the fog in my brain from too much Jane Austen. The streetcar has stopped in the middle of the block. I crane my head out the window and see a car parked close to the tracks.

A discontented murmur arises—will the car move?—and the driver calls, "Sorry, folks, this may take a few minutes."

I can't risk being late, so I climb down and run the last three blocks, my book bag thumping against my hip. I reach the school just as the bell rings and run to my first class without stopping to put my coat away. As I slide into my seat, I pull out a handkerchief to blot the sweat from my forehead before my hair collapses completely.

The teacher walks down the aisle between the desks, distributing yesterday's algebra tests. I look at mine and the neat B- circled at the top almost makes me stop breathing. Beneath my grade is a line of Miss Baxter's neat script: "Well done. Keep up the improvement."

My eyes fill and I blink hard. I won't cry when I finally do good at math; it's brought me to tears often enough when I've failed. I can't wait until lunch to tell Hazel that her tutoring has finally begun to sink into my brain.

A tiny scrap of paper lands on my desk. I look around, but no one is facing in my direction. Sliding it discreetly into my lap, I unfold it to see a note from Peggy. "Such good news!"

She is seated across the room, by the window; her note had probably been making its way to me ever since we sat down. I stare at her until she looks up. Her eyes are bright and even with four rows of desks between us I can tell she's excited about something. When we get up to change classes, I wait outside the door.

"What's your news?" I ask, heading to my locker to stash my coat and the books I won't need until after lunch. "Unless you saw my paper and know that I passed yesterday's test."

"You did?" She grabs my forearms and shakes them. "Congratulations, Pearl! That's wonderful!"

"But what's *your* news?" I ask again, needing to know before we have to separate.

"We got a letter from my father last night." Peggy is radiant, which isn't totally fair since she's prettier than all of us to begin with. "I'll tell you more at lunch."

More than two hours pass before we can meet, and I spend English and biology worrying that Peggy's father is coming home and she and her brothers will go to live with him. It would be for the best, of course, but I have been looking forward to having a sister my own age. Even George and Toby like her—which means they think they can get past her, but she's got brothers, too, so it's not likely.

Hazel and Peggy are already on the roof when I arrive, and Lenny is hot on my heels. It's chilly up there, but those of us who choose to eat outdoors value the garden's privacy even as we huddle deep in our jackets, sandwiches on our laps.

"Is your father coming home?" I can't imagine anything else that would make her so happy.

"No," she says, and her face momentarily falls, "but he sent money and a new address, so we can let him know where we've moved."

Hazel folds her lunch bag, shaking crumbs onto the roof. "If he came back, would you live with him?"

"If he could manage it." She brushes hair away from her face. "Uncle Joe is in a much better frame of mind about taking the boys now."

"Was there ever a chance he wouldn't?" If there was, she'd hidden it well.

"Not really, but this makes it easier."

"For you, too." Hazel says, sounding much more like her old self. She was kind enough to invite me to sit with her family at Mrs. Adler's concert later this month and I'm looking forward to it, even though that means Peggy will be with my brothers and sister.

"For me, too." Her eyes cloud. "I still feel terrible about leaving them."

"If you quit school, you'll never be able to take care of them," Lenny says with her usual bluntness. "Your aunt and uncle are willing to keep them, so you should just say thank you and get on with it."

"You're right, of course." Peggy draws in a hard breath, and strength with it. "Once I graduate and get a job, I can bring Jackie to live with me. And then, when I get more money, I'll send for Ralph."

Her entire life will be spent supporting these boys. I hope the older ones are as good as she is and pull their weight as soon as they're able, or that their father comes back and takes them on, so she can go to college after high school instead of getting a job.

When Peggy elbows me, I look up. "You can't organize the world," she says. "I can see you, wondering how I'm going to do it, and how you're going to help."

"So?" I like being caught out as much as Mama.

"This is for me to do." She rubs the tiny cross at her neck that belonged to her mother. "And I'll do it. I'm just as determined as you are, we just go about things differently."

"That's because you don't have *my* mother as an example."

She hugs me to her and I make a grab at my sandwich before it ends up as food for the pigeons. "I'm looking forward to it so much, even if it's just for a year. My aunt has done everything but pack my brothers in a box. They're just waiting for me to get out."

"So are we," I tell her. "Now, will you hurry up and finish? I want to fit your dress before we go back to class."

Dr. Max was an absolute darling and slipped me enough money to buy fabric so Peggy and I could have new dresses for the concert. "You need a grown up dress," he'd said. "And get something for your friend, too."

Peggy said she would trust me—she wasn't able to get away—so I snuck down to Fourth Street after school last week and bought two colors of crepe at a store other than Mendel's. I like them best, because they've been so kind to us, but I couldn't trust that old Mr. Mendel wouldn't tell Mama I'd spent that much on fabric.

It's a fairly uncomplicated pattern, so I've been able to put the dresses together on her treadle machine while she's at work, and then I take them, folded, in my school bag and do the handwork at lunch time. All that's left now is the hem and the final stitching of Peggy's side seams; I want these dresses to fit perfectly, so that Mama is impressed, even as she wants to shout at someone.

Uncomplicated or not, it's the prettiest dress I've ever owned, and definitely the most grown up. Mine is a dusty dark blue, while Peggy's is wine red. With her pale skin and dark hair, she'll look like Rose Red from the fairy tale.

"Who are you, then?" she asks. "Cinderella?"

I stick out one foot in its sensible brown school shoe. "If only I had glass slippers for the concert."

She shrugs. "It would be nice, but Hazel says concerts like that are really crowded no one will notice our feet. I'm just excited that Dr. Byrne is letting me come with you!"

"You're family now," I tell her. "And family sticks together."

Claire

Is it ever possible for my sister to submit to change without fighting it like it's a wild beast threatening to savage her family? The latest roadblock she's discovered, as we have coffee one morning in her kitchen, is that the children will go to a different public school once they move to Camac Street.

"I hate the idea of them changing schools. It's only October, so there's plenty of time to get used to a new place, but..." She rubs at a lipstick mark on the rim of her cup. "If we have to do this, I wish we'd known sooner."

"Pearl won't have to change, at least," I remind her. "Students come from all over the city to go to Girls High."

"Pearl." She exhales, sounding exhausted. "She'd manage anywhere you put her. It's the younger ones I'm most concerned about."

She's not wrong. Pearl is so set on getting an education that if the schools closed entirely she would move into the nearest public library and only be disappointed there was no one to grade her work.

"What if you used my address?" I ask. "The school won't bother to check. And then you can switch them over the summer and they can start at a new school next year."

"That's a thought," she says. "The boys wouldn't care, but Thelma's made friends. And she likes to come to your house after school."

"That settles it, then." She and Sofie have hit it off, so I'll make certain Thelma comes to the house every day. Hedges can run her home before picking up Harry at the office.

Ava sighs. "Then I guess that's two things off my list."

She doesn't sound like herself, my sister. There's an uncertainty in her voice that is totally unfamiliar. Now that she's done working flat out on Renate's commission, I hope Max can convince her to take a break.

When she leaves, I go upstairs to confront my other problem—this one not related by blood, but just as much mine. Sofie has settled into school well enough. I received a note from her teacher that other than being quiet in class—not unusual, she said, for a student whose first language isn't English—she is a model student, polite and helpful. "Having her cousin in the same class is beneficial," Miss Robb wrote.

It was Thelma who started calling Sofie her cousin, and I'm so grateful to my sweet niece for her willingness to accept new people into her life. She is disappointed that Sofie has no interest in dance, but they have similar tastes in movies and chocolate and they both like to play dress-up with clothes from the attic.

I have had less success bonding with Sofie than either Thelma or Harry. Harry sees her in the evenings, the same as he does Teddy, but having been graced with Leo's approval, she has no problem sitting on the sofa with him, reading aloud from the newspaper to practice her English or asking questions about Philadelphia which I would have been happy to answer, had she asked me.

The door to her room is closed. I knock, and wait for her response. When I enter, she is sitting in the chair by the window, ankles crossed, a book open on her lap.

I smile nervously, and come to sit on the bed. "What did you do in Berlin," I ask, "on the weekends, or when you weren't in school?"

"I studied," she says. "Uncle Leo was often away."

I feel a pang of sympathy; having lost her parents, she should have been able to rely on her uncle for comfort, but Leo's mission to rescue as many vulnerable people as possible did not extend, apparently, to spending time with his niece. Perhaps he couldn't, I realize. As the child of his beloved sister, maybe it was too painful. I choose to believe this, because I don't want to think that Leo abandoned this poor girl to a boarding school when she was grieving her parents.

"Before that," I clarify. "I'm trying to find something we can do together, Sofie. Thelma likes to go shopping, but you don't seem to enjoy that."

She nibbles the end of her long braid. "I need very little. It is pointless."

Good grief, maybe I should offer to swap her for Thelma. Ava and this child would get along like a house afire. There are times when I've hugged my sister and been surprised not to encounter spikes. Although she and I grew from the same soil, we are as alike as a daisy and a thorn bush. Our trials made me uncertain, shy with people who I feared were my betters; they turned Ava into a fighter. She may have fears, but they are invisible to everyone except those who know her best, and often even to us.

I decide to grant the same grace to Sofie and treat her the way I've learned to treat Ava: ignore the worst of the thorns, assume that rudeness often cloaks fear, and find common ground. With Ava, it was sewing, and sending women her way to help build her business. What do Sofie and I have in common? She doesn't want dance lessons, she doesn't like to shop, and she and Thelma do not need me to accompany them to the movies.

"Do you like museums?" I ask, an edge of desperation creeping into my voice. "Paintings? Sculpture?"

"Yes," she says, surprisingly quickly. "My mother and I went very often to the Neues Museum and the Gemäldegalerie."

"It will not be the same as going with her," I say, "but museums are some of my favorite places, and we have quite a number of them in Philadelphia. I'd be happy to go with you any time." I tell her about the parkway museums and the Academy of Fine Arts and Dr. Barnes's home in Merion, which he refuses to call a museum.

Her nose wrinkles at my description of the Barnes Foundation. "I do not like modern art," she says, her child's voice contrasting sharply with her adult opinions. "Mutti and I went to the Kronprinzenpalais to see an exhibition of Der Blaue Reiter before it was shut down. I find expressionism to be shallow."

I flinch, looking at the Monet hanging over her bed; perhaps I can replace it with something more to her tastes.

"Was the exhibit shut down, or the museum?" The Nazis have strong opinions about art, as well as music and books, so it would not be surprising.

"The entire museum," she tells me. "It was...degenerieren."

Is it possible to hate a political ideology as if it were a person? "Art cannot be degenerate," I say. "You can dislike a piece of art or disapprove of its subject matter, but that does not make it degenerate."

"You have proper museums here?" she asks. "With classical paintings? I would like to see one."

That is how we have ended up at the Philadelphia Museum of Art on a crisp autumn afternoon. We drove up in my car, and before we parked behind the temple-like museum, I gave her a quick tour of Boathouse Row, where the local college rowing teams keep their boats.

"Harry rowed for Princeton," I tell her. "That was the university where he met your uncle."

She shows more interest then, peering through the window at the few boats skimming the surface of the Schuylkill. "I don't know if my uncle did that."

"I don't know if he did, either," I say. "It was a long time ago. Harry rowed occasionally when we got married, but he gave it up when his business picked up."

"Also, he is old now." There is no unkindness in her voice, nor any reflection of his recent health issues, only a child's matter-of-fact assumption that anyone over twenty is old.

We walk through the airy galleries together, inspecting Japanese and Chinese ceramics, Renaissance armor, European sculpture, and all manner of decorative objects and furniture. She approves the collection of old master drawings. Finally, we arrive at the gallery holding the American paintings, which I assume she will not like.

I am about to suggest taking a break to find something to eat when Sofie says, quietly, "Oh."

I turn to see what has caught her eye.

The painting before us is an annunciation, but it's not the usual stiff depiction of biblical events. This Mary, sitting on a disordered bed and wearing a blue striped peasant robe, isn't calmly accepting the news given her by the archangel Gabriel, who is represented by a column of blinding light. She looks skeptical and scared and so, so human.

The painting is large, its frame at least seven feet across. Sofie walks up close, tilting her head to gaze into Mary's face. "She looks like me."

"She does." And not even that much older. I read the placard on the wall: *Annunciation* by Robert Ossawa Tanner, painted 1897.

Sofie's hands, nearly hidden in the folds of her skirt, are balled into fists. Every line of her body is alive with tension—alive in a way I have not yet seen from her. I know nothing about this artist, other than that he has painted something which has touched this untouchable, tightly wound girl. For that, I am forever grateful.

Before we leave, we venture to the museum shop, because it has occurred to me that printed reproductions of paintings are often available. I have no idea if the Tanner painting is important enough to warrant printed copies, but Sofie's extreme reaction is enough to warrant further investigation.

"We do have that one," the clerk says, smiling kindly at Sofie. "Only in postcard size, I'm sorry to say, but we do stock it."

She turns to me. "May we please purchase one, Aunt Claire?"

For the unforced use of my name, I would purchase her the entire museum shop. "Of course we can." To the clerk, I say, "Can you tell me anything about the artist?"

The clerk slides the card into an envelope and presents it to Sofie. "Yes, ma'am. Mr. Tanner was born in Pittsburgh and moved with his family to Philadelphia as a boy. He attended the Academy of Fine Arts with Mr. Thomas Eakins, but most of his paintings were done in Paris." She hands me my change. "Oh, and he's a colored man."

"Thank you." Sofie tucks the envelope into her coat pocket and looks up at me. "May we return home now? I want to tell my friend Katie about this."

32

Ava

The new house has more rooms, and those rooms have more space. The scant furniture we've accumulated will swim in them. Max has suggested, time and again, that we go out looking for new furniture, and time and again, I've put him off.

Finally, the day before the concert, he picks me up at the shop as I'm locking up. "I've already told the kids we'll be late," he says. "Pearl has everything under control."

"Where are we going?" I expect him to suggest dinner at Ralph's or some other nonsense. I'm not dressed for going out, and I'm in no mood to be waited on.

"You said you didn't want new furniture." He smiles triumphantly. "I found a place in North Philadelphia that sells used furniture—nice quality stuff, but at better prices. The best thing is, they'll deliver it straight to the new house, so we don't have to move it ourselves."

"But I said—"

"You said you didn't want *new* furniture." He pulls away from the curb and turns on to Fourth Street, a gleeful smile on his face. "This isn't new."

He is worse than the kids for catching me out. If it's not exactly what I said, he thinks it's okay.

"I'd just as soon go home." I crank the window up as the breeze attempts to unpin my hat.

"Not happening."

Once we pass Market Street, I am in unfamiliar territory, reminded again how little I know this city that I call home. Max has worked with so many different organizations, I assume there is no neighborhood left unfamiliar to him. Like so many other things lately, I find that irritating.

It is a silent half hour until he parks in front of a sprawling building with windows running the length of the first floor. The plate glass casts a golden glow over the sidewalk, a combination of overhead lighting and strategically placed lamps.

Cole's Quality Furnishings, the sign shouts. On the next line, in smaller type, it reads, *And Home Goods*.

I can already tell it's too fancy, but I keep my mouth shut. I don't have the energy to argue with him, and hopefully he will see that everything in this store is wrong and we can go home, eat a cold supper, and go to sleep.

I'm not that lucky. His natural friendliness causes him to introduce himself to the salesman who comes to greet us. "The missus and I are moving to a bigger house," he says proudly. "We're going to need a few things."

"Well, that's fine," the man says, his quick eyes taking Max's measure and deciding what we are likely to spend. "Where would you like to start?"

"Bedrooms, I think." He checks with me. "If Pearl's friend is going to be living with us, she needs a bed."

"She can sleep with Pearl." Peggy isn't a real boarder; she doesn't expect a room to herself.

He stops, one hand resting on the side of a china cabinet. "And where is Thelma going to sleep? In the dog bed?"

"We've all piled in together before." The night after Daniel's death, we pushed the beds together and I slept with all five of the kids. I don't tell him about that.

"They're getting too old to pile. They're not puppies." At my frosty look, he suggests, "Why don't we get a new double bed for us, and pass ours on to Pearl and whoever she wants to share with, and then the other one can sleep in the single bed?"

"Fine." Perhaps a bed will be enough. He'll get tired of spending money and we can go home.

But I am wrong. The bed leads to a dresser, and the suggestion of a small desk for Pearl. It's difficult to refuse something that will mean so much to her.

"That's enough now," I tell him. "This is far more than we need."

He doesn't understand. Waving the salesman away, he tugs at my hand until I sit beside him on a lumpy green sofa. "What is it?" he asks. "This is more than your usual hard-headedness. Don't you want to move?"

"Of course." But I don't just want to rent the house—though that will do for now. I want us to own it. I want to know that our home can never again be taken away.

What would Mama think? She'd been so proud that she kept our tied house after Tata's death, at God only knew what cost to her dignity. And she and I had kept it again through the war when Daniel was away, and the lean years after when he didn't make enough to cover the rent. When the mountain came down on the bootleg mine, he hadn't been dead for a day when they told us we had to leave. No insurance, no compassion. No home.

I never want to feel that helpless ever again.

"You could act like it." His mouth turns up at one corner. "This isn't like getting married. We can't change our minds at the altar. There's paperwork involved. Leases and deposits."

"Oh, damn your paperwork." My name isn't on the lease. The kids and I might as well not exist, as far as the law is concerned. We're just something that Max owns which requires more space in which to be stored.

I don't want to tell Max that everything feels precarious. That I'm afraid to stop working so hard, because what happens if we lose him, too? I'm not used to good things happening to my family. It frightens me, and when I'm scared I lash out. I've been harder on Max in the last weeks than he could ever deserve.

"Temper." He points at a set of chairs roped together in the next aisle. "What about those?"

If I have to shop for furniture, I should have Dan with me, not Max. My son knows what he's looking at, what needs fixing and what can be used as is. I don't know if Max has those practical skills—I've never thought to inquire and at this point, I don't really care.

"I suppose they'll do." He has already talked me into a dining room table with a leaf. It's sturdier and more attractive than the door and sawhorses construction Dan knocked together when we expanded into my old workroom. Even I can't call it extravagant; at its full extension, it seats twelve, which is our family, plus Harry, Claire and their kids.

It is still odd to think of them with two. There are times when it jars me that Teddy is theirs, not mine, and now they have this German girl who, according to Claire, will be with them indefinitely. Thelma likes her, so that's a good thing.

"What about rugs?" Max asks. "The one that's in the living room now can go in one of the bedrooms. It's not big enough for the new living room."

A surge of senseless anger overtakes me. "I never had a rug at all until three years ago," I say. "You act like they're absolutely necessities. You're spending money we don't have on things we don't need and I don't like it."

He holds up both hands, surrendering to my wave of words. "We do have the money, and while we don't need all of it, what's wrong with a rug?"

If we have a rug, we'll need a carpet sweeper. If we need a sweeper, that's more money, and the time to do it. It's faster and easier to use a broom on the bare floor.

"I don't care." I fold my arms across my chest. "Let's pay and go home."

"Ava." He tries to take my hand, but I clasp my elbows tightly. "They're just things. Why are you getting so worked up?"

Something snaps. "Maybe to you. You've never had to live like us. It was hard enough to get food on the table and keep the roof over our heads. Shoes on the kids' feet. Any *things* that entered the house were because we scraped and saved for them, and no emergency happened in the meantime to take that money away." I swallow past the lump in my throat. "Forgive me if I don't feel the same way about things as you do."

"I'm sorry." Max rests his hand on my thigh. "Sometimes I don't think. I want to do the best I can for you and the kids."

A worthy goal, and yet I want to shriek at him that it's not his place to provide for us—that I've always managed before now, that I don't need him. I am horrified by my thoughts and leap off the sofa before I can say something unforgivable. "I need air."

"Ava—"

I stalk past the confused salesman. Behind me, Max calls an excuse and chases me out of the store.

"What is it?" He catches my wrist.

"Open the door." My fingers grip the uncooperative handle. "Open the door, Max."

He turns the key and I slide in and slam the door behind me. Part of me wants to hold the driver's side shut, so I can have some peace, but it's his car. And I am his wife. He deserves an explanation and I have no idea what to tell him.

He gets in, closing the door quietly. When I fail to speak, he places his hand on the seat between us, palm up. A wordless invitation.

I consider, then place my hand in his. A tight thread inside me relaxes when he folds his fingers between mine.

"Now what is it?" His voice is calm, waiting for me to gather my thoughts.

What to say? There are no words to describe the pressure that has clamped down over me like a tight-fitting lid ever since we married and he first started making well-intentioned changes to our life.

"Is it me?" he asks softly. "Did I do something?"

"What? No." I shake off the darkness and look hard at his face. He is truly worried. "No, Max. It's not you."

He exhales, and I feel it in his careful grip. "Whenever you shut down like this, I assume it's something I've done."

"It's not. It's all me." Another spike of fear—that I will drive away this very good man by my inability to talk about my feelings. "I don't know how to be what you need."

"Oh, Ava, love." He shifts on the seat and rests his forehead against mine. "All I need is for you to be here, with me, and not try to do everything yourself. So what is it? Do you not like the house?"

The silence builds and builds in me until it erupts into words. "I don't like the house," I choke. "I love the house. I want it so much it hurts when I think about it." My eyes burn and I swipe at them recklessly. "I want to grow old with you in that house. I want to live there until our joints squeak as loudly as our bed. I'm just terrified. Admitting that something this good can happen flies in the face of everything I've ever known."

Tears erupt, and I sob aloud. The place I came from, the life I lived—it shaped me. Those absences in my life, all the pain I buried, they have brought me here, to this new place. To an understanding that I have been handed the pain of generations, but I can set it down at any time, while still honoring my dead. That is new, and still sometimes feels wrong, but I do my best not to steep myself in loss, for the sake of my marriage and my children.

I have never known how to ask for help; Daniel knew what I needed without asking, but because of our lives, he wasn't always able to give it to me. Often he couldn't even be there when I needed him. And I grew accustomed to doing for myself or leaning on my son in his father's place.

It is not fair to Dan to make him into a second Daniel. He has his own life to live. His own complications. I do not want him to grow into manhood with my limitations, or for Pearl to follow my example, as I did my mother's. Let them find their way without my misguided assistance.

"Shh." Max pulls me across the seat and cradles me to him. "You've done so much for so long—you're worn through. Let me help." He tips up my chin, strokes it though it is wet with tears. "Trust me not to get it wrong, or to fix it if I do."

"But what if—" I haven't cried like this since I was a little girl, at least not before witnesses. Even Daniel never saw me this despairing, because I was afraid of its effect on him, that he would feel he wasn't able to provide. Part of my brain wants to examine the fact that I can lose control with Max, but I can't think about that now. "I'm so tired of being strong. Being the pillar everyone leans on." That makes me sound ungrateful, and I cry harder. "I don't mean that. Just that sometimes..."

"Sometimes you'd like to lean on someone yourself," he says perceptively.

"Yes."

He cocks his head to one side. "And you won't lean on me because why?"

My eyes burn and I blink hard. "Because I'm not used to counting on people, I guess. Even when they mean well, they don't always do what they say they will."

"So it's easier to do it all yourself."

"Yes." I see where he's leading me. "Until it becomes too much."

"You can't carry us forever." He gently kisses my wet face, my wet eyes. Eventually my lips. "Give us the privilege of caring for you."

I lean against him, shuddering with sobs, recovering myself, until the darkness in the car makes me realize the lights in Cole's windows have been turned off.

"We've missed the furniture."

"I'll come back tomorrow," Max says. "If you don't mind."

I smile at his careful tone. "I don't mind."

He starts the car. "Do you want to come with me?"
"No." I shake my head. "I have enough to do. I trust you."

Pearl

Mama and Dr. Max went to pick out furniture last night, but they came home well after dark and she went straight to their bedroom. He made tea and brought it up to her, and then went back down again and made sandwiches, which they ate in their room. Toby remarked that the rule about not eating in bedrooms apparently doesn't apply to them, and Dan thumped him and told him to knock it off, couldn't he see Mama was upset.

She was. It's been building for weeks, ever since they made the decision to move. I don't know if she doesn't want to leave this house—I wouldn't, except that we'll have more space—but she's been wound up so tight I'm surprised it took this long for her to blow. I saw her eyes when she went past: redder than traffic lights, and Mama *never* cries. I think the few tears she shed in our view after Daddy died were to prove she was capable of it. Mama's feelings are private things.

Tonight she is late coming in from the shop. I've already fed everyone and sent Thelma off to Aunt's so she and Sofie can get ready together. They're so different, but I like that Thelma has a friend, the way I'll have Peggy when she moves in.

Removing her coat and dropping her bag on the sofa, Mama stands still for a moment. She looks exhausted. "I'm sorry. I meant to get here sooner."

"Don't worry," I tell her. "We ate, and I have sandwiches for you and Dr. Max."

I'm glad she's home: the boys will never get ready without her here, even with Dan yelling at them. She asks me to come upstairs with her, and when I follow her into the bedroom, she shuts the door.

"I wanted to let you know what's going on."

"Me?" I'm not the one she comes to when she needs to talk. "I can keep an eye on the boys if you want Dan?"

Mama sits on the bed, kicking off her shoes. "I'm sorry," she says. "I lean on him too much. I don't want you to feel left out—and you're as grown up as he is. You carry as much of a burden in this family." She sighs, and picks at her nails. "I don't know where to start."

I pick a topic. "Where's Dr. Max?"

"Back at the furniture store," she says. "We looked at things last night but didn't end up buying anything."

Her back is as straight as a rod. "Why not?"

"Because." She sags a bit, then sighs again. "Because I couldn't. I couldn't agree to let him buy all those nice things, because it makes all this real." Gesturing around, she clarifies. "All this *change*. Moving to this big house, being people we're not."

I understand, because sometimes I feel that way—the girl I was in Scovill Run wouldn't recognize the girl I am now, who talks to people with ease, who has smart friends, who dreams of going to college.

"You deserve to have good things happen, Mama," I tell her. "We all do. I think it just takes a while to realize it."

She puts her hands over her face, rubs gently. "It's hard to take in."

"I know." I lean against her, feeling her comforting warmth through my sleeve. "You've worked so hard, you should have a nice house. Look at Aunt—she never did anything to deserve her life except marry Uncle Harry. And you don't think less of her for living well."

Her head tips back. "I know."

I've never seen Mama this uncertain. If she didn't believe in her ability to keep the family afloat, she certainly never showed it before now. "Then what is it?"

The room darkens as we sit in silence. Eventually I lean over and turn on the bedside lamp, which casts a dim yellow glow over the log cabin quilt she and I made together before Daddy died.

"Max saved us." Her voice is weak, at least for Mama. "He rescued us from the kind of poverty you can't climb out of." She thumps the bed. "I can't let go of that."

Is that how she sees it? I take her hands, press them so she pays attention. "You did that," I tell her. "You did it first. You saved us, and then Dr. Max came along and made it better."

She takes a deep breath, holds it until it fills her up, flows into her arms and legs and neck. Once again she's upright, and her eyes have hardened. "It's not that easy, Pearl." With that, she pushes off the bed. "Could you bring my sandwich up? I need to start getting ready."

I'm already dressed in my new dark blue crepe that I made on the treadle machine while Mama was at work. Peggy, who will meet us at the Academy and come back here to spend the night, took her dress home just the other day. I wanted to make something new for Thelma, but Aunt decided to splurge and buy new dresses for both Sofie and Thelma.

Shouts from the third floor follow me down to the kitchen; Dan has his work cut out for him, getting the boys into their Sunday clothes on a weeknight. I take one of the sandwiches I made from the box outside the back door where it's been staying cool, and put it on a plate.

Lingering in the kitchen, I go over our conversation and wonder if she believed anything I said. Why is it easier to tell someone else the words that you need to hear? I told Mama she deserved good things, and it hits me, so hard that I have to sit on the step for a moment, that I have never believed that about myself.

I always thought the bad thing happened because I wasn't good enough, but I'm realizing that bad things just...happen. Was my father bad? No. He was weak sometimes, but brokenness isn't badness, and a mountain fell on him. Not his fault.

What happened with Mr. Nolan was because he was a bad man. It had nothing to do with me, except I was there. I wish I'd screamed or told someone because he's probably out there hurting little girls to this day, but I couldn't. I don't know why. Whenever he touched me, I froze, or submitted to get it over faster. Because I couldn't imagine being strong enough to stop him.

I still freeze when I think about it, so I try not to. Those few times that Tommy touched me were hard because I wanted him to but I was also afraid I would freeze up and he would think something was wrong with me.

I was lucky it wasn't worse. Mr. Nolan didn't rape me, only put his hands on me and in my pants. But he would have, if he'd stayed in our house longer. He was breaking me, bit by bit, so I would be too scared to stop him.

I was too scared the very first time he tried, but he didn't know that. Or he enjoyed scaring me as much as the touching.

This world makes me so angry. Men are allowed to go around hurting people for fun, and yet someone like Dandy would be a target for them because of how he feels. He can stand up for himself, but I wonder, if someone came after him, would he fight back? When he and Tommy fought, Tommy didn't have a mark on him. Did Dandy let himself get hit because he felt he deserved it?

33

Claire

Our box at the Academy seats four. With Max and Ava, who absolutely must be there for Renate's performance, Harry's mother would be an unwelcome fifth wheel.

"She'll have to sit with Aunt Nora," I say. "That won't kill her—her box is almost directly across from ours, and she shares it with the Thurmonds. Irene likes them."

Harry closes his eyes. "She won't be happy, but there's nothing we can do. I'll take her to something later in the season." There has been noticeable softening since his mother visited him in the hospital, but not enough to evict my sister and her husband from our box.

Max splurged and purchased tickets in the amphitheatre for the children, including Sofie, who will be supervised by Dan and Peggy, the girl Ava is taking in. Pearl will be in the parquet with a school friend's family. I'm surprised that the boys wanted to come, but perhaps the novelty of knowing the performer lured them. I hope the Beethoven before Renate's performance is to their liking; if Ava hears her sons' voices, she's likely to go up there and beat them.

The lobby is a crush of well-dressed, overexcited people milling around, greeting each other and exchanging views on the weather, the upcoming mayoral race, and their expectations of Stokowski's special guest. Their voices bounce off glass and marble; it is deafening for someone not accustomed to it.

I find Ava near the stairs, surrounded by a protective barrier of children. Dan holds her hand, speaking quietly in her ear. Pearl is on her other side, wearing her first grown up dress, a simple dark blue dress. Her friend, a strikingly pretty girl, is similarly attired, though her dress is wine red. Ava has obviously made them both, despite how busy she has been with Renate and their upcoming move.

"You look lovely!" I kiss her cheek. She is wearing her black taffeta tea gown, the first dress she remade from our attic, black stockings and proper shoes. "Where's Max?"

"Checking our coats." Her eyes dart around the ornate lobby, from the arched doorways to the gas lamps with frosted glass globes on either side of the carpeted steps to the upper levels. "This is...a lot."

"Wait until you see inside." I'm sorry I never thought to invite her before. This is an important night for her, and she shouldn't be left feeling unsteady, but it's too late now. I step closer, whisper confidingly, "The first time I saw this place, I was terrified."

With Irene breathing down my neck, I spent my first several concerts petrified that I would put a foot wrong, and consequently heard not one note of the music. She finally got a convenient case of the flu and I attended with Harry and two business associates. When I was not stiff with fear, the music found its way in and Irene was never able to glare me into submission in quite the same way after that.

"Max will be back in a moment," Ava says tightly. "I'm sure it's better inside. It's just out here"—she gestures at the crowd—"I'm a little overwhelmed."

Inside is at least as overwhelming, with velvet seats and a painted ceiling as beautiful as anything I've seen in Europe, but the lights will go down before too long and she'll be able to breathe. I stay with her until Harry and Max return, and then we split off from the children to take our seats.

The chatter of the crowd rises to the vast crystal chandelier. Ava sits beside me on the dark red seats, her breathing shallow, her hands clasped tight in her lap. Max manages to be attentive while still carrying on a conversation with Harry around the two of us. Across the space, Irene and Aunt Nora are seated in their box. Irene's lips are set in a tight, unforgiving line. When she catches sight of me, she looks away.

"The chandelier was originally gas," I tell Ava, to distract her from whatever thoughts are plaguing her. "They changed it to electric thirty-some years ago."

"I didn't imagine it was electric to start with," she says, with some of her usual dryness. "Has it ever fallen?"

Did *Phantom of the Opera* make it to Scovill Run, or is her mind just running along disastrous lines? "Not so far."

She looks at me then, a smile twitching on her lips. "Just let me worry, will you?"

The noise fades as the orchestra begins tuning its instruments, and soon the lights dim. I settle into my anticipation of what the evening has to offer.

Stokowski put together a program that would please any concert-goer. We start with Beethoven's Symphony No. 6, easing the crowd into the evening. Irene always criticized the *Pastoral* as trite, but it is among my favorites. I close my eyes and let the music wash over me, imagining myself in the spring landscape which Beethoven saw as he wrote the piece.

As the second movement begins, with its motifs of flowing water, I sneak a glance at Ava. She is bolt upright, her hands folded, but she is paying close attention. Max meets my eyes and gives me a tiny nod, and I settle back into my seat. He is there; he will watch her; I can simply give myself over to the music.

When the music ends and the lights come up, Ava turns to me, a sharp line between her brows. "Isn't Renate going to perform?"

"It's not over," I tell her. "Renate will be the second half. Now it's intermission, and we have fifteen or twenty minutes to go back to the lobby and say hello to people and drink champagne."

"I'm staying here." She crosses her arms, looking as immovable as a mountain.

"Then I'll stay with you." I always enjoy mingling during intermission but I don't want to leave her by herself.

Max leans over. "Let me run out and get champagne for the two of us, and then you and Harry can go."

Ava exhales with frustration. "I'm not an infant. You can leave me alone."

He kisses the side of her face. "But I don't want to, my love. I want to sit here and exult in your beauty and drink champagne with you."

She shoves him with her elbow and he backs away, hands up. "Fine. We'll all go and get tipsy and leave you be."

As we make our way out to the lobby, I ask him, "Is she all right?"

"No!" His amused expression makes it plain that I should have known that. "She's strung tighter than any instrument in the pit."

"Should I—"

Harry takes my arm. "You should leave her alone, as she asked." He guides me to a grouping that includes Prue and Marie. "I'll be back with your drink."

We trade opinions on the music, admire each other's dresses and jewelry, and make quiet, catty comments about people we don't like. Irene is nearby in one of her ingénue dresses, and I smile inwardly when Prue points her out. "There's a woman who could benefit from Ava's expertise."

"She'd never ask." I accept a glass of champagne from Harry, and look around for Max, but he is gone—hopefully back to my stubborn sister. "Ava did make Renate Steiner's gowns for tonight."

"I love them already!" Prue rubs her hands together. "I imagine she's been absolutely giddy, sewing for someone like that."

"That's one word for it." I lower my voice. "I think this whole thing has overwhelmed her. She's hiding in our box."

"No, she's not." Marie tilts her head to the left. "She's over there with Dr. Byrne."

They are near the glass front doors, looking out onto Broad Street. Ava's arm is through Max's, and his head is tipped toward hers, talking earnestly. I hope he's not trying to talk her into staying; she looks like she could make a break for it at any moment.

"Excuse me." I turn toward them and find Harry blocking my path.

"Let them be," he says. "She's Max's job, not yours."

I drop my chin, acknowledging that he is right. "You're my job," I tell him. "Are you having a good time?"

"Other than allowing myself only a single sip from your glass, just dandy." Light glints off his lenses. "Shall we get it over with and say good evening to Mother?"

"Why not?" The chime to mark the end of intermission will save us soon enough.

The second half begins promptly. Stokowski bounds onto the stage, tall and elegant in his black tailcoat. Standing at the center, under the bust of Mozart on the proscenium, he clasps his hands and looks out at the audience.

"This evening," he begins, in his precise, lightly-accented English, "we have a very special treat for you." He runs one hand over his slicked-back pale hair. "When I first learned of Renate

Steiner's presence in Philadelphia, I knew that I would not be content until I saw her on this stage."

Little did he know that Renate, Prue, and I were working toward that same goal. He paces and speaks, giving the little information about the reason for Renate's departure from Europe, focusing instead on her great talent and long career.

"Tonight she will thrill you with her interpretations of the heroines of Puccini," he concludes. "Please enjoy this tremendous honor, and show her your appreciation so that she will agree to perform with us again soon."

Applause rises in a wave. Beside me, Ava stiffens, but I don't look over; my eyes are fixed on the stage, which has gone dark but for a single spotlight. Moments later, Renate walks out to even more frenzied clapping and takes her place in the light. She steps up to the microphone Stokowski left behind.

"I thank you for your warm welcome." She stands for a moment, allowing us to admire the sculpted splendor of her satin gown, and then curtsies, her arms spreading gracefully. Embracing the crowd. "You honor me."

She steps back, and an invisible figure reaches out to retrieve the microphone. All is silence, and then the orchestra crashes into the first notes of *Quando men vo*. Interesting, to sing Musetta instead of Mimi, but I have always preferred this aria, and it shows Renate's voice to perfection. Two male members of the opera company sing the roles of Marcello and Alcindoro, to give Musetta the men she needs for the flirtatious song.

Renate's voice fills the auditorium. I have seen operas in this space for years, but there is something about the solitary staging, and the tiny woman in her beautiful red dress, with a voice far larger than her body, that makes it all feel new.

The orchestra moves seamlessly from *La Bohème* to *Madama Butterfly*. My eyes fill at the first notes of Butterfly's soaring, tragic aria. I have never understood why music makes me cry this way, but I have learned to carry a compact in my bag to repair the inevitable damage.

I sneak a look to my right. Ava sits, motionless, but I feel her straining toward the stage. My sister is not so immune to all this as she tries to make us believe. Smiling, I turn back to the performance.

Two more arias—Tosca and Lauretta—and the spotlight goes out. The orchestra gives us some light Mozart, to cleanse our palate, and voices rise around us as the crowd cannot hold back their reaction.

"Is it over?" Ava asks in my ear.

"Not yet." Renate told me there would be a break for her to change, and then she would come back for one final selection. "Have you had enough?"

She shrugs. "Just curious."

Her expression is interested, and she seems calmer than earlier, but I am disappointed to see her so untouched; she appears no different than when we listen to records on the living room phonograph.

When Mozart ends, the spotlight returns, and this time Renate appears wearing the dress that caused Ava so much grief. The black velvet glows; somehow, instead of absorbing all the light on the stage, it reflects it back to the audience. Discreet beading shimmers on the bodice, and when she turns, the edges of her train sparkle in the footlights.

A few notes, and I recognize Calaf's aria from *Turandot.* Renate stops as a wave of applause sets her back on her heels. When it subsides, she nods sharply—*behave, now*—and begins again.

Nessun dorma has never left me dry-eyed. This occasion is no different. I've never heard it sung by a woman, but Renate is flawless. Her intonation and the way she handles the demands of the aria make me forget every tenor who's ever performed it. When the chorus swells, unearthly, behind her, I hear another, closer sound.

Ava is sobbing, tears running down her cheeks. My mouth drops open to see such emotion from my sister. Max takes her hand, fishing for a handkerchief with the other. He murmurs to her, and she nods and takes it, covering her face for a moment. When she emerges, the tears are gone and the white lawn is smeared with her light makeup. She pushes it back into his pocket and bumps him with her shoulder, and I see the tremulous beginning of a smile.

Ava

We come out into darkness and the brisk air of late October evening. The gas lamps on the Locust Street side of the Academy burn brightly, leaving ghosts in my vision when I turn my head too quickly. Around us rises a wall of chatter, but I can't make out individual words over the rushing in my ears.

"There used to be thoughts in my head," I tell Max, "but I don't know what they were."

I've been scoured clean, whether by the power of Renate's voice or simply the experience of sitting in the darkened auditorium, listening to live music for the first time in my life. I'm slightly wobbly, as if I've drunk too much champagne.

Max settles my coat over my shoulders—somehow I have come away without it—and takes my hand. "I would never tell you not to think," he says, "but right now, let's just leave you empty for a little while longer."

"Where are the kids?" I suddenly realize we are alone in the milling crowd, and I am missing a half dozen of my people.

He draws me along the sidewalk until we reach the front corner of the building. "It's a long way down from the amphitheatre," he tells me. "I arranged with everybody to meet here."

I lean on the sharp corner of the building, letting the ridge of brick dig into my back, to bring me to my senses. I don't even remember leaving the building. "What will Claire think?"

"She understands." He shifts, to block me from the wind. "She has the same reaction to music."

Is that what it is? I've always enjoyed listening to the radio, and Claire's phonograph has been a welcome addition to our Fridays, but other than two old men playing piano and fiddle at the dances back in Scovill Run, I've never seen music performed. It is different, somehow, watching all those black clad musicians, knowing how hard they must work to produce that perfection of sound.

Renate was another story entirely. When she walked out onto the stage and curtsied to the conductor, for a moment I saw a small, complicated woman wearing a dress that took every ounce of my skill. But then, after she began to sing, she could have been any woman, wearing any dress. None of it mattered, even as Max leaned over to me and whispered in my ear, "I'm so goddamn proud of you."

That was when I started crying. His words, yes, but also her voice, and this place, and these people. I wanted to pull my family around me like a blanket, but they were scattered all over—Pearl with Hazel, Dan with the younger kids in the top level, Claire and Harry beside us, in their own cocoon of music.

Max was the only one I could reach. When I lifted my hand, he caught it in his, holding it against his leg. My nails dug into his thigh as waves of emotion rolled over me. Emotions I didn't know I felt, and had never attempted to put names on before. Like waves on the beach, they pulled me under and I began to cry.

I cried for the loss of everything I'd once had—Mama, Daniel, our home—and for the new things that have come to me in their stead. My sister returned to me; a house; happy, healthy kids; the everyday blessing that is Max.

And a new home. A home with the family that he and I have made together.

I blink away more tears, and wonder why I have fought so hard to keep this from happening, even as I acknowledged that I couldn't stop it, that I don't want to stop it. I want to move on, and make the best home I can with the best man I know.

Leaning forward, I press my cheek to his. "When we get home," I whisper, "is it too late to start packing? I can't wait to move."

He grips my shoulders and holds me away from him, his hazel eyes seeking my face. "Really?"

"Really," I say, as the kids surge out the doors and surround us, all talking at once, their voices rising in a chorus. "I want to go home."

Author's Note and Acknowledgments

Considering that Ava and Claire's stories were only ever supposed to be one book—and Pearl didn't say a word in the initial draft—I'm quite pleased to have turned them into a trilogy. It's not the end of their stories, but it's *a good place to end* and that's sometimes the best an author can do.

If you're interested in what happens after Ava and Max move into their new house, and you're not already signed up to my newsletter, please do, because there's a bonus epilogue that's just waiting for a final polishing. Try as I might, I couldn't get it to work tacked onto the end of the book.

Once again, Ava and Claire have given me permission to be both a tourist and a historian in a city that I thought I knew well. Turns out there are always new things you can learn about your home town, and I'm grateful that so many of the locations in these stories still exist, even if the buildings bear different names or slightly different appearances these days.

In addition to the usual suspects, who will be named below, I have one or two more impersonal thanks to offer for their assistance with this story. Have you ever started thinking about something and then seen or read about it—everywhere? I'd already started planning for Claire and Harry to encounter some of WWII's oncoming darkness in Paris when I ran across the Ken Burns' series, *The U.S. and the Holocaust*, which gave me ideas and sent me down more than a few interesting rabbit holes.

Another inspiration was the Netflix series, *Transatlantic*, based (loosely) on Julie Orringer's book, *The Flight Portfolio*, which is a fictionalized account of Varian Fry's efforts to get Jews out of occupied France in 1940. Mary Jayne Gold (a real person) featured in both series and book, and I liked her so much—and she seemed like such a part of Claire's set—that I had to get the two of them together in Paris.

Another real-life inspiration for one of the subplots in this story was the overturning of *Roe v. Wade*, which happened as I was early in the drafting stage. It got me to thinking that 1935 was a time not so different than ours, and the issue of reproductive rights would have been just as divisive among those who could bring themselves to discuss the matter.

It was difficult to put Ava—with her Catholic faith and many children—on opposing sides with Max, who is a doctor first and foremost. While Max will never change her mind, I think Ava got to the place she needed to reach, understanding that there are lives very different from hers and that she can't expect everyone to make the same decisions she would make.

And now for the traditional lavishing of thanks: to Mario Giorno, for his constant love, support, and patience. To Marian Thorpe, Eva Seyler, Laury Silvers, and Erin Rice for frequent character conversations—the best thing about having writer friends is that we're so well acquainted with each other's people that we can talk about them like they're real.

Circling back to my dedication, to the women of my family, all of whom liked to tell stories (but claimed they *never* gossiped), and while they wouldn't recognize any of the people or stories in these books, they nevertheless inspired a lot of it.

And to my great-aunt Margaret—sorry about using your photos for the covers of all three books. You always claimed you weren't photogenic; I beg to differ.

About the Author

As an only child, Karen Heenan learned young that boredom was the ultimate enemy. Shortly after, she discovered perpetual motion and since then, she has rarely been seen holding still.

Since discovering books, she has rarely been without one in her hand and several more in her head. Her first series, *The Tudor Court*, stemmed from a lifelong interest in British history, but she's now turned her focus closer to home and is writing stories set in her native Philadelphia.

She lives in Lansdowne, PA, just outside Philadelphia, where she grows much of her own food, makes her own clothes, and generally confuses the neighbors. She is accompanied on her quest for self-sufficiency by a very patient husband and an ever-changing number of cats.

One constant: she is always writing her next book.

Follow her online at karenheenan.com and sign up for her newsletter to receive a free novella and updates on what's next.

Made in the USA
Middletown, DE
18 January 2024